D0271332

THE NIZAM'S DAUGHTERS

Also by Allan Mallinson

A CLOSE RUN THING

THE NIZAM'S DAUGHTERS

ALLAN MALLINSON

Allan Mallinson

BANTAM PRESS

LONDON · NEW YORK · TORONTO · SYDNEY · AUCKLAND

TRANSWORLD PUBLISHERS
61–63 Uxbridge Road, London W5 5SA
a division of The Random House Group Ltd

RANDOM HOUSE AUSTRALIA (PTY) LTD
20 Alfred Street, Milsons Point, Sydney
New South Wales 2061, Australia

RANDOM HOUSE NEW ZEALAND
18 Poland Road, Glenfield, Auckland 10, New Zealand

RANDOM HOUSE SOUTH AFRICA (PTY) LTD
Endulini, 5a Jubilee Road, Parktown 2193, South Africa

Published 2000 by Bantam Press
a division of Transworld Publishers

Copyright © Allan Mallinson 2000

The right of Allan Mallinson to be identified as the author of this work
has been asserted in accordance with sections 77 and 78
of the Copyright Designs and Patents Act 1988.

All the characters in this book
are fictitious, and any resemblance
to actual persons, living or dead,
is purely coincidental.

A catalogue record for this book is available
from the British Library.
ISBN 0593 04374X

All rights reserved. No part of this publication may be reproduced, stored in a
retrieval system, or transmitted in any form or by any means,
electronic, mechanical, photocopying, recording, or otherwise,
without the prior permission of the publishers.

Typeset in 11/13pt Times by
Phoenix Typesetting, Ilkley, West Yorkshire

Printed in Great Britain by
Clays Ltd, St Ives plc

1 3 5 7 9 10 8 6 4 2

To
the dwindling but gallant band of members of
The Indian Cavalry Officers' Association,
who truly cared about India and their sowars,
this book is with admiration dedicated.

AUTHOR'S NOTE

The Nizam's Daughters is a work of fiction: the princely state of Chintal never existed. However, the story is firmly rooted in what was happening in India just after Waterloo in the build-up to the third Maratha war. And Chintal (even with its singular rajah) is, I would maintain, not untypical of the many minor princely states whose precarious existence depended increasingly on the Honourable East India Company. They were states where young Englishmen like Hervey – as soldiers, administrators or tutors to the royal household – often had disproportionate influence.

So many of the incidents in this book are based on real events that I must make mention of two things, just in case they might be thought improbable. Matthew Hervey's feats of arms are in most cases those of the legendary Rollo Gillespie a decade or so before (Gillespie – in his day known as 'the bravest man in India' – died leading the attack on the Kalunga forts in the Nepali war of 1815) and also of one of the ancestors of a Sikh officer in the army of India today whose help I will acknowledge a little later. Hervey's escapade with the wild boar at the well is, in almost every detail, that of a living man – Lieutenant-Colonel David Garforth-Bles, late of the Guides Cavalry – from whom I heard the remarkable story at first hand. It is typical of the men who officered the Indian cavalry that the incident was considered of no great moment other than for its funny side.

Let me now acknowledge my written sources and point to further reading. First, narrative history. At the risk of offending later scholars and revisionists, I have gone back to two early works, for it seemed to me that that way I might get a more faithful representation of the way men looked at the subcontinent at the time. J. C. Marshman's abridgement of the *History of India* (1873) painted the broad picture, and the detail has come from H. H. Wilson's Volume VIII of Mill's *History of British India* (1846). For topographical and climatic detail at the time I have relied principally on the work of Colonel Sir Thomas Holdich, at one time deputy superintendent of the Survey of India. His truly admirable *India* (1906), in the Frowde 'Regions of the World' series, brings together the observations of many scholars from the previous century. Maria Graham's *Journal of a Residence in India* (1812) and Bishop Reginald Heber's *Narrative of a Journey through the Upper Provinces of India* (1828) have been of particular help in filling in the human detail, as have Bruce Palling's highly recommended *A Literary Companion to India* (1992, John Murray) and Sinharaja Tammita-Delgoda's most readable *Traveller's History of India* (1994, Windrush Press).

In addition to extensive use of regimental histories, I have made free with some of Lieutenant-General Sir George MacMunn's delightful *Vignettes from Indian Wars* (1933, Sampson Low), and much sporting and natural history detail I have taken from Major A. E. Wardrop's *Modern Pig-Sticking* (1914, Macmillan) – most notably the incident of the 'fussunded elephant'. Those of less sanguinary inclination should not be put off by its title: the book is an evocation of the Indian countryside the like of which I know not.

As for the whole business of English attitudes to India at the time I have consulted the usual references. But specifically military attitudes required something else. It seems that fighting men were reluctant to commit to paper any deep feelings: for instance, the Duke of Wellington's many letters at the time of his regimental command there are almost exclusively concerned with campaign narrative and political speculation (and in this connection I freely acknowledge my debt to, and strongly commend by way of further reading, the work of Anthony Bennell, whose scholarly *The Maratha War Papers of Sir Arthur Wellesley* – 1999, Sutton – and *The Making of Arthur Wellesley* – 1998, Orient Longman – root things firmly in military reality). For me, however, there is a sort of Rosetta stone when trying to decode the subject attitudes. This is Francis Yeats-Brown's remarkable *Bengal Lancer* (1930). Yeats-Brown joined the Indian cavalry at the beginning of this century: his experiences were therefore closer in time to those of Matthew Hervey than they are to the reader of today. His candour is (I believe), for the time, unique. And although the Great Mutiny of 1856 swept aside much of what was the way of things under 'John Company', my belief is that Yeats-Brown is not untypical of a thinking, sensitive officer of the earlier period. Readers who know his work will recognize the source of some of the imagery, tensions and incidents in my story.

In addition to *Bengal Lancer*, I have had the great privilege to know – for the past twenty years – Lieutenant-Colonel Douglas Gray, late of Skinner's Horse. His regiment – in Hervey's day irregular cavalry, but later incorporated into the Line as Bengal Lancers – was (still is) of unsurpassed romance and efficiency. Douglas Gray – the sole surviving winner of the legendary Kadir Cup, the blue riband of hog-hunting – also knew Yeats-Brown, and during the many, many hours I have spent listening to him speaking of India I have come to the view that soldiers, horses and the heat and dust of the subcontinent are a widow's cruse of romance (while, I hope, not forgetting the less romantic side that Kipling so famously portrayed). I have also had the privilege of listening to many of Colonel Gray's contemporaries, and of reading their memoirs, privately printed. There emerged a picture of the India of seventy years ago (and in my contention, therefore, closer to the time of my story than to now) that was remarkably consistent. But I am more than conscious that they are men forged in a very different world, and therefore that it is important to keep a respectful distance from any idea that one might know how people really felt: I could only expect to learn what they *thought*, and how they acted. It is to these officers that my book is with admiration dedicated.

There is, of course, another side to the fence, as it were – the Indian soldier. I have had the great good fortune to spend many hours, too, in the company of Colonel (now Major-General) T. P. S. Brar – not a cavalryman, but a Sikh officer of the Maratha Light Infantry. Also, with Colonel M. S. Mhaisalkar, conversely a Maratha serving with the Sikh Regiment. Colonel Brar's late father – whom I knew and revered – had been one of the first Indian cadets at Sandhurst in the twenties, and the first Indian officer to command a regiment of infantry in the Second World War. The Brar caste is the most illustrious of the military castes, and father and son always spoke freely and candidly, and allowed me to consult their distinguished family archives in Chandigarh – on which my climactic battle scene is based. In addition, Colonel Mhaisalkar, a Brahmin, brought an important Central Indian perspective to things, and his wife – a graduate of Nagpore – has been a great encouragement to me in finding what might pass as an authentic Indian female voice; and not least in having as a mother a retired university teacher of Indian history.

Finally, to those who have steered me in the handling of this material I owe sincere thanks. Simon Thorogood, my editor at Bantam Press, has dealt with me at all times patiently and agreeably, but with a sure instinct. And I am, as ever, grateful to soldiers' daughters. Maggie Phillips, my agent at Ed Victor Limited, was a tower of strength with the first draft; Ursula Mackenzie, my publisher at Bantam Press, has been uncompromisingly, but steadfastly, supportive throughout; and my wife, as with the first book, has kept the equine detail technically sound. 'The sex is ever to a soldier kind.'

ON THE EAST INDIA BILL

What is the end of all government? Certainly the happiness of the governed. Others may hold other opinions, but this is mine, and I proclaim it. What are we to think of a government whose good fortune is supposed to spring from the calamities of its subjects, whose aggrandizement grows out of the miseries of mankind? This is the kind of government exercised under the East India Company upon the natives of Hindostan; and the subversion of that infamous government is the main object of the bill in question.

Charles James Fox, to the House of Commons,
1 December 1783

ON LEAVING INDIA

I know that all classes of the people look up to me and it will be difficult for another officer to take my place. I know also that my presence would be useful in the settlement of many points . . . But these circumstances are not momentary . . . very possibly the same state of affairs which now renders my presence desirable will exist for the next seven years . . . I have considered whether in the situation of affairs in India at present, my arrival in England is not a desirable object. Is it not necessary to take some steps to explain the causes of the late increase in military establishment, and to endeavour to explode some erroneous notions which have been entertained and circulated on this subject . . . I conceive therefore that in determining not to go into the Deccan, and to sail by the first opportunity for England, I consult the public interest not less than I do my own private convenience and wishes.

Major-General Sir Arthur Wellesley, to his brother, the
Governor-General, January 1805

ON THE POLICY OF NON-INTERVENTION IN THE AFFAIRS OF THE COUNTRY POWERS

I entreat the Directors to consider whether it was expedient to observe a strict neutrality amidst these scenes of disorder and outrage, or to listen to the voice of suffering humanity and interfere for the protection of the weak and defenceless states who implored our assistance against the ravages of the Pindarees and the Patans.

Lord Minto, Governor-General of India,
to the Court of Directors of the Honourable East
India Company, 1812

CHAPTER ONE

THE AIDE-DE-CAMP

*The Embassy of His Britannic Majesty
to the Court of the Tuileries, Paris, 13 August 1815*

Captain Matthew Hervey had put on his best uniform. It was only the second time he had worn it. He was not even sure he should be in levee dress, for his orders to report to the Duke of Wellington's headquarters had not been concerned with trifles. Yet dress, to a cavalryman in his situation, could hardly be a matter of indifference, and so he had followed the regiment's maxim that no senior officer could be affronted by seeing an excess of uniform, even if he were bemused by it. The newest captain of the 6th Light Dragoons was therefore waiting in an ante-room, with dress sabretache and mameluke hanging long from his girdle, and tasselled cocked hat, with its ostrich feathers, under his arm, in some degree of apprehensiveness. He wore no aiglets, however. He had bought two pair in London on learning that he was to be promoted and appointed to the duke's staff, but he did not yet presume to wear those coveted insignia of an aide-de-camp. Indeed, his astonishment at his preferment was scarcely less than when first he had comprehended it only two days ago at the Horse Guards.

Lying full across the open doorway of the ante-room was a springing

1

spaniel, old and ill-smelling, sound asleep and snoring with perfect regularity and constant pitch. It had not been in the least disturbed when the Staff Corps corporal had shown the new ADC into the room a quarter of an hour before, when both had had to step long over the outstretched animal to avoid entanglement of spur and coat, and Hervey, waiting in the otherwise silent embassy, pleased to find some distraction which might help keep his mind from disquiet, was now timing the length and interval of these snuffling crescendos and decrescendos by the ticking of the clock on the chimney piece. There were five seconds for the inspiration, three for the equipoise and four to complete exhalation – then a further five, where all life seemed suspended, before the sequence was repeated *da capo*. He had counted a dozen of these recitals before seeming suddenly to realize what he was doing. He glanced about anxiously to see if anyone were there, then snapped back to the full attentiveness appropriate for an officer awaiting interview with the commander-in-chief of the allied armies in France.

Outside, the Sunday bells, which had drowned even the sound of hooves on the pavé as he had driven to the Rue Faubourg-Saint-Honoré, had been silent for some time now, and he was relieved that he might thereby be able to hear the duke's remarks, when they came, with absolute clarity. He was in no doubt of the singularity of his position. He was certain that in the whole of the army there could not be an officer below field rank who would not envy him it. Another quarter of an hour passed, the keen anticipation of the honour to come increasing with every minute. Shortly after eleven-thirty a minor commotion in the ante-hall alerted him to the duke's return from his daily ride, though it did not disturb the recumbent spaniel. He snapped his whole body to attention, as well as his wits. And then the field marshal was there, at the doorway, looking directly at him. Hervey stepped forward sharply, halting three paces from him, the spaniel occupying all that remained, and bowed his head briskly. The duke made no bow in return, neither did he extend his hand, saying instead simply, 'Captain Hervey, I am glad you are come. Colonel Grant has need of you. He will be along presently. It will be deuced tricky work, but I should not ask it if I thought it beyond you. Good day then, sir.'

As the duke turned, Hervey saw the young woman in riding dress close by him. She cast a brief backward glance as the duke said something to her, and then she smiled wide and adoringly at the great man as they retired to his quarters. The spaniel woke suddenly and looked up at Hervey with a puzzled expression before breaking wind at considerable length. Hervey sighed as long, and smiled. How the glamoury of aiglets could be so rudely abraded! And how trifling did the appointment of aide-de-camp seem to the great man himself. 'Deuced tricky work' – Hervey had never doubted it would be. He had no experience of staff work; neither did he possess the skills of the courtier, which seemed more necessary now than did any military prowess. But he could read and write French and German and converse in both with perfect fluency. If the duke had confidence in him, then why should not he himself? In any event, he had a shorter time to wait than he expected to find out how tricky was the work, for the corporal returned to announce that Colonel Grant would see him at once. Not the best of news, sighed Hervey, for when he had first met the duke's chief of intelligence, a month ago, it had not been an especially cordial affair. Indeed, Grant had been decidedly livery.

Lieutenant-Colonel Colquhoun Grant of the 11th Foot (North Devon), 'Grant el Bueno' as the Spanish *guerrillas* had called him (to distinguish him from 'Grant the Bad'), was an officer who had spent more time on active service *behind* the enemy's lines than before them. He was impatient of formality, and this had, no doubt, been at the root of his abruptness at their first meeting. This morning, however, although he was brisk he was perfectly civil. Hervey might have appreciated the offer of coffee, but the absence of hospitality was not going to stand in the way of regard for the man whom many believed to be the duke's most trusted adviser.

'Sit down if you please, Captain Hervey,' said Grant, indicating the largest gilded chair Hervey had ever seen, which made him feel that his levee dress was not so out of place after all. 'I shall come at once to the point, sir: do you know anything of India?'

How might he begin to answer such a question? He had read and heard as much as any man in his position might, but he did not expect that it would amount to much for what must be Colonel Grant's purposes. 'A very little, sir – Clive and his campaigns for the most part,' he replied frankly, racking his brains to think what could be the duke's interest in India.

'You know, of course, of the Duke of Wellington's service in those lands – of his signal success in the Maratha war a decade ago?'

'Yes, sir,' smiled Hervey: he had read accounts, of Assaye especially.

'Well, the duke expects to be appointed governor-general in Calcutta when his duties at the Congress in Vienna are concluded.'

Hervey was not altogether surprised, for the duke's elder brother had occupied that office at the time of the Maratha war.

'Just so, Captain Hervey, and it has been the reversal of Lord Wellesley's policies these past ten years that has brought about the enfeeblement of the British interest in Hindoostan today.' Colonel Grant paused before resuming, seeming to want to plant some notion in Hervey's mind. 'It is highly probable,' he continued portentously, 'that the Board of Control will soon relieve Lord Moira of his office and press the duke to accept it.'

'And shall he?' asked Hervey, unsure of the honour that such an office held for a man who was now, without dispute, the first soldier of Europe.

'Yes,' replied Grant emphatically, and then, a little less so, added that the duke would first wish to be assured of certain preconditions. 'But I have no doubt that all these may be accommodated, and so we proceed on the assumption that the duke shall relieve Lord Moira in the new year.'

Hervey was uncertain, now, of his own tenure of appointment. 'Shall the duke want me with his staff in India, sir?'

'Indeed he will, Hervey; indeed he will. So much so that he wishes you to proceed there in advance of him. What say you to that?'

What might any officer say? India – the place that had made the young Arthur Wellesley's reputation! He supposed he would soon tire of Paris in any case, for garrison duties were always irksome, even in aiglets. He presumed he would be given leave in a month or so to return to England to marry Henrietta, and they would have the best of the autumn together in this fair city before balmy days cruising in a comfortable East Indiaman. He would be some distance from his beloved regiment but . . . 'I am all eagerness, sir, for I never supposed I should see Hindoostan. I imagine that the duke wishes me to arrange for his arrival in due course – is that so?'

'In a manner of speaking,' replied Grant, glancing down again at the papers on his desk, seemingly unwilling to answer the question direct. 'Tell me, Hervey – what do you know of the country powers in India?'

'That they are very largely at odds with each other, and at various times with the East India Company too. Beyond that I have no especial knowledge.'

'Have you heard, say, of the kingdom of Haidarabad?'

'Of course, sir: the nizam, as I understand it, rendered the duke considerable service in the war against the Marathas.'

'Just so, Hervey; just so,' nodded Grant approvingly: ' – our faithful ally.'

There was another period of silence, during which Hervey wondered if he were to be given any more tests of his scant knowledge of the subcontinent.

'The point is,' said Grant at length, seeming to search carefully for his words, 'India is far from being in the condition now that it was when the duke and the Marquess Wellesley, his brother, left there ten years ago. There has been fearful mismanagement. Cornwallis, Lord Wellesley's successor as governor-general, died within months of getting to Calcutta. *His* successor, Sir George Barlow, was nothing short of a booby, and thereafter it was Lord Minto – and he would do nothing that might result in any additional cost to the directors of the company. The Earl of Moira, who has been in Bengal for the best part of two years now, is, it seems too, a man in the same mould.'

'And so the duke is chary of what he might find there,' suggested Hervey.

'Yes indeed. And he is firmly of the opinion that the predisposition of the nizam towards us is of the essence. And, too, the condition of his army. Our agents report variously on this latter.'

Our agents – Hervey could not but be impressed by the duke's interest and reach.

'Which is where, Captain Hervey, your immediate duties in respect of your appointment will lie.' Grant was emphatic but still a shade elusive.

Hervey's look conveyed both keenness and curiosity.

'To put it baldly, Hervey, I wish you to go to Haidarabad and to make an assessment of the serviceableness of the nizam's forces, paying especial attention to his cavalry and artillery. And if you are able to gauge anything of the nizam's feelings towards us then such might be of inestimable value to the duke.'

If Matthew Hervey had had a moment's disappointment when, earlier, the duke had seemed dismissive, his self-esteem was now wholly restored, and with interest, for here was a mission of substance, a pivot on which the duke's entire policy in India might turn – and entrusted to *him*, a captain of but a few days. Heavens but there were rewards for Waterloo! He felt his cheeks aglow. He could hear his heart beating. He had a sense of floating, even. He began imagining how, with Henrietta, he might tour the kingdom of the nizam. They would see sights of which they would never dream – perhaps riding with the nizam's cavalry, and hunting all manner of beasts.

Grant called him back to the present. 'There must be great circumspection in this mission, Captain Hervey,' he added; 'it would not do for the nizam to believe that the duke had sent a spy. You will thereby travel to Haidarabad on a pretext.'

Hervey nodded. It need not dull any of the thrill. 'Is that pretext decided, sir?'

'Yes,' said Grant firmly. 'The nizam's cavalry are renowned for their skill with the lance. The duke has already set in train certain measures to form lancer regiments in our own army, consequent on witnessing the great effectiveness of the French lancers at Waterloo.'

Hervey winced at his own memory of that weapon's effectiveness. He was pleased to hear that it was at last to be put in the army's hands.

'And you will therefore be engaged in an ostensible study of the employment of that weapon,' continued Grant. 'Here is a letter of introduction to the nizam, conveying the duke's respect, and so forth, and here is another to the authorities in Calcutta requesting them to make all arrangements for you to travel to Haidarabad. When you arrive in Calcutta you will make contact with a Mr Josephus Bazzard, a writer at Fort William – headquarters of the Honourable East India Company on that continent, as you may know. He is our agent there and he alone knows of this mission. He will render you any additional assistance necessary.'

An uncomfortable thought now occurred to him. There was a certain immediacy in the tone of Colonel Grant's instructions. 'When would the duke wish me to leave for India, sir?' he asked, but with as little concern as he could manage.

'Not quite at once, Captain Hervey, but within the next day or so. The frigate which conveyed you here will at this moment be dropping anchor at Le Havre with instructions to await your rejoining her.'

Much of the colour drained from his face.

'Does that present you with difficulties?' enquired Grant sceptically.

'I am to be married, sir.'

'I see. Do I take it that you therefore wish to decline this assignment?'

If only he might have a fortnight – ten days, even. Something might be arranged . . .

'I am afraid that is not possible, Captain Hervey. This enterprise is already some weeks past due. There was some misunderstanding at the Horse Guards about your appointment to the duke's staff, was there not?'

Hervey would have wished not to be reminded of that unhappy business, and Grant was insinuating that his predicament was of his own making. What *could* he say?

'Very well then, you will leave tomorrow on the frigate *Nisus*,' said Grant briskly but airily: it saved him the distaste of issuing a direct order. 'Now, there is one more thing, Captain Hervey.'

He was beginning to think there was *always* one more thing in staff affairs. How straightforward was regimental life by comparison. 'Sir?'

Colonel Grant cleared his throat and glanced down at his papers again. 'You are acquainted with a Mr Selden, I believe – lately veterinary surgeon to the 6th Light Dragoons?'

No other name could have come as quite such a surprise. 'Ye-es,' he replied cautiously.

'Selden had to take his leave from Ireland owing to . . . ill health,' said Grant, looking up at Hervey for confirmation of this apparently official rendering of events.

Hervey would not confirm or gainsay it. Rather, he returned Grant's gaze in anticipation of what was to follow.

'And he has gone back to India, where he spent the early part of his service, as I understand it?'

'I did not know he had gone back, sir,' replied Hervey, now wholly intrigued.

'Mm,' nodded Grant; 'our agents report that he has an appointment at the court of the Rajah of Chintal.'

There seemed no end to Colonel Grant's information. Hervey, again, made no reply.

'Chintal is a very minor princely state to the east and contiguous with Haidarabad. It would be an entirely regular thing for you to make contact with Mr Selden during your travels, would it not? Chintalpore, where is the rajah's palace, is close to the Godavari river, downstream of the nizam's territories.'

'Make contact for the purposes of acquiring his assessment of affairs?' asked Hervey.

'That might be helpful,' nodded Grant; 'but there is another matter – a matter of some delicacy.' He looked down again and rearranged the papers. 'At the conclusion of the Maratha war the duke was given title to certain *jagirs* – estates, if you will – which lie within Chintal. It is now prudent that these jagirs be . . . *alienated.*'

Hervey did not at first know what to make of this. 'And I am to be an instrument in alienating them?'

'Just so, Captain Hervey. But it is a trifle more complicated than that. You see, it were better if the duke had never had title to these jagirs in the first instance. It were better if all trace, in terms of deeds and the like, were . . . *no more.*'

Hervey understood right enough, but not why.

Colonel Grant lowered his eyes and his voice. 'Captain Hervey, it is one of the precepts of intelligence work that if it be not necessary to know, then a person should not be made privy.'

Hervey looked suitably chastened.

'Well then – let us address ourselves to the particulars of your mission.'

'Hell and confound it!' cursed Hervey, startling even Private Johnson. 'How long has she been like this?'

'A week, sir. She came down wi' it last Saturday after drill.'

Jessye was, it seemed, feverish. She had been coughing a good deal and was off her feed. 'You didn't get her into a muck sweat and then just put her away?'

'No ah didn't, Mr 'Ervey!' Johnson was deeply offended, his broad Sheffield vowels stretching to twice their usual length.

'Oh, I . . . I beg your pardon, Johnson. I said the first thing that came into my head.'

There was no one else about in the infirmary stables, just a couple of box-rest cases. Jessye need not have been there, strictly, but Johnson had been pleased to remove himself from the supervision of the riding master and to give her a bigger stall and more straw. These were fine stables, thought Hervey – the best he had ever seen. 'The King of France's horses are better housed than I.'

'Eh, sir?'

'I was just thinking on something the Elector of Hanover is supposed to have said,' he replied absently. 'It was a good move of Lord George's to get this billet. I'd rather her sweat out the fever here than in the first place we had.'

'It's nowt but a chill, anyroad,' said Johnson confidently. 'Not as bad as that one she got in Ireland last Christmas, either.'

'No,' sighed Hervey, 'I can see that now, but I had a mind to ride her to Le Havre.'

'Where's that? Ah wouldn't take 'er nought but a mile or so.'

'On the coast.'

The coast. Johnson looked at him searchingly. 'Is tha gooin' t'tell me abaht it then Mr 'Ervey?'

He had wished for a better moment, but . . . 'How would you like to go to India, Johnson?' he tried bluntly.

'Wi' thee, Mr 'Ervey?'

Hervey smiled with some satisfaction. 'You mean that going half-way round the world would be conditional only upon the officer you groomed for?'

'Mr 'Ervey, outside Sheffield it's all t'same t'me!'

'Then I take it you will come with me?'

'I'm *thy* groom!'

Hervey smiled again, with much relief: there would be one familiar face at least, but above all a man he could trust in what was bound to be the occasional tight corner. 'And you have heard that it is "Captain" now?' he added rather proudly.

'Ay, I keep forgettin'. It's a bit of a bummy fer me, though, since I'll now 'ave to stand in t'front rank at stables parade.'

Hervey's smile widened yet more. 'You may not be here that long!'

Johnson scooped up a fresh pile of droppings with the clapboards and threw them into a wicker skip. 'When do we 'ave t'go?'

'Tomorrow. And we take Jessye with us. Do you think you'll be able to lay hands on a horse ambulance?'

'In France?' gasped Johnson in astonishment; 'they *eat* their 'orses 'ere as soon as they go lame!'

Hervey frowned, unsure if this half-truth were to Johnson's mind a serious objection. 'There must be an ambulance at the duke's head-quarters – or sprung tumbrils for racehorses somewhere in the city.'

'All right, sir: I'll ask one of t'other grooms to go 'n 'ave a look. I'd go meself but tha'll want all thee kit gettin' ready. If there is one we'll find it.'

'Thank you, Johnson,' Hervey replied softly, gripping his shoulder; 'I would not have split the two of you, and I would not wish to go to India without her.'

'Well,' said his groom with a shrug, 'it's nice te know which of us counts fer most!'

'You know very well what I mean,' replied Hervey, not inclined to flatter him any more.

'And can I ask why we're gooin' t'India, sir?'

'You *may* ask, yes, but I would rather you didn't.'

Johnson whistled beneath his breath.

'Don't make that silly noise. It's just that I am not able to speak of it at present.' He had no wish to deceive his own groom (though he recognized what an inauspicious beginning to covert work that was).

'Right enough Mr – *Cap'n* – 'Ervey, sir! I'll not say another word abaht it.'

All this had been conducted from either side of the bar of Jessye's stall, and Hervey now ducked under it to take a closer look at her. She gave him a snuffling welcome which flecked his jacket, and then proceeded to rub her nose dry on his sleeve. 'Her eye is bright enough,' he concluded: 'she's certainly on the mend. Have you been giving her anything?'

'Mothballs and nightshade for 'er cough to start with. Then iron tonic.'

Hervey nodded. 'Has there been anything else?'

'No, she's been as right as rain. An' if yer 'ave a look, them windgalls 'ave got no worse.'

He felt down each fore cannon to the fetlock joint. The swellings which had been so prominent after they had reached Paris – as with so many of the regiment's horses after the work they had been forced to do in the preceding weeks – were, if anything, less pronounced. 'See,' said Hervey, with a mild tone of triumph, 'I told you blistering wouldn't be necessary. Windgalls generally look after themselves if you leave well alone.'

Johnson smiled thinly.

Hervey recognized the admission. 'Come, then, man: what have you been doing with them?'

Johnson spoke boldly again. 'Tha knows that iodine stuff that Mr Selden were always on abaht?'

It was strange how Selden's name should crop up again so soon. 'Ye-es?'

'Works a treat.'

'How did you find iodine?' asked Hervey, dubiously. It had never been freely available before: Selden had had his smuggled from France as if it were brandy.

'Them Frenchies use it all t'time.'

'You have been . . . *progging* – in the French lines?'

'Ay.'

Hervey smiled as he shook his head.

'An look at 'er shoes: they's saved 'er a lot of strain.'

He picked up her near fore. 'Calkins! You know I don't trust calkins.' But he was much taken by the workmanship. 'Who made them? I've never seen neater!'

'Oh . . . a farrier.'

Hervey's ear was attuned enough to Johnson's Yorkshire to alert him at once to the purposeful absence of the definite article. '*Which* farrier?'

'You don't know 'im.'

'*Johnson!*'

'Well, when ah were gettin t'iodine—'

'You don't mean that you have had Jessye shod by a damned Frog!'

Johnson admitted his delinquency.

'Well, I have to say these shoes appear to do their job well,' he conceded with a heavy sigh, ducking under the bar again. 'She's unlikely to see a set put on so faithfully where we are going.' There was hardly time, anyway, to be talking about the finer points of farriery. 'Now, I shall have to be about some pressing matters. Come to my quarters after evening stables, if you will. And try any stratagem to get a box on wheels for her meanwhile!'

The last thing he expected to see when he returned to the Sixth's mess that afternoon was an express from Longleat, and it was all he could do to escape the curiosity of the half-dozen other occupants of that superior billet to find a private corner in which to discover the condition of his engagement to Henrietta Lindsay. That message from London, composed in half-bewildered haste in the ADCs' office at the Horse Guards after he had learned of his appointment, might so easily have been received with ill favour. Before breaking the seal he made a rapid estimate to assess whether it could have been written after receipt of his own, but his calculation was inconclusive, and he therefore opened it with much uneasiness.

Longleat
11th August

Dearest Matthew,
Be not in the slightest troubled by duty taking you from me once more, for the relief – and excessive pride – which I and all your family feel on learning of your circumstances quite outweighs our dismay at your temporary estrangement from us. We read daily of the difficulties under which the Duke of Wellington labours in bringing a just peace to France, and if your special facilities might be in any way supportive of those efforts then your absence is more happily to be borne.

He sighed, with considerable relief. Here, indeed, was a handsome understanding of his hasty departure for Paris. That much boded well for when she received the letter he had yet to write explaining that their nuptials must be postponed *sine die*. His stomach had scarcely stopped churning since Colonel Grant had revealed the immediacy of his mission, and only the urgency of his domestic arrangements had kept him from complete seizure. He read on, cheered by this beginning.

I know of nothing, however, which indisposes my being with you in these labours, and I shall therefore make haste to Paris as soon as I have my guardian's leave. I send these brief presents to you now by the speediest means so that you might be assured of our great love and my wish to join you at once. Lord John Howard, who has been all kindness in bringing this news, believes that with a fair wind in the Channel I might be in Paris before the third week in this month is out. Pray that it should be so, dearest!
Your most affectionate
Henrietta

His mind was racing even faster than it had at the Horse Guards. He must make himself compute it properly: what was the *earliest* she might arrive in France if the marquess gave her leave at once? He had to try his fingers to keep count of the stages. Longleat to . . . Dover? A day and a night? The crossing – a day, a night? And if she left on the twelfth, early? . . . *Great heavens* but it could be done: she might arrive in France this very evening! He rushed from his room to summon the best man for what he had in mind, and then set pen to paper to explain to Henrietta where his new orders were to take him, and their immediacy. Writing at great speed, without time for circumspection, he found himself penning endearments so direct that he blushed as he reread them, unlike some of the lame affairs he had tried hitherto. By the time the knock came at his door, he was positively fired with excitement. 'Corporal Collins, how is your big French charger?' he asked, still writing hurriedly.

The NCO looked at him a trifle askance. 'In hale condition, Captain Hervey, sir.' The news of his promotion, as any news of note, had not escaped the admirable Collins.

'Good, I want you to gallop him to Calais, intercept Lady Henrietta Lindsay and escort her to Le Havre, to His Majesty's Ship *Nisus*, and by first light on Wednesday! Oh, and I wish you to give her this,' he beamed, handing him the letter.

Corporal Collins remained as unperturbable as he had been the day of Hervey's arrest in the middle of the battle at Toulouse. But he did have questions. 'I take it, sir, that you do not know by which ship her ladyship will arrive?'

'You are correct, Corporal Collins; I am not even sure that she will arrive at Calais.'

'I see, sir. Nor, I presume, *when* exactly she might arrive?'

'Just so,' replied Hervey briskly.

'You wish me, in essence, sir, to patrol the Dover straits and inter-cept Lady Henrietta?'

'You have had less agreeable scouting missions, Corporal Collins!'

'Indeed, sir.' Collins's blithe enquiries could hardly conceal his amusement, though not even Hervey's broad smile could tempt him from his picture of correctness: with a third stripe, maybe, but he still had to secure that precious piece of tape, and correctness meanwhile would be his order of the day. 'And I presume that at first light on Wednesday your ship will set sail for wherever she is sailing?'

'India – yes, perhaps even earlier, but not, probably, later.'

'I shall do my best, Captain Hervey, and, if that is all, I shall take my leave and put my gelding for the coast.'

'Thank you, Corporal Collins: this may turn out a deuced more important ride than the time you galloped for me at Toulouse.'

Collins allowed himself the suggestion of a smile. 'I shall at least receive more than a glower at the end of it, sir, unlike with the major!'

Hervey sighed. 'That you will, though I miss the major's scowls right enough.'

'There is not a man that doesn't, sir. I never imagined we would finish that day in June with so few left in the saddle, but never did I imagine we would see such a battle – just *pounding* all day.'

'Well, Bonaparte is on his way to the south Atlantic, so we are told. There'll be no escape from there.'

'If I might just say, sir – it's nice to see you back, and *Captain* Hervey. I hope you will not be long away, wherever it is you are going.'

'*Thank* you, Corporal Collins,' he replied; 'I am truly very touched.'

And with that, and the most punctilious of salutes, his erstwhile covering-corporal made off for his gallop, leaving him to the first pangs of regret at promotion away from the family of the Sixth.

Having put his trust in the best NCO-galloper in the regiment, Hervey now followed with military prudence to set in place a plan should Collins fail in his mission. He would seek out the picket serjeant-major, whose name for duty that day he had read in regimental orders with a smile. First, though, he must apprise his commanding officer – for such Lord George still was until formalities were completed – of all that had happened, and next he must inform the adjutant of his despatch of Corporal Collins and the possible arrival, after he himself had left for Le Havre, of Henrietta. And then he would look for the man most likely to serve him aptly, for although Lord George Irvine would be all emollience to any wound, Serjeant Armstrong might have a mastery of Henrietta that no officer was likely to gain.

Hervey found him where in camp he habitually was at that time of the afternoon (whether picket serjeant-major or not), the day's work largely done, the dog hour before evening stables. The wet canteen was doing brisk trade, and Armstrong sat outside smoking a long meerschaum (the King's German Legion had made them all the fashion), reading his orders and making entries for such duties as had been completed at this stage of his picket. It was the first they had seen of each other in the best part of a month, and the shared pleasure in the reunion was as much that of friends as of officer and serjeant. Hervey wished first to know how was his arm, for it had taken the glancing point of a lance at Waterloo, and three weeks later – when he had left for England – the wound was not fully closed. Armstrong took off his jacket, pulled up his shirt sleeve and showed him the vivid but dry scar, greatly amused that it was in the shape of a chevron. Which meant, he reckoned, that promotion to serjeant-major was imminent, or – more likely, he sighed – demotion to corporal. Either way, the surgeon had told him that his sword arm would soon regain its full, formidable, power. Hervey told him of his own good news – the promotion and appointment to the duke's staff (though Armstrong, like Collins, knew of it already) and his India orders. At once Armstrong insisted he be allowed to accompany him.

That was not possible, said Hervey: he had no authority to engage a serjeant.

'Aw, Mr Hervey, I'd rather gan wi' 'ee any day than stay 'ere faggin' aboot like Miss Molly!'

Hervey laughed. How he could lay on the Tyneside for effect! 'Geordie Armstrong, let me remind you of scripture – "I have married a wife and therefore I cannot come"!'

Serjeant Armstrong had recently drawn quarters by ballot for Caithlin to join him from Cork, and he looked sheepish at the reminding of it. 'But don't you preach at me, Mr Hervey!'

'I should not dream of it,' he laughed once more: 'not now that you're a good Catholic!'

'Now there's a rum snitch for you! You know I had no choice!'

'No, indeed,' replied Hervey, smiling still. 'Caithlin was worth a mass!'

'Bugger the Pope!'

Hervey frowned in a sort of dutiful disapproval.

Two passing dragoons lost step as they saluted, bringing a blistering rebuke from Armstrong and sending them doubling away as if the sutler were after them at pay parade. 'This new draft from Canterbury – can't even walk in a straight line. I sometimes wish I had that depot squadron!' He took another long draw on his pipe, spat with impressive force and direction into a gutter, and all but emptied his tankard. 'How are things at hind-quarters? Still pushing out horse-shit are they, sir?'

Hervey smiled at the old joke. 'The duke looked well, the little I saw of him. He had a very handsome young lady on his arm – that much I can tell you.'

15

'Ah,' exclaimed Armstrong knowingly; 'that'd be Lady Shelley. She's hot-arsed for him!'

'How do you know that?' he asked, quite taken aback. 'Is it common knowledge?'

'Because I did a stint as brigade orderly serjeant last week and saw 'em every day in the Shamsel Easy. He lets 'er ride that chestnut of his.'

'Well, doubtless it's all innocent enough,' Hervey shrugged. 'He's earned a little recreation, has he not?'

'Ay, no one would deny that. But there's many as wish that he'd put pen to paper again and do his cavalry justice for yon battle. Have you read his despatch yet?' He pointed to the old canteen copy of the *Times*. 'A lame affair if you ask me: you'd think there'd not been a British horse within a dozen miles of the place!'

'No, I have not yet read it – but I have heard say that the duke regrets he did not give more praise. Besides, *we* know the truth, and that is what matters in the end, does it not?'

'Ay,' he sighed; 'and some of it is best not come out, I suppose.'

Silence followed. At length, when Hervey had forced himself to stop thinking of Serjeant Strange and the French lancers (for he could still not wholly rid himself of guilt in allowing Strange to pay with his life so that he might reach the Prussians in time), he steeled himself to his other purpose. 'I have a favour to ask. It may not come to it, but I have to be prepared.'

Serjeant Armstrong looked intrigued. 'Ay, anything sir.'

Hervey recounted the long, involved story – the leaving of Horningsham, the business at the Horse Guards, the frigate, Henrietta's letter, Corporal Collins's dash to the Channel . . . He was beyond being abashed at the muddle and misunderstanding, as once he might have been: life could not be regulated as if it were a handy troop. He sighed and raised his eyebrows, though, for the muddle was unedifying. 'So you will see that things are explained to her, and seen to, if she arrives after I've gone?'

'Of course, sir. And as soon as you can fix for me an' Caithlin to come out and join you—'

'There is nothing I should like better.'

'Ay, enough said, Mr Hervey – *Captain*, I should say. I 'aven't even said "congratulations" yet. It's grown-up stuff being an ADC. You'll be colonel one day soon. Everybody's pleased for you, but sorry you're not staying.'

'I'll be back right enough, Serjeant Armstrong; don't you worry. It's for the best. I know that's what Lord George says. Grown-up stuff, you think? There has to be a time to leave the regimental nest, at least to flap around for a while.' He did not sound wholly convinced.

'Well just don't shite on the Line, as some of them staff seem to like doing when they fly about!'

'No indeed, Serjeant Armstrong,' he laughed; 'I shall be sweetness itself. And I *shall* be back!'

'Ay, well there are going to be too many new faces for my liking – and all as ugly as them two greenheads from the depot just now. So long as Lord George stays commanding we'll be all right, I suppose. But if he goes I've a mind to hand in me bridle.'

'I should be more than sorry if you did that. And in any case, there's bound to be promotion soon.'

'Troop serjeant-major? By God I'd roust some of them corporals about!'

'Just so, Serjeant Armstrong! I'll wager you'll have your crown by the time I get to India.'

'Maybe, but I hear we'll be dropping to four troops soon enough, and that's not a bonny prospect. There are a few ahead of me still.'

'In seniority, perhaps.'

'Now as it's peace, that's the way things will go,' he muttered, cocking an eye: 'seniority tempered by merit, don't they call it? Seniority tempered by dead men's boots more like!'

'Well let us pray not: that's *one* lesson that has been learned these past six years, surely?'

'Ay, perhaps so. At least it's not seniority tempered by arse-licking, like in some regiments! To dead men's boots, then,' he added, thoughtfully, raising his tankard.

'Yes,' agreed Hervey, nodding and lifting his own. 'To absent friends!'

Armstrong tapped it with his: 'To 'Arry Strange.'

'To Harry Strange,' repeated Hervey, his voice muted; 'and Major Edmonds.'

'Ay, an' all the others.' Armstrong emptied his tankard, rose and placed it carefully on the table outside the canteen door. 'Now if you'll excuse me, Captain Hervey, sir, I'll get along to evening stables.' He fastened the button of his collar flap, replaced his shako and saluted. 'Good luck, sir. And don't you worry about Miss Lindsay. She's as good as on the strength now.'

The Duke of Wellington entered Colonel Grant's office without formality and sat in the same chair that Hervey had occupied that morning. His face was a little flushed, as it always was when he had taken leave of Lady Shelley, and he had on a dark blue coat rather than uniform, for he was ambassador as much as he was commander-in-chief. 'Well, how went things with young Hervey?'

'Favourably, I believe, duke,' replied Grant, pouring a glass of hock for him.

'How much did you have need to tell him?'

'He has his general mission and cover with the nizam – he was much taken with it, too. As to the Chintal business, I told him only what he needs to know at this time.'

'And you can trust this agent of yours in Calcutta? Bazzard, his name you say?'

'Well, duke, you will not let me go there in person, so Bazzard shall have to do. And I'm sure he will: he has served me well in the past.'

'You do not think Hervey is in any danger by not knowing all? He did us damned fine service at Waterloo: he doesn't deserve to end as tiger bait – unlike a dozen I could name three-times his rank!'

'I don't see him in any danger, duke. All he has to do is go to Calcutta, and Bazzard will arrange the rest.'

The duke took a sip of his hock, and grunted. 'Who in heaven's name would have thought a bit of dusty land in a place you've scarcely heard of should be such a thorn in the side! Those damned Whigs will have me if they possibly can, and since Warren Hastings' impeachment there isn't anyone safe who's made the slightest profit in India!'

Grant raised his eyebrows in sympathy.

'They'll block any appointment of me to Calcutta however they can. And once I'm back from Vienna they'll want me out of the way here too. Finding me with estates in India will be just what they need.'

'Don't be too cast-down, duke,' said Grant, frowning. 'The mood is swinging against the present administration in India. The calls for you to go back are being heard, I believe.'

The duke grunted again. 'Well, perhaps so. But, in any case, I'm still unconvinced that anything can be done there without Haidarabad wholly in our pocket. And it will hardly do if I am seen to be in any way beholden to Chintal because of those jagirs – which, I might add, have barely kept me in decent claret these past five years!'

18

'I have always believed that were Chintal in the Company's pocket too, there would be greater room for manoeuvre as regards the nizam.' Grant poured more hock and lit a cheroot. 'A small place – yes – but the rajah sits on commanding ground. The nizam could scarcely forbear to take note.'

'Just so,' agreed the duke. 'I should never wish to see Chintal fall to any but the Company. But then neither should I wish to undertake any enterprise against the country powers without the nizam at hand. We need both of them.'

Grant concurred.

'And you are confident – even though we have not told him all – that Hervey will get those damned jagirs disposed of, and without trace? *And* will come to no harm?'

'There is no cause for disquiet on either count, duke,' replied Grant, shaking his head. 'The fewer who know these things the safer it must be: that has always been the principle on which I have worked. All he has to do is take a pleasant enough cruise to Calcutta, and then Bazzard will arrange things.'

The duke took another sip of hock before standing and making to leave. 'And he knows he must make contact with your man before he begins beating about the country?'

'Sir, he has his orders. The reason we chose him for this mission is that he has proved himself devoted to his profession. In any case,' he smiled, standing to open the door for his principal, '*Nisus* is under orders to join the East India Squadron, and their station is Calcutta. I do not think we should have any fears about Captain Hervey's aptness for this.'

CHAPTER TWO

A STAR IN THE EAST

Le Havre, two days later

'Captain Hervey, in my twelve years or more in one of His Majesty's ships I have never heard the like!'

There was no reply.

'Never before have I been asked to give passage to a horse!'

Still there was no reply.

Captain Laughton Peto, RN, struck the taffrail with his fist in a theatrical gesture of exasperation. 'Confound it, sir, she is a frigate, not a packet!'

Captain Hervey smiled sheepishly. 'Sir, you have aboard a goat and several chickens. And I hear that it is not uncommon to see a cow under the forecastle. To what do you object in equines?'

'Damn your impudence, sir!' roared Peto, striking the rail again. But he knew well enough that his protests were to no avail. The frigate *Nisus* had been placed at the disposal of the Duke of Wellington's aide-de-camp – and that was that. 'Mr Belben!' he shouted.

The first lieutenant rushed aft and saluted. 'Sir?'

'Mr Belben, be so good as to find a berth for a cavalry charger,' said the captain briskly.

'*Sir?*' replied the lieutenant, his youthful face contorted by incomprehension.

'Do I have to repeat myself, Mr Belben?' rasped Peto. 'Do you not understand plain English?' And, as his first lieutenant hurried away to contemplate his unprecedented orders, Peto turned back to this agent of the victor of Waterloo. 'Come, Captain Hervey,' he resumed cautiously; 'I think we may better discuss this extraordinary commission of yours at my table.'

Matthew Hervey was, in outward appearance at least, a man transformed from that of a year ago. Then, he had been a lieutenant for but a month, following the deposit of the better part of his savings, and the prize-money accrued over six years' campaign service, with the regimental agents. Into the premises of Messrs Greenwood, Cox & Hammersly of Craig's Court in Westminster he had walked a cornet on his first occasion to visit the capital, and there he had signed an instrument for the purchase of a lieutenancy in the 6th Light Dragoons. He had signed another for the sale of his cornetcy to an officer in the Twentieth anxious to avoid service in India, whither that regiment was posted, and had put his signature to a further instrument for the assignment of arrears of pay, held by the agents, towards the difference in price – £350. Other regiments were cheaper (and a few were markedly more expensive), but Hervey would never consider the option of changing horses. He loved the Sixth as if it were his family – which, in all but the literal sense, it was. Its commanding officer, Lord George Irvine, had always shown him the greatest kindness. Its choleric major, Joseph Edmonds, a soldier who had known almost nothing but campaigning in his thirty years' service, had encouraged him in every particular of the profession, and had exercised a protecting, paternal hand on many an occasion. Sir Edward Lankester, his troop leader – urbane, coolly, almost contemptuously, brave – had been his idol, like an older brother. His fellow cornets, and lieutenants too, who had filled the mess with laughter and good company in the darkest of times, had been his people as surely as were his blood family in Horningsham. And Hervey would add yet more to that family, for in it he counted, as did any officer worth his salt, the companionship of the ranks – the non-commissioned officers who put his orders into action, and the dragoons, the private men, whose life turned and occasionally depended on those orders, and whose daily routine was either miserable or tolerable depending on the aptness and humanity of the officers. The Sixth, however, were a family that had seen misfortune. Waterloo, though a battle gained, had been, in the duke's own words, hardly better than a battle lost. True, the Sixth had suffered not half as much as the infantry, but shot, shell and lance had plucked some of the best from its bosom. Hervey may have been in two minds about his new appointment – this mission especially – but before Waterloo he could never have contemplated having a choice at all.

And so now he was *Captain* Hervey, with aiglets and the patronage of the duke himself, and no longer so impecunious that economy was for him strict necessity. Yet in one respect at least Matthew Hervey was unaltered: to frigate captains he was still in thrall. Captain Peto was, in any case, an officer to whom no ordinary mortal could be other than in thrall. Every reef and hitch, every furl and coil, even in the very extremities of the *Nisus*, was made in the expectation that his eye might at any time alight on the endeavour. And all was therefore perfection. What was more, however, he achieved this exemplary regimen without resort to flogging. Peto was, indeed, renowned as much for his implacable opposition to the practice as for his boldness in closing with a foe. He had once hanged a man for cowardice in the face of the enemy, but long before the Admiralty had put a stop to it he would not permit a bosun's mate even to start a laggard.

Captain Laughton Peto was in age two years, possibly three, Hervey's senior. He was the same height and build, though his back was a little longer, and his hair was dark, full and straight and looked as though it might once have been pulled into a queue. His manner was not easy to fathom – at times the utmost insouciance, and at others zest for the merest detail of his ship's routine. He might talk discursively one minute, and then in the next his clipped quarterdeck speech would seem almost incomprehensible. Hervey wondered if he were married, for it would go hard with any wife to live with so contrary a man. When they had first met, at Chatham not a week ago, there had been something of an edge to their intercourse. Peto had not been well disposed to the notion of holding his frigate ready for the conveyance of a staff officer, even an aide-de-camp of the Duke of Wellington, and wished only to be about his passage to the Indies before the winds became any less favourable. When Hervey had gone aboard *Nisus* he had been presented with sealed orders marked, 'To be opened only at sea', and so it was off the North Foreland that he had learned that he was to report to the Duke of Wellington with all possible haste, and to request that the ship on no account leave for the Indies without word from Paris – to which Peto had replied, with no little irritation, that he was not in the habit of disobeying Admiralty orders, for those were his instructions too from their lordships. Yet neither man had anticipated that there was to be any congruence in their instructions. So here where the Seine, having flowed peaceably through Bonaparte's erstwhile capital, became salty by the Channel – for mastery of which Englishmen like Peto had fought since Drake's day – the captain of the *Nisus* found himself once more at the disposal of the captain of light dragoons.

Captain Peto's quarters comprised a day cabin running to half the length of the stern windows, a dining space – the steerage – and two sleeping cabins, one of which, as on the short passage to France, he now gave up to Hervey. The principal cabins were well furnished. Comfortable chairs, as well as a large desk, occupied the day cabin, while a highly polished dining table of Cuban mahogany, and eight chairs, graced the steerage. There were even some pleasant-looking pictures on the bulkheads, including one or two small oils of indeterminate landscapes, and the table was laid with silver.

'Take a seat, Hervey,' said Peto, indicating a comfortable armchair; 'one of my French Hepplewhites.'

Hervey assumed them to be booty, acquired in one of the many dashing engagements he knew Peto to have seen. 'I presume they are—'

'I began with ten, but clearing for action takes its toll.' He said it almost with relish. 'There are many who consider the Hepplewhite chair in the French taste to be the acme of English cabinetmaking: there is not a single straight line anywhere in it,' he continued absently, waving an outstretched palm towards one of the objects of his admiration. 'I bought them in Bond Street when last I was attending at the Admiralty.'

Bond Street? *English* cabinetmaking? Another fox's paw he had nearly made of that!

'You will take some Madeira with me, will you not?'

Hervey nodded approvingly.

'A rather fine Sercial, I fancy – an eighty-three,' continued Peto, pouring from a broad flat-bottomed decanter. 'And a vintage, mind – not a solera.'

Hervey took a sip and agreed that it was indeed special. 'It puts me in mind of some German wines, in both colour and taste,' he said.

'You are well acquainted with Rhenish, are you?' enquired Peto, evidently impressed.

'The wines of Alsace to be precise. I had a governess from there who first told me of Gewürztraminer, and then the King's Germans gave me the taste for it.'

Peto nodded, favourably. 'They say the Sercial derives originally from the Riesling grape, so there is an affinity with the region.' He paused, his mind seeming momentarily to be elsewhere, before clearing his throat and returning to his original intention. 'Captain Hervey, you had better, I think, give me some account of what you are about so that I can best order my ship's affairs. Start, if you will, at the beginning, for I must know it all.'

Hervey waited first for Peto's steward, a Suffolk man who had been almost twice as long at sea as his captain had been on earth, to finish laying the table, and then he began to explain, though not without some misgivings. 'I am bound by confidentiality in this matter,' he warned; 'or, at least, by discretion.'

Peto looked at him indignantly. 'You do not suppose that I, myself, am without discretion in such matters?'

'No, indeed – forgive my incivility,' he stammered. 'In truth I am as yet uneasy with the circumspection required.'

Indeed he was. He was also unsure of his capacity for such an assignment. He had been wholly – headily – flattered, as would any officer, when the Adjutant General had made the offer on the duke's behalf of his becoming an ADC. But all his service had been with the Sixth, and though he knew the elements of staff practice he was by no means confident of his aptness for employment beyond regimental duty. But there was, immediately, the question of secrecy. He looked at Peto resolutely: 'I see no good reason, sir, why I should not tell you all, for I shall be much in want of counsel these coming months. How long is our passage to Hindoostan?'

'Four months at best; six at most.'

'Oh,' said Hervey, sounding a touch discouraged; 'I had imagined half that time.'

Peto frowned again. 'Captain Hervey, do you know *anything* of navigation – of sea currents and trade winds?'

Hervey confessed he did not.

'I imagine you suppose we shall merely cruise south, round the Cape of Good Hope and then make directly for India?'

Hervey's smile, and the inclination of his eyebrows, indicated that that was exactly what he had supposed.

'Well, to begin with,' sighed Peto, 'we are making this passage at the least propitious time. To have full use of the south-west monsoon, which blows from October until April, we should have set out in the spring. Come,' he said, rising and indicating the table on which there were spread several charts. 'See here' (he pointed with a pair of dividers): 'we shall pass about ten leagues to the west of the Cape Verde Islands and continue westward, almost crossing the Atlantic to the coast of Brazil to get the south-east trades on the beam. Then, at about three degrees south of the Equator, we shall pick up the westerlies to bring us around the Cape. And in the Indian Ocean we shall need to stand well to the east of Madagascar to find what remains of the monsoon.'

Hervey apologized for his nescience as they returned to their chairs. But of greater moment was the disclosure of his assignment, for he was again seized by doubts as to what discretion he legitimately possessed in the matter. He had not been sworn to secrecy – quite – but in everything that had passed between Colonel Grant and the duke's new aide-de-camp, there had been the very proper presumption of it. And yet Hervey knew too that he had been appointed to the staff principally because of what the duke himself had referred to as his 'percipient exercise of judgement' at Waterloo. He had neither experience nor training in work of a covert nature (though his present commission scarcely, to his mind, gave him the appellation *spy*). He would therefore have to trust his instincts, and these now told him that he could trust in Captain Laughton Peto – trust absolutely. 'Then if we are to spend so long in each other's company it is the very least I should do to apprise you fully of my business,' he said, with a most conscious effort to avoid any further semblance of condescension. 'I shall tell you each and every detail – though as yet they are few.'

The door opened and in came Flowerdew again. 'Beg leave to bring a pudding, sir,' he said, in a voice that called to mind Serjeant Strange's mellow Suffolk vowels. Hervey shivered at the remembrance.

Peto eyed his steward gravely. 'It is the Welsh venison pudding?'

'Ay, Captain,' replied Flowerdew, equally solemnly; 'and there is a redcurrant jelly with it, and your cussy sauce.'

This news was received with evident satisfaction. Peto took both the greatest pride and the greatest pleasure in his table. It was, perhaps, unsurprising since he appeared to take the greatest pride in everything about his ship. Hervey knew enough about Admiralty to know that a ship in the hale condition that was the *Nisus* – with her fine fittings, new paint and gold leaf – was not found by chance: Peto would have had to go to endless pains to flatter the dockyard commissioner into providing that which was routinely denied to other, less persuasive, captains. Or else – and he suspected it was this latter – it was Peto's own purse that had embellished his ship. As to his taking pleasure in his table, albeit somewhat self-consciously, Hervey was likewise not in the least surprised, for in his experience men exposed as a matter of course to great privation rarely persisted in a taste for frugality in times of plenty – and Peto had, more than once in his service, been reduced to a diet of biscuit and water.

When Flowerdew was gone the captain conducted his guest to the table and bade him resume his explanation.

'It seems that the Duke of Wellington expects at any moment to be appointed governor-general in India,' he confided.

Peto merely raised an eyebrow in disbelief – or in dismay.

'He has been given to understand that Lord Moira will soon be dismissed,' he continued, 'since that gentleman apparently has little appetite for reversing the policies of Sir George Barlow – which, it is commonly supposed, were too feeble with the native princes. You will know, of course, that the duke's own brother prosecuted a most vigorous policy before Sir George.'

Peto's brow furrowed. 'And yet, from all I read and hear, the Court of Directors do not appear to be developing any appetite for intervention. Quite the contrary, in fact.'

Hervey sighed briefly, but aptly conveying his own frustration with the limited intelligence imparted to him in Paris. 'The Company, perhaps – yes. But I am to suppose that the government – the Board of Control, that is – takes the opposite view.'

'And do you share these opinions?' he asked, leaning across the table to replenish Hervey's Sercial, a distinct challenge in the tone.

'I confess for my own mind I know only what I read in the newspapers and the *Edinburgh Review*, and these are frequently contradictory accounts. I am the duke's aide-de-camp and it matters only at this time that I understand perfectly what is in the duke's mind,' he answered resolutely.

'And what is his need of you in Calcutta?'

'I am to go in advance to India and to make certain appreciations of the situation.' Hervey's reply lacked just a measure of his former resolution.

Peto now had about him a decidedly disapproving air, though he said nothing.

'I am sorry, Captain Peto, but you appear to object to this assignment,' countered Hervey, puzzled.

'The Honourable East India Company, sir,' began Peto, 'is neither honourable nor a company worth the name, for its monopoly has perverted trade. It is a body which maintains armies and retails tea.'

Hervey hesitated. 'You speak as someone with a very singular grudge.'

'My father might not have lost what little he had by way of stocks – his sole provision for the future – if, during the late blockade, the East Indies markets had been open.'

'But the opening-up of trade – has not the Company's monopoly of the eastern markets been repealed?'

'The reform of the charter was only two years ago. It came too late to save my family's interests.'

'I am sorry to hear it,' sighed Hervey, 'for heaven knows the country has need of every enterprise now to repay its war debt. Your father – he is a merchant still?'

'No, Captain Hervey, he was never a merchant: he had merely invested what little capital he possessed in an ill-starred joint-stock company.'

'I fear that my father might have had the same story to tell had he not already purchased a modest annuity with his capital. Well, there is great need of enterprise nevertheless: the duke says we have spent eight hundred million fighting the French, when before the war it was scarce eighteen a year.'

'Then there will be more slaughter in the east to pay for it. It will be the very devil of a business. That is why, I suppose, your principal is to go to India – to pay his way these past dozen years and more!'

Hervey frowned.

'Do you know much of India, sir? I have made something of a study of that continent,' Peto challenged.

'I confess I know little, sir. I have with me a new history of the enterprise but I have yet to make more than a beginning with it.'

'Well, I tell you that no good will come out of our enterprise there. I have read extensively of the trial of Warren Hastings, and of Mr Fox's speeches in parliament on the East India Bill. What is our object in India, Captain Hervey? It is too ill-defined, I tell you. We shall be drawn ever greater into the wars that are endemic in that place, and our outlay will vastly exceed any receipts.'

'So I may take it,' smiled Hervey, 'that you are not greatly enamoured of the activities of the Company?'

'Hervey, mistake me not: we are a mercantile nation. But our business overseas is trade, not conquest. Read your book and then speak freely with my secretary, who was once a writer in Calcutta, and then we may talk of it with more felicity. And he may be able to teach you one or two words which might be of use – how to get a palanquin or a clean girl or some such. But come,' he added, and with a lighter touch, 'have some burgundy with that pudding.'

'Thank you; it is an excellent pudding,' replied Hervey, taking another large piece of dark meat on his fork. '*Welsh* venison, you say? I had not supposed anyone might be so particular in choosing their game.' And he took a large gulp of wine.

Peto smiled – not triumphantly, for that would have been to overvalue his success, but certainly with a degree of satisfaction that alerted Hervey to another imminent revelation of his innocence of the ways of the 'wooden world'. 'My dear Hervey, know you not that prime eight-tooth mutton – *wether* mutton – fuddled and rubbed with allspice and claret, may be ate with as much satisfaction as the King's own fallow deer?'

It was not as disconcerting a revelation as might be supposed, and Hervey professed himself most pleasantly surprised by the discovery. 'Especially so since I come from a county with a great many more sheep than people. I have scarce dined so well, ever, as I have aboard your ship,' he concluded.

Peto seemed more than happy to leave weightier matters aside for the moment. 'I have, I fancy, one of the best cooks in the fleet. He was in the service of the Duke of Northumberland until there was some . . . misunderstanding. My coxswain found him adrift in some alehouse on the Tyne. He has been with me over a year and seems content. But here, some more burgundy: what do you think of it?'

'I think very *much* of it,' he replied, feeling its warmth reach the extremities.

'I am glad, for it is one of my best – a Romanée-Conti. So much so-called burgundy has been passed off during this war. Any old sugared red wine laced with brandy seems to take the name. And nauseous it is – frequently poisonous, too. Ever to be avoided, Hervey – ever.' He took another large draught. 'But I am careful of its taking: it is a very *manly* warmth that a Nuits-Saint-Georges brings – invigorating, whereas claret merely . . . *enlivens.*'

Hervey chuckled. 'I am astonished that, with such good provender, you avoid any tendency to stoutness. I fear much for my own figure these coming months.'

They both laughed, vigorously.

'But what of this commission of yours?' demanded Peto, though his manner was now thoroughly congenial. 'Why must you go in advance of the duke to India – before, indeed, his appointment has been made?'

Hervey was wondering how best he might explain, when the door opened again. The silence continued as Flowerdew cleared away the remains of the pudding, returning at once with an even larger tray, from which, with considerable ceremony, he placed on the table a greengage tart, an almond cheesecake, several custards and a bowl of figs. Hervey made more appreciative – and despairing – noises, and Peto again reached for the decanter of Madeira. But before he could remove the stopper – or Hervey begin his explanation of his early passage – there was a knock at the door.

'Come!' called Peto, as Hervey sliced large into the cheesecake.

The first lieutenant entered, his fresh face and fair curls making an even greater impression of youth than before. 'I beg your pardon, sir: I had not thought you were dining. The carpenter is knocking up a stall for Captain Hervey's horse in the waist. Might I ask him to approve the dimensions when it is convenient?'

Peto looked at Hervey.

'If you will permit me, sir, I shall do so at once,' he replied, rising (and none too steadily). 'My groom should be here with her before the evening.'

The Marines sentry at the doorway presented arms as Peto emerged. Hervey took the opportunity to speak to the first lieutenant, whose acquaintance he had made only briefly during the crossing a week before, while Peto bantered with the sentry about some amiable business of the shore. 'Mr Belben, we have not yet been able to exchange more than formalities. I hope I have not made impossible demands. No doubt it would have been better for me to seek passage for my horse on a ship of higher rate.'

'Not at all sir: *unusual* demands, perhaps, but not impossible. Nor indeed would a first-rate have been any more commodious – quite the reverse, in fact.'

Hervey looked at Peto, puzzled by the notion that a frigate offered as much space as a ship-of-the-line. 'That is so,' the captain affirmed. 'The biggest first-rate is two thousand and three-fifty tons, with a complement of nigh eight-fifty. She has less than three tons per man, whereas we are a thousand tons and two-fifty.'

'It sounds as though I might have brought my second charger,' tried Hervey, and he was pleasurably surprised to see Belben smile.

'Captain Hervey, we are at your disposal,' said Peto from behind, smiling equally. 'However, in the event of our having to clear for action then I am very much afraid that your charger will go overboard!'

At this Hervey looked plainly ill, and said no more. Lieutenant Belben led them along the waist towards the forecastle and stopped between the third and fourth gunports on the larboard side. 'I thought we might construct the stall here, sir, between numbers three and four guns,' he said to the captain.

Hervey looked worried. '*Between* the guns, Mr Belben? But that will give about eight feet at most.'

The lieutenant looked puzzled. 'I cannot very well move the guns, Captain Hervey. How much room does your horse need?'

'She must have twelve feet square, with a good strong bar to shorten it into a standing stall if the sea gets too high.'

'Twelve feet!' said Belben with dismay; '*I* only get eight, sir!'

'Yes, but you at least have freedom to exercise over the rest of the ship. My mare will be confined thus for six months.'

'Mr Belben,' said Peto, wishing to bring the issue to a resolution, 'dismount number four gun and be ready to remount it if we clear for action. The crew can take turns to exercise on another.'

'Ay, ay, Captain!' replied the lieutenant. There was no dissent: he was not responsible for the captain's decisions, only for implementing them.

'And might some padding be fastened here?' asked Hervey, touching the beam above. 'Her head will be—'

'Mr Belben, canvas and straw, if you please,' sighed Peto. 'We addle enough men's brains with timber; let us not have a cavalry charger strike its head too.'

And with stabling thus arranged, Peto and Hervey returned to the cabin and the table – and began on the plum tart with renewed appetite. However, Hervey was still troubled by the captain's warning of Jessye's fate should they clear for action.

'Do not distress yourself,' replied Peto reassuringly as he took another slice of the greengage; 'the most that could disturb us is a pirate or two, and we shall be standing too far to the west to encounter those who swarm from the Barbary Coast. And in any case, there is not a pirate afloat who – in his right mind – would tangle with a frigate!'

Hervey was now reassured.

'So, as we were saying, what is the imperative behind your early despatch to the Indies?' Peto was not to be deflected from any course, once set.

'Well,' sighed Hervey, 'as you recall, the duke expects that the government will shortly replace Lord Moira and appoint him in his place to carry through the policies of his brother in the decade before. The duke is especially keen to know the condition of the forces of the state of Haidarabad, which he regards as crucial to any enterprise by the Company. I am therefore to make a tour of that place in order to be able to report to the duke immediately on his arrival in Calcutta.'

Peto's brow furrowed again. 'Do not mistake me, Hervey, but is there not an official of the Company's in Haidarabad? Would he not be infinitely better placed to render such intelligence? I hazard a guess that at this moment you would be hard pressed to point to where is Haidarabad on a map!'

Hervey nodded and simply raised his eyebrows. The ancillary duty in Chintal was not something he intended to divulge, for it was in his judgement of little moment to the mission as a whole.

'Doubtless the duke knows his business,' tutted Peto, 'but treating with Mussulmen is a risky enterprise at the best of times.' He poured himself another glass of wine.

'You have experience?'

'Indeed I have – at both ends of the Mediterranean! But that is of no consequence. The material point is that the nizam's religion is alien to the continent of Hindoostan. The importation of the Mughal invaders – and not so many centuries ago at that. As I understand, it does not go well with the native Hindoos, and there is ever a restiveness. You must be at great pains to avoid its worst effects, Hervey.'

He assured him that he had every intention of doing so.

'But how shall you keep this enterprise secret?' pressed the captain. 'Do you intend dressing as a native or some such thing?'

Hervey smiled. 'No! If news of the duke's appointment precedes us – as well it might – I shall go about my business openly. If, however, there is no such news then I have letters from the duke requesting that Calcutta lend me every facility to make a study of the employment of the lance. The duke was much taken by the French lancers at Waterloo and wishes to equip some of our regiments of light dragoons so. And in India are some of the most proficient lancers – in Haidarabad especially.'

Peto looked sceptical. 'You do not think that some might suppose it would have been easier to go to Brandenburg to see the Uhlans, or even to Warsaw?'

'That is as maybe, though we are not on entirely the best of terms with the Prussians. However, I think mine a plausible enough mission – do not you?'

Peto took this to be rhetorical. 'Here, have one of these sweet sisters of the vine; they are come from Turkey – the Locoum variety, very much better than the pressed ones.'

Hervey took a fig and again voiced his appreciation of the quality of the captain's fare.

'Well, I must tell you that it's unlikely to remain thus in so long a voyage. It will be pocket soup and biscuit by the time we reach the Cape.'

Hervey replied that, for his own part, he was perfectly accustomed to any hardship in respect of rations, but his horse could not be expected to fare well on a long voyage without a proper regimen. 'And I must ask your leave to go ashore soon, sir, to attend to it. I need to find hay and straw, and hard feed.'

Peto said he was happy to accompany him, 'For there are things of which I have need, too.'

'Shall you have to find extra provisions?' asked Hervey without thinking.

The arched eyebrows told Hervey at once that he had somehow impugned Admiralty efficiency. 'Captain Hervey, I have heard of the dilatorious condition of the army's commissary department, but I would have you know that a frigate is provisioned so that she might sail without interruption for six months!'

*   *   *

'Very well, then, Mr Ranson,' said Peto once he had seated himself.

The crew of the captain's gig pulled with a good rhythm, seen to by a midshipman who looked not very much older than Hervey when first he had left Horningsham for Shrewsbury. *Nisus* lay three cables from the quay. Peto kept his eyes fixed ahead and said not a word during the seven minutes which it took for Ranson to pilot the gig through the slack water. As it neared the quayside steps, Peto rose before the midshipman had ordered 'easy-oars', and then stepped confidently to the landing stage even as the gig ran alongside with oars just raised. He was almost at the top of the steps before Hervey dared trust himself to alight from the now motionless boat. Hervey thanked the midshipman, who looked startled by it, and raced up the steps to regain Peto's side, pausing at the top to replace his spurs which, as was the custom, he had removed aboard ship.

'From *your* parts, young Ranson,' said Peto as Hervey caught him up; 'Somerset. A pity he's unlikely to see a fleet action ever. But it can't be helped. He cut his teeth in the 1812 affair: blew off a Yankee's head with his pistol, right in front of me, though the damned thing broke his wrist! And he club-hauled a prize lugger from a lee shore off Madeira. A little too inclined to drop his head and escape the bit, as you would say, but he'll do.'

Oh, such a man would do all right, thought Hervey. Some officers needed driving with long, rowelled spurs; most with the touch of the whip; very few needed the curb. And it did not do to judge from a man's aspect which were the proper aids. Ranson, for one, looked no more like a plunger than did his father's first curate. Peto's matter-of-factness intrigued him, though. Studied, perhaps? He had not seen the like except perhaps in Adjutant Barrow. And with Barrow it was more a device to compensate for having risen from the ranks. With Peto he could only suppose it a self-imposed distance, a necessity for command in otherwise close and familiar quarters. It seemed he might be in for a somewhat oppressive six months, the hospitality of the table notwithstanding.

Hervey changed step to walk in time with his senior, spurs ringing on the cobbles while Peto's heel struck the ground in the less emphatic way that was the sailor's. It was a sound that always gave him a certain prideful satisfaction. 'I saw a corn merchant on the way here, a little further along this street,' he tried.

'Space is pressing in a frigate, Captain Hervey – even in peacetime.

I do not wish it too filled with oats,' replied Peto peremptorily.

'No, indeed not,' said Hervey, taken aback somewhat. 'I have calculated very precisely how much she – my charger – shall need for a six-month passage.'

'*She?* Captain Hervey – a mare!'

Hervey sighed to himself. This was to be heavy going. 'Yes, a mare, but not a chestnut, you will be pleased to know.'

'Captain Hervey,' frowned Peto, '*any* mare, with any number of legs, is much the same to me: I have little use for them.'

He chose to ignore the proposition. 'I trust that mine will be no trouble, sir.'

'I trust not, too,' replied Peto, still looking straight ahead. 'Just so long as you do not fill the orlop with oats.'

'I shall give her no oats whatever,' replied Hervey, sounding surprised, 'otherwise she will likely as not suffer setfast.'

Peto turned his head and eyed him quizzically. 'I can keep a horse between myself and the ground tolerably well, Captain Hervey, but beyond that I make no claim.'

'Setfast is sometimes called Monday-morning sickness, which describes the symptoms aptly. The horse shows great stiffness; in extreme cases unable to move.'

'Why *Monday* morning?'

'It generally follows from inactivity after vigorous exercise – a day's rest on Sunday after a Saturday's hunting is common. There can be muscle damage, which is evident if the blood becomes azotous – discoloration of the urine, I mean. And then the kidneys may fail. Mares seem especially prone.'

'Captain Hervey, my surgeon would be intrigued to hear of such a systemic catastrophe resulting from a day's rest, for he is a great advocate of them!'

'I make no claim to know anything of human physic, sir,' countered Hervey, not immediately catching the attempt at humour.

'No,' smiled Peto at last, 'I am sure you do not. I am, however, impressed that your veterinary knowledge goes beyond that of many of the run-of-the-mill officers I have met.'

Hervey said nothing.

'So, your horse—' he continued.

'Jessye is her name, sir.'

'So, Jessye – a fine thoroughbred no doubt – how shall she maintain condition during the passage?'

'She is not a thoroughbred. Indeed, were she to be one I would as soon see a caged beast aboard. No, she has some good Welsh Mountain in her, and she is, therefore, just sufficiently tractable for the adventure. I shall give her hay *ad libitum* to reduce the risk of colic or her gut twisting. No doubt we shall have to pay over the odds – it's not a good time to be buying old hay, and I dare not risk new to begin with. But if we can find good Timothy it should keep her in modest fettle. I shall feed her some barley each day – say, three pounds – and a pound of bran with chop to keep her interested.' He took out a notebook and opened it to consult his earlier calculations. 'We shall need, therefore, two hundredweight-sacks of bran and five more of barley, and forty hundredweight of hay.'

'Great heavens, Captain Hervey! I haven't the—'

'I have resolved on deep-littering her, you will be pleased to hear, and so I shall need only the same again of straw. Barley straw unless we can find no other, for she has a partiality to eating it, and wheat straw can blow her up something dreadful.'

Peto halted and turned full towards him. 'Captain Hervey,' he said, portentously; 'I am full of admiration for the attention you lavish on your mare – by your own accounts, a female of not especial breeding. Is that affection returned, do you suppose?'

Hervey wondered where this line of questioning was leading. 'I *do* suppose – yes.'

Peto nodded. 'I had imagined thus. See, therefore, Captain Hervey, the distraction that affection demands,' he sighed, his head shaking pityingly.

As they neared the head of the great avenue leading from the quay to the Paris highroad, where stood the gendarmerie building as the street turned ninety degrees to the right, they came on a large but silent gathering. Curious as to its purpose, they joined the rear of the crowd, but the onlookers soon recognized the import of their uniforms and shifted to one side, affording them a clear view of the object of interest.

'Well,' said Peto after some moments' consideration; 'I own that this is the closest I have come to General Bonaparte's *Grande Armée*. What a sight they are!'

What a sight indeed, thought Hervey. The last he had seen of officers of the *Garde* was on the field of Waterloo, in the final moments of the battle when he had led the Sixth up the slopes which had been French ground all day, and on to the inn called La Belle Alliance, far in advance of any others of the Duke of Wellington's army. What a moment that had been. What a heady mix of joy and sorrow, of anger and pity. 'Yes,' he replied; 'officers of the Imperial Guard – grenadiers and *chasseurs à pied, les vieux des vieux.'*

They were as he had seen them at Waterloo – the white breeches and top boots, the white facings of the blue coat, with its long tails and bullion epaulettes. Above all the 'bearskin', the plateless fur cap with its red-tipped green plume. He had watched hundreds upon hundreds of them advance on the duke's line in perfect order, and thought that all before must surely be swept away – until the duke's own Guards, who had lain concealed in the corn to the very last moment, sprang up and opened a withering fire, sending the French columns reeling back down the slopes.

'They are formidable-looking, even in defeat,' acknowledged Peto. 'I can well understand, now, how an army with such as these men might gain so much – might march to Moscow and back, and fight every mile of the way.'

Yes – *formidable*, thought Hervey. And yet, without their swords they had perhaps lost something of their menace. 'I had not supposed I should ever be so close again myself,' he conceded.

'*Lion* is at anchor waiting to take them to join Bonaparte at St Helena. I spoke with her captain yesterday. He's hoping to meet the man himself there.'

There were thirty of them, perhaps more – Hervey could not see all – and they stood, arms folded, in the middle of the wide street. Some were smoking clay pipes, and all had the appearance of sublime indifference to their fate. In the sky above, swallows circled and dived, soon themselves to be southbound. The French were eyeing them too, envious perhaps of the freedom to pick their own moment. The escort, two dozen men of the 104th (North Derbyshire) Regiment, and evidently weary of the task, stood easy in a circle about them, bayonets fixed but muskets at the order. The captain, a tall, languid man, perhaps a year or so older than Hervey, but no more, on noticing the two officers touched his peak in salute and raised his eyebrows as if in search of sympathy for his role as gaoler. He gained none from

36

Hervey, though, who was affronted, indeed, by the want of collection in the escort. The men looked tired and insensible, a picture neither of vigilance nor good order. Never would the Sixth have paraded themselves thus in front of a French crowd, let alone before their captives! There was a price to aiglets, he told himself: duty required that he say something. He began pushing his way to the front.

He was too late, though. In an instant a dozen of the French officers rushed the sentries furthest from where he stood. The others formed line with their hands raised above their heads in submission, confusing the disengaged half-circle of infantrymen from rushing to the aid of their comrades. It was done in seconds. The sentries had not even time to bring their bayonets to the port before they were assailed with the greatest ferocity by the French, fists and boots flailing. Those on the edge seemed dumbstruck. Had they rushed in at once from the flanks it would have been over quickly. Two of them fired their muskets in the air, but then the weapons, discharged and harmless, were wrenched at once from their hands. Hervey and Peto drew their swords and rushed at the fray, but the crowd had doubled in size and women and children arrested their progress so effectively – whether by design or not – that by the time they had pushed through to the other side the captive officers had wholly overpowered their guards. They began withdrawing along the street towards the prefecture in model fashion, half of them doubling a dozen yards and then levelling the muskets while the others doubled further to take up the same covering position. The North Derbyshires' officer recovered himself and shouldered his way through the crowd with the remainder of the escort, ordering his men to give the French a volley. The report was deafening, and smoke filled the street, making it difficult to see its effect. The French did not fire back, however: Hervey supposed it because the street was full of civilians. 'Reload!' shouted the captain. As the smoke cleared, the Derbyshires furiously ramming home new charges, the effect of the first volley was revealed: a dozen or more bodies lay not thirty paces up the street, and only a handful in uniform.

Hervey was as appalled by the recklessness of the volley as he had been by the escort's bearing. Why had they not charged first with the bayonet? He called to the captain, but the man did not hear, having now decided, it seemed, to follow with steel after failing to lead with it. Hervey rushed forward but a French leg was put in his way and he fell sprawling atop one of the sentries lying senseless from a butt-stroke. A ragged volley of musketry came from windows on both sides of the street fifty yards ahead, knocking down redcoats like skittles at a fair. It would have struck down Hervey, too, for some of it flew his way, striking the walls of the house where he lay, making little puffs of red brick-dust, the lead balls flattening and falling to the ground – where iron shot would have ricocheted. He turned his head to look for Peto, relieved to see him crouching safe in a doorway. The remnants of the escort fell back along the street, the half-dozen or so remaining on their feet trying to pull their wounded comrades with them – though several were beyond help. At least as many were left for dead. Another volley came, felling two more. Hervey sprang up and rushed to one of them, lifting him across his shoulder and taking up his musket in his free hand. Peto did the same as another welter of musket balls assailed them. One struck the silver pouch of Hervey's crossbelt, and with such force that he was knocked clean to the ground. Peto, having dropped his man in a doorway, dashed to him, but he was already on his hands and knees retching with the pain and gasping for the air that had been knocked out of him. And still the firing continued as Peto half-pulled him to the safety of the side street where the ragged remains of the infantry were rallying, then ran back to the wounded corporal whom Hervey had been carrying, dragging him too to safety.

The crossbelt pouch was so twisted that the gilt 'GR' was no longer recognizable. The ball was embedded in the silver cover, but it had been the hardened leather of the pouch itself that had stopped it. Where precisely on his back the pouch had been when the ball struck Hervey could not tell, for the ache there was too general. But had it sat as it usually did, when he walked or rode erect, the pouch would have rested directly on his spine. Here, likely enough, was the closest that death had kissed him in seven years' campaigning – and the first time in his life that England was truly at peace with France!

'You fell so hard I was sure you were shot through,' gasped Peto, still out of breath.

'It felt so,' he muttered as he glanced across to where the Derbyshires' officer lay dead. They had to do something – and quickly. Peto was indisputably his senior, but the responsibility was surely his. There were now a dozen or so infantrymen crowding his corner of the side street, including their serjeant, whose earlier lack of address was still manifest in a look of stupefaction. 'Serjeant,' said Hervey, shouting almost and shaking the man's arm, 'where is the rest of your company?'

The NCO continued to stare straight across the main street, as if relief might come from that direction at any second. Hervey shook him again, but could get no answer. He looked at the others, who looked back at him like so many sheep. Yet these were men who, not two months before, had stood their ground at Waterloo against Bonaparte's finest. Only one of them was showing any activity: he lay prone, squinting round the corner whence the firing had come. Hervey shook the man's leg: 'What do you see?'

The soldier, who had taken off his shako so that as little as possible should betray his surveillance, did not move. 'They 'ave just picked the cartridge bags off 'em, sor. An' by the way, sor, them French is in the gendarmry building now. They'll 'ave powder and shot aplenty there.'

Hervey recognized the soft vowels of Cork. For an instant his mind was filled with his tribulations there. Then he noticed the stitching holes on the arm of the man's jacket: evidently the sleeve had borne two chevrons lately. He came back to the present. 'Where's the rest of your company, Corporal? Where is the garrison?'

'The company's at 'Arfleur, sor. There's a review or some such. And it's "Private" now.'

Harfleur was ten miles away: he had ridden through it that very morning. 'How many marines do you have on your ship, Captain Peto?' he asked, turning to see Peto deftly applying a tourniquet above the shattered knee of a private little older than a boy.

Peto looked surprised. 'Thirty-eight, the same number as she has guns – and a lieutenant. Are you asking me to—'

'With only these men here all we can do is *watch* the gendarmerie: we can't assault it,' he replied, shaking his head to emphasize their powerlessness.

'Would it not be better to recall the garrison? What about the town major?'

'If we don't act swiftly then we run the risk of every Bonapartiste in Le Havre throwing in his hand with them. The whole town might be taken!'

Peto thought it unlikely, but recognized the possibility – and therefore the necessity. 'Very well, Captain Hervey,' he replied grimly, 'you shall have my marines,' and he turned to make his way back to the quayside.

But he had no need, for his gig's midshipman had come up. 'I heard the firing, sir, and feared there might be trouble.'

Hervey smiled to himself. Right place, right time – he'll do!

Peto, his hat removed in the heat of the afternoon (though he had kept it square during the action), simply raised his eyebrows, and even managed to look irritated by the blood on his white breeches. 'Yes, yes, Mr Ranson, it is nothing. Be so good as to signal to *Nisus* and request Mr Locke to bring his men ashore – sharply if you please.' The midshipman doubled away with the greatest enthusiasm, and Peto turned to Hervey, raising his eyebrows again. 'His first time within earshot of French fire,' he drawled; 'it's as well to behave with as much indifference as possible.'

Hervey was minded of Edward Lankester, though nothing of that patrician's manner was at all studied. Even the way Lankester had ridden the length of the Sixth's line in the closing hour at Waterloo, risking every tirailleur's parting shot, was – he was sure – born of the most natural impulse. However, Peto's bearing, studied or not, was as cool as ever he had seen. Did its impulse really matter?

But now he saw an even greater service that *Nisus* might render, for as he lay prone, snatching the odd glance up and down the street (and grateful he was too that he wore his second coat, for the cobbles had sharp edges), he tumbled at last to it – the apt line of fire. 'Captain Peto, do you see your ship yonder?' he called excitedly.

Peto, without thinking, looked back towards the roads where *Nisus* lay at anchor, and then quickly back at Hervey again, irritated. 'Of course I see her, Captain Hervey; to what do your powers of observation lead?'

'The gendarmerie is at the end of the street. It stands in direct line from her.'

Peto looked astonished. 'You surely do not wish me to undertake a shore bombardment?' he gasped.

'Not a *bombardment* – a shot across their bow. Except it must needs be a shot *into* their bow.'

Peto looked even more astonished.

Hervey failed to understand.

'Captain Hervey, how far is the gendarmerie from us?'

'Sixty or seventy yards I should say,' he replied.

'And a further hundred or so to the quay. And by my reckoning *Nisus* stands three cables out – a total of seven hundred and fifty yards. Eight hundred perhaps.'

Hervey was yet more puzzled. 'That is not an extreme range, sir?'

Peto raised his eyebrows a third time in as many minutes. 'It is not an extreme range, sir, but the parabola is such that—'

'Oh yes, Captain, I know the intricacy well,' he interrupted, but somehow managing not to contrive offence. 'If you aimed low, however, the ricochet could be to our advantage.'

Peto said nothing. Indeed, he looked aghast. And then he appeared to be contemplating the proposition. Slowly he warmed to it. 'There is no guarantee of line, mind you. The shot is not tight in the barrel as with a rifle. It might fly wide.'

Hervey was silent. It was not his place to give a lesson in gunnery to a frigate captain, though he knew that, at a thousand yards, the shot could not be too far out of line if the gun were laid dead-centre on its target.

'Very well, Captain Hervey, though heaven knows what shall be our fate if this is misdirected. I dare say a court martial awaits us both.'

'Quite so, sir,' smiled Hervey, taking another look round the corner.

Peto said he would go back to *Nisus* himself. 'I suppose you are capable of the business ashore – mounted or dismounted. But I need to see that gun is laid truly.'

Hervey asked if he would leave his midshipman. 'I shall need an officer with the cordon around the gendarmerie.'

Peto approved. 'And shall we agree to fire on the place at a given time?' he asked absently, brushing brick-dust from his seacoat.

'I should prefer a signal,' replied Hervey. 'Something always seems to make a given time too early or too late as it approaches. Shall we say three powder flashes from this corner?'

'Very well,' said Peto, 'three powder flashes it is. I shall make "Affirmative" when ready.'

'And if the first shot is insufficient,' added Hervey, 'we shall await another; then you will see us rush the building.'

A quarter of an hour later Lieutenant Locke and thirty marines (even Peto would not leave his ship entirely without marines) came doubling along the side street to where Hervey and the midshipman were observing – the one with his telescope trained on *Nisus* for the ready signal, the other still prone and peering round the corner at the gendarmerie. The marines looked eager, bayonets already fixed, sweat running down their faces. There was no time for introductions or other pleasantries. Hervey quickly explained his intention, the lieutenant

41

lying prone beside him to peer round the corner at their objective. 'There's no place for skirmishing. When the ball makes a breach we must rush it at once!'

Ranson's telescope awaited the red flag with white cross that would signal his ship's readiness. Suddenly he started. '*Nisus* makes "Affirmative", sir!' he called excitedly. 'She is ready!'

'Very well, then, Mr Ranson, please take charge of the watch I have sent to the rear of the gendarmerie. There are a dozen private men there, but I fear their serjeant is unsteady.'

The midshipman looked disappointed. He wanted to draw his sword and join the storming party. But a sharp look from Hervey sped him away to join the dozen infantrymen who were all that stood between the gendarmerie and its reinforcement. Hervey had retained the Cork man, however. His job was to make four powder flashes – three for the signal and one as reserve, for powder was never as reliable as supposed, even on a hot day, with not a drop of moisture in the air. However, before he signalled the frigate there was one more thing Hervey felt obliged to do. Taking a white silk square from the pocket of his coat, he tied it to the soldier's bayonet. 'Are you ready, Corporal McCarthy?' he asked, not needing to explain for what.

'Yes, sor,' said the man resolutely. 'I shall get an NCO's funeral, then?'

'I shall see to it myself,' smiled Hervey, cheered not for the first time by an Irishman's black humour. 'Come then,' and he marched boldly to the middle of the street with McCarthy by his side.

Musket at the high port so that the trucial white would be plain to all, the erstwhile corporal laughed as they advanced on the gendarmerie building. 'Jasus, sor, but I hope them French is still willing to go by the rules!'

'Officers of the Garde?' replied Hervey reassuringly. 'I should think honour is *everything* to them. We need have no fear.'

At that very moment a musket exploded not a dozen yards to their front, the ball flying a foot or so above their heads.

'You was saying, sor?'

Before he could make reply a voice from within the gendarmerie commanded them to halt and state their business. Hervey looked about until one of the shutters opened further to reveal the moustaches of a colonel of the chasseurs à pied, a man with so great an air of indifference that he began wondering what they might know which he did not.

In his best French, and with proper deference for rank, he explained that there could be no escape. 'You have fought with great honour on the field of battle. I myself saw the gallant conduct of the Garde at the late battle in Belgium. And today you have fought with determination. But further resistance will be to no avail: the guns of one of His Majesty's ships are at this very moment laid on you. I call upon you to lay down your arms.'

The shutter opened full, and the colonel called out one word. '*Merde!*'

'What's that he says, sor?' asked McCarthy, who had stood patiently but uncomprehendingly throughout Hervey's peroration.

'He does not wish to lay down his arms,' he replied, bruised. 'Come.'

They turned about and marched back with the same composure as they had advanced, the ringing of Hervey's spurs on the cobbles seeming twice as loud, for all else was silence.

'What was their answer?' asked Lieutenant Locke.

Hervey, his pride not a little damaged, felt the need of paraphrase. '*La Garde meurt mais ne se rend pas!* Like Cambronne at Waterloo,' he sighed. 'Well, so shall it be if they insist. Are the flares ready, McCarthy?' he called, seeing him light a portfire.

'Yessor!'

Hervey drew in his breath and drew out his sabre. He could not remember the last time he had gone into action dismounted. He thought it wise to pull off his spurs. Then glancing once about to see his storming party were ready, he gave McCarthy the word. '*Fire them!*'

Private McCarthy put the portfire to the powder trails, and seconds later three flashes, one after another, told *Nisus* it was time.

Hervey hardly expected delay, for there was no swell for which to compensate in laying the gun, but even he was surprised by the frigate's response. In an instant one of her eighteen-pounders belched a long tongue of flame, the report reaching them almost at once in the still air. But they saw the shot approaching even before hearing the discharge. It first flew higher than he expected, but then its falling trajectory became apparent, and it crashed into the very doors of the gendarmerie building – so accurate a piece of gunnery that for a second Hervey was speechless.

'*Charge!*'

Up! Forward! Boots pounding on cobbles – slipping, sliding. It seemed so *slow*! As bad as plough, almost. But they made the breach before the French rallied – hardly a shot from any quarter. The double doors were no more, the jambs pulled in with the force of the round-shot. Hervey was through first, a fraction ahead of the big lieutenant of Marines. Inside was all dust and wreckage – more than expected, and a sight he hoped never to see again after Waterloo: broken bodies of fine French officers. Marines rushed past him to the rooms beyond, almost knocking him down. This was their business: close-quarter fighting, confined. And they were eager for it. Not for them long lines and squares, wheeling, fronting and volleying like the infantry. They held their muskets close instead of at high port, ready to thrust with the bayonet or swing the butt up to groin, gut or chin. Brute strength – brutal – brut*ish*. They worked in pairs, with no commands, with the utmost violence, and without check. *Forward, forward, forward* – momentum was everything to Marines!

There was nothing for Hervey to do. He had led them in. He was a hindrance now. He turned for the breach, but a blow like a prize-fighter's knocked him flat on his back. The Waterloo stars and the dancing lights were back, and the blackness rolled in as a cloud. Like a wounded animal, writhing in hopeless rage, he blindly slashed this way and that with his sabre. It made no contact.

'Are ye all right, sor?'

Sometimes a voice was as welcome for its tone as what it brought. 'Yes,' groaned Hervey; 'I'm all right, thank you,' cursing inaudibly in language fouler than even Joseph Edmonds might have been tempted to.

Private McCarthy helped him to his feet and out through the breach. 'Have a care here, sor,' he warned as they ducked the lintel – the same that Hervey had run full tilt into.

Outside, his wits were restored soon enough. The shako had taken some of the force, and spared him an open wound, but his pride bore a bruise much worse than his forehead. Then it was all shouting again – *Allez! Allez!* – and those officers who had not taken Cambronne's words literally were bustled out at the point of steel.

Later, the town major and the mayor expressed fulsome gratitude, the mayor assuring them that Le Havre wanted no truck with what remained of Bonaparte's ambition. 'Do not be too dismayed at the 104th, Captain Hervey,' said the major; 'they are not a bad regiment. I stood close to them at Hougoumont, but they lost a good many of their best officers and NCOs there.'

Hervey did not doubt it, and felt meanly for having condemned them so roundly. The Line battalions had, after all, borne the brunt of Bonaparte's onslaught all that day in June. Waterloo had changed things. He knew himself to be changed. The army was now divided into two distinct parts: those who had been there, and those who wished they had been. And to those who had been there, the world would never be the same again; for they each knew they had escaped death by the chance of the fall of shot or the line of a musket ball, and were determined either to enjoy their deliverance to the fullest or to learn why fortune had favoured them above other men.

Hervey returned to the *Nisus* at six o'clock with three carts in tow. On the first were two one-hundredweight sacks of bran and five more of barley. On the second, a much bigger waggon, was the best part of two tons of hay, and on the third the same of straw. *Nisus* had come alongside one of the wharves, and her crew, under the eagle eyes of her marines, now made light work of stowing the forage. They showed a pleasure in doing so, even, with more than one nod of respect sent Hervey's way, for the assault on the gendarmerie had been retailed through the ship.

Peto shook his hand as he came aboard but allowed himself few words on the affair. Hervey expressed himself much taken by the skill and speed with which the carpenters had erected a most solid-looking stable for Jessye – with a roof that would carry rainwater over the side, and the gunport allowing for good circulation of air – adding that he had not imagined they would have it done so quickly. But Peto had resumed his former peremptory manner. 'Great gods, Captain Hervey!' he spluttered. 'My carpenters are not country cabinetmakers: their business is with battle damage!' And a short time later his sensibilities were even more severely assaulted by the arrival of Private Johnson and a travelling horsebox, for when the *cochers* let down the ramped door to the rear, and Johnson led out Jessye, her lack of blood was at once apparent. Neither was she on her toes – and her ears were flat. Indeed, the effects of her fortnight's chill were all too evident, so that the contrast between what was expected to emerge from the box and what in reality did was all the more pronounced.

And to compound the affront to Peto's notions of good and handsome order, Hervey's groom now hailed *Nisus*'s quarterdeck, only

45

just remembering to touch his shako peak: 'Bloody 'ell, Mr 'Ervey! What was all that firin'?'

Peto looked askance. 'Does he address you, sir – aide-de-camp to the Duke of Wellington?!'

Hervey shifted uneasily at the rail, making awful comparison in his mind with the captain's steward. 'Yes,' he replied simply, 'we have been together some time.'

'Most singular indeed!' concluded Peto, shaking his head as he turned for the other side of the deck.

Hervey glanced back to the quayside. So unmilitary a sight, indeed, was Johnson, and so unprepossessing did Jessye look, that he could find no reply.

He was blowing into her nose and pulling her ears as the marines' commanding officer approached. 'I took you for a dandy,' the lieutenant laughed; 'your horse tells me you are not!'

Hervey had not cared for the look of the lieutenant on the crossing to France, though he had seen him only at a distance, and his impression had not changed when he had come doubling along the street with his marines. His face – knocked-about and horribly scarred – was that of a pug rather than an officer. But how he could fight! He had gone at the breach with as much vigour – and even more strength – than Serjeant Armstrong would have. And his smile was not the sneer Hervey had first thought, but a warm, almost familiar one. 'I will wager she could beat anything *you* have seen over two miles!' smiled Hervey back.

'I don't doubt it for a minute. Why else would the Duke of Wellington's aide-de-camp have such a hack?'

He was about to try another riposte when the lieutenant laughed out loud. 'You have scarce changed a jot since Shrewsbury, Matthew Hervey!'

He stared back blankly.

'No, you do not recognize me! You were once my doul, but I was bonnier then. A Yankee frigate did for me – grape sweeping across the forecastle just as we boarded her. Lucky to keep my sight. Locke – Henry Locke, of Locke-hall in the county of Worcester.'

Hervey remembered – *indeed* he did. But a boy whose looks were the envy of his house at Shrewsbury. 'My God,' he started, before checking himself. 'I mean . . . no, I should not have recognized you. But how very pleased I am to make your acquaintance again. What are you doing in His Majesty's Marines?'

'I might ask you the same manner of question. And I believe the answer to both is that we have been fighting the King's enemies.'

'Just so,' laughed Hervey, 'just so.' He recalled him well enough now – a kindly senior to serve for a term, but no favourite of the masters' common room, for sure. 'I hardly saw you when first I came aboard at Chatham.'

'No, I was ashore at musketry. We joined by cutter once she was under way.'

'Ah,' said Hervey, now comprehending; 'I was being most handsomely entertained at your captain's table by that time.'

'No matter. But that was a famous action this afternoon. Are you recovered of your blow?' he smiled.

'Yes, thank you,' he coughed (mortification was perhaps too strong a word for his condition).

'The cannonade was your idea, I hazard?'

'Yes, it seemed best,' he replied lightly, relieved to be let off the subject of his collision with the lintel. But the affair of the gendarmerie could hardly be counted a great stratagem.

Locke's expression indicated otherwise. 'You are deuced lucky *Nisus* is a frigate: even a seventy-four would not have done.'

Hervey was puzzled. 'How so?'

'Hah! You should *see* those first- and second-rates at gunnery: they simply lay alongside the enemy and blast away – broadside after broadside. There's no *science* in it: there's hardly need. "Engage the enemy more closely": that's what an affair of big ships amounts to.'

'Oh,' replied Hervey, disappointed – not to say disconcerted – by the intelligence. 'I had imagined their gunnery to be more expeditious than that.'

'Then you are in error. It is not to be compared with Woolwich. Don't mistake me, mind: the celerity with which those guns are served is magnificent. But it's broadsides – volley fire.'

'In a frigate less so, however?'

'In a frigate less so, yes. But that was rare shooting this afternoon – very uncommon shooting indeed. You know that Captain Peto laid the gun himself?'

Hervey did not.

'Peto is that sort of captain.'

'I am full of admiration. I had not supposed he took so great a risk firing on the gendarmerie. And that he should shoulder the responsibility so personally is, as you say, singular.'

'Just so, Hervey. I doubt there is any bolder frigate captain in the navy. But let us to other matters: what brings you to *Nisus*?'

Faced with his first occasion for subterfuge, Hervey all but foundered. 'Well, er, yes . . . you may. You see, I am to go to India to study the employment of the lance with the native cavalry regiments. The Duke of Wellington intends raising lancer regiments and wishes to know how best they should be ordered and trained.'

Locke seemed puzzled. 'The cavalry leads a queerer life than the Johnnies, that's for sure. It seems a deuced mazy way to find how to carry a spear!'

Hervey smiled. 'The duke is very particular about things.' How easily came the deception now.

'Well, we must get your mare aboard. Yon crane and hoist – see? A dozen marines is all it should take.'

And, indeed, a dozen marines was all it took to hoist Jessye aboard. She lay in the sling with neither a swish of her tail nor a whicker (but looking, thought Hervey, distinctly sorry for herself) as she was first hoist aloft and then lowered into the waist. No more trouble than a gun barrel, said the boatswain. The sling's fastenings loosed, she stepped into her box as if from the paddock, and was promptly rewarded with carrots by Johnson, his face now changed from one of anxiety to satisfaction. A promising beginning, said Hervey, though he knew it by no means certain she would survive the passage. Nevertheless, she had enough space to turn about freely and to lie at full stretch – which was more than the horses to and from the Peninsula had had. The stall was airy (it could hardly have been otherwise), yet there was enough shelter from rain and spray. Not too heavy seas to begin with – that was what he prayed for.

'You are prone to seasickness, then, are you?' asked Peto, though the tone was of indifference rather than sympathy.

'Oh no, I manage quite well. It's my mare I have a care for, since a horse has not the facility to vomit. They get the colic instead, and in the worst event they die.'

Several hands had gathered about the stall, intrigued by the addition to *Nisus*'s complement. One of them held out something in his palm, but she only sniffed at it and snorted disapprovingly.

'What's tha givin 'er?' demanded Johnson.

'Only baccy,' replied the hand.

'Tha daft bugger!' frowned Johnson. 'An 'orse doesn't chew t'bacca!'

'Will 'e 'ave a bit o' salt-pork?' asked another.

'Saints alive,' cursed Johnson, 'tha's as daft as 'im! An 'orse doesn't 'ave meat! And "he's" a she!'

Peto, observing from the quarterdeck and by now much diverted, hailed his first lieutenant. 'Mr Belben, I think the boatswain should be advised to instruct the crew that this important animal be given no titbits!'

'Ay, ay, sir,' replied Belben, with a long-suffering raise of the eyebrows.

Later that evening, while Peto attended to his papers, Hervey went up to the quarterdeck to take the air. First he stopped at Jessye's stall. The feverish chill, the long haul from Paris and the hoisting aloft would have put many a blood on its side, but Jessye stood square in her stall chewing hay with slow but regular rotation of the jaw, grinding out the goodness from the Timothy. He had nothing to trouble himself about.

On the quarterdeck he found Henry Locke leaning on the taffrail and gazing out into the busy channel that was the estuary of the Seine. The light was failing fast, but a dozen vessels of various sizes could be observed under way, and as many more lay at anchor. The steady light from a lantern threw the lieutenant's features into sharp relief, the hollow of his nose and the empty space that had once been his strong chin all too apparent in profile. Hervey shivered a little, and then hailed him.

'Good evening, Hervey,' replied Locke without looking round. 'Might one ever tire of such sights?'

Hervey perceived the ambiguity in the question but could not be certain that it was intended. 'I can see why some do not, though I am a landsman,' he said. 'Is this what drew you to the Marines?'

'No, but it is one of the things that keeps me: Worcestershire is not notably a naval county. So, we're all set fair for the Indies?' He did not alter his gaze as he changed the subject.

'Yes. Do you know India?'

'Only from the telling of others. A place where a man might live like a prince on a lieutenant's pay.'

Hervey smiled. 'So I hear. You have not been tempted, then?'

Locke turned to him. His face, insofar as his disfigurement permitted any range of sentiment, bore an expression of melancholy. 'I have only one desire, Hervey, and that's to win back Locke-hall.'

Hervey was intrigued. 'Do you wish to speak of it?' he enquired solicitously.

'Gambling debts mostly.'

Hervey sighed to himself – an old story. 'You gambled away your inheritance?'

Locke stood upright and looked at him with a frown: 'No! It was gambled by my father in his dotage. I was to have a cornetcy in the Blues: every penny for it went on the tables.'

'And that is why you went to sea?'

'I tried my hand at one or two ventures, but I have no head for business and no stomach for a profession. Admiral Jervis was a cousin of my late mother's, and it was on his recommendation that I received a commission.'

'You said *win* back Locke-hall?'

'Ay, with prize-money. But since a lieutenant of Marines ranks merely with a navy warrant officer for pay and prizes, we shall need to capture a treasure fleet!'

'And we are at war with no one.'

'Ay, just so. Do you have a wife, Hervey?'

He explained his circumstances, and now the hope – vain as it sounded in retelling – that Henrietta might at any moment appear with the gallant Corporal Collins.

'She sounds to have capability,' replied Locke. 'Ward of the Marquess of Bath, d'ye say? Money, too. Well, let us hope this letter you say you wrote is sufficient. Many a woman would suppose herself proper jilted by a lover who runs off to the east. All her grand friends will have to be told . . . explanation after explanation.'

'She might yet arrive, and—'

'And you would ask the captain for another berth?' smiled Locke.

'No . . . I had not thought . . . that is—'

He smiled again. 'A wife isn't something to pack in a marine's dunnage. We fight light, as they say. And I dare say, too, they don't stow so well on a bat-horse either!'

Hervey frowned. 'That is a cynic's counsel indeed!'

'I myself was married once,' replied Locke, claiming thereby a right to the philosophy.

Hervey studied him for a second or so, trying to gauge his earnestness, and then pressed him to the details.

'She took one look at my face when I returned home and away she went. She hardly took much to living in lodgings in Portsmouth in any case.'

Hervey expressed himself sorry.

'I cannot say I blame her,' sighed Locke, 'but I thought I had married into stock made of sterner stuff. We had known each other since . . . well, since we shared a pew.'

Hervey did not think it appropriate to reveal that his attachment with Henrietta had an equal gestation. 'And Locke-hall shall be without a mistress?' he tried, curious as to the force which bound the man to his vision.

'Never again should I marry, even were my wife to have us put asunder in law.' And then he smiled: 'But as lord of the manor there'd be lasses enough to keep me content. As long as the candle was blowed out!'

Hervey smiled, perhaps less fully than he might.

'Matthew Hervey, don't you preach at me. You think on how life would be if *your* fair looks were rearranged by grapeshot or a sabre-cut. Even the whores in Portsmouth run when they see my face.'

'What, *all* of them?' he asked in disbelief.

'Well, I've not tried *all* of them, to be sure. But *one* whore who's too particular is a powerful insult to a man's . . . manhood.'

Hervey clapped his hand on Locke's shoulder and smiled broadly. Even through the thick serge of the scarlet coat he could feel the brawn built of hours at exercise, the cutlass-swinging for which the Royals were renowned. Locke stood an inch in excess of six feet, taller than any man aboard – a powerful, if artless, fighter held in affection as well as respect by his marines. 'I think you are as lucky in your ship as I am in my regiment,' proclaimed Hervey.

Locke returned the smile as broadly. 'Yes, she's a fine ship. And what service she's seen! That night before Trafalgar – she and *Euryalus* did work to make the meanest heart proud.'

'Indeed,' nodded Hervey, 'there can be few who do not know it. And what poetic fortune it was, too.'

Locke seemed puzzled. '*Poetic* fortune?'

'Yes,' said Hervey; 'that it should be *Nisus* with *Euryalus*, of all ships.'

'Hervey,' replied Locke, now looking quite decidedly puzzled, 'I do not have the slightest idea of what you speak.'

'Oh,' said Hervey, surprised, but anxious not to cause embarrassment, 'were Nisus and Euryalus not Trojans, Trojan warriors?'

'Well,' said Locke, his brow obviously furrowed, though concealed under the roundhat; 'Nisus was a Trojan warrior – that I know. But of his attachment with Euryalus I know not. What *is* the connection?'

Hervey was relieved his remark seemed not to have caused his erstwhile idol to be abashed. 'It's just something I remember from those hours in the classroom at Shrewsbury,' he said lightly. 'Nisus and Euryalus were friends, the closest of friends – David and Jonathan, Pylades and Orestes.'

Locke nodded his understanding.

'Together one night they stole into the enemy's camp and killed many as they lay sleeping. Euryalus was wounded, and Nisus rushed to save him, but both were slain.'

Locke made no reply for the moment, and then sighed. 'Well, had *our Euryalus* got into trouble that night, *Nisus* would not have been able to go to her aid: she could not afford to lose contact with the French. But I for one, in ordinary, own that the measure of a man is his steadfastness towards his comrades in battle.'

Hervey seemed uneasy.

'"Greater love hath no man than he lay down his life for his friend," it says somewhere in the Bible does it not?' said Locke by way of explanation.

'Yes, in St John. For his *friends*, indeed.'

'But I'm very much taken with the Trojan legend. I did not know it.'

Hervey smiled again, but his expression was still a little pained. 'Would all *Euryalus*'s crew have acknowledged that *Nisus*'s captain did the right and proper thing – leaving her to her fate in order to stay on the tail of the French?'

Locke gave a sort of half-shrug. 'The usages of battle are well understood in the Royal Navy. Why do you ask?'

Hervey asked because of Serjeant Strange, and for an instant he was tempted to tell Locke of it. But that was not his way, nor was this the time. 'Oh, nothing – merely that I wished to have some notion of the way things are in the wooden world.'

'They are different in the detail, for sure, but in the spirit I reckon not,' said Locke. 'You must learn of it. Mr Belben would, as a rule, take you round the ship, but I shall do it – to explain things with a landsman's eye.'

'Thank you,' said Hervey eagerly, flattered by Locke's attention as if still the schoolboy.

'But now you must excuse me: there's the watch to set, and we shall have many hours to talk during the passage to the Indies. And I tell you, Matthew Hervey, I am right glad to have the opportunity. It is curious, is it not, how a couple of shared years at the same school make the intervening ones as nothing?'

Hervey smiled, eased by Locke's frankness and warmed by his congeniality. How fortunate he was, always, with his comrades-in-arms.

He left the quarterdeck, returning the sentry's salute with a touch to the brim of his hat, and strode purposefully to Jessye's stall where he hoped to find practical business to occupy his mind for an hour or so before he turned in. But Jessye was lying down, eyes closed and breathing soundly. He crossed the deck and clambered onto one of the guns to sweep the quayside with his telescope in the dying light. But there was no sign of Collins. He snapped the glass closed, sighing, and stepped down. It was early still, but he was not yet at ease enough to go to the wardroom so instead he went to his cabin. There he undressed, threw some water over his face, cleaned his teeth with the expensive powder bought in Paris, and climbed into his swinging cot (with less difficulty than hitherto, he was relieved to find). He read the psalm appointed for the evening and then closed his eyes, leaving the safety light burning. He lay listening to the ship's night-noises – the lapping of the waves, made audible by the open gunports either side of his cabin, and the creaking of timbers as the ship rolled ever so gently in the swell. The motion was seductive, and the manly burgundy invigorating. If only Henrietta had been beside him.

CHAPTER THREE

FIGHTING INSTRUCTIONS

Off Ushant, in the afternoon, two days out

A fresh north-easterly was blowing down the Channel. *Nisus* was running with all but her royals set, and the wind, the groaning canvas and the creaking of timbers in every quarter of the ship tried the intimacy of conversation. Next to nothing now could be made of Ushant and the coast of Brittany. The heavy cloud made it difficult, at this distance, to tell even where the sky ended and the sea began, though a telescope might yet pick out the great lighthouse of L'Ouessant. The sea was becoming a forbidding grey. The waves were long, with white horses running, and the spray was persuading Hervey that his cloak would have been prudent. Great shearwaters skimmed the troughs with rapid wing-beats, rearing up over the wavetops in long glides and plunging from time to time in search of a finny bite. Soon they too would be leaving to winter in the warmer islands of the South Atlantic, not many miles distant from where Bonaparte himself would pass both his winters and summers. Hervey shivered, if only slightly.

Captain Peto had spoken hardly at all since leaving Le Havre. His lieutenants were, it seemed, men in whom he had every confidence, and his sailing-master had been long years with *Nisus*. He spent much of the day in his cabin surrounded by sheaves of Admiralty papers and charts, visited only by his clerk, content for the most part to observe the set of the sails from a quarter gallery. Once or twice in the morning, and then again in the afternoon and evening, he visited the quarterdeck for his solitary promenade, when, as was the custom, the whole of the windward half was instantly cleared for him. No one ventured to address him without leave, and although this ritual aloofness seemed perfectly regular to the ship's officers, Hervey felt keenly the loss of the earlier intimacy. Now, though, he and Locke had the quarterdeck to themselves, with only the officer of the watch, the quartermaster and two mates by the wheel.

'I shouldn't brood on matters were I you.'

'Do you take your own counsel in this?' smiled Hervey by return.

'No,' he laughed, 'but that need not stop me. Is advice so great an insult to judgement?'

'No, indeed it is not!' laughed Hervey, thankful for Locke's forthright cheer.

'Then tell me more of your lady: that is your trial, is it not?'

How queer, thought Hervey, that he should feel disposed to speaking his heart to Locke. He knew him now only two days. And at Shrewsbury their situations had been so different they could scarcely be called old friends. But common years could root trust deeper than first supposed, and he was content enough to speak with a man who shared something singular. And besides, they had gone through the breach almost shoulder to shoulder. The gendarmerie was hardly Badajoz, but at the point of any assault the scale of the affair was merely theoretical. 'Well, in truth, I should not have let my hopes rise so high,' he admitted. 'The odds against seeing her before we set sail could scarcely have been longer. I believe the captain might have been offended that I asked for one more day.'

Locke smiled. 'Well, the captain isn't known for his patience where women are concerned. But I shouldn't let it trouble you.'

Hervey sighed. How he wished, now, that he had not thought of the interception stratagem, that he had trusted instead to the arrangements in Paris, where Henrietta might be told of things with due propriety, instead of harum-scarum along the coast with Corporal Collins. 'No, I have fudged things. And I thought myself so clever!'

'Tell me of her, in any case,' pressed Locke.

'I told you of her family,' he began resolutely; 'or, rather, of her guardian – for her people died when she was scarcely more than an infant. We have known each other since the day she came to Wiltshire, to Longleat. We shared a schoolroom together.'

'Not solely the lady of fashion, then? Not someone courted to be an adornment to a man's ambition?'

Hervey glanced cautiously at him. 'She is not someone who owns to nothing *but* fashion. She has read widely and has many accomplishments.'

'And she's pretty, I'm sure.' His tone suggested he was leading to some general proposition.

'She is *very* pretty. I do not have her likeness with me, else I would show you.'

'An officer should take care only to fall in love with a woman of beauty and a good fortune, for these are necessary in the advancement of his career, are they not?'

Hervey frowned as much as Locke smiled. 'That is very ill! It is bad enough hearing the same from Captain Peto!'

Locke smiled even more broadly: 'Hervey, these are new and opportune times, but the day a pair of pretty eyes and connection in society do not count in the advancement of a husband will be very long in its coming. Our system is different, but I have observed that officers who rise to the highest ranks always marry the right wife!'

Hervey laughed too, but overcame the temptation to tell him he was already beholden to Henrietta's connections – for although it seemed now a trifling affair in Ireland that required her influence, it would be wrong to underestimate her capacity to persuade. Heavens, but how he wished she were with him! Or had seen her for a few moments before sailing, even. Had it been unreasonable to ask Peto for one more day? The captain's reaction had said as much.

'Will you give me a straight answer if I ask a straight question?' said Locke, breaking the vocal silence.

'That or none at all,' replied Hervey briskly, pushing as far away as he could the unpleasant realization of his failure, and wiping another bit of spray from his eyes.

'Are you entirely disposed to this enterprise?'

Hervey started. It seemed a damned impudent question. 'What the—'

Locke grasped his quarrel at once: 'I mean the India enterprise! I've no cause to question your matrimonial affairs, I assure you!' and he clapped a hand on his shoulder.

Hervey sighed to himself. Here was what came of speaking about matters which properly remained interior. 'It's the first time I have been detached from my regiment,' he conceded. 'I had not imagined I would feel quite so . . . well, at *sea*.'

Locke drew his head back, and then both began laughing at the absurdity of the unintended play on words.

Private Johnson had been unable to perfect any better means of communicating with the quarterdeck than by standing at the foot of the companion ladder to await the passing of an officer or mate. He had been deterred from the obvious and direct method – ascending the ladder – on their first morning at sea, by the Marines sentry. The exchange had been forthright, soldierly and ultimately bruising, leaving Johnson with little taste for the ways of the wooden world, but nevertheless a healthy respect for its discipline. This morning he had prevailed upon a midshipman who looked not half his age to convey the message that Jessye was ready for her tonic – which he himself would have mixed and administered, except that, with no locker space, the bottles were kept in Hervey's cabin.

Hervey's mare was on the mend. She was already on that road in Paris, but the sea air was doing her a great power of good. That and the tonic – two pinches sulphate of iron, a half of powdered nux vomica, and two each of gentian and aniseed. It had been the regimental standby since Major Edmonds had been a cornet. Hervey sprinkled the mixture into some molasses syrup and then rolled half a dozen barley-favours from the sticky paste. Much ado, they agreed, but the surest way to have her ingest.

'Tha thinks she'll be all right, Cap'n 'Ervey?'

'Heavens, yes: I don't think we need continue this tonic beyond a day or so more.'

'I meant will she be all right cooped up in 'ere for six months?'

A month's box-rest was the longest Hervey remembered seeing any horse confined. 'There's no reason why she can't stay the course, as long as the ship remains afloat. If the sea gets too high we can brace her into a standing stall. The real worry is the wasting of that muscle,' he sighed, indicating the rounded quarters, testament to many hours of careful schooling. 'It will take all of six months to get it back. But she'll have fewer ailments this winter – of that I'll be bound. No damned stuffy stable, with every cough of a morning becoming three by evening.'

'Isn't she gooin' to go barmy, though?' Johnson had hung up a turnip on a length of string so that she might have something to amuse herself by, but she hardly paid it notice, so taken was she by the constant activity about the deck.

'Well, there's plenty to keep her interest, and she's not having any corn to hot her up. And she has space enough to stretch.'

Johnson was not entirely convinced.

But then neither was Hervey. 'If I spend an hour each day with her, brushing and strapping, and you likewise, then we might keep the muscle hard. Come on, I'll lend you a hand to skip her out.'

They were picking out her bed as the captain's steward came up. Johnson had never found the job easier, for droppings and fouled straw went straight through the gunport, giving the following gulls the brief promise of a feast.

'Begging your pardon, sir,' said Flowerdew, knuckling his forehead, 'captain's compliments, and would you join him for dinner, at six, sir?'

'Who'd be a bloody fart-catcher afloat!' said Johnson when Flowerdew had gone.

'Private Johnson, I never cease to be amazed by how ill you consider anyone in service. And yet you show no appetite for going back into the ranks of a troop yourself.' Hervey was more puzzled than offended.

'I'm 'appy to be of service, but not all this "by your leave" palaver. Like a lot of Susans they are! An' tha knows I'm not frit by gooin' back in t'ranks: it's just that there's too much frigging abaht – *that's* what!'

One of the hands nearby was laughing.

'For heaven's sake, man, mind your language!' appealed Hervey.

Johnson looked astonished. 'Language? Tha should be on t'mess deck! It's—'

'Yes, very well – let's not have all of it,' Hervey protested, somehow wishing he had saved himself the trouble. 'You know the captain's strictures on profane or low words on deck.'

'Suit thisen, Captain 'Ervey.'

Truly, it was not difficult at times to see why Johnson had been passed on from two lieutenants within the space of a couple of months. And why he had been the bane of the corporals in his troop. Yet it was his very irrepressibility that recommended him – that and the undisputed fact that he was a deuced fine groom. And then there was his resourcefulness. Never would Hervey forget that Waterloo dawn, rain still beating down, every dragoon skulking under his cloak until all but kicked from under by the picket. But not Johnson. *He* had spent the opportune hours progging, and managed to wake Hervey with a canteen of hot tea – the only officer in the Sixth, besides the major, to have that privilege. Sheffield vowels and brusquerie was hardly a great price to pay, whatever others thought.

Hervey dressed for the captain's table with particular care that afternoon. He put on white cotton breeches, and court shoes instead of hussar boots, hoping, however, that the buckles might not look so obviously like the pinchbeck they were. He put on one of his fine lawn shirts, turning up the collar so that the points would project. Then he took out his best coat, finer cloth than his service tunic. How diligently Johnson had wrapped the buttons in paper to preserve their shine, he noted. Ten, top-to-bottom on each side of the bib front – he took care not to touch any as he hitched-to the tunic hooks. He fastened the belt and girdle, smiling again at how he and his fellow cornets had complained of the new pattern with its red hoops – the colour of the legionary infantry – which 'vulgarized' them. That and the new cross-belt with its deuced red stripe. And all because a new colonel – long gone – had wanted to be able to see instantly which were his officers. How trifling had been their concerns.

And so they both sat, with Peto likewise more formally attired than hitherto, sipping the presents with which Hervey had joined *Nisus* – all blue coats, gold lace and white breeches. The wind had fallen away in the early afternoon, and they were running very smoothly now through the water, the flatware on the table making not the slightest noise. At first, conversation was merely polite – the weather, Jessye's sea legs, Hervey's engagement with the language of the Mughal court. Not a word of the gendarmerie, however. A paltry affair, unworthy of mention? He simply could not judge.

Quite suddenly, Peto changed his tack. 'Captain Hervey,' he began, 'you may think me overly curious, but I have observed you closely since our first meeting. This business of yours in India: it seems hardly patrician sport.'

Hervey's frown said he was not sure of Peto's meaning.

'Officers who are well connected have little appetite for the Indies. They would rather do their soldiering in Brighton, would they not?' replied Peto, with a note of the accusatory.

Hervey laughed. 'I have no blue blood, sir – well, none to speak of, that is. Why did you presume otherwise?'

Peto looked surprised. 'The Duke of Wellington, by my under-standing, chooses his ADCs from the nobility. You are a *Hervey*, are you not?'

'So distantly am I related that the Earl of Bristol would not know of my being on this earth!' he smiled. 'Indeed, those Herveys pronounce the name as if it were spelled with an *a.*'

'*Oh.*' Peto now seemed disappointed. 'So neither are you descended, in any direct sense, from Admiral Augustus Hervey?'

'I am afraid that I am not descended in any sense whatever,' he smiled again.

'Then by what influence did you become aide-de-camp to so great a man?'

'You have a decidedly low opinion of the way the army conducts its business, Captain Peto!'

'I know what I know, sir!'

'Well, the duke chose me – that is all there is of it.' He hoped that it would put off further interrogation on the subject, but it did not.

'Fiddlesticks, Captain Hervey! There's a great deal more of it – of that I'll be bound. I have observed an officer with a true instinct for his profession – if as such it may be dignified – and one with an uncommon eye for a horse in respects other than its bloodlines. I'm pleased the duke recognizes your aptitude, but I'm sceptical.'

'I surmise that you are sceptical by nature, sir,' replied Hervey, still smiling.

'Like the philosopher, Captain Hervey, I deny nothing but I ques-tion everything.'

'In what do you place your faith, then?'

'I always strive to gain the weather gage and the first broadside!' Peto said it with such relish that it made Hervey blink. 'But I am forgetting myself: I have a very passable Bual that I think we may enjoy before our dinner.' Champagne was evidently not the captain's ultimate pleasure. He opened a locker and took out a bottle of Madeira from an inclined rack made to keep them fast in the heaviest of seas. He drew the cork deftly and poured two glasses. 'It will not need tasting: Blandy has never failed me. My first captain had barrels of the stuff as ballast. Two or three times across the Atlantic and the Equator and it was very finely matured indeed.'

'You buy direct from the island?'

'Captain Hervey, Madeira has been my second home these past three years, for that was my station during the American war. And, I might say, it was the place of some fortune, for we took a frigate and two merchantmen in a year.'

'That would mean prize-money, then?' Hervey was gaining his ease.

'Do not think ill of it, sir: the greater part goes to the officers, but then so does the enemy's shot!'

Hervey assured him he meant no disrespect. 'You have bought a handsome estate somewhere, no doubt?' he added.

'Not at all. It is invested in Berry Brothers in St James's Street: a good wine, sir, will have a better return than bricks and mortar.'

'You do not have a wife?'

'Captain Hervey, I have scarce spent seven successive nights ashore since leaving Norfolk to be a captain's servant, and I should scarcely wish to spend any more with a wife!'

Hervey laughed. 'Well I, too, am not well acquainted with soft pillows. The army has not been idle these past years.'

'Bah!' said Peto; 'I have followed events with the closest attention, and it seems to me that if your Duke of Wellington had shown a little more address you would have been over the Pyrenees two years before. And he was humbugged at Waterloo, I hear.'

'Oh come, sir!' spluttered Hervey, but still with a broad smile. 'You can have but an imperfect conception of the difficulties the duke faced at Waterloo. He had few battalions which had seen service – most of those were in America. And his allied regiments were – at best – untried. It is astonishing that he did as he did.'

They had moved to the steerage and a very handsome table of salt-pork collops, a veal pie and crabs dressed with olive oil. Peto poured him burgundy again. Here was no less generous or attentive a host than poor d'Arcey Jessope himself, thought Hervey – though that delightful Coldstream dandy, killed stone dead by a tirailleur's bullet at Waterloo, had been almost self-mocking in the fare he offered. Captain Laughton Peto would have been mortified by any want of gravity. For him the table was a serious affair, comparable, it seemed, with the very business of seamanship itself.

Peto was keen, however, to press his censure. 'But the duke's attachment to purchase, Captain Hervey, and his favouring of fellow nobles, his promoting their sons: is *that* conducive to efficiency?'

Hervey sighed to himself again. What was he meant to do – defend the inexplicable, though it worked nonetheless? 'I think,' he began tentatively, 'that the duke has always been in want of men in whose capability he could place confidence. It is the Horse Guards who appoint officers to command, and sometimes these appointments are inapt. I myself have served a brigadier who was both a coward and an incompetent. The duke ensures that at least his own staff are of his mind. But he's by no means closed to the appointment of men who have recommended themselves by service.' He paused briefly to sip his wine and crack open a claw, and he wondered to what Peto's questioning might be tending. He thought it prudent to rehearse the duke's opinions a little more fully. 'And as to purchase, it has its iniquities but yet its recommendations: I think it well to have officers with a stake in the country when the army is the means of maintaining public order – and might indeed be the means of overthrowing the government.'

'And yet the nation may entrust its wooden walls to officers with no such stake, only patriotic sentiments!' countered Peto, unimpressed.

'Does the navy not have its patronage too?' asked Hervey, hoping the doubt sown might allow them to pass on to other things.

'Not for the advancement of knaves and imbeciles, that's for sure. Do you know our system?'

Hervey indicated that he knew it but imperfectly.

'I was taken on as a captain's servant at fourteen – or "volunteer" as we were by then more properly known.'

'And how was that arranged?' Hervey interrupted.

Peto smiled. 'By Lord Nelson's recommendation to Captain Blackwood, but . . .'

'So influence has its place in the navy, too?' smiled Hervey by return.

'There must be a start *somehow*, Captain Hervey. All that Lord Nelson did, though, was to recommend me as from an honest family, that I was clean-limbed and eager! From volunteer, advancement is on merit alone. I was a midshipman the following year – 1805 – though in truth I had not spent the regulation four years at sea. But yellow-jack had carried off three of our mids. I passed for lieutenant at nineteen

– the earliest I could do so – and was appointed to a first-rate almost at once . . .'

'But again, Captain Peto,' Hervey pressed, 'there must be more midshipmen who pass for promotion than there are vacancies for lieutenants? How are appointments thus made?'

'Some by favour, to be sure; but no captain would appoint an officer in whom he could not have confidence.'

'How did *you* obtain your appointment?'

'By Captain Blackwood's recommendation. I was one of his signalling midshipmen on *Euryalus* at Trafalgar. But as I was saying, I was first lieutenant on *Amphion* at Lissa, and from that action got my command the following year. And do not forget that promotion is ever open to those of ability on the lower deck: both Cook and Benbow served before the mast.'

'Trafalgar was hot work for you?' asked Hervey (he intended, firmly, to deflect the conversation from purchase).

'Not for *Euryalus*: we had done our work during the night, keeping contact with the French and signalling to the fleet, to let Nelson bring them to battle at daylight on terms of advantage.'

'So you saw little of the action?' Hervey asked, with a note of disappointment.

'On the contrary,' smiled Peto, 'we saw everything. We were in the thick of things throughout.'

'Then how might you not describe it as hot work?' said Hervey, surprised.

'Because in a fleet action a first-rate does not fire on a frigate unless fired upon first.'

Hervey looked puzzled.

'Captain Hervey, do you have any conception of the firepower of a first-rate compared with that of a frigate?'

'Well,' began Hervey awkwardly, 'evidently I have failed to grasp the magnitude of the difference.'

'Just so; a first-rate has three times the guns, and her lower-deck battery has thirty-two-pounders – almost twice the weight of mine. At the Nile, there was a French frigate that opened fire on the *Goliath* – who was but a seventy-four. *Goliath* fired back, and with a single broadside dismasted her and shattered her hull so that she sank at once.' Peto took a sip of Madeira with intense satisfaction at the thought. 'No, from a line-of-battle ship a frigate must stand away, and she may invariably do so with ease and honour both. At Trafalgar *Euryalus* repeated the flagship's signals and so on – first for Nelson, and then for Collingwood – and we helped several ships which were otherwise disabled: we towed off *Royal Sovereign* – she was dismasted. But we had no damage ourselves.'

'I did not know of the convention,' admitted Hervey, taking another long draught of Peto's excellent burgundy. 'But I can see its purpose, now. It is very gallant: *tirez les premiers!*'

'*Gallant?* I tell you *I* would have none of it were I Admiralty. A frigate is an instrument of war as much as is a first-rate. Fighting chivalrously is always at someone's expense – and usually those who are least able to afford it! All this *tirez les premiers* is so much cant. Fontenoy it began at, did it not? "We do not fire first, gentlemen: we are the English Guards!"' Peto made a loud huffing sound.

Hervey thought there had been something pragmatic in the Guards' invitation but could not recall the particulars, and, in any case, it was Trafalgar he wished to discuss, not Fontenoy. It was not every day a man might hear of it from so close an observer. And so they sat well into the night, Hervey pressing him to every detail of the battle, with more burgundy and Madeira than he had ever drunk at one sitting. When at last he rose, unsteadily, to retire to his quarters, he put a final question to his host. 'How came it about that Lord Nelson was able to recommend you to Captain Blackwood in the first instance? Are you from a naval family, sir?'

'No, I am not,' replied Peto with a smile. 'Not, that is, in the literal sense. Lord Nelson's father had the living at Burnham Thorpe, and my father was once his curate. At the time of my going to sea he had the neighbouring parish.'

'Then,' smiled Hervey, 'we have something in common.'

They began comparing their relative ecclesiastical fortunes, but since the tithes were either impropriate to the patron or modest, the comparison was brief.

'So we each must seek for our prosperity in uniform,' concluded Peto, dabbing with a napkin at the Madeira which had found its way to his waistcoat.

'Just so,' smiled Hervey, 'and at a time when there is peace on earth!'

'Ah,' said Peto, shaking his head optimistically, 'but there is little goodwill towards men!'

The wind had backed, and a moderate westerly was making the air chill. Hervey had on the thinnest cheesecloth shirt, yet he was sweating. Half an hour's brushing followed by another's strapping would maintain his own hale condition as surely as it would Jessye's. And he had just been struggling to remove her shoes too, for they served no purpose standing on deep straw. He looked up to see Peto eyeing his labours intently. Feeling the need to say something, for he knew the business must gravely offend the captain's sensibilities, he thought he might express his gratitude once more. 'I do very much appreciate what a trial this is, sir,' he began.

Peto surprised him by his reply, however. 'Captain Hervey, I should not have risked the regularity of my ship had I thought your horse posed any danger,' he smiled. 'On the contrary, a horse has a most civilizing effect. The hands feel better for seeing her. I would be chary of that, perhaps, were there not peace on earth, but I see no cause now for keeping the crew quite as tight as the bowstring they have been hitherto.'

He seemed in excessively good spirits this morning. Hervey smiled with some relief.

'We see eye to eye, I think, on many matters. When you are quite finished with your day's exertions join me, if you please, on the quarterdeck. I wish to apprise you of something.'

Hervey put on his cloak before leaving the shelter of the waist. Sail was stretching fuller in the freshening westerly, and spray was now visiting the deck. No land was visible, even by telescope, and seabirds were fewer by the hour. Peto was wrapped likewise in a cloak and stood alone at the stern rail, legs braced a little apart, a hand fastened on one of the shrouds. Hervey walked as close to the rail as he could without actually placing a hand on it, the ship's motion sufficiently pronounced now to make him a shade insecure. Peto smiled as he reached the stern. 'Worry not: in six months you'll be rushing to the tops like an old hand!'

Hervey looked unconvinced, and then not a little anxious as it occurred to him that Peto might have summoned him to begin this very practice.

The captain's preoccupations were otherwise, however. 'Since you are evidently an officer of singular attachment to your profession, I judge that you might be an availing interlocutor in the art of war.'

Hervey had no idea of what he alluded to. 'You flatter me greatly, sir—'

'Yes, yes, yes – but do I suppose correctly that you have an eye for more than a horse?'

He smiled. It seemed that the duke, at least, believed so. 'Try me, sir,' he replied.

'Certain notions of warfare, acquired these past six years, I am minded to commit to the page.'

Hervey wiped the stinging salt spray from his eyes and pulled his shako lower. 'Notions particular to war at sea?'

Peto thought a moment before replying. 'At first I should have considered them so, but I am no longer sure, for it seems to me that the general precepts ought equally to apply on land. What do you know of the affair at Lissa?'

Hervey now had his legs braced twice as wide as Peto's, and a tighter grip on a shroud line. 'I know that an English squadron defeated a French one twice its strength.'

'Just so, Hervey, just so.' Peto's voice was beginning to rise against the wind. 'Four of the French's were forty-gun frigates, too – though to say *French* is not entirely true, for one was Venetian, and another couple of thirty-twos as well. A damned fine fight they put up, though!'

Hervey made respectful noises.

Peto now revealed he was writing a memento. 'I gave a public lecture on Lissa – at Gresham's College in the City. A publisher approached me thereafter.'

His evident pride in both was endearing. Hervey nodded in appreciation.

'I intend, in a supplementary chapter, to draw lessons from the action, developing a more general theory,' he added.

Hervey asked if he would be challenging any Admiralty document thereby.

'There are the Standing Instructions, yes. And these are added to by fleet instructions. Lord Howe's are still the basis for our fighting.'

'And these are deficient?'

Peto looked rather irritated. 'They don't want for quality! I wish merely to develop a general design for captains of frigates – and it's only of frigates I speak, for the future is with them.'

'And the import of Lissa?'

Peto looked happier again. 'In the Royal Navy it is a precept, by which an officer is taught, that navigation precedes gunnery.'

Spray was now beginning to reach high, yet Peto was not inclined to move. Hervey pulled up his collar and further inclined his ear towards him.

'Captain Hoste prevailed at Lissa because he handled *Amphion* superbly, not because her gunnery was superior – though it was. He placed his ship where her fire might be to greatest advantage, and he drove the French onto the shore. *That* is working a frigate, Hervey!'

Despite the distraction of having to keep his balance, Hervey saw how it must be so (indeed, he wished they were a little closer to the shore themselves). In any case, there could be no doubting the captain's aptness for such a treatise, for Peto had walked the quarterdeck with Hoste, who had himself walked the deck with Nelson.

'And I tell you this,' he continued, now so fired by his subject that his voice had risen well above the wind, 'there is wonderful pleasure to be had cruising, but it's nothing to manoeuvring to advantage in shallow waters. The Nile was, to my mind, the most famous of victories!'

Hervey would not have gainsaid that.

'Do you recall Bonaparte's lament? "Wherever you find a fathom of water, there you will find the British!" Oh yes, Hervey, believe me: it's shallow waters that truly test a captain.'

'I shall remember it,' he replied, smiling. 'A fathom only, you say?'

'It is all that *I* should need,' Peto asserted. 'Come below and I'll read you my account of it.'

Even in the cold and the spray – and the effort to stay on his feet – Hervey could see the vigour in Peto's thinking. And if he could pass just a little of his time at sea in discourse such as this he might well increase his own fitness for command, for it was evident that in the handling of a frigate and a troop of cavalry there was more than a little similitude. As to this being any more than a theoretical fitness, however, he could only confide, for everywhere, they agreed – even in India – there was peace on earth.

CHAPTER FOUR

A PROSPEROUS VOYAGE

Approaching the coast of Coromandel, 6 February 1816

Hervey had written so many letters during his otherwise idle hours that they filled one of his hatboxes. But to one man he had yet to commit his thoughts, for Daniel Coates was neither family, nor regiment, nor superior. Daniel Coates was a man who would wish to hear of his thoughts as they touched upon his military condition, so that he might compare them with his own experience, which, in the space of the ten years he had been Hervey's self-appointed tutor in practical soldiering, he had shared unsparingly. Daniel Coates, formerly General Tarleton's trumpeter in the first American war, had lived peaceably on Salisbury Plain for twenty years, first as shepherd, then as agister, with sheep so numerous they had made him rich even by the wool standard of that county. Hervey would hold that he owed his life on a dozen occasions to that veteran's generosity and tireless instruction – and never more so than at Waterloo, when Coates's clever new carbine had been all that stood between him and a French lancer's bullet. He had left the letter until this time so that he might reflect properly on the half-year he had passed in the wooden world.

My Dear Daniel,

I write this as the end of my passage to Hindoostan will soon be come. You will know, I trust, since my father will have told you, of my great good fortune. Of my affiancing I can say nothing but that it is more than I ever thought possible, and I pray daily that its consummation will not be too long delayed. Of my attachment to the Horse Guards, you may be skeptical, but I believe I may assure you that on that account you need have no anxiety, for I come here to do the bidding of the Duke of Wellington, about which more I am unable to say in this present but that the duties seem fitted to me. I do confess, though, to some unease, for, having pondered on my orders these past months, I feel the need of more intelligence than that to which I have been made privy. However, I can have nothing but the utmost faith in those who have despatched me hither (as they must have reposed their faith in me), and I am confident that when I attend on the offices of the Honourable East India Company in Calcutta I shall be given every facility and courtesy, and that all shall be well.

Six months at sea has seemed a great many more than six months in the saddle. No day has been the same as another, although the ship's routine is so regular. Wind and weather may change with such rapidity – sometimes, it seems, almost perversely within but a few minutes – and hands must race aloft to set more sail or to shorten it. As a soldier, changes in the weather have rarely meant more to me than variations of discomfort. You, of all men, will remember talk of the campaigning season, but you, as I, have fought in the depths of winter often enough. But, on the whole, weather might mean putting on capes and oilskins, or taking them off, and the difference between a hot meal and a brew, or biscuit and a nip. But beyond that the weather troubled us nothing much. Once or twice in Spain we had posted extra sentries during storms at night, when hearing was made difficult and it was feared the enemy might pass through our vidette line undetected, but these occasions were exceptional. To a soldier, changes in the weather bring no habitual extra duties. But the captain of this ship, the Nisus, *owns that that is the first purpose of a frigate's crew, to trim the ship to the weather, and declares that fighting her is secondary.*

And I do so very much see what he has of mind, for without apt sailing, her gunnery is to no avail. Indeed, Dan, I have learned so much from this captain that might with profit be taken up on land by light dragoons. Captain Peto says that, in the navy, navigation precedes gunnery, and I can see how likewise it should be with light cavalry, for if one could but manoeuvre one's force to advantage, and with surprise, there might scarce be need of a single shot. These past months have been the first time that I have had any leisurely opportunity to address affairs of strategy, and in Captain Peto I have found a most unexpected teacher.

Likewise have I greatly enjoyed the companionship of the wardroom, cramped though it is. To a man, I declare, the officers are fine fellows, and, would you believe, the lieutenant of Marines was my senior at Shrewsbury. I like him very much, though he is at times melancholy, though that is in large part accounted for by a most unhappy history. But I shall be most sad to part from him and all the Nisus's *crew.*

I do not know, Dan, if you were ever tempted to go to sea, or, for that matter, were ever close to the press gang, but I must say that, this companionship apart, I have not seen anything that might recommend the Service to a free man in place of going for a soldier. There are the evident advantages, of course, a bed and a roof over the head for at least part of the day, regular if in-different food, and, perhaps, a little prize-money, but beyond that it seems the meanest existence. Drink keeps order here, where in the Peninsula it was the cause of so much disorder. Here the officers control it with strict regulation and precise appli-cation, for no liquor could mean mutiny and too much could mean dissent. Nisus's *officers are what others call, charitably, enlightened. Captain Peto would not have it otherwise. He promotes self-respect in the way that the Sixth does. The purser has told me that the ship's victuals are better and more varied than on any other he knew of, and that it is the captain's own pocket which causes it to be so. And so, too, with the crew's uniform, for it is not provided at Admiralty's expense, as ours is by the Horse Guards. Every man has a smart, round japanned hat with a gold-lace band with 'Nisus' painted on it in capital letters, a red silk neckerchief, white flannel waistcoat bound with blue piping, white canvas trousers and a blue jacket with three* rows of gold buttons. The crew parades on Sunday mornings in their best dress, and after divine service come pickles and beer, and there is music from two black fiddlers whom the captain engaged in London at a not inconsiderable premium. Sometimes, too, there is much skylarking, as they call it. In the middle of November, when we crossed the Equator for the first time, King Neptune paid us his apparently customary visit. In truth, this king is always the longest-serving rating, and I and the other first-timers (one of the lieutenants and all the midshipmen) had to do homage to the briny deep, as they say, and with as much good humour as we could manage. This we did in a great bathing tub of seawater on the deck, and there was much skylarking which followed, until I was grateful that a sudden squall doused us all and sent the larboard watch aloft to shorten sail. And then there was Christmas, a day which I confess I found uncommonly difficult to bear, for my thoughts kept returning to Horningsham, where I have not seen Christmas in nine years. But the southern seas were heavy all that night and throughout the morning, and Captain Peto had his work cut out keeping the rig balanced while allowing the crew what they considered their rightful merrymaking. I do not envy him this command, Dan, as once I might, and I confess that he exceeds even Major Edmonds and Sir Edward Lankester in my estimation, for he sits on a powder keg in more than just the actual sense. Can you imagine, Dan, that a sentry should ever be posted by the headquarters of your old regiment or mine to guard the colonel from assault by his own dragoons?

I have dined with the captain on so many occasions during this voyage, for he has been kindness itself to me. Our table has become less rich of late, and preserves of all kinds are now our staple, as well as fish, of course, and, for one week in January, turtle. But the captain's cellar has good wine still. I long for a plate of your best mutton, though!

I should tell you that Jessye has borne the voyage very tolerably well. Only once has she given me true anxiety, and that was lately in what they call, aptly, the 'horse latitudes', but it proved no more than a common chill. I cannot tell you (though perhaps you will know) how much I ache to have her feet on dry land again so that she might enjoy a run. She is the best of horses. I *could not imagine what it might be like to take a blood on board, but I should not want to put her through the confines of a journey such as this for a long time to come. For the moment, though, I am only too relieved that she is well.*

I have been able to learn a little of one of the native languages from the captain's clerk, who has spent some time in Calcutta, and I have had much opportunity for reading and contemplation. Milton I have read copiously; and Wordsworth and Coleridge, for Henrietta gave me a little collection of the latter's work as yet unpublished – you will not know, I think, that she meets and corresponds with some who are called the 'romantic poets' (how strange to think that Coleridge once shared our calling, albeit briefly!). I confess they give me intense pleasure. Milton is as ever improving, though. Do you recall how you used to say that 'Paradise Lost' was the best of gazetteers? Too much of its alle-gory eludes me still, but it is apt to conclude with it, for the passage describes our position and condition almost perfectly:

'As when to them who sail
Beyond the Cape of Hope, and now are past
Mozambic, off at sea north-east winds blow
Sabean odours from the spicey shore
Of Araby the blest, with such delay
Well pleased they slack their course, and many a league
Cheered with the grateful smell old Ocean smiles.'

Well, Dan, I trust that so it shall be until our proper landfall, and ask, when at last you receive this, to pray for a safe passage for Henrietta by these same waters, or for my return by them in due course – whichever it is to be.

Your ever most loyal friend,
Matthew Hervey.

As evening came on, he took a turn on the quarterdeck. There was the lightest breeze, and in consequence a full set of sails, but it was quiet enough to hear the contented purling of the hens in their coop as they settled for the night. It was warm, though without the sultriness of the latitudes through which they had lately sailed, and there was a scent of land on the breeze, part dust, part spice. In any event, it seemed to bear a scent of mystery. Yet he could see no lights, and therefore no shore. It must be just beyond the horizon, and he wondered whether it were desert or rainforest. He knew nothing at first hand of the former, nor indeed of the latter. But he had read, and he had listened to others, and he knew which would be his choice if pressed to make one, for even the thought of what things would be in such a forest repelled him – what creatures crept, stalked or slithered unseen. He shuddered at the schoolroom visions. Nothing short of absolute necessity would ever compel him to enter the jungle. *That* he swore.

Peto came upon him just as he turned his head from landwards. 'I'm pleased to say, Hervey, that I shall have no further call on your admirable travelling library, for I have now completed my manuscript.'

Hervey expressed himself pleased, not that Peto should have no further need of his books, but that he had evidently reached a conclusion in his strategical conception.

'Yes, and I am quite certain that it is a true model for the future,' he said emphatically. 'I have called it *The Action off Lissa, A Latter-day Punic Victory*. Note, mind, that I choose the word "action" rather than "battle", for it was the manoeuvre before the engagement that was the really significant.'

Joseph Edmonds would have approved. That much Hervey was sure of, for Hannibal's outwitting of the consuls at Cannae was his constant inspiration. Indeed, Edmonds had a notion that all military truth was extant in the three centuries before Christ, and that gunpowder merely hastened things rather than changed any fundamental principle. 'Acceleration' was what he called it.

'I should have liked to meet your Major Edmonds,' said Peto. 'Indeed I believe I half-know him, for scarcely a week has passed that you have not spoken of him. Well, Hervey,' he smiled, 'you may now read my monograph at your leisure since I have had my clerk make a fair copy. He finishes it even as we speak.'

'Captain Peto, I am very grateful—'

'And you will mind, mark you, the inscription I have placed in it.'

Hervey inclined his head and raised an inquisitive eyebrow.

'*De l'audace, et encore de l'audace, et toujours de l'audace!*'

'Danton?' Hervey smiled by return. '*Pour les vaincre, pour les atterrer!* Goodness, how it must give you satisfaction to turn the words of the enemy so!'

'The *enemy*? Hervey, let me remind you: there is now peace on earth!'

It amused them each as much.

Flowerdew came up, knuckled his forehead and went to the hen coop. A few moments' searching through the bedding produced two good-size eggs, and a little smile of satisfaction. 'There, Captain, I said as they'd start layin' again. It was that foul weather off Madagascar that stopped them up!'

'Yes,' shrugged Peto, 'and I was the one who wanted to put them all in the pot! An egg for breakfast: oh what a prospect again! Captain Hervey shall have the other.'

'Oh no, Flowerdew should have it by rights.'

'As you please, Hervey, but Flowerdew will sell it to the highest bidder in the wardroom – isn't that so?'

His steward merely grinned.

'In that case,' grinned Hervey back, 'I shall claim the right to be the highest bidder. You will let me know the final price?'

'Ay, sir, that I will! Right generous of you, sir.'

'That egg may cost you more than a whole breakfast in St James's, Hervey. A nice gesture, though. You're a good sort. Men will always follow you, even though they'll curse your ardour at times.'

Hervey was rather flattered.

'How is your horse? Still out of sorts?' Peto seemed done with fighting for the time being, theoretical or otherwise.

'Out by the merest degree,' he replied, 'but it's nothing more than a chill – nothing like as bad as that she came aboard with. It was that same foul weather near Madagascar, I think. The worst is over.'

'She looked rather sorry for herself this morning, I thought.'

'Well, she would wish for a good gallop, but her stall allows her plenty of movement. She's borne it handsomely. Neither heavy seas nor heat appears to trouble her. I'm intensely obliged for your allowing her so much of your gundeck.'

'And you yourself have not found things too . . . confining?'

Hervey smiled broadly. His ordeal was all but over, and he had much to thank Peto for. 'My dear sir, for me it has been pleasure without alloy. I have read much, I have learned a language in no little measure, for your clerk has been a most excellent schoolmaster, and I have greatly enjoyed – and profited from – our colloquies.'

'I am glad to hear it,' replied Peto, with genuine satisfaction; 'and you have maintained a most vigorous regimen: I see you racing to the tops from time to time with the alacrity of a seasoned hand.'

'And I believe that I am stronger than before through the exercises that Mr Locke puts upon his marines.'

'Very probably,' smiled Peto. 'Locke is a diligent officer, though life has dealt him ill indeed.'

The stern lights were being lit, and Hervey lowered his voice lest the mates heard. 'You know, when we were at Shrewsbury he was . . . well, an Olympian to us younger boys. He seems now . . . altogether cut down, diminished.'

Peto understood. 'He would take no leave when last we were in Portsmouth. He broods too much. Sea air seems to revive him, though. I warrant he could swing one of those cutlasses clean through the best Baltic fir sometimes.'

It was curious how little they had spoken up to now of *Nisus*'s officers. In the Sixth they would have talked freely about those who shared the regiment's badge, for the officers and men *were* the regiment. Unlike His Majesty's Ship *Nisus*, the 6th Light Dragoons had no other corporeal form. But Hervey and Peto could only agree: Locke needed a more clement diversion than a cloister with wooden walls.

When Peto broke to speak with the officer of the watch, Hervey went to the main deck, to Jessye's tranquil stall. There she stood four-square, a little back from the door, grinding hay in her mouth in a slow, rhythmical motion, as content as he had ever seen her. She had lost the roundedness whence came so much of her supple agility, but not as much as he had feared, and he prayed again that soon they would be ashore to begin restoring that muscle. He pulled her forelock gently, and rubbed her muzzle. She whickered. Just loud enough for him to hear – no one else. So many thoughts crowded in upon him – the years they had spent together, the shot and the shell, and the terrible sights and the terrible sounds. Could there be any secret closer, or safer, than that between a man and his horse? Thank heavens, then – for her sake at least – that there was peace on earth. She had seen and heard and done enough. India would be kinder to her, and he left for his cabin with a smile of satisfaction at the thought.

In his cot he turned to the psalms appointed for the evening – for the sixth time of reading during the passage. He smiled again when he saw them. 'Be ye not as the horse, or as the mule, which have no understanding,' said Thirty-two. He frowned in dissent, for Jessye gave the lie to any literal rendering. 'A horse is counted but a vain thing to save a man: neither shall he deliver any man by his great strength.' Again, he dissented at Thirty-three. But in Thirty-four he could at least acknowledge a lament for Henry Locke's condition: 'Great are the troubles of the righteous.' 'Righteous' was perhaps too preachy a word, but that admirable officer of Marines deserved something of equal worth. Without doubt, though, he brooded too much. Perhaps Locke would see his fortune restored in some future action, but with peace on earth it seemed unlikely. Jessye's deliverance – and Hervey's too, if he were to own to it, for only peace was likely to see Henrietta restored to him – would therefore be Locke's damnation. It was, he pondered, a rather wretched sort of corollary to the adage of the ill wind.

Next morning

Captain Peto was standing with his clerk on the quarterdeck, dictating letters of presentation to the authorities in Calcutta. He had been minded to address this courtesy for some days now, seeing *Nisus*'s progress, by the chart, northwards along the coast of Coromandel towards the Bay of Bengal. And yesterday he had known it to be pressing when the crew had seen sea snakes swimming alongside – a sure sign of being in those waters, said his trusty almanack. They were vivid serpents, their sinewy lengths – dark blue with yellow bands – gliding effortlessly at the ship's side alternately on and just below the surface. Peto had not cared for the sight, and even less when one was netted, and displayed later in a bottle of pickling fluid by an old hand who delighted in collecting such curios. This morning there were no serpents, but they were joined by a pair of squawking parakeets, as appealing to Peto as the snakes had been repulsive, their greens and reds all the more brilliant for the drab contrast of the quarterdeck in whose rigging they now sat whistling and calling. 'Shall I try an' catch one, sir?' asked one of the mates at the wheel, in gentle Devon: ''E'd be a 'andsome thing in yome cabin.'

'No,' replied Peto, shaking his head; 'we should only get the one, and then the other would fret. Leave them be.' And in truth he had no special regard for the thought of the bird's squawking the while in his quarters. He turned back to his clerk: 'I shall take it as a propitious omen for our run into Bengal – like Noah's dove!'

Peto was, indeed, well pleased with the fair winds of late. At the outset of the voyage, as they crossed an uncommonly tranquil Biscay,

Nisus had all sail set and, though Peto had chafed at the need (for they could make no more than five knots), Hervey had been pleased at the opportunity it gave for him to learn the sail plan – and he had gained some approval from the crew by his eagerness to visit the tops. By the time they had reached the Cape Verdes the wind had freshened and they had cruised then on, for the most part, without jibs and staysails. On the run south-east to the Cape they had topsails only, and occasionally the foresail, and she had come up past Mauritius and the Maldives on the south-westerlies of the dying monsoon without Peto once needing to set the topgallants.

These were unknown waters for him, however. He had seen the River Plate a year or so after Trafalgar, he had crossed the North Atlantic half a dozen times, and he had regularly patrolled the Azores. But his fighting had been in the Mediterranean. The sultry breezes of the Indian Ocean were as new a pleasure as they were for Hervey. He was mindful, though, of the greater need for caution in the tropics, for the heat of the sun played tricks on sea currents and wind alike. But these breezes held a sensuous promise too, the breath of the Spice Islands – the 'Islands of Spicerie', an earlier locution that had fascinated him since first he had seen it, as a captain's servant more than a decade before, on an old chart. He stood by the rail now, luxuriating in the warmth and the recollection.

'Do you wish you might be with the East India Squadron for some more definite period?' asked Hervey, having joined him from a full half-hour's strapping.

Peto nodded thoughtfully. 'I should wish to see the great anchorage at Trincomalee: it has no equal, I have heard. And yes, I should welcome a cruise in warm waters. Any seaman would. I should wish to weather a typhoon once in my service. The China Sea's reckoned the most dangerous in all the oceans – shoals and reefs so steep-to that the sounding line can give no warning of their proximity.'

'But . . . ?'

Peto sighed. 'I have no appetite for squadron work, unless I should be commodore. Now that peace is come, advancement will be slow. I shall not see a seventy-four, likely as not. I should as soon take my pleasure under Admiralty letter in a frigate, therefore.'

Hervey would have imagined it thus. Peto, he now knew, was his own man.

*   *   *

Within the hour the wind was falling unaccountably, and by late morning *Nisus* had every yard of sail set but could make little steerage way. In the afternoon Peto conceded that they were becalmed and was contemplating the unwelcome prospect of dropping anchor for the night: being in unfamiliar waters, he was doubly wary of drifting closer to the shore than he would wish. And, thus becalmed, her crew were put to making and mending, and a boat was lowered so that Peto might take a closer look at the bottom, for he very much feared that weed was growing, she being overdue for recoppering. By the chart they were but a few miles south of the old French settlement of Pondicherry – Hervey climbed the mainmast for a glimpse of the place whose name had possessed almost magical qualities since his first schoolroom meeting with Robert Clive. But the great fort there remained just a little too distant for his telescope, and so he had to content himself with listening to one of the mates recounting how he had weathered a typhoon in an East Indiaman before the turn of the century.

The long warm hours were a great pleasure for the crew, now able to aerate their hammocks and wash and hang to dry all manner of things without the usual risk of salt spray spoiling their hussifry. Peto was pleased with this contentment, for there were few favours remaining in the purser's store with which he might reward them, and he had of late been increasingly exercised by the leak below the water-line, as well as, now, by the accumulation of weed. The leak was too near the keel for the carpenters to make good, and several times a day hands were sent below to the pumps. This back-breaking work, in the hot and stuffy conditions below deck, had not made for the happiest of crews before this day's respite and, with weed as well as a leak, Peto resolved to put his ship into dry dock as soon as they reached Calcutta.

For the rest of the day *Nisus* lay motionless in the water – at least as far as forward progress was concerned, for by late afternoon it was evident that she had drifted west towards the coast, with now not twenty fathoms beneath her. And so Peto, for the first time since they had left France, ordered that her anchor be dropped for the night. He did so reluctantly, but he had no wish to find himself on a lee shore when dawn came. At about eight-thirty, however, a south-easterly blew up, as if from nowhere, and at once *Nisus* was a bustle of activity again, hands piped to their stations with an alacrity which would have done them credit had they been beating to quarters. And much to Peto's satisfaction it was too, for at that time of an evening it was a very fair test of a crew's handiness to have the best part of half of them turned out from their hammocks or recreation so fast. Hervey had been sponging Jessye down when he felt the first breath of wind, and he began drying her off as the mates' pipes began shrilling. Yet even in the short time it took him to rub her down the capstan was turning, the muscles of three-score marines and seamen straining at the bars, and the topmen were making ready to loose sail. *Nisus* was under way in less than a quarter of an hour from Peto's first order, the breeze freshening throughout that time, so that by nine-fifteen, when at last the captain went to his quarters for some supper, she was making six knots with unreefed topsails and her foresail set. Now very much gratified by the address which all had shown, he lit a cigar, resolved to open his last bottle of malmsey and sent Flowerdew with an invitation for Hervey to join him.

'Well, Captain Hervey,' he began, as they each took a chair by the stern windows, Peto looking out at the wake for any sign of increase in their speed, for the evening was still light; 'we should make Calcutta in ten days if we can count on this wind, and then, I think, our paths must diverge.'

Hervey sipped his malmsey and lit a cheroot. Though he looked forward keenly to release from his confinement, he would nevertheless miss these opportunities for intimacy. 'Captain Peto, I cannot thank you enough for the kindness you have extended. As I was saying to you only yesterday, the passage has been all ease.'

Peto inclined his head slightly, a gesture of both acknowledgement and pride. But before he could make reply there was a sudden commotion outside, making him sit bolt upright with indignation. 'What in heaven's name—'

The door burst open. A midshipman stumbled in, and quite overcome by the surroundings seemed unable to say a word. '*Fire*, sir!' he shouted suddenly.

Peto was on his feet at once, dousing his cigar in his glass. He raced from his cabin to see smoke billowing from the galley ventilators and long tongues of flame sending sparks into the foresail. He bounded up a companion-ladder to the quarterdeck, roughly pushing aside another midshipman: 'Hard-a-lee!' he bellowed.

The officer of the watch had already put the helm over and *Nisus* was answering to starboard.

'Beat to quarters, Mr Belben,' he barked. 'Close starboard gunports!'

The Marines bugler sounded 'Alarm'. Firemen, one from each gun, raced to their posts. Gun captains on the weather side slammed closed the gunports (even on an open deck Peto was not about to risk additional vent). The carpenters were already connecting hoses to the suction pumps. There was – thank heavens, he sighed – enough water to be able to get up force at once rather than having to wait for the seacocks to be opened. The decks were all activity, but perfect order. *Nisus* had a well-drilled crew. Peto had heard too much as a young midshipman of the explosion aboard the *Boyne*, and the loss of the first *Amphion*, ever to take fire drill for granted. Men at their quarters, with the officers under whom they worked in action, were less susceptible to the blind panic which had overtaken the *Boyne* in its dying moments. He cast his eye about: no sign of panic here, thank God. But why was this fire so fierce? What was fuelling it?

At the alarm the surgeon and his mates took station on the quarter-deck rather than the orlop, and soon they were attending to burns, the Marines sentries at the companionway first satisfying themselves that the wounds were serious enough for prompt attention. The fore-sail was now well alight but the hoses were at least having some effect in keeping the flames from spreading, dousing as much canvas as the jets could reach, with one playing directly into the galley ventilator. Two lines, one of sailors, the other of marines, were passing buckets to and from the cisterns at the head of the chain pumps by the mainmast. Hervey had gone straight to Jessye's stall, where Johnson was already trying to calm her, and he got the marines to throw water over the roof and onto the bed. He pulled one of her blankets from the tackling chest, plunged it in her water butt and threw it over her head and shoulders, then pulling out a second, dousing it and throwing that over her back. Even with her head covered, with Hervey and Johnson standing by, and her head collar on, she was almost frantic, for nothing could keep the smoke out of her nostrils, and it was smoke that tokened fire – as she had known more than once in stables in Spain. She reared and struck her head on the roof. She reared a second time and dislodged one of the timbers. Never had Hervey seen her so terrified. He called to the marines, who were reluctant at first to come into the stall until Johnson's tongue left them no other honourable course. 'We must get her on her side,' called Hervey above the din. 'Johnson, turn her head this way. You men get your shoulders to her flanks and be ready to push when I get her forelegs from under her.'

Wary of her hind legs, the marines edged around the stall. 'Keep alongside 'er,' snapped Johnson; 'if she does lash out you won't take t'full force of 'er feet that way.'

'Ready!' called Hervey, a hand on each fore cannon. 'Now!' And he snatched both feet back. She fell not too heavily, sliding down the side of the stall, and he whipped off the blanket from her head so that she might see him as well as hear his voice. Johnson lay across her flank as the marines edged back towards the stall sides to be clear of her still active legs. But in a few seconds she was calm again and Hervey dismissed them, to their obvious relief.

He kept her down a full fifteen minutes, calming her the while – stroking, talking softly, lying on her neck, though she had more than enough strength to throw both him and Johnson aside had she wanted. In that time the crew managed at last to put out the fire, but smoke still drifted from below, and the smell of charred wood and rope hung heavily on deck. He would keep her down a while longer – until the wind and the hoses had got rid of the worst of it.

Captain Peto was receiving the last of the damage reports from the carpenter when Hervey joined him half an hour after the flames had been finally doused. Things were bad; but they could have been much worse, of that Peto was sure. Before they had got up pressure on all the hoses, oil had run, burning, along the lower deck from the galley towards the hay and straw in the orlop. Two men were dead – both victims of their own panic more than the flames. One had missed his footing racing from the tops, falling across a spar and breaking his neck. The other had sunk like a stone when he threw himself into the sea, somehow persuaded by drink that it was the safer station. Midshipman Ranson had dived after him at once, but it was an hour before a boat fished the man out. Several of the crew were sorely burned. The cook, whose galley had been the source of the conflagration, was so badly scorched about the face that the surgeon did not expect him to live. His skin looked for all the world like that of the pig which had been roasted for the crew when they left France. Peto knew he was unlikely to learn, therefore, what had caused so fierce a blaze, or one so hot, for it had driven all back at first, even when pressure had been got up high on the hoses. Hervey could see well enough his chagrin, and he resolved not to be the first to speak.

81

'You shall be delayed as little as is expedient, Hervey,' said Peto – not sharply, but with exaggerated briskness nevertheless. 'But I shall have to put in somewhere before Calcutta. To begin with, I have broken pumps, and we have shipped so much water – the hoses have sluiced us from top to bottom. I want to put the injured men ashore, too. I fear, in any case, that all your bedding and fodder is ruined.'

Hervey nodded. It was some time before he summoned the nerve to ask where they might put in.

'Madras,' replied Peto, 'though there's no wharfage there: everything has to go through the surf.'

He left the captain to his thoughts, and the occasional brisk word of command, for a good ten minutes. 'How long might we be at Madras?' he ventured when he sensed the ship's routine was returning.

'Four days, perhaps five.'

'Then, with your leave, I would take Jessye ashore: she was excessively restive during the fire, and it will be well to let her run about. And it *has* been six months, sir: I am all anxiety myself to see what the country is about.'

CHAPTER FIVE

THE HONOURABLE COMPANY

Madras Roads

Nisus dropped her anchor at two the following afternoon within sight of the great fort of St George, where Robert Clive had begun his service – a beginning that had taken him, as Hervey knew from his earliest lessons in the schoolroom, to Plassey and immortality. He climbed the shrouds better to spy their landfall, and soon he was able to make out the palaces extending for a mile or so along the shore – perfectly white, colonnaded, bespeaking a dignified wealth, a confident power. The massive walls of the fort – as big as those of any fortress he had yet seen – enclosed buildings of such grace and proportion as to suggest that Wren himself might have been here, the fine spire of St Mary's church looking almost as if it were standing in the square mile of the City of London. How strange it seemed. He had expected an altogether more . . . *native* picture – the jungle encroaching, perhaps; domes and cupolas instead of the colonnades. Meanwhile, the quarterdeck having regained its spirits, Captain Peto was engaged in an exchange of signals with the fort, from which he emerged tolerably content to give instructions to make ready the boats.

The marines reassembled the sling tackle which had brought Jessye aboard, and lowered the canvas cradle into her stall. Private Johnson deftly fastened her in, and two dozen sweating men heaved on the halyards to lift her out of the square twelve feet that had been her stable these past months. She was swung out over the side with nothing more than a whicker, as she had been swung aboard, to Johnson's evident relief and satisfaction. Hervey was already in the captain's barge as the cradle descended slowly, watching apprehensively as Jessye began the instinctive treading motion when her feet felt the water. When she had reached her natural buoyancy and begun to swim properly, although still restrained by the sling tackle, Hervey leaned out to clip a leading-rope to her head collar. Although he did not suppose she would have difficulty following the boat, he knew she would feel more secure if he were leading her. As soon as it was fastened and the strain on the hoisting rope slackened, he leaned out as far as he could to unfasten the tackle and free her from the sling. Once she was safely astern, the oars struck for the shore, Hervey encouraging her the while.

At first all was well. Jessye kept up easily with the stroke of the oars. As they left the calm of the ship's lee, however, she began to fall back, and the swell kept putting her out of sight. She was rapidly becoming distressed, and though there was but a half-mile to the shore, Hervey became anxious too, for at Corunna he had seen strong horses drown in their panic. 'Captain, will you hold the rope?' he asked. 'I'd better go to her.'

Peto raised an eyebrow. 'Of course, if you must,' he replied, sighing as he handed the rope in turn to the midshipman in command of his barge.

Hervey threw off his coat and shoes, and slipped over the side. He had a moment's vision of the sea snakes, shuddered at the thought, but then struck out for his mare. The water was warm, perhaps even warmer than the mill-race at Horningsham in summer, and he reached her in a couple of dozen strokes. She settled at once, with a whicker of contentment as soon as he touched her neck, and, the current taking them easily towards the shore, he even thought he would have a pleasant time of their swim. He was not as fast through the water, however, Jessye swimming in the only way she knew. A little abashed, he had to grab hold of her mane, taking care to keep his arm well stretched to stay clear of her busy legs. Once settled to the rhythm, however, they both seemed to enjoy it as much – more, for sure, than the times they had swum the half-frozen rivers of northern Spain. Then, sooner than expected, they were amid the breakers. The beach shelved gently and Jessye found her footing before her master did. But as soon as his feet touched bottom he sprang astride her.

The joy was instant – to be up on his little mare again after so many months – and she, kicking up through the surf, was likewise full of spirit once more. He was sure he could never describe it in any letter home – though try, in due turn, he must. He looped the rope about her neck and put her (or allowed her) into a canter along the water's edge of the flat, sandy shore. She did not even buck. Months of box-rest, and here she was as good as gold! How genuine a horse could a man want? He could imagine no other as they slowed and turned after a quarter of a mile (for he wanted no strains), and he talked to her every yard of the way, encouraging, praising. She had stood patiently in that stall, in fair weather and foul, for half a year, and now she was responding to his leg and voice as if she were in the riding school at Wilton House. If only his old Austrian riding master could see them now: what pleasure would that eminent equestrian take in seeing the practical effects of his instruction!

Spain had been hotter – much hotter. But there the heat had come unquestionably from the sun. Here it was as if the air had been warmed in some vast oven, for it touched every part of him the same. There was no hiding from it, no shade. Seeking shade was anyway of no help, for the sun had no especial strength. This was the heat of the land, collected, stored, year after year. This was a heat that annealed rather than scorched, invigorated rather than weakened. He looked about as they trotted back to where the captain's barge was being hauled ashore. Faces were turned towards them – open, warm-looking. It took a while for him to tumble – *black* faces. Or rather, brown; darker, certainly, than he had somehow imagined, and in stark contrast to the pearl-white buildings behind them. And the colours of their clothes – so bright, so unrestrained. Never had he seen their like. Heavens, but these women were arresting – shapely, graceful, smiling unself-consciously. He wanted to jump from Jessye's back to embrace them. How a head could be turned in this place!

Up on the embanked promenade bearers were porting richly caparisoned palanquins. Only an elephant would have been needed to complete his schoolroom image of the Indies. And, though separated by half the globe from all he loved, he was roused once again by his commission here – and already thinking of how Henrietta too might one day, soon, thrill to such a landing.

As he came up to the captain's barge he saw the ambassage engaged with Peto. 'And this, we must presume,' said one of the officials, turning, 'by his most obvious and characteristic mounted landing, is the captain of cavalry of whom you speak?'

The voice was a little precious, the language over-florid, but it was nonetheless warm. Hervey, soaked to the skin and barefoot, jumped down and held out his hand. 'This is Captain Hervey, Mr Lucie,' said Peto; 'Hervey, Mr Philip Lucie, fourth in council at the presidency here.'

Lucie was a little older than Hervey, about the same height, though with a sparer frame, and he wore his clothes with a studied elegance. 'You are half-expected, sir,' he said with some bemusement.

Hervey was even more bemused, for Madras formed no part of the itinerary given him by Colonel Grant. 'Indeed, sir? How so?'

Lucie smiled. 'My sister has received a letter from Paris informing us that you were to come to India.'

What in heaven's name, he wondered, might this man's sister have to do with Colonel Grant? 'I am honoured to be the subject of such correspondence – though, I confess, somewhat puzzled.'

Peto made a restive noise which hastened Lucie to full revelation.

'My sister has some affinity with the lady to whom you are engaged to be married. Which lady wrote to her here from Paris, though she did not imagine you would see Madras.'

Hervey looked astonished. 'No, we . . . that is . . .'

'I have explained our circumstances, Hervey,' huffed Peto. 'May we proceed to business, Mr Lucie? I have no time to waste.'

'Of course, Captain,' he smiled. 'I have already alerted the naval commissioner to your presence. But since you expect to be engaged here these several days, perhaps I might extend to you and Captain Hervey the hospitality of my quarters at the fort? I believe we may offer you a table worthy of the Company – or, I should properly say, of the Governor and Company of Merchants of London trading into the East Indies.'

Peto, though tempted to make some remark touching on the propriety of that company, contented himself with a brisk acceptance for the following day; 'For there is much to attend to aboard my ship while there is still light. But Hervey, here, is entirely free to avail himself of the Company's hospitality at once.'

It took no time at all for Philip Lucie to arrange for Captain Peto to see the naval commissioner, and that officer, though about to proceed on home leave, threw himself with the greatest energy into the expedition of the captain's several requests. The injured crewmen of the *Nisus* were brought ashore soon afterwards to the naval hospital – a fine-looking two-storey infirmary with an airy balcony running the length of the upper floor, and with separate quarters to isolate contagion. It stood half a mile or so outside the fort, surrounded by palm trees, and when Peto called on his return from the shipwright's office he was quickly reassured in leaving his men in the care of its native staff, though their faces were more than ever alien to him after so many months at sea. His final business was with the storekeeper, and this was conducted with the same brisk efficiency as at the shipwright's, so that Peto was afterwards able to express himself much privileged to meet with officials capable of such address. Even so, he declined once more Lucie's invitation to dine at Fort George that evening: 'My compliments to the governor, sir, but I must first superintend the repairs to my ship. Captain Hervey will, no doubt, have much to speak of with your sister.'

Madras was one of the most agreeable places Hervey had ever seen. Of that he was sure, even on so short an acquaintance. Most of the houses and public buildings which lay along the shoreline were extensive and elegant, limed with chunam which took a polish like marble, putting him in mind of pictures of Italian *palazzi*. Most had colonnades to the upper storeys, supported by arched, rustic bases, and it was not difficult to imagine himself somewhere along a Mediterranean rather than an Indian coast – though perhaps the minarets here and there might place him further towards Constantinople than to Naples. It was the pagodas which settled his true location, however, and it was as well that he should see them now, for a short distance away Fort George, with its lines and bastions, its Government House and gardens, and St Mary's church, suggested that despite all contrary indications Madras was a place as British as Leadenhall Street – the distant headquarters of this remarkable company.

Madras, the captain's clerk had told him, was a place that had turned its back on India, looking out to the east rather than to the country itself, unlike Bombay and Calcutta. Here, said the clerk, the English conducted themselves as if in London. The displays of fine equipage along the Mount Road of an evening, where to be seen at the cenotaph in memory of Lord Cornwallis was to attain the acme of society, rivalled anything that might be observed in Hyde Park. And afterwards, if there was no meeting at the racecourse nearby, whose graceful stand would have been the envy of Newmarket or Ascot, the occupants of these elegant carriages would return home, dress in great finery and dine to the accompaniment of the most superior wines. Then, perhaps, having dressed once more, they might repair to a ball, to dance until the early hours before at last retiring. And when husbands had, next day, gone to their offices, blades would visit from house to house retailing news, or to ask commissions to town for the ladies, to bring a bauble that had been newly set, or one of which the lady had hinted before – one she would willingly purchase for herself but that her husband did not like her to spend so much – and which she might thus obtain from some young man, a quarter of whose monthly salary would probably be sacrificed to his gallantry.

The captain's clerk might warn that Madras was become depraved, but to Hervey that morning it was simply alive. 'Then you must stay with us at Fort George for as long as you are able!' said Philip Lucie. 'Let us show you how civilized a country this may be.'

Nothing could have been more welcome to him, for the entreaty meant the indulging of Jessye in the presidency stables. Above all, it meant he might have some intimation of Henrietta's response to his leaving Paris in such haste. The mere fact of her writing to a friend suggested she was not unsympathetic; but he was more than ever fearful that he had likely trespassed a journey too far.

That evening, as the oven heat of the day gave way to a balminess that seemed from the pages of an old Indiaman's recollections, Hervey and the fourth in council dined together in the place of England's first footing on the subcontinent. In the short time at his disposal, Philip Lucie had given considerable thought to their fare, at first supposing it apt to display the culinary glories of Madras, a taste to which he was wholly devoted. But he had later thought better of it, for he knew that the privations of a long sea voyage did not always render the digestion welcoming of assault by spices (he had not been in the east for so long as to forget his own first, tumultuous encounter with Madrasi spices). So, instead, he conceded to digestive prudence: after a mild native pepper soup they would proceed to the finest beefsteaks in India.

They were to be made four at dinner, he explained. His sister would soon arrive, having spent the day driving in the peace and quiet of the hills west of the city, and they would be joined by another, whose company he was sure Hervey must admire. 'But first allow me a quarter-hour's leave. I have to sign articles of authority. Here,' he said, handing him a sheet of paper, 'this will entertain you – the bill of lading for our gallant general who left for England with his staff yesterday.' And with that Lucie courteously abandoned him to the sights and sounds, and most conspicuously the smells, of his new surroundings.

Hervey, wearing the lightest clothes that Lucie was able to find him, stood on the terrace of this gentlemanly residence, closed his eyes and listened to the rising chorus of cicadas from the gardens all about. What the sources were of the procession of smells he could scarcely imagine, for, beyond the occasional wisp of smoke, he had not encountered them before. None was rank, and most were agreeable. They were, he expected, restrained compared with those he might find in country India, but they were wholly alien nevertheless.

To his side came, without a sound, a khitmagar bearing a silver tray. Hervey started on seeing him, then felt foolish, and then appeared as such by asking for whiskey and seltzer in Urdu. It was only after several exchanges that he realized Urdu was as strange a tongue as French would have been – except that later he remembered the French held sway in the Carnatic for many years. When the khitmagar returned he simply took the glass and bowed in the universal sign of gratitude, at which the little Tamil looked even more bemused.

Hervey took refuge in the paper Lucie had given him. It was, as he promised, diverting; a list to make any commissary envious.

Articles Put On Board 'The Fortitude', Packet, Captain Bowden, For His Voyage To England, For The Use Of Major-General Stuart, &c, &c.

Licquors	Dozens
Claret	60
Madeira	60
Arrack, half a leaguer	
Brandy	18
Hock	12

Porter				24
Bullocks	12	Hams		15
Sheep	60	Tongues	Casks	5
Fowls and capons	30 Doz	Cheeses		6
Ducks	12 "	Fine rice	Bags	12
Turkies	2 "	Fine bisquit	"	30
Geese	3 "	Flour	Casks	3
Hogs and pigs	30	Tea chest		1
Sows and young	2	Sugar-candy	Tubs	10
Milch goats	6	Butter	Firkins	5
Candles	Mds 8			

salt-fish, curry-stuff, pease, spices, lime juice, onions, &c, &c, cabin furniture, table linen and towels, glass-ware, China &c, &c. Standing and swinging cots with bedding and curtains complete. A couch. Also a great number of small articles of provision, care having been taken that nothing material should be omitted.

(Signed)   W. M. SYDENHAM,
Town Major.

FORT ST. GEORGE
3rd February 1816.

'You are, I imagine, in some degree impressed by the care with which we treat a general officer?' said Lucie as he returned.

'I am all astonishment,' replied Hervey truthfully.

'Then let that invoice speak by itself of the wealth and address of the Honourable East India Company, sir. Nothing is left wanting for its servants. Were you a lieutenant-colonel on the duke's staff you would not receive as much as a captain on the Madras establishment! You will find it tempting to stay when your essay for His Grace is finished.'

How he wished he could tell him that he himself expected to be installed at Fort William before too long. Instead he contented himself with the first thing he could think of: 'Are you very much concerned with bills of lading and the like?'

'We are a trading company, Hervey.'

'Oh, indeed, I—'

'However, my principal occupation as fourth in council is the affairs of the country powers,' he added with an indulgent smile. '*Very* much more interesting than bills of lading!'

The khansamah entered and announced Lucie's other guest, an apparently youngish man but with a decided look of the dissolute. Lucie reversed the strict formulary by introducing *him* to Hervey. 'May I present Mr Eyre Somervile, who is Deputy Commissioner of Kistna and Collector-Magistrate of Guntoor district in the Northern Circars.'

Hervey bowed. A most imposing appellation, he thought, and for one whom Lucie now intimated was but a little younger than Lucie himself. The collector of land revenues bore the customary marks of the Company's service – at least, as imagined by those whose knowledge was limited to salacious gossip. His face seemed puffed up, though the remnants of fine features indicated that once it might have been described as distinguished. His thinning hair was bleached by the fierce sun, of which he evidently had little regard (for his puffy skin was the colour of some of the native men Hervey had seen on the beach), and though his raw silk shirt was generously proportioned, it did not conceal the swelling that was his stomach. But he had kind eyes.

Then came the fourth for dinner. 'My dear,' said Lucie, positively beaming, 'you know Mr Somervile. May I present Captain Matthew Hervey of the 6th Light Dragoons.' A tall, slender woman, close to Hervey's age, serene in a shot-silk dress cut in the late Empire fashion, made a low curtsy in response to their bows. Her skin had not the pallor of the other European ladies he had seen on his way to the fort, for she – like Somervile – evidently took no especial shelter from the sun. But how well did it complement her raven hair! 'Captain Hervey, my sister, Emma.'

It was not difficult for Hervey to be captivated. Emma Lucie had the same engaging smile as her brother, an unthreatening self-possession, and – revealed quickly but charmingly – a keen mind. They chatted freely for some minutes (though with no mention of Henrietta, for Hervey was nervous of hearing anything that would trouble him any greater at this time), and then she turned and greeted the collector more intimately. Somervile dabbed at his neck with a small piece of towel as he took a glass of claret from the khitmagar, drank it at once and then took another. Emma Lucie addressed him in French so eloquent that Hervey might have thought himself a beginner.

'He is a most exceptional fellow, I assure you,' said Lucie quietly, taking Hervey to one side; 'he is the cleverest man I have ever met. Not only does he seem to speak every language in southern India, he knows everything of their etymologies. And he has such a remarkable facility with the native people too: he knows everything of their religions and customs, and they hold him in the very greatest esteem and affection. He will be able to tell you everything there is to know about the country.'

'I should like that very much,' he replied, glancing across at Somervile. 'Your sister – she has been here some time?'

'Almost five years! She refused flatly to be presented, saying she would have no more of London. That is where she knew your affianced.'

Hervey concluded that, with so distant a connection, the acquaintance might not have been as intimate as he supposed.

'She and Somervile would appear to be conducting the longest courtship the presidency has ever seen,' added Lucie with a smile. 'But come, it is time to supplement all that ship's biscuit you have been subsisting on with some red meat!'

When they were seated, after grace (from which Somervile's 'amen' was conspicuously absent), and as hock chill enough to bring a mist to the side of the glasses was poured, the collector looked directly at Hervey and frowned. 'And so are you come, sir, to seek your fortune in the east, or to inform us of some delinquency the duke considers us guilty of?'

He had scarcely taken two spoons of soup before having to protest that he had no other designs but acquiring skill with the lance.

'I am in any case much relieved to learn that you are an emissary of the Duke of Wellington, for he can do little harm,' replied Somervile, raising an eyebrow.

Hervey could not, from either words or intonation, gauge Somervile's precise meaning. 'In what sense might the duke do *any* harm, sir?' he enquired.

'I mean that as a military man there is little to fear from the duke. If he were to return and put all of the Carnatic to the sword he would do little lasting harm. If, however, he took cloth and returned with a bible he would have most of India in revolt.'

Hervey looked astonished at the proposition – both its parts.

'Generally speaking, Captain Hervey, the Hindoo does not fear death half so much as he fears baptism,' explained the collector. 'I am more greatly exercised by the emissaries of Mr Wilberforce who wish to convert the heathen to their especially repugnant form of Christianity!'

92

Emma Lucie sighed and raised her eyebrows with studied amusement. 'Mr Somervile includes me in his strictures, Captain Hervey, for I take a Sunday-school class and there are native pupils.'

'But Miss Lucie's is a most accommodating form of religion, Captain Hervey,' replied Somervile without looking at her. 'It stirs up little ardour. You have read, I hope, of Warren Hastings?'

This was become remarkably like dinner at Cork, thought Hervey, when that assembly of patriots had tested his understanding of history. 'Yes, I have read of his trial,' he replied cautiously.

'Trial? Impeached before a lunatic House of Lords! Seven whole years they vilified his comprehension of this country!'

'The collector feels a keen affinity for Warren Hastings, Hervey. They were each at Westminster, a very superior school, you understand!' said Lucie gravely.

The collector smiled. 'I admit it.'

'He will admit, too, of equal scholarship at Winchester and Eton,' added Lucie with a look of mock despair; 'but the likes of Shrewsbury – where I received my education – he holds in scant regard.'

Hervey looked back at him. 'I was at Shrewsbury too, sir.'

'Indeed?' said Lucie, agreeably surprised.

'I left just as the war was taken to the Peninsula.'

'My time was past somewhat before then. Trafalgar was done in my second year at Cambridge.'

'And did you know a boy called Henry Locke?'

Lucie recalled at once. 'Adonis?'

'Well, yes,' sighed Hervey, thinking how he might explain the change in his appearance.

'He was a year or so below me,' said Lucie, the recollection of him evidently pleasant; 'but what an athlete! He could throw a ball clear across the river.'

'Well, sir, he is with me aboard the *Nisus*. He is commanding officer of her marines.'

Lucie nodded, agreeably again. 'Then I should very much like to see him.'

Somervile evidently thought it time to make some amends for the impression given of him. 'Ultimately, Lucie, the only means of judging a school is by its alumni. Captain Hervey, here, is a distinguished enough soldier to attract the attention of a field marshal, so I should suppose him to be a man of sensibility. I have a high regard for men under discipline. I conclude from this additional evidence, therefore, that Shrewsbury school is a diamond of the first water.'

'Just so,' agreed Lucie, wishing to move on. 'You were saying of Warren Hastings?'

'I was saying that his comprehension will be vindicated, if indeed it has not already been so. To succeed in any measure in India you must treat with the native from a position of close association. Have you heard of Sir Charles Wilkins, Captain Hervey?'

Hervey said he had not.

But Emma Lucie had: 'The Sanskrit scholar, do you mean, Mr Somervile?'

'Yes indeed, madam,' he replied with no especial notice of the singularity of her knowing – nor indeed, of the reason. 'He was the first Englishman to gain a proper understanding of Sanskrit. He translated the *Bhagavhad-gita.* Hastings wrote a foreword and in it he said that every instance which brings the real character of the Hindoo home to observation will impress us with a more generous sense of feeling for their natural rights, and teach us to estimate them by the measure of our own. These are wise sentiments: there are too many which contemptuously deny them.'

'*One* may be counted too many, Somervile,' said Lucie promptly, 'but do you really suppose there are enough to imperil the Company's situation?'

'Let me put the question to *you*, sir,' he replied. 'How many in the service of the Company hereabouts make any concession to native custom – beyond smoking a hookah or taking to bed dusky, lower-caste women?'

Lucie blanched and protested.

'Do not trouble on my account, gentlemen,' urged Emma; 'you forget I have been in these parts quite long enough to know the way of things.'

Somervile pressed on, not the least abashed. 'You, Lucie, are an honourable exception here in Madras, but how many of your fellows have troubled to learn any more of the language of the natives with whom they speak, other than to facilitate satisfaction for whatever are their appetites at that moment?'

Emma Lucie intervened to enquire of Hervey's culpability in this respect.

'I have been learning Urdu these past six months, but have not yet had any chance to practise with a native speaker,' he explained.

'I am gratified to hear of it, Captain Hervey,' said Somervile. 'Urdu is as serviceable a choice to begin with as any.'

'But you object to the preaching of the gospel, even in that tongue?'

'I do.'

'We want no repeat of the Vellore mutiny,' added Lucie, signalling to his khansamah to have the soup dishes cleared.

'Mutiny?' Hervey's voice carried the chill which the word had brought.

'Not ten years ago,' said Lucie, shaking his head as if the memory were personal and vivid. 'Vellore is about a hundred miles distant, to the west of here, and less than half that distance from the border with Mysore. You must understand that at that time Madras and Mysore were in the midst of a most hostile dispute. The sepoys at Vellore rose during the night and killed very many of the European garrison. They would have prevailed, and thrown in their lot with those devils in Mysore had it not been for the address shown by Colonel Gillespie.'

Hervey was at once roused by the image of this gallant officer. Might he know more?

'Indeed you might, Hervey; and right pleased you should be of it, for Gillespie was a cavalryman – though I cannot recall which regiment exactly—'

'You should, Lucie, for it was the first King's regiment of cavalry in the Company's service,' said the collector archly, surprised that a Madras writer should not know his history more perfectly. 'The Nineteenth, Captain Hervey – light dragoons.'

'Ah,' said Hervey, mindful of the Nineteenth's reputation, 'the victors of Assaye – the battle which the Duke of Wellington counts higher than Waterloo in his estimation.'

'Just so,' replied the collector approvingly.

'Well,' coughed Lucie, taking up where he had faltered, 'Colonel Gillespie's regiment were about three leagues away at Arcot. Word was got to him and he set off at once with a portion of dragoons and a couple of galloper guns. With a determined assault he was able to overcome in excess of fifteen hundred mutineers. The bravest man in India, he was called.'

'And he died but a year ago,' said the collector, 'a major general – sword in hand fighting the Nepalis. A fine soldier and an equally fine gentleman. But this is to stray from the material point, Lucie: we were discussing the *cause* of the mutiny.'

'Indeed we were. Well, Hervey, the cause, lying in a nutshell, the *ostensible* cause, was the activities of missionaries.'

'Did you know the Abbé Dubois, sir?' asked Hervey, the abbé's book having lain open in his cabin for much of his voyage. 'He was a missioner was he not? I have been reading his study of the Hindoos and their customs. It seems to me an admirable work.'

'I knew him imperfectly: I met him but a half-dozen times – to converse with him on his perceptions of the country. I do not include him in my general censure. In any case, the French here had a rather different intention.'

'So you will be acquainted with his book?'

'Indeed I am. I first read it at Cambridge. Lucie, you must surely have a copy?' he said, in a manner implying a request.

'Why, yes – but in translation only, if such you do not disdain!' he replied, already on his feet at the collector's challenge, searching the shelves which ran the whole length of one wall. 'I saw it only a day or so ago . . . Yes, here!' He pulled out a handsome leather-bound volume and presented it to the collector.

'Then I shall now quote to you from it,' he said, leafing through as if he knew it well. 'This is a most telling passage: "I venture to predict that Britain will attempt in vain to effect any very considerable changes in the social condition of the people of India, whose character, principles, customs, and ineradicable conservatism will always present insurmountable obstacles." How say you to that?'

'Just so,' agreed Lucie.

'A counsel of some despair, however,' sighed Emma Lucie, 'for India had the Word of Our Lord before our own lands. The apostle Thomas brought the gospel to these shores.'

'Madam,' began the collector, leaning forward with a look of keen anticipation, 'I should like very much to speak with you at greater length on these matters, but a question of Captain Hervey has just this minute occurred to me, and which I should wish to put instead at this time.'

She nodded obligingly, while Hervey braced himself for what he sensed was a question that would test his guard.

'Urdu, Captain Hervey, was the language of the Mughal court and is the language of those parts where the heirs of Babur still rule. Yet these parts are largely to the west and north, and you are – you say – making for Calcutta?'

'That is correct,' replied Hervey without difficulty; 'propriety demands that I first present myself to the commander-in-chief at Fort William. But I understand that the finest exponents of the lance are to be found, however, in Haidarabad, where I believe my Urdu would be most apt.'

'Haidarabad?' said Lucie, in a tone implying that this was somehow to be deprecated.

Hervey was put on alert. 'It was the duke's remembrance thus, sir. It is of no necessity that I go to Haidarabad if there be some difficulty, and if there are other apt exponents of the weapon. No doubt the commander-in-chief will direct me appropriately.'

Lucie clearly wished the condition of Haidarabad had not been broached, and his discomfort was now compounded by Somervile's blithe indifference to his sensibilities in this respect. 'There is some uncertainty in our relations with the nizam at present, is there not, Lucie?' he called from the other end of the table.

There was nothing for it but to brazen things out, as if it were of no great moment. 'There is indeed,' replied the fourth in council, 'and want of intelligence is our greatest affliction. I fancy that the commander-in-chief would welcome your seconding there, if such could be arranged – which I very much doubt. Haidarabad is a closed book to the Company.'

'Why do you doubt it?' asked Hervey, with as little air of concern as he could manage.

'Because,' smiled Lucie, 'the nizam appears to be in one of his periodic bouts of inscrutability.'

'And not helped by the Company's resident, and the Pindarees,' added the collector.

Lucie shot an urgent look at him. 'Somervile has also the rather tedious difficulty of having as a neighbour a small state which seems to be permanently at odds with Haidarabad. He is especially sensitive thereby, for when elephants fight – so to speak – they trample on a good deal of their neighbours' crops. You understand what is the function of a Company resident, I take it?'

Hervey took the opportunity to learn more. 'Perhaps if you would remind—'

'By all means, sir. The Company's policy for some years – initiated, indeed, by the brother of your Duke of Wellington when he was in Calcutta – has been to conclude treaties with the country powers whereby their security is guaranteed by the Company in exchange for their surrendering the right to engage in war on their own account. These subsidiary alliances, as they are known, are bolstered by a force raised and officered by the Company but paid for by the country power itself. And a resident is appointed to the court as an ambassador of the Company.'

Hervey was intrigued by the earlier intimation of difficulty with the Haidarabad resident – and the Pindarees (whoever they might be). He judged it inexpedient to pursue the question, however, for there was more than a suggestion that the nizam might be not nearly so well disposed towards the Duke of Wellington as imagined. He would try to change rein for the time being at least. 'And this state which is at odds with its neighbour?' he asked, again as innocently as he might.

'Chintal,' replied the collector, helping himself to whiskey and seltzer from the decanter making its slow progress around the table. And the Rajah of Chintal was largely to be pitied, he continued, for he was a Hindoo and wholly in awe of the nizam, in whose territory the princely state of Chintal would have occupied no more than a fraction of a corner. 'If all the nizam's subjects spat at once in the same direction,' he sighed (to Lucie's evident distaste), 'Chintal would be drowned out of sight.'

'Just so, Somervile. I myself would have described Chintal as a nine-gun state, however. Less colourful than your description, but more telling.'

Hervey seemed not to understand the claim.

'I mean that the rajah receives a nine-gun salute from the Company – the minimum.'

'The nizam gets twenty-one,' added the collector; 'as do only four others.'

'Others?' enquired Hervey.

The collector looked at Lucie, who took up the challenge: the country powers were his business, after all. 'Mysore, Gwalior, Kashmir . . . and Baroda, though heaven knows why, for it is a trifling place.'

Hervey wondered how he might enquire of Chintal's condition, but could think of no way that might not arouse suspicion.

Lucie was growing more agitated by the minute, however. The collector had often enough made known his view that circumspection was no asset in India, so he now sought emphatically to deflect the conversation away from matters that might lead to graver indiscretion. 'Come,' he said firmly, 'it is time for some air. Shall we go and see your horse, Hervey? And perhaps Somervile will show us his too, for they carried off all the trophies at the racecourse last evening!'

The stables at Fort George were solid, whitewashed affairs which would have been the envy of London. The Governor's Bodyguard, a hundred native troopers under a British officer, were as pampered as His Majesty's Life Guards – though hardened by not infrequent forays into the field. The numerous little fires about the yards, lit in the evenings to drive away the flying insects which otherwise plagued the occupants, were dying down, and although it was now much cooler, the punkahs were still swinging. The syces had gone to their own charpoys some hours ago, leaving the lines to the chowkidars, each of whom made low namaste as the visitors passed.

Jessye was lying at full stretch, perhaps pleased at last there was no motion beneath her bed. She raised her head as the four approached, her ears pricked with her habitual alertness, and she drew up her forelegs in preparation to rise should the disturbance threaten her. But on seeing Hervey in the lantern light she relaxed visibly, her ears flattening to the sides in anticipation of some word from him, and she whickered – scarcely more than a grunt, but enough to alert the other horses in the lines, each of whom echoed the sound of pleasant expectation. Hervey bade her stay down, pulling her ears a little and giving her candied fruit which he had stuffed into his pockets as they left the dining room.

The collector made approving noises: he could see her obvious handiness, he said.

Lucie was less restrained: 'She is not a looker, but I can vouch that she swims well!'

Her master pulled a face, but the collector beckoned him towards the further stalls, where his own mares stood.

'Arabs!' exclaimed Hervey. 'I have never seen them this close before.' And both mares flattened their ears and flared their nostrils, intending that he should get no closer.

The collector smiled. 'I prefer to call them Kehilans – the Arabic for thoroughbred.'

'More literally, "of noble descent", I think,' said Emma Lucie.

'Just so, madam,' replied the collector, surprised. 'I defer to your uncommon facility with languages!'

'No,' she laughed, 'merely a good memory. I was once shown the Kehilan in Newmarket. I wanted to see what was *your* facility.'

'Oh,' he replied absently, 'just the here and now.'

Lucie would not hear of this modesty. 'Somervile has studied at the university in Fès, Hervey. The languages of the Orient are his passion.'

'And horses, evidently,' replied Hervey, who had coaxed one of the mares forward to take candy from his hand.

'Indeed yes,' replied the collector; 'a measure of a civilization may be largely had from its horses. You will never comprehend, say, a Bedouin unless you acquaint yourself with that which he holds above even his most favoured wife.'

'And rather more prosaically,' said Lucie, 'Somervile takes from us a prodigious number of rupees each time he brings his horses here to race!'

The collector smiled, with satisfaction. 'Tomorrow they return with me to Guntoor. Why don't you do the same?' he said to Hervey. 'You would see more of India than hereabouts. In Madras you may as well be in Brighton. There is a brig leaving tomorrow. And you, too, Miss Lucie. You were saying only yesterday that you had calls in Rajahmundry which were overdue. It is a short distance only, and a good time of the year to be travelling.'

With the knowledge that *Nisus* would remain in the roads for at least five more days, it was, said Hervey, a capital invitation. 'Might you extend it to my friend Mr Locke?'

Somervile seemed content.

The invitation held its appeal for Emma Lucie too. 'There is also a ship leaving for England tomorrow, Captain Hervey. It will take letters of ours; do you wish it to take any of yours?'

Indeed he did. And he would write an additional one to Henrietta to tell her of this fortuitous meeting. 'In her letter to you, madam, was there anything that I might know?' he added cautiously.

Emma Lucie considered a while. 'Not really, sir. Henrietta merely says that you are to come to India on affairs of the Duke of Wellington. She asks that we receive you, if it is expedient – for she knows you are bound for Calcutta rather than here. She says that she hopes herself to make the journey here soon.'

'Oh?' said Hervey, quickened – though he had said in his letter that he thought it better he should first return.

'That is to say, *perhaps*,' added Emma promptly, 'after you are married? For her letter bore the marks of being written in some haste, and her meaning was not altogether clear in that respect. I shall, of course, write to her and say she is welcome here at any time – subject, of course, to your wishes.'

Hervey seemed confused. 'I don't know what is best. I am under orders, and cannot therefore vouch for my movements at this time. She may come here and we never see each other!'

'Then I think it best if that is said. Henrietta will make up her own mind – as she always has.'

Hervey agreed somewhat ruefully. 'How long shall this ship take to reach England?'

Emma Lucie turned to her brother, who was still engrossed in contemplation of Somervile's champion Kehilans. 'How long shall our letters take home, Philip?'

'It is one of our fast pinnaces with despatches for Leadenhall Street: two months.'

'Only two months? *Nisus* took the best part of—'

'The pinnace goes to Egypt,' explained Lucie, 'and then the despatches are taken overland and by the Mediterranean: two months, at most, this time of year. That is the way your affianced's express came.'

CHAPTER SIX

LICENCE TO PLUNDER

Guntoor, 23 February – two weeks later

No pleasanter beginning to the month of purification could Hervey remember. Candlemas, which had come as *Nisus* had only lately recrossed the Equator, had been so warm that he could scarcely comprehend that this same day in Horningsham might be chill enough to freeze his father's breath as he said the offices in church, and numb his fingers so much that turning each page of the prayer book became a labour. The nights were a little cold in Guntoor, perhaps, but each morning came as the one before, and the days followed the same course – a warming which progressed precisely by the clock, and with it the lives of the people who depended so much on its regularity. 'Brighton', the collector had called Madras, and Hervey might have believed it when he attended morning prayer in St Mary's church the following day. But now he was seeing India beyond the Company pale. The strangeness of its gods, its beliefs and superstitions, the dangers which attended routine things, the revolting deformities, the sensual possibilities in the dirtiest of corners – it was a heady, elemental place as alien and fearful as the pagan lands of the Old Testament. But it was beginning its work with him as surely as it had with the collector and thousands before him, for none but the most desiccated could be untouched by the promise of so much. Not that Guntoor was Babylon, or even Gaza.

Hervey, Emma Lucie and Henry Locke (to whom Peto had seemed relieved to grant arrears of furlough) had spent a week in the collector's company, a week equally pleasing to each, for Mr Eyre Somervile was generous, cultivated and sporting to an uncommon degree. Dinner had just finished, Emma Lucie had retired to her quarters, and Locke had repaired once again to the bazaar, whose unselfconscious delights had instantly captivated him. Hervey had accepted the collector's invitation to a final brandy and seltzer, and they were sitting in the comfortable leather armchairs of his drawing room, wondering which of two brightly spotted geckoes would reach the ceiling first. 'They are singularly lazy beggars,' opined Somervile after a while. 'The house snake will have them by morning if they don't look sharp.'

'*House* snake?' said Hervey, suddenly alarmed.

'House *snakes*, I should say, for there are two,' replied the collector casually.

'Oh! I am very unpartial to snakes,' confessed Hervey, lifting his feet and looking all about him. 'What kind are they?'

'One is a wolf snake, the other a cat – both female, I reckon. And there is a big male rat snake which comes in from the garden from time to time.'

Hervey was now certain he had been living within an ace of death these past seven days. 'Are they *very* venomous?' he asked, shuddering.

'*Venomous?*' said the collector, incredulously – but thoroughly warmed to his teasing. 'Not in the least, though a rat snake killed one of the writers at Fort George last year!'

'How so then?' asked Hervey, quite horrified.

'It looks somewhat like the cobra, but it has a more pointed head – and bigger eyes. And it doesn't spread a hood, of course. But to a writer not long from England it can *look* like a cobra – or several if you've taken too much whiskey. As it seems had Mr Fotheringham as he fell headlong down the residency steps in his fright.'

Hervey frowned at Somervile's wry smile, recovering his composure somewhat.

The smaller of the geckoes had finally reached the top of the wall when one of the collector's babus entered with a despatch. 'Read it for me, if you will, Mohan: I have left my eyeglass in my dressing room.'

The babu put on his own spectacles, and lifted the paper to the light of a wall sconce. 'Sahib, it is from the deputy collector in Tiruvoor subdistrict. He writes: "A body of Pindarees, by estimates one thousand strong, entered the Circars three days ago from Nagpore and have laid waste villages along the Tiruvoor. There is much destruction of property and life, and the horde proceeds unchecked."'

The collector's donnish affability vanished in an instant. He sprang up, seized the despatch from the babu, held it up close to the oil lamp on his desk and scanned its details with increasing dismay. 'I knew it! I knew it! I've been warning for months but Fort George didn't wish to hear!'

Hervey, on his feet now too, pressed him for details.

'There are twenty villages along the Tiruvoor, probably ten thousand souls at the mercy of these devils. And there's not a standing patrol in miles!' He was railing so loud his bearer and khansamah came running.

'What's to be done?' asked Hervey, having no notion of the proximity of the villages, and therefore of the predators.

'What men are there in the garrison at present?' said Somervile to the babu.

'At present, sahib, there are being only one troop of cavalry. Infantry will not be returning inside of one week.' His head rocked from side to side in the manner of babus offering news that might be disagreeable.

'Very well then, be so good as to have it parade here at five tomorrow morning ready to take to the field. I shall ride with them myself: I wish to see at first hand the scale of these depredations.'

The babu took off his spectacles, made namaste and scurried from the room. Later he would tell his wife he had seen the collector in a rage, and she would not believe him, for the Collector of Guntoor had never been known to raise his voice. The meanest bondsman who had ever heard of his magistracy, or of his administration of land revenues, knew him to be of the purest fire and the most gentle, generous heart, and the most fastidious Brahman knew him to be of an intellect and sensibility no less remarkable.

And yet the collector's gorge was now so risen that he could barely contain himself. He sank into his chair and struck the table with his fist, sending coffee cups spilling from their tray. 'I dearly wish I could believe in your god, Captain Hervey, so that I might be assured that the fiends who inflicted such evils on their fellow humans would savour the same!'

Hervey poured a large glass of brandy and seltzer for him. 'Do you have any objections to my accompanying you? And Mr Locke would, I know, wish to come too. As long as we may return within the week, for *Nisus* will be off Guntoor then.'

'No objection at all. I should be glad of it,' said the collector, springing up again and searching the maps on his desk.

'Locke will be the best of men in a fight,' continued Hervey. 'I'm glad his captain felt obliged to be so generous with leave.'

'Yes,' replied Somervile, having found the map he wanted. 'Your Mr Locke is a good sort, though I regret there'll be no need of his sword arm, for there won't be a single Pindaree east of the Ghats by now.' He sank down in his chair again and wiped a hand across his face. 'I've been warning of it, I know; and yet I can hardly bring myself to believe it can have happened – that a native body has deliberately violated the territory of the Honourable East India Company, ravaged that which is under the Company's protection' (he took another large gulp of brandy), 'plundered its villages, tortured and murdered native people under the dominion of the Company and, therefore, of His Majesty!' He took out a large silk square and dabbed at his eyes.

Hervey tried to think of something that might help him regain his composure, but could not. 'Somervile, I have not enquired before, since I formed the impression that it was Company business of a confidential nature,' he tried, refilling both glasses and fixing him with a look that demanded serious attention, 'but I should be very much obliged if you would tell me all that there is of the Pindarees.'

The collector paused a moment before laying aside the map. 'Very well, I shall tell you all. And, I might add, if your Duke of Wellington were here I have not the slightest doubt that this would never have happened, for the policies which the previous governor-general pursued were too yielding, and the present one, though more vigorous, has yet to make his mark.'

'Though he has subdued the Ghoorka tribes, I understand?'

'I fear he was driven to it. I doubt he had any real appetite.'

Hervey was reassured that his principal was held in high regard by one official of the Company at least. 'The Pindarees, then: what is their peculiar menace?'

The collector sat in his armchair again. 'From the beginning? The Pindarees are a body – several bodies – of irregular horse who serve without pay and who have licence to plunder wheresoever they can: chiefly south of the Nerbudda river, in the territories of the nizam and the Rajah of Berar and the peshwa.' He dabbed at his brow again and loosened his collar. 'They originated – as far as we may know – a century and a half ago in the Dekhin, in the service of the Mughal rulers, but as Mughal power declined they transferred their services to the Marathas – against whom your duke fought with signal success a dozen years ago. As Maratha power declined in turn, the Pindarees have become even less disciplined and predictable.' He emptied his brandy and seltzer, peered at the motionless geckoes for what seemed an age, and then resumed as they began their descent of the wall. 'They've separated into three clans, each led by the most odious of men. These chiefs rarely themselves lead a plundering foray; rather they appoint sirdars. That band which has penetrated hereabouts is led, it seems, by one Bikhu Sayed, who is known for his especial insolence and depravity. I fear we shall see and hear things that will make the strongest stomachs turn.'

Hervey was confident of his stomach, but the notion of lawlessness on a regimented scale was wholly alien to him. 'How many are they?'

'The estimates are varied, but the best formulations are probably those of the Bengal office, which put the number of horse at twenty-five thousand. That is the figure which their spies estimated to have assembled at the Dasahara festival five years ago – the most reliable intelligence in our possession, if a little dated.'

'And all these may operate as one body, with effect?' asked Hervey, incredulous, for he knew that no such body of European cavalry had manoeuvred to advantage during his service.

'Again, so little is known,' said the collector, frowning. 'Captain Sydenham, from the Bengal office, has estimated that only some six or seven thousand may be counted truly effective cavalry.' He shrugged. 'But there is a saying here: "What cares the ass or the bullock whether his load be made of flowers?" It matters little to a ryot whether the cavalry that has ravaged him is counted effective or ineffective.'

'No, of course,' Hervey agreed, 'but it matters more if some oper-ation to extirpate the menace is being contemplated.'

The collector sighed and nodded. 'Forgive me. Indeed it does. I am too distressed at the knowledge of what these demons have done. That and the certain knowledge that there will be *no* concerted campaign of extirpation.'

Hervey wished profoundly that he might reassure him on that point: the duke, for sure, would not sit idly by once he was appointed to Fort

William. 'What does this incursion portend in the wider sense?'

'Hah!' said the collector, getting up and pouring yet another glass. 'That is the very question which should most be exercising the minds of those at Fort St George and Fort William – ay, and in Bombay Castle too. There must be some great concerted action on the part of the three presidencies, else we shall never be able to continue our business unmolested. More immediately, I fear for the peace hereabouts since the Rajah of Nagpore has evidently been unable to prevent Bikhu Sayed from traversing his lands, and this will put Chintal in a most perilous position – squeezed by the nizam to their south and west, and by the Pindarees to their north and east. It bodes ill for trade along the Godavari river if Chintal declines into chaos.'

Tempting though it was to question him directly on Chintal, Hervey held himself in check, though they sat talking for an hour before the collector thought fit to retire. Hervey penned a brief note for Henry Locke and hoped he would return before dawn. When he turned in, he lay for a full half-hour trying to think how Somervile's estimate might affect his mission. But beyond the obvious conclusion that it could not make things easier, he was at a loss. Perhaps Bazzard in Calcutta would have a clearer picture, though he was inclined to think not, for Colonel Grant had seemed to suggest he would be little more than a facilitator, a clearing office. Was that why Selden was so useful as a point of contact in Chintal? Not for the first time he began to feel the want of that fuller exposition which Grant had said was not necessary.

There were just the remains of the night's chill in the air as dawn came to Guntoor. The first rays of the sun were quick to pick out the whitened, single-storey residences of the civil lines, the verandahs, where sat the chowkidars, becoming for a time darker pools as a consequence. Smoke was already rising from stoves and ovens behind each residence as bearers prepared chota hazree – tea and poori, or chapatti perhaps. The collector's household had risen earlier this morning, however, and after a fuller breakfast – eggs and cold beef – Somervile, Hervey and Locke were now gathered in the carriage drive at the front. Birds sang in every quarter – not as many as in Horningsham, but shriller, although a bulbul was giving out its melodious, liquid call from deep inside a leafy shrub. A pair of night herons flapped overhead, from the direction of the river, their distinctive 'kwaark, kwaark' more than ever importunate in the quiet of the dawn. Hervey breathed deep, in both senses, eager to begin.

A minute or so later and the sound of hooves on hard earth quickened him even more. Wiry little horses, country-breds, not Arabs, led by equally wiry syces, came up the carriage drive in a restive jog-trot. There had been some heat in Jessye's leg after their ride yesterday and Hervey had told Johnson that she was to have box-rest for a day or so. These country-breds looked handy enough, however, and he had sufficient respect for the collector's eye for horses to trust that he would have under him an honest gelding. As the three mounted, each with the help of as many syces – one holding the bridle, one on the offside pulling down the stirrup leather, and the third with palm on knee in lieu of a mounting block – there arrived from the cantonment the patrol that was to determine whether the Pindarees' incursion was the precursor of another fierce predation, or whether it had been a single freebooting action. And as the Godavari river was to be the limit of their reconnaissance, they carried with them – or, rather, bullock carts would follow with – camp stores and provisions for a week's essay.

Had the officer commanding the cavalry troop been attired according to the regulations, he would have looked more magnificent than Hervey himself on a full-dress parade, for the Madras Light Cavalry's uniform was a French-blue hussar jacket, with silver lace across the chest, sky-blue overalls and a Greek helmet with a shoulder-length, white horsehair plume. But this morning, as most days, the officer (as his troopers) wore the same shako as Hervey had at Waterloo, but instead of a black oilskin cover it had one of buff cotton with a piece of cloth to shield the neck from the sun. The officer saluted the party from the civil lines eagerly with his sword – the straight-pattern sabre, unlike Hervey's. 'Cornet Templer, sir,' he said, smiling.

'Yes, Mr Templer,' replied the collector; 'I am not likely to forget. I shall not wager my mare against yours quite so soon again, unless I find a more talented jockey than that jackanapes who calls himself your lieutenant! You should take her to Madras: she will win you a small fortune.'

Cornet Templer looked not much more than a boy. His tanned face was framed by curls the colour of autumn corn, and it now seemed to be but one large smile. Hervey took to him at once, for his liveliness was infectious, his eagerness admirable. Just the sort of cornet he would have wanted for his own troop – a clean young Englishman.

There was a deal of handshaking following the saluting. Lieutenant of Marines Henry Locke took to the cornet too, though, as his seat was less certain than once it might have been, it was not without some difficulty that he managed to press his mount to within handshaking distance. Cornet Templer looked him straight in the eye, seeming not to see any disfigurement. And that to Locke – more than Hervey or even Peto might have supposed – meant a very great deal.

There was one more introduction to effect. Cornet Templer turned his head towards his troop. 'Subedar, sahib,' he called, still smiling. A tall Madrasi, dressed almost identically to Templer, jogged up on his big gelding – an animal in better condition than Hervey had yet seen in the country. 'Gentlemen, this is Subedar Thangraj. He will not permit us to get into too much trouble.'

Subedar Thangraj straightened his back still further, and saluted high, almost touching the crown of his shako. 'Captain, sahib, it is an honour to meet with one who has fought at the great battle of Waterloo,' he said in clear, confident English, looking directly, and with much solemnity, at Hervey.

'Thank you, Subedar sahib,' he replied formally, though astonished that these details should already be known to this native officer – and that the man should be so wholly confident of recognizing to whom the distinction applied. But he was puzzled by the rank. 'Templer, you said "Subedar"; I understood that in the cavalry the rank is "Rissaldar".'

'In the armies of Bombay and Bengal, yes sir, but not in Madras.'

'And is this so for the other ranks?'

'It is. All our private men are sepoys, not sowars.'

'How so?' asked Hervey, vexed with himself for being unaware that there should be this difference.

'I do not know,' said Templer, with the elements of a frown now added to his wide smile. 'But since Madras was the *original* presidency, it is for the others to explain why they changed, sir.'

'Quite so,' smiled Hervey, recognizing the propriety. 'Is there very much difference in other respects between the three armies?'

'Indeed there is, though I have not been in the country long enough to see at first hand. But when we make camp tonight I shall be glad to tell you what I know.'

There was evidently more to Cornet Templer than his broad, easy smile – and Hervey liked him even better for it.

When all were satisfied that the necessary salutations had been made, Cornet Templer asked the collector for leave to begin the patrol.

Somervile nodded.

'Walk-march please, Subedar sahib,' he called. It seemed to Hervey more a friendly invitation than a command.

'Very good, sahib,' replied the subedar, who barked the orders in turn to the patrol, but in a tongue Hervey did not recognize. The sepoys straightened their backs once more and the column moved off in a cloud of dust fetlock-high, out of the civil lines and on to the wide palmyra avenue that led directly to the high road north to the Krishna river – and thence, if they were to remain on it rather than branching north-east (the latter being their intention), to the Rajah of Chintal's capital at Chintalpore.

Dust rose higher as they settled to a brisk working trot, kicked up by the more extravagant action of one or two of the horses, fresh and eager to stretch their legs after a night in standing-stalls. The dust quickly reached his nostrils, yet it was not wholly unwelcome, for it seemed no different from the spices to which he was becoming accustomed. Indeed, he was already of a mind that this taste of baked earth was rather the essence of India, like the light which transformed the way he saw things, or the heat at midday, as if hands were touching him. It was not possible, even momentarily, to be insensate in this land, for the presents to each and every sense were so potent as to be almost compelling. Already he had observed that no bird had anything but the gaudiest plumage. Not even an insect concealed itself by drab colour. No noise was restrained, no taste – in either sense – was mild. No smell was anything but pungent, no belief incredible, no notion too outlandish. And all this within the civil lines of the Company's very regular station at Guntoor. Now he would see Hindoostan – the country beyond the chunam and the chintz, beyond the exaggerated English manners of the Company's officials and their liveried servants. He would see it just as he had wanted to see Ireland beyond the Pale, a year and a half ago. The experience of native Ireland had taught him, however, that although he might cross such a divide physically, to do so with his heart spelled ruin. He would be on his guard.

But home thoughts were with him yet as they jogged past pretty bungalows (the word new to him), whose white fences and trim gardens would not have been out of place in Sussex. 'Which part of England are you come from?' he asked, Cornet Templer now having drawn alongside him.

'I don't call any part home, sir,' replied Templer, still smiling; 'I spent three terms at Harrow but went thence to Addiscombe, for I was first meant for the Company's sappers. My people are from Wicklow.'

So much for his instinct for people, thought Hervey – *English* indeed! They talked freely, however, especially of Addiscombe (for Hervey had little knowledge of the Company's military academy), until, leaving the town limits, Templer excused himself to go forward to attend to some detail with the point-men.

Hervey rode thereafter with Locke and the collector, several yards off to the flank in order to avoid the dust. They wore mixed dress, with overalls of light canvas made up for them a day or so before in Guntoor, and their sword belts were simple affairs with snake-fastening and no sash. Locke wore a marine man's hat of black glazed leather, with a neck shield pinned to it, and Hervey wore his own shako with a cream cover and neck flap – like Templer and his men. But neither of them had on a tunic of appreciably martial stamp. Hervey's was a coat of hunting length, the same colour as his shako, and he wore a yellow silk stock. Locke had on a cutaway of the same weight of cotton, but of a dusty pink colour, together with a white stock and his treasured gorget. Despite this mixture, however, neither man could have appeared to an onlooker as anything other than military, whereas nothing could have been further from the case with the collector, whose black coat made no concession to what Hervey supposed would soon be the excessive heat of the day – though his wide-brimmed straw hat would provide considerably greater protection from the sun than the short peak of Hervey's shako or the pulled-up brim of Locke's headdress.

'It seems a distant cry from trade, this,' smiled Hervey.

'Then let me disabuse you, sir, of any notion that trade is what the Company is about nowadays. At first, yes – in Queen Elizabeth's day. Then it was truly a company of merchants trading spices from the east. It began to change with King Charles's Braganza dowry – Bombay – and then later when that enfeebled Mughal Shah Alam made the Company his dewan – his administrator – for the Bengal revenues. But this much you surely know?'

Hervey was relieved that the collector had some appetite for conversation, even at this hour, for Locke was bearing the signs of little sleep, promising to be no sort of companion at all. 'I have not heard it stated so definitively, sir.' He was not without the art of flattery in a good cause.

The collector was more than happy to continue, definitively. 'Mr

Pitt's India Act established the Board of Control. Doubtless he would have preferred to appropriate the Company lock, stock and barrel, but that would have put too much patronage in his hands for the Whigs to stomach. It was a half-baked scheme, for it gave no one the necessary freedom to act. And it made worse the differences between the three presidencies. Madras and Bombay were all but pursuing contrary policies towards Mysore at one juncture.'

Hervey pressed him to more as he leaned forward to remove a monstrous horsefly from his gelding's ear.

'The amending act three years ago has done much to tidy things up – the president of the Board now has a seat in the cabinet and such like – but it spells the end for the Company. Of that I'm sure. We are in all effects a department of state even at the present, and it will not be long, in my judgement, before parliament sees fit to wind up all trading interests. What worries me, Captain Hervey, is that our new administrators are becoming too imperious in their dealings with the country powers and with the natives in the presidencies. Warren Hastings *knew* the continent, you see, from his engagement with trade. The new breed does not.'

Hervey thanked him for his candid opinion.

The collector made light of it. 'But I heard you asking Templer if there is any difference between the armies of the three presidencies.'

'Yes; he said he would explain when we made camp tonight.'

'He will indeed, but I shall first tell you the root of those differences.' He flicked his whip against his mare's quarters, she having become disunited. 'You would say that there is a difference in the fighting qualities of men from the various parts of our own islands, would you not? You would no doubt say that the Scotchman is a fearsome soldier, but without his officers he is at a loss; that the man from East Anglia is steadfast in adversity and so on. But these are but fine shades in men whose red coats make of them all fine soldiers. Here things are a matter of greater extremes – as they are in all things. From a military point of view there is no doubt that the Rajpoots of northern India are the noblest, the finest of the races. The Rajpoot is tall and well-built, clean-limbed. He may not marry a woman who is not of a Rajpoot family. Where you find him – in the Bombay regiments – he is peerless.'

Hervey nodded in appreciation. 'Then I hope I shall soon meet them.'

'Not this side of the Nerbudda river, I think,' replied the collector, shaking his head. 'You shall have to go to what is Hindoostan proper

– to the north of the Nerbudda. But that is as may be. The Bombay presidency's forces are well-tried: that is the material point. And, incidentally, what a city Bombay is, Captain Hervey! You would consider it alone worth the journey to see what its women will dare in the matter of dress! Nowhere on earth will you see any more colourful sight than a Parsi girl – brilliant beyond measure!'

Hervey and Locke were all attention.

'A Bombay street is as splendid and lively a sight as a Calcutta one is ugly and dispiriting.'

'I think you have no very great regard for the Bengali, sir?'

'Not in the main. He's feeble and effete beyond measure. He holds personal cowardice to be no disgrace. Do you know of any other race in the world to which that accusation might be directed?'

'Which leaves the soldiers of the presidency of Madras,' said Hervey, smiling.

The collector sighed. 'The glories of the ancient Telinga kingdoms are long past, and – it must be said – their martial spirit. When the French occupied the Karnatic, and when Clive was campaigning in Mysore, the Telinga fought with ferocity and intelligence.' He touched his mare's flank again with the whip as she fell back half a length. 'But the Madrasi now is a man of peace, a better servant than a soldier. The Telinga makes a better-looking sepoy, being of superior physique, but he possesses on the whole less stamina than the Tamil. The Tamil can exhibit fine fighting qualities, mark you: Subedar Thangraj overcame more than a dozen mutineers at Vellore with only a clubbed carbine.'

Hervey glanced across at the subedar. In his native dignity there was the stamp of Serjeant Strange. He looked back further along the column, seeing in a face here and there more than a vestige of that fighting spirit which the collector said was now dimmed. He found it hard to believe that men who wore their uniforms as well as these did, or who sat their horses so, were not as determined when it came to drawing the sword.

The collector strove at once to correct the impression he had given. 'Captain Hervey, do not suppose for one moment that I am saying these men lack fighting spirit. It is only that by *comparison* Madras is not thought to have so martial a people. If you were to see the men of the northern parts – Rajpoots, Sikhs, Jats, Punjabis, Pathans – big men, not enervated by climate, you would understand my meaning.

Have no fear: Cornet Templer's men will fight as well as you would wish. And I for one am content to place my security in their hands.'

Next day

The sun had been up for only an hour, but in that cool, fresh, first sixty minutes of another Indian day the patrol had made ten miles. Chota hazree – sweet tea and a plantain – had been brought to the officers in their bivouac tents a half-hour before sunrise, and they had been in the saddle as the first shafts of light searched them out on the plateau from behind the hills to the east. Nothing that Hervey had seen before made him so conscious of his own insignificance.

The collector had intended to ride for another hour, at a reduced pace, before halting for a breakfast of cold chikor, of which they had bagged a dozen brace the afternoon before. But there was to be no burra hazree just yet. 'Pindarees, sahib,' exclaimed Subedar Thangraj, his eyes seeing clearly what Templer and Hervey could only confirm with the telescope.

From a mile away the village, which had no name that any in the patrol knew of, and none on any map, bore the signs of having been assailed. More than the usual number of vultures circled above, and there was a continual glide earthwards. And instead of the many wisps of smoke that would ordinarily have marked the cooking fires and ovens of a village of this size, there was a single, large pall of black smoke.

Cornet Templer's face changed at once from ease to tautness. 'Subedar sahib: extended line, draw swords!'

Hervey had to check his instincts. Templer intended, it seemed, to gallop straight to the village without any preliminary reconnaissance or indirect approach. This was dangerously more than audacity, surely? This was more than the boldness which Peto's book advocated and which Hervey approved. It was recklessness, was it not? He looked at Henry Locke, who shrugged. 'He orders the troop to form line and draw swords,' he explained; to which Locke simply raised both his eyebrows.

'Captain Hervey,' said the collector with perfect calm, seeing his concern, 'in the Company's cavalry it is the practice to charge the enemy at once – instantly, without hesitation. He invariably outnumbers you and hesitation is fatal; by the very action of attempting to throw over the greater number there somehow comes the *ability* to do so. And the enemy, who in his rational appreciation would know that such a thing is impossible, is denied the time to think, and so is afeard that it must in truth be so. Rarely will he stand his ground – unless his escape is closed off.'

By the time the collector had finished his elegant if somewhat elliptical explanation, the troop had extended into line. 'Draw swords!' ordered the subedar. Fifty and more sabres came rasping from their scabbards. Hervey winced at the noise, as he always did – the sound of sword edges blunting. But he also suspected that these sepoys had begun the patrol with blades as sharp as razors.

'Walk march!' called Cornet Templer, his voice carrying easily to both flanks – in all a frontage of 150 yards.

All Hervey could think of was the duke's instructions to his cavalry commanders: 'Cavalry is to attack in three lines, four or five hundred yards apart when facing cavalry; a reserve must be kept of two-thirds of the whole, to exploit a success or to cover a withdrawal.' And here was Cornet Templer and his troop in one extended line, and open order!

He fell in by the collector's side at the rear and drew his sword. The collector pulled his straw hat down firmly and reached inside his coat for the diminutive pistol he always carried (but had not thought to prime). 'Keep an eye for any who wish to throw themselves on our mercy, Hervey. I should wish to interrogate them.'

Hervey smiled to himself at the collector's absolute confidence in the outcome, struggling meanwhile with his gelding, which seemed to have had little by way of formal schooling and was reverting to its instinct for the herd. The line was soon in a brisk canter. Dust billowed, horses were pulling and blowing at the same time. Hooves drummed and bits jingled. He looked left and right at the half-hundred troopers: from behind they could have been from any one of the armies that fought Bonaparte. They could have been from the Grande Armée itself, except that they rode shorter than any regular cavalry he had seen before – and in open order and extended line! Yet it was not difficult to understand how these men felt invincible in that headlong rush at the Pindarees, of whose number they had not the slightest intimation, for there was dust enough to conceal a thousand cavalrymen.

'Charge!' roared Templer, with fewer than a hundred yards to run to the village. The line of sabres lowered to the 'engage', expecting to catch the enemy on foot.

Hervey could see nothing of what they were charging. He thought he saw horses but he could not be certain, for dust swirled everywhere. He was more anxious still: even if there were no ambuscade, the line, once it had collided with the village, would rapidly lose cohesion – when a half-capable enemy could take them from a flank.

And then they were in the village, and it was all he could do to keep his seat as his little gelding, effortlessly changing leg, swerved this way and that to avoid tumbling at an obstacle, any number of which would have brought down a less balanced horse. They jumped something he didn't even see, and the gelding landed with its head still up and ready for the next challenge.

Some of the sepoys were far ahead, and he could see that the charge had become a pursuit. Here and there was a fallen horse, but mainly they were human shapes which lay sprawled and bloody – and none was wearing a French-blue tunic. He galloped on, looking about for the collector. The ground was rising slightly but there was no cover. As far as he could see in front of him there were sepoys furiously raising and lowering their sword arms. He began to check, for the gelding was blowing hard – when the best of horses could stumble. A lone Pindaree came towards him and threw down his sword, falling from the saddle to his knees and clasping his hands together, pleading. Hervey was trying to find the words to tell him he was made prisoner when one of the sepoys galloped up with a different intention. He shouted that the man had surrendered, but whether or not he was understood, it made no difference, for the sepoy sliced at the Pindaree's neck from behind, severing the head as neatly as Hervey had seen Serjeant Strange cut a swede in half in the tilt-yard.

It was not his fight, he told himself, and the sepoy gave him a most respectful salute with his bloody sabre as he circled back to join his comrades. He turned and slowly trotted back to the village, recalling what the collector had said two nights before about the strongest stomachs turning. There were bloody bundles of flesh and homespun about the village, but no other human presence that he could see. He heard the bugle, and looked back to see the line at last rallying. Then the collector appeared, in a lather every bit as prodigious as that of his horse – and blowing almost as much – though he had kept up remarkably well. 'A sorry business this, Hervey,' he called, dismounting by one of the bundles and clasping a handkerchief over his nose.

Hervey said he did not expect there would be anyone for him to interrogate, to which the collector seemed not overly surprised, nor even very disappointed.

'We had better begin searching the huts, however,' he suggested, still clasping the silk to his nose. 'There may be something that tells us what these fiends are next about.'

They regretted doing so almost at once. The sight in the first hut made the collector rush out clutching the silk to his mouth, and throw up noisily. Inside, Hervey stared in disbelief. Here was a lesson in anatomy he had not seen even in a textbook – the womb hacked open and its full-grown contents ripped away and sliced like meat on a butcher's slab. And, as if that could not have been enough to satiate the most depraved, the wretched woman had been impaled hideously and severally. Hervey now wished he had struck off the Pindaree's head himself, for though he had seen the horrifying work of cannon, never before had he known sheer surgical brutality. He was numb with incomprehension.

'You had better search the well, Mr Templer,' said the collector as he recovered himself, seeing the troop coming into the village.

Before it occurred to Hervey why the well should be searched, one of the havildars revealed why. 'It is full of bodies, sahib,' he called.

Hervey, Templer and the native officers doubled over to him, covering their noses as they did so. The well was large, twenty feet across, with a three-foot wall, and it was deep. There were many bodies (perhaps fifty – it was difficult to estimate), and as far as Hervey could tell, peering into its darkness, most – perhaps all – were women. Those uppermost in the tangled mound were naked.

'They were the ones who either had not the time or the courage to jump for themselves,' said the collector.

'What do we do now?' asked Hervey, beginning to sicken at both the sight and the stench.

'What do you think we should do?' enquired the collector, with a mild challenge in his voice. 'We roll up our bloody sleeves and get them out!'

The officers took turns to descend to the bottom of the well, to where the ordure was most nauseous, and tied ropes round each body, the sepoys hauling them to the surface. For over three hours they laboured thus, until the remains of every one of forty-seven women and girls – and eleven infants – were brought into the heat of the mid-morning sun. Meanwhile, the other sepoys had collected the bodies of a dozen men, mostly aged, and had lain them in the shade of the village's banyan. Now they began building a massive pyre on which they might all be cremated according to the rites of Vishnu.

'The village men would have been in the fields, by the look of things,' said the collector, 'and there they will have hid since. We shall not be able to tempt them in for a day or so.'

Hervey simply nodded.

The collector lowered his voice, until it had almost a note of despair. 'This is an especially brutal raid. The women are always susceptible, but they are by no means always defiled, nor the men killed if they offer no resistance.'

'It's the mutilation and . . . the brutishness, the *method* of their violation,' said Hervey, matching his tone.

The collector nodded grimly. 'If I were to suppose what happened, I should say that the village was taken wholly by surprise – at about three o'clock yesterday. Some of the women would have screamed, gathered up their last-born and run at once to the well, throwing themselves in within sight of the marauders. This would have excited the worst of them – a freebooting band among freebooters without what passes for the discipline of some of the Pindaree cohorts. Some of the old men would have made a show of protecting the women and been cut down for their trouble. The first blood would have excited the appetite for more, until there was a frenzy of rape and slaughter. You are dealing with a savagery here, Captain Hervey, the like of which you would find hard to imagine even in your battles in Spain. I pray this cohort we surprised is not typical of what we may expect.'

'And how many rupees might the Pindarees have supposed a village such as this would render up?' asked Hervey incredulously.

'Just so, just so,' the collector replied, shaking his head again. 'We are, as a rule, spared these sights in the Company's territories, and half of me wishes to believe that this incursion was but a misjudgement. However, I fear this and the earlier forays have been somehow to test our strength, and that we shall see more unless we do something. Yet I can't suppose that anything which is done in a small way shall have any effect. No, it must be something undertaken on a bigger scale – encompassing the whole of the country. I hold the extirpation of the

Pindaree menace to be the greatest, and most pressing, necessity of the Company. And yet the Court of Directors in London will have no truck with it.'

Cornet Templer told off a jemadar's patrol to follow the Pindaree spoor, then came up and saluted. 'Do you have any further orders, sir?'

'No, Mr Templer, I think not. How many did we account for in all?'

'Villagers, sir, or Pindarees?'

'The latter.'

'Seventy, not fewer.'

The collector nodded approvingly, even though a prisoner or two would have been helpful. 'You showed great address, Mr Templer. I shall commend your conduct this day to Fort St George.'

'Thank you, sir,' replied Templer, flatly, for there was too much otherwise to dull any satisfaction with his exertions.

The jemadar's patrol left with little expectation of catching any more of the fleeing Pindarees. If they could trace their route of withdrawal from the Circars it would at least indicate something of what freedom of movement they enjoyed in the neighbouring states. Meanwhile, all that the remainder of the troop could do was wait in the hope that some of the ryots would return to the village, and that they would be able to say something which might help in any subsequent encounter. It was a mournful bivouac that night.

The first hour of daylight the following morning was given over to what Hervey's regiment called 'interior economy'. Saddles, bridles and other tackling were laid out with great precision for the scrutiny of Cornet Templer and Subedar Thangraj. And after inspecting every piece of leather they went to the horses with the farrier-naik. Hervey walked with the collector through the lines of country-breds, recalling as if yesterday the condition of his own regiment in Spain after a similar march.

'What do you think of them, Captain Hervey?' asked Somervile.

Hervey replied that he found them very much better than he had been led to believe, that they compared very favourably indeed with the remounts they were receiving towards the end of the campaign in the Peninsula.

'The Company of late has been much exercised by the need of good horses. Left to itself, India breeds indifferent mounts, though there are a dozen or so native breeds. Seven or eight years ago – before my time here – the directors engaged a distinguished London veterinarian – a Mr Moorcroft. Do you know the name?'

Hervey said he had some notion of it.

'It was he who began the reform of the Company's stud department. And great work he has done, too. But much buying is still, perforce, in the hands of regimental purchasing officers.'

'Then I perceive that the Madras Cavalry's purchasing officer has an affinity for Arabs.'

'You would be right,' replied the collector, smiling. 'Mr Blacker has bought many hundreds of pure Kehilans, and is most adept at putting them to native mares.'

'You are very evidently an apostle of the breed,' Hervey smiled back, conscious of the energy of the little horse the collector rode, though he had not yet become accustomed to its curious lines.

'Yes, indeed I am. See how full-chested those troopers are, how broad across the loins, and how round-sided and deep-barrelled they are. You will not see one horse in ten in England as short-limbed yet with such qualities. That chest is what gives the Kehilan his endurance. You would scarcely ever be able to exhaust him, unless unreasonably. And he can live on air if needs be. The only inconvenience I perceive is that the entire needs considerably more bleeding than does an English stallion, and in this country he is more prone to miasmic fevers. You will see the farrier bleed as many this morning as he finds in need of a new shoe.'

Hervey expressed himself surprised at the number of entires generally. 'I'm afraid we find them altogether too untractable. We cannot pick and choose our remounts whilst on campaign, and they must stand side by side with the mares.'

The collector understood. 'But there is none so brave as a stallion. I would not wish to surrender such an advantage were I a military man.'

Hervey smiled. He had to acknowledge the point. Though, as he explained, when considering the normal method of operation of European cavalry – in squadrons, knee-to-knee – some concession had to be made to the need for tractability.

'But if you are pleased by what you see with our native *regular* cavalry, Captain Hervey,' the collector added, 'then you should see our *silladar* regiments.'

Hervey paused while he searched his mind for the meaning of the Urdu. 'I do not know this word,' he concluded.

'A Maratha corruption of the pure Persian *silahadar*,' said the collector quite unaffectedly, for he had studied both languages. 'It means simply a soldier bearing arms, or wearing armour. In this case it refers most approximately to British yeomanry, except that they are more or less permanently embodied – and, I hazard, a great deal more effective. Each man provides his own horse and all necessities, except firearm and ammunition. And for his services he receives thirty rupees a month. We shall soon have one such regiment on the Madras establishment – one of Colonel Skinner's Horse. They are at present in the north of the Circars where the first Pindaree band struck earlier this year. You would, I believe, approve of them!'

Hervey was intent on learning more. What, for instance, impelled a sowar to hazard his horse if this were the means of his livelihood? But Cornet Templer reported that the troop was ready to resume, and the collector was keen for the off. The jemadar's patrol had already sent word that the marauders were a half-day's forced march ahead of them and had crossed into the Rajah of Chintal's territory. They would remain on the border to watch for a day and then rejoin. Hervey asked if Chintal was where they would take refuge, but the collector thought not. They would plunder the place and pass through with as much impunity as they had here, for the rajah's forces were meagre and ineffectual. But Somervile wished nevertheless for a reconnaissance along a fair length of the border to be sure there was no doubling back, and so he asked to be left with an escort to conclude his business with the village – a business which, Hervey soon learned, was impelled by humanity rather than any actuarial concern of the Company's – and pressed Templer to make a good show along the border en route for home.

Templer was about to leave, and Hervey and Locke with him, when there came another of what Somervile called India's infinite curiosities. A solitary trail of dust, not very high, first revealed the presence on the road from the east. One by one the soldiers of the patrol turned to watch, until all were fixed on the little bullock cart as it made its slow way towards them. Two of the thinnest-looking oxen Hervey had seen, yoked side by side and standing no higher at the shoulder than Jessye as a yearling, plodded patiently before the hackery, their cream-coloured tails swaying with the movement of their quarters but otherwise still, not yet needed for relief from the plague of flies that would beset them in an hour or so. And in the cart itself sat a shrivelled little figure, sun-hatted, smiling. Without any apparent urging, the oxen made for the shade of a banyan at the edge of the village, and there they stopped. The little man took off his hat and bowed his head.

Hervey looked quizzically at the collector.

'The priest,' explained Somervile.

'Ah,' said Hervey. 'I had imagined someone more . . .'

'The Catholic priest, I mean.'

'*Catholic* priest? I had not imagined—'

'Well, do not suppose the roots are as deep as St Thomas would have wished. In these villages it is but a superficial creed – to the unread ryots merely an intelligible alternative to unintelligible Hindoo. The Virgin Mary is to them but a beneficent goddess, and the transition from Krishna to Christ is one which offers no material difficulty to their limited faculties.'

It seemed a harsh judgement, but it was said with kindness. 'Where does he come from?'

'Who knows?' shrugged Somervile. 'The cart is his travelling residence, but beyond that . . . Rajahmundry perhaps? But priests were ministering here before the French came. And he will go on ministering and hoping for the best until he dies. And then a few sticks with rags tied to them will decorate his grave, and he will rank as a departed fakir or yogi.'

The collector seemed full of admiration. Hervey would never have thought it.

'Oh, mistake me not, sir. I do not hold with any faith, but I cannot but be moved by the devotion of these bullock-cart priests – and the constancy of their flock by return. There are easier things to be in India than a native Christian.'

The noise was like that which the greenhead recruit makes when, wagered by the sweats that he cannot get a clear note from a bugle, he blows hard with full lungs and open lips in a terrible, straining distress-call. Except that no human lungs could blow so long and so loud.

'Elephant, sahib,' said Subedar Thangraj, seeing Hervey's astonished look. 'Elephant very angry, very not-content.'

Hervey had somehow supposed elephants to be entirely mute. There had been no reason to suppose otherwise. The stuffed specimen in Mr Bullock's Museum of Natural and Artificial Curiosities, at No. 22

Piccadilly, had engaged him a full quarter of an hour when he had visited with d'Arcey Jessope two years before, but had, naturally, revealed nothing of its stentorian powers. And those living beasts that tramped, with the greatest docility, along the thoroughfares of Madras and Guntoor had likewise made not a sound. He now supposed they must bellow like cattle, and was suspicious at first of the subedar's assurance that the noise came, indeed, trumpet-like from the animal's trunk. Johnson had once assured him that an elephant was able to prospect for precious stones in the ground, and Lieutenant Locke now insisted, even more improbably, that elephants were able to throw stones with great accuracy at a mark.

The Sukri river, explained Templer, was the border between the princely state of Chintal and the Northern Circars, and there was held to be common title to its waters. Thus it was not evident whence the distressed elephant, thrashing knee-deep at the edge of the river with its attendants, had come.

'Elephant fussunded, sahib,' concluded Subedar Thangraj.

Hervey looked at Templer, to whom the problem did not seem novel. 'Mud or quicksand it will be,' said the cornet. 'The great beast will have sunk and struggled, and now he will be well and truly stuck.'

'What shall we do?' asked Hervey, assuming they must do something.

'I've seen a gaur caught this way. I fear there's nothing we can do that is not already being done,' he replied, indicating the ropes on which the attendants were pulling as the elephant continued its trumpeting as loud as before, and its two companions on the far bank added to the uproar.

'Save me, O God: for the waters are come in, even unto my soul.'

Cornet Templer looked at him strangely.

'Psalm Sixty-nine,' explained Hervey, with something between a smile and a grimace. '"I stick fast in the deep mire, where no ground is: I am come into deep waters, so that the floods run over me."'

'And does the psalmist have any notion of how the elephant may be delivered from the mire, sir?' asked Templer, smiling too.

Hervey racked his brain for the rest of the psalm – one of the longer ones. '"As for me, when I am poor and in heaviness: thy help, O God, shall lift me up."'

'Then we had better go and do God's work down there, sir,' laughed Templer. 'Subedar sahib – shoulders to it!'

*   *   *

123

The attendants had cut grass and branches from the few trees there-abouts, and had thrown them for the elephant to tread on. But it had been no use. They even tore planks from a ferry moored nearby and put them in reach of his trunk, but he seized each one and angrily threw it aside.

'Elephant will tear off his mahout to step on, sahib, if he has need,' said the subedar; 'it is most strange he will not take planks. Better for stay clear, sahib.'

The attendants – a dozen or more – were now hitching the ropes to the two other elephants in a last bid to haul out the stricken animal.

'That will cut through to the bone, surely,' said Hervey, seeing them only manage to secure a line round one leg. He sprang from the saddle, unable to remain a spectator any longer – even if he had no other ideas.

Templer and the subedar dismounted too. 'I think we could wedge some of those planks under his belly to prevent his sinking any further,' said the cornet.

Subedar Thangraj barked orders to the attendants and the patrol. He had advised they kept their distance, but now that his cornet had decided on this course of action he would direct the operation with all the vigour the sahibs would expect. Meanwhile, Templer and Hervey removed their boots and jackets to cross the quicksand.

The attendants spoke a dialect unintelligible even to the subedar, but several understood Hervey's Urdu and in a few minutes, with the help of half a dozen sepoys, they succeeded in getting up a platform around the beast, with wedging planks angled under its great bulk. By now, however, the elephant had sunk so deep that all but a part of his back and head were under the sand. He could no longer struggle, only wave his trunk in the air and trumpet feebly – though the clamour of the attendants and the calls of the other two elephants were as strong as before.

'Sahib, elephant will soon go under quicksand. Better for we shoot him now and take him from his misery,' said the subedar.

When Templer put this to the attendants they howled in protest and waved their hands about in horror. It was only then that Hervey, who had been standing on the platform for some minutes, dismayed that he could not think of any solution to the worsening problem, thought that he might have an answer. 'Great heavens!' he exclaimed, as it occurred to him. 'Templer, do you remember your Ovid?'

Cornet Templer was taken aback.

'Come, man: how did Hercules cleanse the Augean stables?'

Templer thought a moment. 'He diverted the river through them. But what—'

Hervey did not let him finish. 'See, there's a bend in the river yonder,' he said, pointing upstream; 'we can cut a channel and let in water. It should loosen the quicksand and we might then be able to get him out – that, or it will be over quickly for the wretched beast.'

Templer gave the orders at once to Subedar Thangraj. He in turn got the sepoys and others who had gathered on the bank to work with their bare hands, and in half an hour they had made the cutting, and water began to flow towards the fussunded elephant. At first it looked as though all that would happen was the merciful drowning of the beast, now utterly exhausted and seemingly resigned to its fate, but after a few more minutes the quicksand started to loosen. The attendants put ropes around the animal's quarters and the combined strength of fifty men and two elephants now braced for a final effort. The water was fast rising, and the ropes might not bear the strain. But at the signal, all pulled as if their own lives depended on it – and out he came, like a cork from a bottle.

The beast was done for. He had been stuck fast for a full five hours and every rib showed. He stood, swaying, as if he might collapse at any moment. 'Brandy, Subedar sahib: fetch him some brandy,' said Hervey.

Subedar Thangraj found a bottle from the bat-horse packs and, mixed with water in a bucket, the brandy was proffered to the exhausted elephant by his mahout. And it seemed not without some effect, for although he continued to sway on his feet, he began to step from side to side, showing no sign of wanting to lie down. The attendants were overjoyed, and began an incoherent babbling which nevertheless conveyed appreciation of the sahibs' ingenuity. And then suddenly there was excited pointing and more jabbering: '*Salutri*, sahib, salutri!' shouted the one with some Urdu.

Salutri? Hervey was baffled: where in all of Hindoostan were they to find a veterinarian? He tried to tell them this, but they pointed more insistently: 'Salutri, salutri!' Hervey turned to look – astounded.

'Matthew Hervey, I never supposed for a moment that you would take my advice,' said Selden as he rode up, followed by a half-dozen lancers, saffron pennants fluttering – the distinguishing colour of the princely state of Chintal.

The last time Hervey had heard that voice was in Dover the best part of two years before. Hatless, he held his arm out to the side and made the smallest bow of his head, smiling with incredulity as he did so: 'Mr Selden, by what providence is it that we should meet thus?'

The salutri laughed. 'Doubtless you would say it was the will of God, but I should not wish to debate divinity again with you – at least, not here. It is a great world into which we are born, but a small one in which we choose to live. Who are your friends?'

'Oh, forgive me,' said Hervey, conscious now of Templer and Locke standing silent next to him. 'Let me present Mr Locke, lieutenant of Marines in His Majesty's Ship *Nisus*, and Cornet Templer of the Madras Light Cavalry.' Both made bows. 'Gentlemen,' continued Hervey, turning to them, 'may I present Mr Selden, lately veterinary surgeon to the 6th Light Dragoons.'

Selden, now dismounted, held out his hand to each. 'Well, gentlemen,' he said, smiling the while, 'you are standing on the left bank of the Sukri. May I therefore welcome you on behalf of the Rajah of Chintal to his domain.'

They expressed themselves grateful but explained that the crossing was unintentional. One of the mahouts began to talk rapidly in his own tongue, and Selden quizzed him with considerable fluency. He turned to Hervey again. 'It appears, too, that I must thank you on the rajah's behalf for rescuing one of his favourite hunting elephants. The rajah is a great *shikari*: we have been in these parts for a week's sport and these elephants were bathing before their return to our hunting camp. Come, let me offer you some refreshment. Our camp is but a mile away, and we don't strike until tomorrow, though the rajah has returned to Chintalpore, unfortunately – the Nizam of Haidarabad visits and there's much to attend to.'

Here was fortune indeed. He was met with Selden, an object of his mission to India, and a month, surely, before he might be able to do so through the offices of Calcutta. And the nizam himself was about to pay a visit to Chintalpore. Hervey was turning over the possibilities in his mind even as he accepted Selden's invitation.

Templer, however, was concerned for the propriety – and the legality – of Company troops entering the rajah's domain, even with an invitation.

'Very well, then,' Hervey concluded, with as indifferent an air as he could manage, 'it seems that Mr Templer shall have to return directly to Guntoor. However, Mr Locke and I accept with the greatest pleasure!'

CHAPTER SEVEN
FALSE CIVILIZATION

Chintal, princely state

The Rajah of Chintal's hunting camp lay at the forest edge, where great mathi and tadasalu trees provided shade over the best part of three acres of mown grass. There were a dozen large tents, one bigger by half than the others, with saffron panels and streamers, evidently the rajah's former quarters. In the middle of the camp was the *maidan*, on which several Arab ponies were being schooled by bare-legged riders. Xenophon would have approved, smiled Hervey, for they rode without saddle too, the sweat of the ponies' flanks giving the necessary adhesion.

'Come: you will feel the need of a bath,' said Selden, as their horses were led away; and he called after one of the syces, in a tongue Hervey did not recognize, to fill two tubs for the sahibs.

Hervey was glad of the offer, and Locke too, for the quicksand had a rankness that had travelled with them to the camp. And for a half-hour they each luxuriated in leaden baths of warm, perfumed spring water brought by relays from a huge vat heated by a charcoal fire. And to slake their thirsts a khitmagar brought silver cups of cold beer.

'Upon my word,' exclaimed Locke after his first, long, draught, 'this is uncommonly good ale. This Chintal nabob has a damned fine brewer. And so cool it is too, as if it has been in a cellar. A man might be tolerably content in these parts!'

It was a half-hour of indulgence. And all the more pleasurable for its being well earned.

'Did you find the arrangements to your satisfaction, gentlemen?' enquired Selden as they joined him outside his tent.

They had. Towels, brushes and clean shirts from the rajah's quarters, and breeches from the packs carried by the bat-horses, had made new men of them.

'May I offer you more ale, or perhaps you would prefer wine?'

Both preferred the cold hops.

'An uncommonly good brew,' said Locke again, emptying his cup in one motion, which a khitmagar refilled at once from a silver pitcher.

'Yes,' said Selden, with some satisfaction, 'I too am fond of Burton ale.'

Locke was intrigued. 'You do not mean that which *we* call Burton ale, do you?'

'Indeed I do,' Selden assured him. 'The rajah is especially favoured of it. Twice yearly it is shipped from Madras at sixty rupees a dozen.'

They made noises of appreciation, though at such a price Locke was not now so assured that a man might be advantageously set up here without a small fortune.

The khansamah led them to the dinner table, which stood under the double shade of both a giant mathi and a saffron canopy. The table was so solid that even when Locke half-stumbled against it as they sat nothing was put awry. Had they been able to see beneath the crimson tablecloth, richly decorated as it was with images of the chase worked in semi-precious stones, they would have been astonished that anything so massive as this teak board, its legs carved voluptuously, might be brought to the jungle's edge. The plates and flatware – everything, it seemed – were gold, and by this sumptuousness Hervey was left in no doubt as to the rajah's rank and wealth, though he could not, with any certainty, discern thereby his character. He had seen like displays of nobility and wealth at Longleat and Lismore, albeit more restrained. His preference was still for a white tablecloth and silver; though how long might a man be in India, he wondered, before it was for brocades and gold?

Henry Locke, evidently, was occupied by no such thoughts, setting about the fare without seeming much to notice the richness of the plate on which it was served. His thirst was already proving prodigious, and one khitmagar was engaged almost entirely in replenishing his cup. 'How d'ye manage to chill it so thoroughly in this infernal heat?' he asked. 'You cannot stand it in the river alone. That wouldn't cool it thus.'

'Ice,' replied Selden in a matter-of-fact way. 'The rajah has ice houses in Chintal and blocks of it are brought down here each night.'

Hervey was minded of the ice cart in Chelsea, and how his arresting officer's reserve had begun to thaw, with the ice, on that hot July morning. What an extraordinary change in his fortunes that day had seen. And what extraordinary circumstances had brought him since to this table at the edge of the jungle on the far side of the world. He could not help his thoughts wandering back to the vicarage garden in Wiltshire, where his father might now be pottering – perhaps to see the first snowdrops. His mother, his sister, and quite probably Mrs Strange too – all would be at some good work or other. And, of course, Henrietta. He could not suppose with any exactness what she might be doing, nor where she might be. London was not improbable at this time of year. Bath, too, perhaps – there were fashionable assemblies there throughout the winter. She might be at Chatsworth – the new duke was the staunchest of her friends. Indeed, she might be at any of two dozen great houses in England, for such was her beauty and wit that her company was constantly sought.

Selden recalled him to the forest's edge. 'How do you find your fish, Hervey? I'll warrant you've not tasted its like before.'

'No, I think not,' he replied, much pleased with the fullness of its taste.

'It is mackerel, brought fresh from Rajahmundry.'

'Mackerel?' said Hervey, curious.

'Yes, the rajah is inordinately fond of them. And they're so much fatter than those you will find in England. The warmer waters make them lazier.'

'And the special taste they have?'

'One of the rajah's cooks is from Bombay. He has a clever way with a marinade – coriander and other spices. I tell you, the rajah's table is second to none.'

He was becoming happily accustomed to good tables, declared Hervey.

But the most fulsome praise was reserved for what followed. 'Pig!'

exclaimed Selden, as two khitmagars advanced with the spitted bulk of his delight carried high on their shoulders. 'There is no better sport than spearing pig, Hervey, and the more so because he tastes so fine. Shooting tiger is nothing to hog-hunting!'

Great slices of meat were hacked from the boar's loins, and soon both Locke and Hervey were confessing that they had never had such choice game. The meat was fine-grained, not at all coarse – darker, more promising than pork, but not offensively strong.

'You had better have some claret with it to appreciate its fullness,' said Selden, beckoning to a khitmagar holding a magnificently chased ewer. 'I could eat pig every day. Have some of this too,' he continued, nodding as another khitmagar proffered a bowl of preserve. '*Sev, aroo, aur kubani ki.*'

'Apple . . .' began Hervey, racking his brains for the other words.

'Apple, peach and apricot – *chatnee*. And some of this – there's nothing more sensuous than dhal!' A tall, loose-limbed youth, clean-shaven, with effeminate features, dabbed at the little beads of sweat on Selden's forehead, smiling confidentially as he did so. Selden returned the smile before waving him away with a playful gesture.

Hervey affected not to notice.

'He is the most amusing boy,' said Selden, 'a Bengali I engaged in Calcutta when I came back here last year. A trustworthy bearer is a prize, Hervey.'

'Indeed,' replied the latter, taking another slice of pig. 'You will recall that I found it thus with grooms. With me still is the very same dragoon from that last winter in Spain.'

Selden nodded approvingly. 'Tell me of this battle – *Waterloo*. Not how went it, for I was never much occupied by fighting – but how the regiment fared.'

Hervey recounted the tally of officers, and the men whom Selden might recall.

The veterinarian heard it in silence, here and there shaking his head at a name. But Joseph Edmonds's brought more. 'The major was a humane man. He treated me with not a little kindness.'

Hervey supposed he must be referring to events on campaign, and latterly to his manner of leaving the regiment in Cork. 'I owe Major Edmonds everything, perhaps, too,' he confided; 'no man I ever met combined such zeal for perfection in his profession with such benevolence towards an individual.'

'Indeed?' smiled Selden with an irony that was lost on his visitor. He had always regarded Hervey as having excess of both.

By the time coffee was brought by the khansamah, Henry Locke had slid deep into his chair and a profound sleep. He made little noise, however (beyond the occasional snuffle), so that Hervey and Selden were able to continue without distraction. 'Well,' said the latter, with a sudden and curious insistence, 'you have not spoken one word of your purpose in coming to India. I don't suppose it was anything I said in Toulouse when I recommended this course to you? And I don't suppose you have voluntarily quit your precious dragoons.'

Hervey smiled. 'No, I have not left the regiment. I am with the Duke of Wellington's staff. I am here to study the employment of the lance with a view to its being taken into service in our cavalry.'

Selden looked puzzled. 'The duke's staff, you say; in what capacity?'

'I am aide-de-camp.'

He now looked positively wary. 'So you are *Captain* Hervey?'

'Yes.'

'Forgive me,' he continued, his brow furrowed, 'but when last we met you had not two sovereigns to spare, and there was some general or other after your hide. This is a remarkable change of fortune, is it not?'

Hervey smiled again. 'I have been fortunate, yes. In the wake of the battle there were many positions to be filled.'

Selden looked sceptical. 'Well, whatever your business in India,' and he seemed not yet inclined to believe that it was entirely stated, though he would ordinarily have staked his last rupee on Hervey's candour, 'I am very glad to see you again. You will know of the circumstances of my leaving the Sixth in Cork. It's better that we have it out.'

Hervey made some protest, not without embarrassment, but Selden bade him stop.

'I freely admit that my tastes have been seduced by years in the tropics,' he continued, 'and it's as well that I am returned here where they cause less offence – indeed, go entirely unremarked.'

'And better for your health?' asked Hervey, grasping the opportunity to change the subject.

'That I do not know, but I don't imagine that I should have enjoyed many winters living beneath a fountain – which is what it seemed to me that Cork was.'

'How did you come to this employment?'

'By letters of introduction from the Company in Calcutta. I had once been their buying agent there.'

'And the rajah wished to have a veterinarian?'

'Someone to buy horses – *that*, yes, but more: I am become his adviser in other, general matters. He has a most efficient dewan – minister, that is – and a sound treasury. Which is as well, for he has much wealth, but he has made no treaty with the Company and there is no resident, therefore.'

It was now Hervey's turn to look puzzled. 'But if he is so afeard of the nizam, as I hear tell, why does he not conclude such a treaty with the Company?'

'He values his own sovereignty, of course, and there is always a fear among the princes that a resident is but a covert viceroy. But principally he fears that the very act of approaching the Company would provoke the nizam into invading Chintal. And since we know that Haidarabad is presently at the mercy of the nizam's lunatic sons, I shouldn't wonder but that he is right.'

Hervey paused thoughtfully before making what seemed the obvious retort. 'But the rajah could surely conclude his treaty in secret, and then it would be for the Company to protect Chintal.'

Selden smiled – laughed, almost. 'My dear Hervey, you have a very great deal to learn about India. War is made here with bullocks, money and spies. The rajah would not even be able to *think* of such a treaty without the nizam's hearing of it. Several of the rajah's own khitmagars are in the pay of the nizam!'

'Surely if you know that, then—'

'Hervey, it is better that we know who the spies are than that we dismiss them and begin again.'

'Perhaps so,' he conceded. And then he frowned, as if something troubled him. 'Bullocks, money and spies, you say. What about guns?'

'*Battle* is made with guns. You of all people know that!'

They lit cigars, yet not even the smoke made Locke stir. 'Not, I fancy, an officer of your fastidiousness,' suggested Selden, contemplating his repose.

'There are two suppositions in your saying so, and I am not inclined to remark on either,' replied Hervey with a smile. 'He is a most gallant and faithful officer.'

'As you please,' conceded Selden.

'One more thing, however: what manner of forces does the rajah possess?'

'About five thousand of infantry and two risallahs of cavalry – five hundred each.'

'And guns?'

'A few siege pieces hardly worth the name; and each risallah will have a brace of gallopers. The Company has always been anxious to see as few cannon as possible in native hands.'

'I have heard that a galloper gun deployed with some address might have considerable effect here, though – the mutiny at Vellore? I was sorry on more than one occasion in Spain for their passing.'

'Indeed,' nodded Selden, 'but the nizam has copious artillery, including a battery of siege pieces that seem able to go where even our own horse-gunners would have difficulty. They blew apart the rajah's forts on the Godavari river a decade ago when he tried to levy tolls on Haidarabad trafficking. The nizam's beautiful daughters, they are called.'

'Yes, I had heard. I should very much like to make their acquaintance, but as a friend of course,' laughed Hervey.

Selden frowned. 'Hervey, as I remember, you once professed to having little facility with women – though I believed I had observed otherwise. Do not suppose that you will find any woman in India fathomable, not least one belonging to the nizam!'

Hervey blushed.

'But why, in any case, should you be so interested in these details?'

There was nothing in Selden's tone to cause him alarm, but he thought nevertheless to dismiss the matter with a certain lightness. 'You once chided me, too, for being excessively interested in my profession – and that it would do me no good if I wished to be advanced!'

Selden smiled. 'That I did! Though I did say, also, that the Honourable Company would take a different view of your aptness, did I not? I even urged – as I recall – that you throw in with the Company and see that aptness rewarded!'

Hervey was content that his diversion had worked, even if at some cost to his pride. Locke made a loud snorting sound, then whimpered, like an old dog dreaming of rabbit-chasing, and slid even further into his chair.

'It is the custom of the Hindoo to take to his charpoy for an hour or so after such a meal,' said Selden, looking with some amusement towards the lieutenant. 'Your friend will be honoured by the khansamah and his staff for so doing. Do you wish to do likewise?'

'Not especially,' replied Hervey, looking about him; 'I am not in the least tired and there is so much of interest hereabouts that I should very much like to see more.'

'In that case,' said Selden, sitting bolt upright and with a glint in his eye, 'let us ride out across the *kadir* – the river plain. We shall very probably see pig, and you'll be able to observe from how they run what manner of sport I speak of. I tell you, Hervey, there's nothing of its like. Chasing the fox is for dullards when you've run after pig!'

Hervey was all attention.

'And, then, perhaps, before too long, we might get you to carry a spear.'

Now he was all eagerness.

After a half-hour's respite – so that, in Selden's words, they would not get the colic – he went to make the arrangements. Hervey watched him stride purposefully across the maidan towards where the syces were taking their ease in the shade of a huge palmyra. That he seemed so well in both body and spirits was a happy thing indeed. In Spain and France he had never looked more than well enough, and there had been times when he was far short of that – Toulouse, notably, after the battle, when the hot and cold remittent fevers, his malaria, from years in the Indies, rendered his diagnoses so unreliable that more than one troop-horse escaped destruction only by the hand of Providence (or, in one case, by Hervey's own). He was at times the very model of black bile. Yet here in Chintal his humours seemed wholly restored. The irony – that India had been the cause of his original ill humour, and was now the restorative – seemed apt. Concerning the manner of his leaving the Sixth, details of which Hervey knew only through Private Johnson (for no one in the mess seemingly had much stomach for them), he was content to let things lie. It was a pity that Selden's proclivities in that direction had been further complicated by a specific taste, and it was a cruel temptation, therefore, that in the regiment's band there should have been a cymbalist from the Ivory Coast who, had he been in skirts, would have passed pleasingly for a young woman. In these parts it was of no particular matter, however: there were no interests of discipline to be attentive to, nor even propriety, and Hervey could simply enjoy the company of a man whose fellowship had sometimes been disdained by the mess but whose knowledge of horses he greatly admired.

Selden returned with two Arab ponies, and two of the same breed built bigger. Hervey had never ridden a pure-bred Arab, though he had ridden many a horse that had profited by Arab blood in its lines. Jessye, indeed, Welsh crossed with thoroughbred, had in consequence such blood on both sides. All the rajah's hog-hunters were Arabs or Turkomans, explained Selden. The Chintal kadirs were trappy country compared with those in the north, and with a jinking pig, as long as the cover was not too heavy, a pony was a better bet, though if it came to a straight gallop then the pony would naturally lose. Those who could ride under twelve stone, said Selden, were therefore at an advantage, and it was ever to his consternation that the rajah, who rode considerably in excess of that, should find himself so often defeated by even an elderly boar.

Hervey tried one of the two ponies, a flea-bitten grey about thirteen hands and three inches. The saddle was English, as he would have chosen for the hunting field at home, yet never had he felt less secure as he cantered her in a large circle, for even with Jessye he was used to having shoulders in front of him. This little mare – Gita – seemed unusually high on the leg, and narrow-chested. But he could feel the power beneath him. She had a good length of rein and her mouth was a deal less hard than he expected: he managed to turn her so sharply at one stage that he was almost parted from her. He expressed much satisfaction, and Selden said he should be pleased with his choice for that was the rajah's favourite, which no one as a rule but his own daughter – the raj kumari – rode. Hervey voiced surprise, and then admiration, that the rajah's daughter should trust so active a horse with a side-saddle. And he admitted even greater surprise when Selden told him she rode astride.

Selden himself rode at a little over thirteen stone, and took the reins of a fiery-looking Turkoman bay almost two full hands higher. He explained that, since he was not hunting, he would prefer the extra height to observe. His own preference with a spear was the other gelding – at fifteen hands, a near-perfect mount for this kadir.

'He looks uncommonly like an English blood,' said Hervey, admiringly.

'The Turkoman's breeding has much, I think, in common with the thoroughbred,' Selden conceded. 'Without doubt, there's much Arab in him. And I'm convinced that the Byerly Turk – on which you know that much of the thoroughbred's blood is founded – is in fact from Turkomania. You have only to look close at the paintings of him to see the similarity – the head, principally.'

'And is he as fast?'

'Not, perhaps, over so short a distance as would a blood usually race. But I'll warrant that I could gallop this one most of the day and he would stand it well. Especially since he's been fed on *nahari* for over a year.'

'Nahari?' asked Hervey.

'Flour and fat: it means "never get weary". Now,' he began, as they left the camp, 'the first thing on which we must be clear is that we hunt only the *boar*.'

'How do I tell him?'

'Both he and the sow have tushes, so the only way to be sure are his testises – they'll be prominent enough beneath his tail. Now, a hog will lie concealed until he's beaten out, and then he'll run fast for the nearest cover – and I truly mean *fast*. He can go at a gallop, and you'll need to go flat out to stay with him. That's why you must have a horse you can trust, for you yourself will have no time to help it out of trouble. I have had some crashing falls: it's all part of the sport. And the faster I've been going as we tumbled, the less damage has been done.'

Hervey nodded, accepting the proposition, illogical as it might at first have seemed, for it was indeed better sometimes to be put on the ground with no time to flinch than struggling to save oneself.

'Remember,' continued Selden, 'a horse can go where a pig goes. And in this country there's so much grass and dhak in the season that unless you stay right up with him you'll lose him as soon as he makes his first cover, and in any case the pig will make a good pilot. Now, if you *do* lose him the golden rule is to cast well for'ard: do *not* look for him at the point you lost him. Cast for'ard a mile or so on the line he was running, for believe me, the pig will soon cover that distance. And then find a hillock, or a nullah, or some such feature, and wait for him to break.'

The camp was now a mile or more behind them. In the heat of the afternoon, though Selden warned him that it was not a fraction of what was to come in July just before the monsoon broke, Hervey felt the curious sensation of coming alive, like the basking lizard which manages, just, to crawl onto its warming stone and then, after sunning itself for an hour or so, is suddenly disposed to scuttle off at great speed. And though this heat was not enervating, as sometimes he had found it in Spain, neither was it a burning heat, from which, instinctively, all tried to shelter. It was an invigorating warmth, annealing the muscles of his arms and legs, and he had not felt its like before. Perhaps, he mused, this was the beginning of what Selden had said so often in France – that India sweated out the false civilization in a man (though there was as yet scarce a bead of sweat on his brow).

They picked their way through a patch of untended sugar cane, Selden falling silent and crouching low in the saddle to peer between the dhak for a sight of his quarry. 'If you come out for pig on your own – "gooming", we call it, as opposed to on a big hunt – it's best to try to get on top of him before he breaks, rather than beating him out, otherwise he may get too great a start on you. Beware, mind: you'll likely enough find a leopard in these places, and that can be tricky.'

Hervey was more and more intrigued by Selden's transfiguration from the fever-ridden cynic he had known in the regiment. 'And tiger?' he asked. 'Do you find tiger in such patches as these?'

'Be assured, Hervey,' said Selden half laughing, 'if I suspected tiger were here then I should not come within a mile. You may take your chance with a leopard in thick country, but you have none with a tiger. Leopard's not so intent on killing, merely escaping. Whereas tiger – man-eater or no – is so prodigiously strong that it makes no odds why he attacks, for he'll crush you instantly.'

Hervey had entertained a notion of killing his own tiger and sending the skin home to Horningsham – just as he had pictured Midshipman Nelson battling with the polar bear so as to send the skin to his father at Burnham Thorpe.

'If I were you, Hervey,' said Selden on hearing this, 'I should put the notion from your mind. I have been on perhaps a dozen tiger hunts and only once did the enterprise come off without mishap. The rajah was almost killed last year when his most practised elephant went must. Now, let us return to the king of sports. If you are gooming, then it does not matter so much, but if you are hunting hog properly then there are certain observances. First, we don't as a rule hunt pig that is not full-grown – two feet at the shoulder at least – unless the villagers say their crops are being sorely ravaged.'

'How big can pig grow?' asked Hervey, already surprised by the idea of one standing even two feet at the shoulder.

'I have killed one that measured forty inches.'

Hervey made a rapid calculation, and concluded that such a pig, if it were to charge him on this pony, would gore him in his thigh, and almost certainly would be heavy enough to bowl them both over.

'The biggest pig in India are to be found in these parts, although Nagpore has recorded the largest – forty-four inches, I believe it was.'

Hervey wished he had his carbine with him. He did not suppose the sabre at his side would make much of an impression on a boar that size.

'Once a pig is flushed then the nearest man must get onto his line at once and press him for all he's worth. If he gets his wind he'll take you a long way, and you'll need to settle down to his pace and keep close. You've got to see the ground – waving grass, dust and the like – to keep you on his line. Believe me, it's a lot more than merely chasing like a lunatic.'

'And how is the lance used?'

'It's not a lance, rather a spear. And different ways are favoured depending on what country you're hunting in. A decade or so ago you would only see throwing-spears, but now it's the practice to close with the hog and spear him from the saddle. In Chintal, for the most part, a short spear is carried, and used overhand for jobbing. There's much thick cover, and it's generally preferred if a pig charges. In open country, such as that in the Bombay presidency and in the north, the long spear, couched, is better. In Chintal we usually have a couple of long spears out, too, for they can be handy when a boar is running away in the open.'

'I imagine that one can carry through the weight of the horse's speed better in the long spear,' suggested Hervey.

'Ah, but it's a mistake to think that brute strength is all. With a jobbing spear it should be more the rapier than the bludgeon. The merest touch through the heart or the lungs – or, indeed, the spine – ought to be sufficient. But more of spears anon. I want only today to show you how a sounder breaks and how to get onto the line of a good-size boar.'

As they came through to the far edge of the sugar cane, Selden had just embarked on an explanation of riding second in the hunt. He was intent on emphasizing the sovereign importance, in awkward ground or thick cover, of riding wide or behind the spear who was on the pig to give him all the time he needed. 'But as soon as the pig's into easier country you must challenge the man who is "on" at once. Make the pace as hot as you can! You may override the odd young boar who doesn't know when to make for cover, but you'll kill more pig that way than by trying to wear him down.'

'I cannot wait!' declared Hervey, wishing they were carrying spears now.

So intent on his instruction was Selden that what happened next took him wholly by surprise. A big old boar – Hervey's weight and then half again – burst from the cane to their left and took off across the kadir like a greyhound on a hare. Hervey (or perhaps it was his pony) did not hesitate for a second, and they were at full stretch in less than a dozen strides. Selden was close behind, however, shouting for him to ride on a loose rein. He had, in any case, instinctively begun to do so, for even in the relatively open country into which the pig was heading there was little he could see of the ground as it came at him.

After half a mile the boar ran into a cotton-field. Hervey checked for an instant to be sure of its line, for he could not see any of the grass moving. Then he saw the merest, but tell-tale, waving ahead and to his right, and he spurred his pony to flatten out once more, leaning so far forward himself as to be almost head to head with it. Out onto the plain rushed the boar again. Hervey began to make up ground but there was another patch of dhak ahead and off to the right. He saw the boar check, as if trying to decide whether to turn for it. The instinct was too strong merely to continue chasing, and he reached for his sabre. The pig's momentary hesitation cost it the distance over his pursuer, and as it jinked right for the dhak Hervey managed to give him the point of his sword in the loins.

'Spear well forward next, Hervey!' shouted Selden, close up behind and already turning for the dhak. 'He'll crouch in that cover. Go through and wait for him to break the other side. I'll wait to see if he doubles back.'

Hervey galloped round the dhak to take post in a nullah beyond. His pony was blowing, but still, he sensed, she had plenty in reserve. He had yet to accustom himself to her lack of shoulder, though, and he scolded himself for misjudging his sabring, for he had put his leg on precisely at the moment of driving home the thrust, and the mare had not responded as would Jessye. He would have liked to dismount to give her a little respite, but he knew enough not to. He was not there more than a minute when the boar, squatting close by but unobserved, jumped up and charged. Though Selden had not got so far in his instruction as to explain how to take a charging pig, Hervey swung round instinctively to meet it at an angle rather than head-on, and dug his spurs hard into his pony's flanks. Even though her momentum would have been nothing to that of Selden's Turkoman, the sabre went deep into the boar's shoulder. But still it fought, and he had to struggle for all he was worth to keep his leg on, pressing the pony up close to use the weight to hold off the furious animal.

The struggle seemed to last an age, with no sign of the boar's weakening. Until Selden galloped up and gave him a thrust with his own sabre. The pig staggered and then fell dead with Hervey's sword still deep in his shoulder. Indeed, when Hervey dismounted and pulled it out there was more than a foot of grease on the blade.

'Hervey, let that be a lesson to you. I wonder that your sword didn't break. Mine has not been out of its scabbard except to salute since coming here, and I shouldn't have wished to trust to its tensility!'

Hervey smiled sheepishly.

'But by heavens, what a run you gave him! He's no squeaker, and he had a lifetime of rancour in him – of that there's no doubt. I'll be able to tell the rajah that you tackled a boar without benefit of a spear. He'll be mightily stirred if I am not much mistaken. And his daughter, the raj kumari – she'll be gratified her best pony rode so faithfully.'

Hervey looked pleased. 'And what do we now do with our quarry?'

Selden pointed to the village a quarter of a mile away. 'They shall have pig for the rest of the week. Come, let's go and tell them. We shall drink their rus while they bear him in, and wait for them to cut and boil out the tushes. See, I reckon those will be all of nine inches. The raj kumari will be much favoured by them.' And then another thought occurred to him: 'Hervey, why don't you return with me to Chintalpore to make these presents in person? The place will quite beguile you!'

CHAPTER EIGHT

DESPATCHES

To Lieutenant-Colonel Colquhoun Grant   *c/o Fort George*
at The Embassy of His Britannic Majesty   *Madras*
Paris   *22 February 1816*

Sir,
I have the honour to report my arrival in India. My ship had
perforce to put into Madras for repairs and during her
inactivity I availed myself of a most opportune re-acquaintance
which has placed me within the state of Chintal very
considerably earlier than might otherwise have been arranged.
    I report that predatory bands of Maratha horse are
marauding along the Eastern Circars but, from accounts I
have, they do not trouble the Nizam's territories, nor very
greatly that of the Rajah of Chintal. I have it on the same and
other authorities that the Nizam's forces are formidable and
respected, and that especially he is well served by artillery.
    I have further to report that I am in contact with Mr Selden
and shall be proceeding with him soon directly to the Rajah's
capital at Chintalpore. I am very mindful that my orders are to
report first to Mr Bazzard in Calcutta, and I shall, of course,

communicate with him at once, but the opportunity presented by my encountering Mr Selden is one which I feel sure you would wish me to avail myself of, for it is probable that I shall shortly make the acquaintance of the Nizam himself since His Highness is to visit with the Rajah. I have accounts, by officials of the Honourable East India Company, that relations between the Nizam and the Rajah are infelicitous. However, by Mr Selden's own accounts, relations are – if not cordial – sufficiently tolerable. I believe – though I may only surmise – that this disparity of opinion is occasioned by the want of intelligence available to Madras, for it seems that Haidarabad and Chintal are interests of Calcutta's rather than of the former. I have to report, however, that there appears to be certain resentment between Fort George and Fort William which may stand in the way of unity of effort in terms of intelligence.

This must therefore be but a brief account of my assessments so far. I pray that this fortuitous beginning shall yield full and timely results, and with little attention drawn to His Grace's agency here.

I remain, Sir, Your Most Obedient Servant

M. P. Hervey
Captain

From the Deputy Commissioner of Kistna,   Guntoor
the Collector of Land Revenues, and Magistrate

To The Governor's Secretary
Fort George
Madras   24 February 1816

Sir,
Be pleased to lay before the Governor at the earliest opportunity this assessment of the recent incursions into the Company's territory of the Eastern Circars by the irregular Maratha horse become known as Pindarees. At attachment is a schedule of depredations, together with the relief authorized.

In all probability the route of the incursion lay through Nagpore, and it is most evident therefore that that country is enfeebled to a degree alarming to the Company's peace. My agents report that the Rajah of that place is so enfeebled as to be incapable of exerting his dominion. His son is but an imbecile and a prey to the most malevolent influences. It is my very strongest recommendation that the treaty of subsidiary alliance be advanced as rapidly as possible ere the country descends to lawlessness, and I urge you most fervently to press upon Fort William the absolute imperative of concluding the said. For the present time I urge that the subsidiary force be assembled in anticipation of said conclusion so that not the least time is lost in bringing Nagpore under regulation.

I have in the past urged a similar course with Chintal and my entreaties have been met with ill favour at Fort William on account of their conviction that Chintal represented no threat as a conduit for Pindaree attacks upon the Circars, neither that the Nizam retained any ambitions towards attaching that country to his own by force of arms. I must tell you now that my agents report most emphatically that the Nizam is about to begin a campaign against Chintal by subversion and intimidation. I do not have to tell you how parlous would be the condition of Madras, and the Circars, were such a unity to be opposed to the policies of the Company at some time in the future, for it would render mutual support of the two Presidencies by land most perilous. I therefore urge once more that Chintal, as Nagpore, be pressed to conclude a subsidiary alliance, if necessary on terms unusually advantageous. The situation, believe me, is very grave.

I have the honour to be etc etc

Eyre Somervile C.B.

CHAPTER NINE

THE RAJAH OF CHINTAL

Chintalpore, 25 February

Half a mile west of the city, the Rajah of Chintal's palace sat prettily on a shallow hill just visible from the rooftops of the humblest dwellings of Chintalpore – imposing, therefore, rather than dominating. It had been built in the middle of the seventeenth century on the birth of the rajah's great-grandfather, whose own father had visited the water gardens of Italy and had wished to create fountains and cascades of like grace. He had therefore excavated a canal to take water to his new seat from the tributary of the Godavari on which Chintalpore stood, and the palace's precise elevation was determined by the Venetian engineer who had laid out the gardens. The rajah's ancestor had thereby sacrificed the eminence of a hilltop situation for the elegance of a less elevated one. It was a compromise of which successive generations had approved. At least, that is, to this time, for the present rajah was without male issue.

The palace itself was an eclectic structure, a mix of Hindoo and Mughal architecture in which domes and pyramidal roofs stood harmoniously side by side – symbolic of the harmony in which the Mussulman population of Chintalpore lived with their more populous

Hindoo neighbours. Everywhere there was marble and alabaster, some of it almost pure white, but some richly veined with a shade of red that Hervey would have been hard put to describe. There was a tranquillity, in part wrought by the continuous tinkling of water in the fountains, inside and out, which stood in the starkest contrast to the city through which he had just ridden. And, though the heat outdoors was hardly oppressive in this early month, he found the cool shade the greatest relief after their long march.

'"High on a throne of royal state, which far outshone the wealth of Ormus and Ind . . ."?' he declaimed, turning to Selden with a smile.

'You are beginning to sound like Major Edmonds.'

'I had all Milton's works with me during the passage.'

'You suppose this is paradise, then: you shall have to wait and see.'

They had been met at the foot of the droog, the great earth ramp that led to the palace, by the rissaldar of the rajah's life guard and thence borne by palanquin to the turreted gates which commanded the ascent. Here they observed the customary propitiatory offering to Pollear, the protecting deity of pilgrims and travellers. One of the bearers stopped before the gates and, with considerable ceremony, silently unwound his turban. Then, giving one end to another bearer, he placed himself the other side of the gateway so that the turban was stretched across the entrance at about waist height. Hervey and Locke, at Selden's urging, placed some silver into the outstretched palms of the bearers before passing over the lowered tape and through the portals into the courtyard.

They were shown to their quarters at once – high, airy rooms with fretted windows overlooking the water gardens – for it was afternoon and the household followed the custom of retiring until the sun had fallen half-way to the horizon, even in this cooler season.

'*Nimbu pani, sahib?*' said the khitmagar, indicating a silver ewer in a cooling tray.

'*Mehrbani*,' replied Hervey, pleased at last to be able to say 'thank you' in a native tongue.

The khitmagar filled a silver cup, placed it on a tray by his side and took his leave with a low bow.

Lime juice, sweetened, with something giving it an edge: it was a prompt restorative. Selden had said they would have the afternoon to themselves, until seven, when the rajah would show them his gardens and menagerie and then feast them with the honour due to those who had saved one of his most favoured elephants. And if Hervey had been in any doubt as to the veneration in which the rajah held the elephant then the number and magnificence of the carvings of that animal about the palace would soon convince him. So, with Selden's assurance that he would be called to bathe an hour before the appointed time, he lay down on the wide divan and gave himself to the pleasure of rest.

His Highness Godaji Rao Sundur, the Rajah of Chintalpore, spoke English with clear, precise diction, and without the inflections of other than an educated Englishman. Selden had told him that the rajah had had both an English nurse and governess, and a tutor from Cambridge, though he had travelled little beyond the frontiers of his princely state – except, in his youth, for a journey through the Ottoman domains to Rome, whose history enthralled him and whose religion still intrigued him. Although his native tongue was Telugu, the language of the majority of his Hindoo subjects, he was fluent in Urdu, and he even had a very passable acquaintance with French. But he preferred to converse in English, and many of Chintal's officials were proficient, too. Indeed, with so many languages alive in Chintalpore, it was almost impossible for a visitor not to be able to make himself understood. The rajah's daughter, Her Highness Suneyla Rao Sundur – the raj kumari – had likewise learned English at her nursemaid's knee, but she had retained a religious sensibility – said Selden – that was wholly native. So native, indeed, as to be unfathomable, for, he confessed, after all his years in India he was still unable to give any account of what the Hindoo religion truly held to. The rajah, he believed, was at heart a good man, but for the raj kumari he could not speak, for she would never converse with him other than of mundane matters.

The rajah was all ease at their meeting. He greeted Hervey as if he were the saviour of one of his children, and Henry Locke hardly less. 'In my father's day, gentlemen, such an act as the rescue of a royal elephant would have been rewarded by the gift of a dozen virgins,' he smiled; 'but I much regret that I must offer you less than that.'

Hervey was momentarily unsure whether the rajah's undoubtedly fine command of English embraced the difference between 'less' and 'fewer'. Henry Locke failed to register any distinction, and wondered merely – and with keen anticipation – what would be the precise, if reduced, number of maidens who might be sent to his chamber.

The rajah was a figure of dignified restraint, and evidently of sensibility and cultivation, concluded Hervey – in spite of his apparent jesting. His face was clean-shaven and fine-featured, his sallow complexion clear, and his shoulder-length hair was pulled back with slides. Around his eyes were darker rings, like those of the elephants to which he was so devoted. Perhaps it was a natural coloration, but so marked were they that Hervey thought them of cosmetic making. He was not tall, nothing like as big as the bazaar Hindoos who thronged the streets, yet he was possessed of a stature which, if it did not actually *command* respect, then otherwise induced it. Indeed he possessed an air of tranquillity that was at once appealing, while all about the palace there were images of the elephant, in statuary and inlays, which spoke too of the measured dignity of his court. And now, as they neared the menagerie, a big, old bull with full if fissured and yellowed tusks, his skin scarred from many fights, trod slowly into their path from behind an acacia screen. His mahout, standing nearby, shrivelled and as ancient as his charge, made low namaste as the rajah approached, but did nothing to take the animal in hand.

'That is Seejavi,' whispered Selden. 'He was one of the late rajah's war elephants. Now he is allowed free roam of the palace. His mahout is with him only because he has always been. Seejavi may trample anything and anyone he pleases.'

'And does he?' asked Hervey.

'How are we to know? No one would admit evidence of Seejavi's ill behaviour.'

The rajah took a sugared favour from a silver tray which a khitmagar carried ready, and held it out in his palm – not at arm's length, but close to, making him hostage to the elephant's forbearance.

'Your Highness,' said Selden, more wearied than anxious, 'I do urge more circumspection with Seejavi. He is old and may not always remember his place.'

The rajah smiled, without turning, and took another favour from the tray. 'An elephant not remember, Mr Selden? The notion is an intriguing one. Seejavi would never be disloyal, of that I am sure.'

Selden made no reply.

The next voice was female. 'You are too trusting, father. Constancy is no more an animal virtue than it is a human one.'

Both the appearing and appearance of the raj kumari was of some moment. Hitherto she had been hid by the acacia screen, a slender figure, of about Hervey's age and not much less than his height, her

147

skin lighter than the Madrasi women whose complexion he had admired at Fort George (so close in colour as they were to Jessye's bay), though her hair was blacker and her eyes larger. She was, by any estimate, a beauty of considerable degree, and, after the formalities of presentation, both Hervey and Locke found themselves, temporarily, less than fluent in their replies to her questions – which she asked without any of the coyness or reservation they had been led to believe was the mark of Hindoo women.

At first they walked side by side along the aviary, and neither Hervey nor Locke felt able to look but ahead. When, however, she went a little in advance of them in order to attract the attention of a favourite peacock, Hervey saw that she wore not the saree but something divided, allowing her to walk with singular grace. In consequence he almost failed to hear the rajah's enquiry as to how he liked the aviary, and thereafter he was all attention as they processed back to the palace down an avenue of deodars. 'My grandfather grew them from seeds brought from a great hunting expedition to Kumaon,' said the rajah, with no little pride.

The raj kumari herself had shown no dismay on seeing Locke's face. She spoke with warm civility, unafraid to look at him fully as they talked of this and that brightly feathered species in the aviary. Hervey saw nothing but the same warmth as that of her father, nothing that suggested a need for the circumspection Selden had advocated.

The tamasha that evening was a regalement such that Hervey and Locke might never forget – as, indeed, was the rajah's intention. The brilliance of the hundreds of candles and scented oil lamps, reflected by the white marble in the great dining chamber, seemed no less than the midday sun. The guests sat on cushions at a low table covered by a richly embroidered white cloth, on which were laid dishes of pomegranates, grapes and jujubes. To Hervey was accorded the honour of sitting on the rajah's right, while Locke was seated to the raj kumari's left, she herself being next to her father. Selden, who sat at the angle of the table, but in view of their host, had correctly predicted this arrangement, explaining to them that, unlike in other native, even princely, households, the raj kumari did not take a retiring role. Her mother, the ranee, had died within a year of labour – a conception for which there had been many years' unanswered prayers – and the rajah had placed the overseeing of the palace in her trust from an early age, while he had withdrawn increasingly to his menagerie and his library. He had even shown less pleasure in the chase of late, though this was, thought Selden, because he disliked leaving the palace, fearing perhaps that on his return he would find it no longer in his hands, the possession instead of the nizam or one of his acolytes. Throughout his life, and his father's before him, Haidarabad had laid claim to Chintal, a claim which, had not the late Maratha war diverted him, the nizam might by now have made good.

But this evening the rajah was in good spirits. Musicians in a gallery at the other end of the chamber played lively ragas, and there was laughter among the two dozen courtiers enjoying his hospitality. A well-drilled troop of khitmagars brought more fruit to the table: oranges, peeled and dusted with ginger, finger-lengths of tender young sugar cane, and mangoes whose soft, peach-coloured flesh and abundant juice especially became the evening's sensuality.

'I am informed, Captain Hervey,' said the rajah, casting an eye over the procession, 'that in England you would not begin a feast with sweet things, that you must earn sweetness, so to speak, by progression through much sourness – as in life itself. But in India we have no such coyness in our pleasures. We have each earned title to indulgence in this incarnation through preparation in earlier ones.'

Hervey was as much engaged by the elegance of the rajah's phrasing as he was intrigued by his theology. 'You know, sir,' he replied, with considerable delicacy, 'that our religion holds these things differently.'

'And I shall look forward keenly to our being able to speak on these matters, for you are the son of a sadhu, a priest, I am informed – whereas Mr Selden, there,' he nodded, smiling, 'is as much an atheist as was my tutor.'

'Your tutor an atheist, sir? Mr Selden informed me that he was a fellow of Cambridge.'

'Oh, indeed – both. He was sent down along with Coleridge for his opinions. Do you like Coleridge's poetry, Captain Hervey?'

'Very much, sir,' replied the latter, hoping to conceal his surprise at hearing of Coleridge here.

'I am much diverted by the notion of his enlisting in the cavalry afterwards. It was not your regiment, was it, by some chance?'

'No, sir,' said Hervey, even more surprised. 'His was the Fifteenth Light Dragoons, and mine the Sixth. He was, by his own admission, a very indifferent equestrian!'

'It is as well, Captain Hervey, otherwise we should have been deprived of some sublime poetry.'

'Just so, sir,' agreed the other, but with a resigned smile, for the rajah evidently held the two to be incompatible occupations.

However, the rajah did not press the matter, returning instead to the subject of his gardens and menagerie, and the plans he had for their enlargement. The khitmagars entered once more in procession. 'These will delight you especially, Captain Hervey,' he smiled, as one of them proffered a salver. '*Mandaliya*. I have a cook from Bengal who makes it as no other I know. There is nothing else of worth in Bengal, I assure you, Captain Hervey!' he added with an even broader smile. 'He takes the entrails from only the youngest of lambs and then fills them with marrow and a mixture of spices known only to him, and then he roasts them over charcoal. They are the very apotheosis of taste, are they not?'

Hervey agreed readily, and he would have indulged himself liberally had he not a concern for how many such dishes he would have to savour before the feast was ended. He glanced across at Selden and saw him eating modestly, and then at Locke, who was attending to each dish as if it were his last.

'Why are you come to India, Captain Hervey?' asked the rajah suddenly, though without trace of anything but approval.

He sighed inwardly. He had no wish to deceive this generous and civilized man. 'I believe you will have heard of Sir Arthur Wellesley?' he began.

'The Duke of Wellington?' replied the rajah.

He was much embarrassed by his presuming the rajah's ignorance. 'I am very sorry, sir; I had no reason to suppose that the duke's elevation to the peerage would have been of interest in Chintal.'

'But indeed it is,' replied the rajah. 'The duke rid India of the Maratha plague – Sindhia and Barjee Rao, and the other devils. I met him once, in the company of his then more illustrious brother. I was gratified to see him made a marquess, and then duke. Are you acquainted with him?'

'Not intimately, sir. I am recently appointed aide-de-camp, a very junior capacity, and am sent here to learn the employment of the lance. We suffered from it at the hands of the French, and the duke intends forming lancer regiments forthwith.'

'*Indeed*,' was all that the rajah would say by reply, although after a while he appeared to remember his own lancers. 'My sowars would be able to instruct you most ably,' he said, nodding.

'I am grateful, sir. I believe I have also heard that the nizam's cavalry have lances.' Hervey wished at once he had not said it – a clumsy stratagem.

The rajah, after the briefest flicker of consternation, recovered his composure. 'You may know that we are to receive the nizam in Chintalpore in a month's time,' he said, dipping his fingers in a bowl of scented water.

'Mr Selden so informed me, sir.'

'We hope to show him some sport.' And he embarked on a lengthy praise of Chintal's hunting promise.

The musicians were by now less animated in their playing. A leisurely tala weaved its way in and out of the conversations around the rajah's table, a perfect accompaniment to the sweet confections now brought by the khitmagars – sweeter even than the madhuparka in the Venetian glasses.

'But on the matter of the Duke of Wellington's bidding,' said the rajah at length, and seemingly absently, 'there may be some quality that the duke seeks in *numbers*: the nizam's cavalry has the most lancers in all India.'

'So I am informed, sir. But in terms of how well the weapon itself is handled, and how handily are the rissalahs trained, I understand the Company's irregulars too have much to teach.'

The rajah nodded. 'And in our own modest way, Chintal may boast of a handy rissalah. Indeed, you saw some upon your arrival today, did you not? Though they stood at the gates of the palace for ceremony.'

'And, may I say, sir, their bearing does them great credit. I should much like to see them at exercise.'

'Then you shall, Captain Hervey,' replied the rajah. 'You are our guest: I would not suspend any pleasure of yours that it is in my power to prolong.'

One of those pleasures was the fine claret which the rajah kept. But Hervey was abstemious, for not only was its taste ill-matched to the harlequin dishes paraded before them, he was uncertain of the potency of the madhuparka. He could afford no indiscretion which might suggest his mission were any more than he had declared, especially having once aroused, if not the rajah's suspicion, then certainly his curiosity. The same was not the case with Locke, however, whose robust spirits seemed wholly pleasing nevertheless to the raj kumari.

The rajah spoke of hunting again: Hervey would not leave Chintal without a tigerskin, he promised, as bowls filled with boiled rice, dyed with saffron and much spiced, were placed before them. They talked of tiger and leopard and the wild boar, and the differing dangers and pleasures in the pursuit of each. And much satisfaction the rajah seemed to gain from Hervey's keen anticipation.

A light soup followed, and then all was cleared, bowls of hot water scented with lotus flowers were brought, and the rajah began speaking of his stables, of the merits and otherwise of the Arab and the Turkoman when compared with the native breeds – the Kathiawar, Marwari and Waziri. And the air was then filled with yet more, and different, scents as perfumed dishes of curds were laid before them, and the musicians once again became lively, an insistent tabla presaging a turn in the course of the evening. The rajah's guests ate greedily, even after so much, and when the curds were gone a whole army of khitmagars crowded in to sweep away the residue of the feast so that the entertainment might begin.

The raj kumari herself had arranged their evening's diversions, explained the rajah. First came an elaborate nautch in which twelve tall, extravagantly dressed girls moved about the wide floor of the banquet chamber with a grace the like of which Hervey had never seen, as if floating – bending this way and that like tall grass in a breeze. From neck to ankle, they were aflash with mirrors, bracelets and rings, and in each bare navel shone an emerald.

'They are come from Maharashtra for the delectation of the nizam when he visits,' explained the rajah. 'I am pleased to see you approve, Captain Hervey.'

How could he not approve? 'I do not think I ever beheld a more beautiful sight, Your Highness!'

Henry Locke was altogether transported, and even Selden seemed rapt. The nautch girls danced for a quarter of an hour without respite, leisurely in all their movements, mistresses of time as well as of their sinewy muscles; until, though it was grown very warm, their spirited climax of much shaking and turning brought to a sudden end the now frantic raga – and with it the prostration of the dancers. There was great applause and calls of approval, and the dancers stood as one and bowed low to their audience. That they did not smile only added to their allure. Truly, he confided again, he had never seen anything so exquisite!

The entertainment next took a less elevated form. A half-naked, wiry little man entered carrying a basket and a caged mongoose. 'A vulgar thing of the bazaar, Captain Hervey,' smiled the rajah indulgently, 'to fascinate the indigent of the country and visitor alike. You may now write home to tell of your seeing a snake-charmer.'

He was puzzled by the rajah's need to explain, but thought it kindly meant. The wiry little man placed the basket not a dozen paces before them, and the cage to one side, then sat on the floor, crossing his legs. He took a pipe from the waist of his dhoti, removed the lid of the basket and began to play. The mongoose at once began jumping up and down excitedly, urinating as it did so – to the amusement of the guests – and soon from the basket came the head of a snake, drawn, it seemed, by the pipe's lugubrious melody. It was not, to Hervey's mind, of any great size, but it was no rat snake, for its spreading hood was unmistakable.

'The *cobra di capello*, Captain Hervey,' said the rajah; 'prettily named is it not? – by the Portuguese when they built their missions on the Malabar coast.'

Hervey recalled it well enough from his schoolroom lessons in natural history.

The rajah sensed that he had expected to see a more impressive reptile, and sounded a note of warning. 'Be assured, Captain Hervey, that the cobra, if its fangs could pierce the skin, has enough venom to kill an elephant.'

Hervey looked suitably warned. Indeed, he looked mildly alarmed.

'Do not concern yourself though,' smiled the rajah. 'The cobra's mouth is sewn together.'

The raj kumari leaned Hervey's way a little. 'To see the largest – the king of cobras – Captain Hervey,' she began conspiratorially, 'you must go into the forest. There it is called the hamadryad. You must understand why?'

He did. But Locke looked puzzled, leaving Hervey to whisper as best he could, 'Wood nymph – Greeks – dies with the tree? Remember?'

Locke nodded in faint but indifferent recollection of his Shrewsbury classicals.

Once the rajah was satisfied that Hervey understood the principles of the art before him, he waved for the little man to cease his playing. The cobra descended at once into the basket, and the mongoose, which had not let up its jumping and turning throughout the performance, settled quietly on the floor of its cage.

'My groom would be delighted by the mongoose, Your Highness,' said Hervey, smiling. 'He is inordinately fond of ferrets, an animal very akin to this.'

'Is he here in Chintalpore with you?' asked the rajah.

'No, sir: he remained in Guntoor with my charger. But I am assured he will soon arrive.'

'I am very glad of it, for I hope that you will avail yourself of our hospitality for some time yet,' for, declared the rajah, he was in constant want of conversation since the demise of his tutor some years past.

And then curiously, as if to be done with every vestige of the grace and dignity that the Maharashtri nautch had given the evening, there came a raucous chorus of voices the like of which Hervey had never heard, accompanied by cymbals and tambours in a fearful cacophony. The voices wore sarees of the gaudiest colours imaginable, festooned with bangles, necklaces and ankle bells. They were taller even than the nautch girls, and older. Some, indeed, were counted in riper years. They were as thin as laths, without any of the voluptuousness of the nautch. And their singing – if such it could rightly be called – was incomprehensible, their husky voices rhythmically repeating words that Hervey sensed had little meaning. They were to the nautch, indeed, as sackcloth was to silk.

They did not dance, they cavorted. Cavorted for a full five minutes. And their gestures became increasingly lewd until the rajah, smiling indulgently, clapped his hands and shooed them away, at which they besieged the seated audience with little begging bowls – and made hissing noises if they considered the contributions mean. As they recessed to the outer chamber, keeping up the cacophony still, Hervey, astonished by so tawdry (but undeniably amusing) an intrusion, asked the raj kumari who they were. She, like her father before, smiled indulgently. 'They are known variously, but we call them *hijdas*.'

Hervey was unenlightened. 'Meaning?'

'It is an Urdu word – "neither one thing nor the other".'

Still Hervey had not understood.

'Neither male nor female,' she explained with a sigh.

His embarrassment made her smile.

'They appear from nowhere at gatherings such as this – weddings, tamashas. They make a great deal of noise and accept money to go

154

away. They always seem to know when there is such an assembly, but I suspect that your Mr Selden told them of this evening. He enjoys their confidence.'

Hervey looked across at Selden, who seemed content.

'There is a small company of hijdas in Chintalpore, though their greatest number is in Haidarabad, for they are in truth more relics of the Mughal court.'

'Will they come when the nizam visits?' asked Hervey.

'You may be assured of it,' replied the raj kumari with a smile; 'whether invited or not. And they will expect generous alms from so rich a ruler and his following.'

When the last strains of the hijdas' chorus were gone, the rajah and the raj kumari took their leave, satisfied that the banquet had been a worthy gratuity for the service which Hervey had rendered the favoured elephant. The rajah looked forward, he insisted once again, to being able to continue that hospitality in a manner especially appropriate for one of Hervey's calling, 'for I believe you will hold with me that hunting is the most noble of our pleasures.'

Hervey thanked him fulsomely.

The raj kumari bowed, smiling also, and thanked him once more for his present of the tushes. 'They are a handsome trophy, Captain Hervey. And you won them without permitting my Gita to suffer a single mark. Truly, the English are not to be trifled with!'

'Take a turn with me about the gardens,' said Selden as the khansamah's men began the lengthy business of extinguishing the candles and oil lamps.

Hervey was glad of both the air and the chance of broaching at last the subject of his being there. When they were outside, and some distance from the ears of the palace itself, Selden gave his opinion of the evening. 'The rajah has, quite evidently, taken to you. But I observed him closely as he questioned you on your purpose in coming to India, and I don't think he was disposed to believing that your mission is concerned solely with the lance. As, indeed, do I not. The rajah is perforce both hospitable to and suspicious of strangers. He knows – without doubt – of the Wellesleys' late affinity with the nizam, and it will not be beyond possibility that he is thinking of your being an agent of Haidarabad.'

This he had not imagined. He felt at once anxious as he realized that

155

had he first made contact with Bazzard in Calcutta he would have been forewarned of this diplomatic complication.

'The Pindarees are again making depredations on Chintal's borders,' continued Selden. 'The rajah bought them off last year but they've paid his gold little heed. It can't be long before they come within, for his forces would be hard-pressed to deal with them without leaving Chintalpore open to attack from the west, from Haidarabad.'

Hervey looked about him, anxious there might be ears closer than the palace. His mind was beginning to race and he tried hard to check it as it dawned on him how awkward was his predicament – and of his own making. 'Selden, may we speak in absolute confidence?'

'Here is as good as anywhere,' shrugged the salutri.

'I mean, may I divulge things to you confident they will go no further?'

Selden paused only for an instant. 'I would never betray anything that might harm my country – on no account. But if it is something that might harm the rajah then I beg you would not try my loyalty.'

Hervey took the plunge he knew must come. 'The duke has title to several jagirs in Chintal. They're governed on his behalf by an official of the Company's in Calcutta.'

'Is this of great moment?' asked Selden, the tone a shade bemused.

'I don't know. All I have need to know is that the duke wishes to dispose of them in as discreet a manner as possible.' Never did Hervey imagine he would dislike a business so.

'If he has an agent in Calcutta, why should you be concerned in this?'

'Again, I don't know why. I understand that not even the jagirs' steward here in Chintal knows their true ownership. It's the duke's wish that they are disposed of as advantageously as possible, within Chintal, and that their former title remain privy.'

Selden inclined his head in a manner that suggested he was now well apprised of Hervey's purpose. 'And you wish me to assist in this disposal?'

'Yes,' said Hervey quietly, but emphatically.

Selden sucked his cheeks. 'So your meeting with me was not coincident: you sought me out?'

'The meeting on the Sukri was *entirely* coincident, but my orders were that I should go to Calcutta and meet an agent of the duke's. He was to see to my entry here. I told you about our diversion to Madras;

it seemed opportune when I did meet you, and little point then in my going to Calcutta. It was a misjudgement, I see now.'

'Indeed,' nodded Selden, '*quite* a misjudgement! There might no longer be the glittering path ahead, then?' The tone was of sympathy, even if a little brutal.

Hervey hardly needed reminding of the personal consequences.

'And so, who now has the title deeds?' he asked, wanting to pick something from the ashes.

'I do,' replied Hervey, quick to respond to the suggestion of help. 'But since they bear the duke's name they will need to be transferred through a third party. My instructions were to request that you yourself fulfil that role. And, further, that you ensure any reference to the duke in the land registry is expunged.'

Selden smiled. 'Hervey, you – or, I suppose, the duke's agents – astonish me. Assuming that I would have access to the registry, you would wish me, say, to spill a bottle of ink on the offending page – or to set the entire ledger alight?'

'Whatever is necessary,' he replied bluntly; 'but my principal had hoped that the original document might be delivered up to him. He is quite willing to meet all expenses.' This last troubled him. He had rehearsed it many times so that it might be rendered lightly, but it smacked none the less of a crude bribe.

Selden saved him further discomfort by ignoring it – at least, on the surface. 'My dear Hervey, I think it time I made a clean breast of one or two things too.' They sat on a low wall by one of the fountains, its fall of water a further aid to their seclusion. 'Now,' he began, dabbing at the edge of his mouth with a silk square, 'you must not suppose me to occupy any great office of state here – or even position of influence.'

Hervey looked worried. 'But—'

'Let me finish. I am the rajah's salutri. There are few of us in India, and most of them are quacks, men who would scarce make a good farrier's assistant. I know my worth in this respect, and so, I flatter myself, does the rajah. I am the only Englishman at his court, and since he places his trust in my facility with his horses he is inclined to seek my opinion on other matters. He's not obliged to take it, of course.'

Hervey was not now so discouraged, but it was far from what he might have wished. 'And do you have dealings with the Company?'

'I am not a spy, if that's what you mean. Periodically I have given my opinion on this matter or that when in Calcutta – as any loyal subject of the King would.'

Hervey thought for a moment, for Selden evidently had more to give. 'Are you therefore able to help me dispose of the jagirs?' he asked plainly.

Selden smiled again. 'One of the many things I have learned in India is that what one supposes to be a secret is known as often in the bazaars.'

'Are you telling me that the duke's title to them is known of?'

'Not, I suspect, in the bazaars, but the rajah knows – certainly.'

'Oh,' sighed Hervey, now even more anxious that his misjudgement would see his mission come to nought.

'The jagirs are, indeed, something of an insurance to him.'

'How so?'

'The rajah has always supposed that as long as the Wellesley family held title to land in Chintal the country would be secure from predation by others.'

'You mean he expects the Company would be prevailed on to come to his aid?'

'Just so.'

'I'm astonished. It would be little better than—'

'There you go again, Matthew Hervey: false civilization, still to be sweated out!'

He frowned. 'You will tell me next that the duke is somehow a party to this pretence!'

'I would presume no such thing,' replied Selden, a little archly. 'But I tell you two things – or, rather, I *ask* you one thing first.'

'Very well then,' said Hervey, squarely.

'Ask yourself why the duke has jagirs here in the first place.'

'Is there reason why he should not? His family has wealth, and he was here a half-dozen years.'

'Quite so,' conceded Selden. 'You have heard of Seringapatam?'

'Of course: the Sixth still spoke of it when I joined.'

'And well they might – the loot was prodigious!'

'What has that to do with the duke? He put a stop to as much of it as he could, as is commonly known.'

Selden looked thoughtful for a moment. 'See here, Hervey: I have no wish to sully the name of a great man – and one you serve so admirably. But there are persistent stories in India that he sequestered

158

some of the prize-money that should by rights have gone to General Baird, the man whom he superseded after the capture of the fortress, and it's supposed that the Chintal jagirs are part of that . . . shall we say, *artifice*? Do you not suppose that that might account in some degree for the needy discretion in disposing of them?'

Hervey protested that there were too many suppositions.

'And I must further inform you,' pressed Selden, 'that the jagirs themselves have yielded meagre revenues these past years. The rajah supplements them handsomely.'

Slowly it began to occur to him that he might have been kept in the dark by Colonel Grant for no better reason than to conceal something that was – at best – unbecoming. And then he tumbled to the notion – but prayed it was not true – that his mission to gauge the effectiveness of the nizam's army was no more than a diversion. He sighed heavily. How clever of the duke's chief of intelligence if it were so, for in conniving with him at the diversion of the lance, he diverted himself from the truth that the business of the jagirs was Grant's real purpose – and an infamous one at that.

Still he did not dare share this with Selden. Yet his look must have spoken of some sense of betrayal, for the salutri placed a hand on his shoulder and warned him of the consequences of judging things too keenly. 'For I dare say the duke believed he did nothing dishonourable. He broke the Marathas at what might have been no little cost to his reputation, or even his life, had things not gone well. "To the victor the spoils", Hervey!'

It was all supposition in any case. And, indeed, Hervey could ill afford too many scruples in his position.

Selden was prepared to agree with him – for the purposes, at least, of lifting his spirits for the time being. 'Who, by the way, were you to meet with in Calcutta?'

Hervey wondered if this were information he might not rightly divulge. 'I think it better if—'

'It wasn't Bazzard, was it?'

'Why do you name him?'

Hervey's surprise encouraged Selden to assume it was. 'Because he is the writer who forwards the revenues to London.'

'I should not say more.'

'It makes no difference, my dear fellow,' frowned Selden, 'for Bazzard has been dead these past three months.'

'*Dead?* You mean . . . *killed?*'

'By the fever.'

Hervey saw at once some mitigation of his misjudgement. Going to Calcutta would have proved fruitless after all. A pity he had written already to Grant telling him it was his own choice. But at the same time the death of Bazzard meant the loss of his best means of recovering the situation. A picket officer's duty in the Paris garrison seemed suddenly attractive compared with aiglets. At length he steeled himself to his purpose in Chintalpore: 'Do I assume from this you are unable, and unwilling, to help me dispose of the jagirs?'

Selden let out a deep sigh. 'Hervey, I'm not sure I would do this for anyone else. Let us not be too sentimental by recalling Androcles and the lion, but you were rare among your fellow officers in showing me more than sufferance. I have no notion how to begin the jagirs business, but begin I shall. It will take time, though. And meanwhile I advise you to be most attentive to the rajah, and not to give him any grounds to suspect you have come on business other than the lance. Play the simple soldier, in heaven's name!'

CHAPTER TEN

THE BOURRH LANDS

A few days later

'Choose which you would, Captain Hervey,' said the rajah. 'You will have an eye for quality, and Mr Selden has told you of the requirements for hunting the boar.'

The rajah's stables were indeed full of quality, and punkahs in each stall drove air over the fifty saddle-horses that were his pride. However, he had had all the stall-names covered for Hervey's visit so that he might choose one horse above the rest without knowing anything of them (though since the Sanskrit names were written in the Devanagari script he could hardly have gained anything from seeing them).

'A greater test than merely spearing the biggest boar,' Selden had smiled as Hervey began to appraise each animal.

Fifty horses and ponies, perhaps two minutes to run over each – there were two whole hours before them, unless he was to come across perfection before then. The trouble was that he knew little enough about the Arab, let alone the other breeds, to make a choice. What made one better than another? All he could do, therefore, was apply the trusted principle of eye, wind and limb. Wind would have to be judged by depth of chest alone. As for limb, the feet, and leg blemishes, seemed his safest indicators, since these were horses too superior to possess significant faults of conformation. Up and down the lines he went, into each stall – Arab, Turkoman, country-bred, Akhal Tekke (much prized for their legendary endurance) and the hardy Khatgani from Afghanistan. He looked at every eye. More, even, than with a man or a woman, it could tell so much. He glanced at the chest and ran a hand up and down the legs, then looked at each foot, lifting one here and there. It took him the best part of two hours, but no one – the rajah especially – showed the least concern, until at length he chose a jet-black Turkoman gelding, about fifteen and a half hands.

'Why do you choose him?' asked the rajah.

'Your Highness,' replied Hervey, his hesitation speaking of the difficulty he had, 'I could say that it was his quarters, which seem especially powerful, and his legs, which look to me to have exactly the right amount of bone to make him at once both hardy and fleet. His chest is deep; I like his head, too, which is set on well, and gives him a most noble appearance. But above all, this horse has a look of intelligence. His eye says to me that he would see what I could not, and would take the right course in spite of my inaptness.'

Selden had smiled broadly during the verdict, the reason apparent when the rajah clapped his hands together and made a little sound of delight. 'Truly, Captain Hervey, I could not better have expressed why this gelding is my own favourite. And you shall ride him when we hunt the boar. His name is Badshah.'

'"The King"?' replied Hervey; 'Your Highness, I am greatly honoured.'

Next day, Private Johnson arrived with Jessye and two bat-horses carrying the remainder of Hervey's baggage in yakhdans almost as big as the horses themselves. He had lost no time in setting out, but progress from Guntoor to Chintalpore – a full ninety miles – had been slow. As soon as Cornet Templer had returned with Hervey's message to join him, Johnson had assembled his little equipage and demanded that one of the sepoys accompany him as guide. This brought no great advantage, however, for the Madrasi sepoy had no English – though even had he been able to speak it tolerably well he would have found that Johnson's vowels and the truncation of his consonants rendered his speech incomprehensible. There was certainly little chance that Johnson himself had acquired any native words that might have aided discourse: four years in Spain had not seen him with more than a dozen, and these of a basic, alimentary, nature. And yet, as they arrived at the gates of the rajah's palace, where Hervey was just returned from morning exercise with the lancers of the palace guard, Johnson and the sepoy, formerly a cinnamon-peeler from the southernmost part of the presidency, were enjoying some joke together.

Later, as he and Hervey were sluicing a hot but still fresh-looking Jessye, with the aid of a chain of syces passing buckets from one of the running-tanks, Johnson at last spoke his mind. 'Captain 'Ervey, sir, what are we *doin*' 'ere? I thought we was gooin' to Calcutta.'

Hervey paused before answering, but he had already concluded that it was time to take his groom into his confidence. 'See here, Johnson,' he said at length. 'I will tell you all we're about, since I may have to rely on you to act independently, and you'll be no earthly good if you don't know everything.'

Once in the seclusion of Jessye's stall, Hervey began to explain his purpose, while Johnson continued with the sweat-scraper as if it were nothing of any moment. The best way to judge the nizam's general disposition, suggested Hervey, was indirectly, by observing him during the coming visit to Chintalpore. And as for the business of expunging all trace of the jagirs – well, he would have to trust to Selden's address. 'And so, in the circumstances the very best thing is to remain here in Chintalpore for the time being. If I were to go directly to Haidarabad I don't see that it could fail to arouse suspicion, both here *and* there.'

'Tha knows best, Captain 'Ervey, sir,' shrugged Johnson, taking a stable rubber to Jessye's head. 'But tha's in a spot o' bother right enough.'

The environs of Chintalpore were not the best hunting grounds, but a dozen or so miles to the north, across the Godavari river, at the jungle's edge, there was game to be had in large numbers in the sandy undulating downs – the bourrh lands. Here, gaur (or bison, as some knew them) left the seclusion of the dense forest occasionally to graze. Muggurs sulked on the shoals, great gaggles of wild geese crossed the sky in one direction and then another, and the sorrowful cries of Brahminy ducks made the solitude yet more desolate. Hervey was captivated by its wild emptiness. The far-distant forest, the small scattered groves of mangoes, with here and there a lordly banyan rising unmistakably above the jhow, but above all the graceful palmyra palm, told him they were elsewhere than the Great Plain of his own county.

But the emptiness of that wonderful downland came at once to mind, and his rides there with Daniel Coates. How *he* would love the talk of horses, of reading the country and the pursuit of so worthy an opponent as the boar.

Selden closed up. His horse's ears were pricked, nostrils flexing at what the country promised. '*Agar firdos bah rue zameen ast, Hameen ast, wa hameen ast, wa hameen ast!*'

Some of the words were familiar, and so sensuous that the English must surely be as arresting. 'Meaning?' enquired Hervey simply.

The salutri smiled. 'An old Persian couplet: "If there is a paradise on earth, It is this, it is this, it is this!"' He smiled broadly. 'Ride hard, Matthew Hervey!'

The rajah was unusual in his pleasure in the chase, Selden had explained, for in his experience princely Indians had no great appetite for it – and those who had, confined themselves largely to the pursuit of tiger from the lofty vantage of the howdah. The rajah's favourite hunting ground for pig was the Sukri kadir, where Hervey had first made his acquaintance with Chintal, but the bourrh lands were within a day's ride and could provide sport for his lancer officers – although compared with the Sukri kadir the country was rather too treacherous for his liking. He explained that the rissalahs were soon to take to the field for their last drill before the onset of the hot season, and today was the rajah's last opportunity to give them a run.

The mounted party numbered near twenty, the rajah himself accompanied by a jemadar and an orderly. The raj kumari, who rode astride, as Selden had told him, was escorted by one of the shikaris as pilot – an express provision of the rajah rather than of her own choosing. She carried a jobbing spear, but only to gain first blood with, for to hold off a charging boar required every ounce of a man's strength. Her pilot was therefore her covering-spear. Locke, Selden and Hervey were accompanied by six of the lancer officers, by any measure an intriguing group. The commandant (as in Chintal the commanding officer was called) was a Piedmontese, a minor member of the House of Savoy who, shamed at the surrender of Turin to Bonaparte seventeen years earlier, had come east. Hervey liked him from first meeting. Commandant Cadorna was about Joseph Edmonds's age, and it was this connection, perhaps, as much as anything that accounted for the immediate affinity. Cadorna's captain was German, a Württemberger who had likewise sought his fortune elsewhere once the Confederation of the Rhine had required him otherwise to take an oath of loyalty to his former enemy. Captain Steuben was not many years older than Hervey, but his face was lined and sun-dried, and unlike his commandant he spoke no English. Yet he seemed to have little regard for Hervey's facility with his own language. Indeed, he seemed almost to resent it, displaying a distinct coldness from their first meeting at the rajah's banquet. Hervey was doubly puzzled by this want of the fellowship of the 'yellow circle' – the universal spirit of the cavalry – but for the time being at least was content to let it pass. The third European officer was another Württemberger, but of a different stamp. A big, coarse-featured man with a walrus moustache, he littered his speech – a blend of German, English and Urdu – with expletives in the fashion of the serjeant-major he had once been. Captain Bauer, *Alter Fritz* as this venerable old soldier, now the rissalah's quartermaster, was known, had come to India not by choice but as a prisoner of the British. He had enlisted in a regiment of mercenary infantry for Dutch service and had been taken captive at the Cape twenty years ago, remaining a prisoner until the regiment was disbanded in Ceylon thirteen years later. But Alter Fritz bore the British no ill will. Besides his fair treatment, he explained, his incarceration had kept him from the campaign of 1812, which had seen a whole corps of Württembergers in Bonaparte's service reduced to but a few dozen by the end of the winter's march from Moscow. The three native officers were fine-looking men who sat their horses well. All of them – native and European – wore jacked boots, white breeches and green kurta, and the saffron sasa which was the distinctive headdress of the rajah's cavalry. Commandant Cadorna, Selden explained, was not only commanding officer of the cavalry but in overall command of the little army of Chintal. His rissalahs, together with the infantry (commanded by two German officers and a Swede), were housed in cantonments built lately some ten miles east of Chintalpore, whence the officers had ridden that morning.

It took but two hours to reach the place where the rajah hoped to give them their sport. He was at first discomposed by the sickness of the shikari who knew the lands best, but he was confident nevertheless they would be able to find game enough to give some memorable runs. For the finest sport they should have been here at dawn, said Selden, but the day was hastily arranged: a *proper* bandobast could not be improvised. The shikaris had been out the day before to reconnoitre, however, and to visit the villages to recruit the long line of beaters which he pointed out to their front. 'They will be hidden from view in the jhow for most of the time, but you will always tell their whereabouts from the chief shikari on the big she-elephant in the middle of the line. He is the man on whom our sport depends.'

Unlike a line beating *on*to guns, this line was silent, and the spears now quietly took up their places to the rear of the beaters at intervals of thirty yards. When all were in position, the rajah – with Hervey away to his right – nodded to the chief shikari. He in turn waved a white flag, signalling the line to begin its stealthy advance to take by surprise – they hoped – a lone boar. Hervey could scarcely bear the wait; like scouting, when at any second the hunter might become the hunted, with the numbing surprise of the ambuscade. He felt more alive than ever. He looked to his right, where the raj kumari stood with her pilot. He had never seen a woman ride astride, her legs covered for most of their sinuous length in silk, the sweat from her pony's flanks ensuring the cloth traced their form faithfully. His thoughts were as primal as the chase itself.

Suddenly there was pandemonium – grunting, squealing, shouting. A big sounder had burst, and everywhere was pig. But neither the rajah nor the raj kumari moved, for the line was the commandant's and the officers' on the right. They spurred headlong after the boar, crying 'On! On! On!' and Hervey was only able to contain Badshah with a struggle, anxious not to have him bolt in front of the rajah. The chase did not last long. Perhaps the boar was reluctant to leave the sounder, and hesitated just a fraction too late before making for the cover of some jhow, but Commandant Cadorna stopped him in his tracks by a deft thrust with a jobbing spear between the shoulders.

'I don't suppose there will be any pig left in miles of here now,' sighed Hervey as Selden rode up.

'Do not imagine it!' replied the salutri, looking pleased there had been an early and successful run. 'There will be pig aplenty, I assure you!'

Bearers strung the boar to carrying poles and trotted back towards the rajah to display the first blood. He was big, though not quite as big as the one Hervey had sabred. The rajah was pleased and signalled for the beaters to form line again. Spears began taking post to the rear, as before. The raj kumari rode over and asked Hervey if the tushes he had presented her had been so quickly won, and he answered that they had not, confessing to the impasse of sabre and indestructible boar. She had not spoken much since the banquet, though he had sensed her surveillance as he walked each day in the water gardens. Selden's warning had been prescient, for there was something in her manner which said she distrusted him. On the other hand, she had engaged Henry Locke in the most animated of conversation whenever she had seen him, even encouraging him in his fledgling dalliance with one of the nautch girls. Now the first sounder was burst, there was an easing, and she seemed more candid. Indeed, for a few minutes at least they spoke freely and agreeably of the natural history of the bourrh lands. But the potency of her allure was overmatched for just this. Her black hair fell about her shoulders, and there were flecks of red dust on her face, thrown up in the gallop to see the commandant's kill. She had a look as wild as the Spanish women who rode with their guerrilla lovers. They were raw peasant girls, however – gypsies. *Her* allure was the more for its high-born underlay. Here was danger as exquisite as the cobra that had swayed this way and that at the rajah's banquet. Hervey knew it, and was on his guard, but was fascinated nevertheless.

Silence once more descended on the company as the white flag from the centre of the line signalled another drive. They advanced with scarcely a sound for almost two hundred yards, through grass so high in places that the beaters were entirely lost from sight. Ahead was a particularly dense patch of jhow – uncut tamarisk grown to about twenty feet, with prolific sideshoots difficult to ride through. Hervey knew there would be pig here; and it would be his line, too. His blood coursed twice as fast, energizing muscle and heightening the senses.

Out burst another sounder – smaller, faster. On the rajah's line, though, but giving Hervey a run as second. The rajah fixed on the boar at once; Hervey slapped Badshah's quarters with the bamboo shaft of his spear and dug his spurs into his flanks. The gelding sprang forward like a leopard, flattening in a few strides to a gallop. 'Keep behind and to the side and at a right angle to the boar's line!' He could hear Selden still. He made up ground with the rajah in under a minute, and when he was almost in line he hooked back just enough to keep in place, settling to a hand-gallop.

He looked right. There was the raj kumari, pilot at her side. Her little Arab pony – the one he had sabred the Sukri pig from – raced head low through the long grass, and the raj kumari's hair flew like streamers, her legs long in the stirrups but quite still, even at that taxing pace. Hervey looked ahead and to his left: the rajah was almost on the boar. Then it jinked right so quickly that he overshot it. It ran obliquely across Hervey's front, thirty yards ahead. It couldn't have been making for cover, for there was none in sight. He pressed Badshah to charge for what he was certain must be a kill. The gelding's stride lengthened once more and in another hundred yards he had closed with it. Hervey stood in the stirrups and raised his spear to job well forward. The boar jinked left so sharply in front of his line that Badshah jumped to clear it. Hervey was astonished as he gathered back the reins, for the horse could have had no sight of the pig so close in and must have jumped by some instinct. Nor was it the end, for although they had overshot, the gelding had of his own made a flying change to the nearside leg and was already turning onto the pig's new line. Hervey glanced right, left and behind. The raj kumari had likewise overshot. Behind him the rajah was circling and about to come onto the old line. The boar himself was well clear of their front and heading away on the left, putting the rajah's jemadar now on his line. That officer lost no time spurring for his quarry and claiming it – 'On! On! On!' Hervey galloped after him, determined to be close enough to spear the boar when – as he expected – it jinked back right. Badshah needed no telling to keep the line, and he gave him all the rein he wanted. It was only the third time he had ridden him but he trusted him as much as Jessye. They covered the best part of a mile at a furious pace, the pig running straight and showing no sign of tiring, until Hervey was only thirty yards behind.

Then suddenly the jemadar was gone – disappeared. A second later and Hervey almost went too. Badshah lost his footing, the near-fore slipping and throwing all Hervey's weight to the left – when the horse needed all he could on the right. They were going in – into a chasm as black as Hades. A fraction of a second and every bone must be broken. And then somehow Hervey was on Badshah's neck the other side. How in heaven's name . . . he had cat-leapt, on three legs, at a gallop, with weight bearing on the wrong foot! 'What a horse! What a horse!' was all Hervey could say as they scrambled to recover. He turned at once, springing from the saddle when he reached the chasm's edge. He looked down – into a well thirty feet across. And in the water, a full twelve feet below, his eye lighted on the astonishing sight of the jemadar, his horse and the boar, each desperately treading water.

He raced down the steps still carrying his spear, relieved to find just enough space on the ledge to haul out the jemadar, whose shoulder was badly broken. The horse was frantic. Whereas Jessye might have swum placidly round and round, confident of her rider's purpose, the jemadar's desert-bred Arab was wild-eyed and squealing with fear. The boar, enraged or equally fearful of the water (though Selden had told him what prodigiously good swimmers pigs were), was squealing and grunting in equal measure. Hervey picked up his spear and edged to the other side where the animal tried to scramble out. He stabbed between its shoulders with all the force he could manage, the spear going in deep and the water at once turning red. The boar struggled furiously, but this time Hervey hadn't the secure seat in which to brace himself until it collapsed. He lost his footing and fell headlong into the water. The boar turned on him. All he could do was use his feet to fend off the maddened creature. So ferociously did it attack that one of its tushes cut through the leather of his boots, deepening the red of the pool. But Hervey managed at least to grasp back the spear, and found just enough of a footing on the well's edge to get a full purchase on the shaft, forcing the brute underwater. It seemed an age but eventually the boar ceased struggling, and his side of the well was at last calm.

Now he could edge round the side to grasp the Arab's reins, for mercifully the bridle was in place. The saddle had slipped full under her, adding to her distress, and he knew he would need to support her soon, for she could not tread water for ever. The girth strap would be the best point to secure her, but he judged it best to free her of the encumbering saddle, and this he managed eventually to do – though not without kicks and more than one ducking. At once she became less frantic, but she was exhausted.

Hervey was still in the water when the others began arriving. First down the steps was Captain Steuben, who lapsed into a string of Rhenish expletives. Next came Locke and Selden, followed by the rajah and the raj kumari until there were more of the party below ground than above. Two shikaris carried the jemadar up the steps, his right arm hanging limply like a rag doll's, but he made no sound ther than alternate gratitude and apology.

There was now just enough room for Locke and Steuben to pull Hervey out. 'Does the bottom shelve?' asked Locke. 'Can she get a footing?'

169

'I think not,' replied Hervey, still holding the pony's reins as she continued to tread water. 'She's been all around the edge and found nothing firm. We'll have to haul her out. Fasten as many girth straps together as possible to make a sling: she'll soon tire and go under if we can't at least support her. And we must find some rope and a means to lift her.'

Selden looked at a loss; Steuben likewise. The rajah, the raj kumari, the other officers, the shikaris – all seemed to find it beyond them. But Locke saw it at once. 'Just like lifting a gun from the lower deck – pulleys and braces. Come!' he cried to the idle hands as he ran up the steps. 'We need twenty men, a dozen yards of timber, all the girths and thirty feet of rope. And an axle!'

Hervey smiled ruefully at the rajah. 'If we are without an engineer, Your Highness, a marine is not a bad standby! I doubt we shall be too long here.'

It was near to dark as they rode back to Chintalpore. Hervey had managed to get the girth sling under the pony (not without difficulty, for even free from the slipped saddle her legs were extravagant) and they had thus been able, with reins and other leathers, to keep her afloat for the three hours it took for Locke to construct the derrick, with its axle pulley, attach the sling fashioned from the howdah trappings, and to marshal the thirty beaters to heave on the rope to hoist her out at last. And then they had done the same with the boar, for not only did they not wish to see the well – ancient and abandoned though it was – poisoned, but the beaters were to be rewarded by its meat, as the day's rupees were customarily supplemented.

Locke and Hervey were heroes once more, Hervey the greater for his having fought off the boar, suffering a wound in the process. He protested it was nothing, but it was as well that the veterinary chest provided Selden's sworn-by iodine. Exhausting as the encounter and exertions in the water had been, however, and aching though his leg was, instead of being pulled down by the affair he was quickened by it. Indeed, the raj kumari's attention excited him. It was attention not born of inclination to minister, as might be supposed of female instinct, but by the chase, the lusty killing of the boar – Hervey's *mastering* of things. Selden, Locke and even the rajah rode apart from them.

When they reached the palace, as the sun was almost gone in the hills beyond Chintalpore, Hervey's exhilaration could increase no more. He spent but a moment with Badshah's syce before seeking out the raj kumari in her mare's stall, but she seemed anxious, glancing about her, and she dismissed him, awkwardly, saying she must hurry to her quarters. He made to follow, but the syces were watching. Instead he turned for his own.

As he threw open the door of his chamber, the girl looked up – a slender, trembling thing, her doe-eyes wide with fear, as if she had been a crouching fawn, and he a ravening leopard. His wild eyes told her he would spring, as the leopard springs when he finds the fawn. She dropped the bowl of fruit she had been so carefully arranging, and fell in a dead faint.

CHAPTER ELEVEN

FORESTS ANCIENT AS THE HILLS

The following morning

'Good morning, Captain Hervey; I gave instructions that you were not to be disturbed.' The rajah motioned to his bearer to bring tea. 'But I must know how is your wound.'

Hervey made to rise from his divan but the rajah would not have it. 'No, Captain Hervey, there is not the least reason for you to rise. I now bow to you as a man of most exceptional courage and resourcefulness. But I wish to know how is your wound.'

'In truth, sir, I can barely feel it,' replied Hervey. 'Mr Selden has as much facility with a man's limbs as he does with a horse's. And I asked him for something that might make me sleep.' By now he was standing, despite the rajah's protestations, and agreeably surprised that there was scarcely any stiffness in his leg.

The rajah sat by the window as the bearer poured tea. 'You will be pleased to hear that the little thing who so charmingly fainted on seeing you last night is fully recovered,' he smiled.

Hervey reddened.

'Your sanguinary appearance must have been more than she was able to bear.'

He nodded, much relieved with the explanation.

'Captain Hervey, I would speak with you concerning several matters that occupy me,' pressed the rajah, changing course pointedly. 'I know that you had intended taking to camp with my rissalahs, but you may just as well meet with them tomorrow, for they will do no more than carouse on their first night under canvas. Will you dine with me?'

Hervey said it would be his privilege, but that he feared his opinion would be inadequate in any matter.

'Captain Hervey, your counsel will be more valuable than any other that might be had.'

'I am obliged, sir,' he replied, making a small bow, intrigued by the response.

The rajah returned the bow and took his leave. 'I regret that our sport yesterday was brought to so sudden an end,' he added, turning at the door. 'I shall arrange more at once, but for today I must be about other business. I have asked the raj kumari to see to it that all you have need of is provided.'

Hervey dressed and made his way to the maidan at the foot of the droog, where all but a quarter-guard of two dozen sowars were parading to join the rest of the rajah's lancers for the last evolutions before the hot weather. From a quiet corner he studied them carefully, trying to assess how they compared with a King's regiment. There was first the obvious difference in complexion, although there were times in Spain when his own dragoons were so sun-baked that they might easily have passed for natives of Bengal, if not quite of Madras or Bombay. There was the lance, not yet in a British trooper's hand. The uniform, too, had not the appearance of one of the King's army. It bore, indeed, a passing resemblance to an Austrian heavy's – green kurta, white breeches with long jacked boots. Yet it was neither the dark skin, the lance, nor even the uniform that revealed these men to be other than British cavalry. Rather was it their bearing, for in a British regiment Hervey had always observed a certain animation, even when sitting at attention. With these sowars it was different. They held their heads higher, their eyes set on something distant – an altogether unfathomable look which he had not seen even in the Madrasi sepoys. Perhaps it was the German method in which their regulation seemed bound. He watched the rissaldar and Captain Steuben exchange salutes as the native officer handed over the parade. It was as ceremonious as if they had been at the Horse Guards, but there was a certain something . . . a stiffness. In any case, it was not how it would have been in the Sixth, where discipline and ceremony never wholly suppressed the spirit. Nor, for that matter, with the Madrasis: Cornet Templer held himself not nearly so aloof as this German. But for all that, he was much taken by the good order in which the rajah's lancers paraded. Whether they could use the lance as well as they could carry it – beyond the exercise yard – he could not yet judge.

A trumpeter sounded 'Walk-march' and the rissalahs left the maidan in fours, the quarter-guard remaining at attention throughout, only their lance pennants making any movement. The jemadar in command of the guard, his charger's saffron throat plume as brilliant as the displays in the rajah's aviary, lowered his sabre to salute the standard as it passed, carried proudly by a veteran nishanbardar, and dust swirled knee-high in spite of the best efforts of the bhistis to damp it down. As he turned back for the palace he saw the raj kumari watching from the shade of a huge parasol carried by a bearded giant of a sepoy. 'Good morning, Your Highness,' he said, taking off his straw hat and bowing, keen to put the ardour of the previous day at some distance by a display of formality. 'Have you been watching long?'

'Yes, Captain Hervey – I have been admiring the horses especially. I think your Mr Selden has much to be satisfied with. He has transformed my father's stables. And I understand that he has worked the same wonders with your leg.'

Hervey smiled. 'I think it was in no danger, madam; but yes – he is very sure with his potions and stitches.'

The silk breeches had given way to a chaste saffron saree, recasting the raj kumari as a figure of nobility rather than of sensuality – but a figure of no less appeal. 'Will you walk with me a while?' she asked. 'I would speak with you of certain things.'

Despite his intent on formality, there was little he would rather have done.

They strolled together in the water gardens. A host of Java sparrows, red-vented bulbuls, flycatchers and wagtails – and several others of which the raj kumari did not know the name – were drinking and preening in the fountains before the growing heat of the morning sent them to seek the shade. She turned to him suddenly. 'Why did Mr Selden leave your regiment, Captain Hervey?'

'Oh,' he said, more than a little alarmed, hoping the expression of surprise might also give him time to find a satisfactory answer.

She dropped her gaze, helpfully.

After what seemed an age he found the words. 'You know that the climate here is more to his liking. He was sorely troubled by fevers.'

The raj kumari looked at him directly and raised her eyebrows. 'So it is not true that he was . . . *obliged* to leave, following . . . shall we say, an *indiscretion* with a fellow officer?'

Hervey blanched. His dismay at the hint of the vice – and from the lips of the raj kumari – was partially eclipsed by his admiration for her remarkable facility with the language. But as stated, the detail of the concupiscence was untrue.

The raj kumari was not inclined to afford him time to consider. 'Captain Hervey, do not be abashed: such things are not regarded as of any great moment here.'

Hervey knew that his continued silence would only serve to condemn, yet he could not bring himself to confirm any part of her supposition. 'Forgive me, madam,' he tried, 'but it is a practice which we abhor. Such accusations are not to be made lightly.'

'Then we may suppose, Captain Hervey, that your coming to Chintal was not occasioned by vice?'

Hervey boiled, and would have let his rage show had he not had to weigh the consequences for his charge from the duke. 'Madam, such a thought gives me great offence – more than I can say. I beg that you speak no more of it!'

The raj kumari looked, for an instant, genuinely contrite, but soon regained her self-possession. 'Very well, Captain Hervey,' she smiled; 'I shall not.'

He bowed.

She was as good as her word, but he could not know how pleased she was that his reply had permitted her to strike the notion from her mind at last. 'Captain Hervey, do you recall your disappointment with the diversion at your first night here in the palace?'

'No, madam,' he replied cautiously, 'I do not recall any disappointment.'

'The cobra – it was not as you had imagined.'

He smiled. 'Disappointment? *Perhaps* – in that I had imagined the cobra to be a much larger serpent. But I had a very healthy regard of it, I may assure you!'

When the raj kumari smiled, though it invariably presaged her own pleasure, the effect was always great – no matter with whom. 'I am resolved to take you to the forest to see the hamadryad. *There* is a serpent of which you will stand in awe,' she promised, nodding emphatically.

'Madam,' he began hesitantly, '. . . the jungle – do you think it would be wise?'

The raj kumari laughed. 'Captain Hervey, you cannot be afeard? Not you – not the fighter of boars in deep caverns!'

He had heard that mocking tone before, and Henrietta's smile flashed before him. 'Sometimes discretion is to be preferred,' he said softly, hoping she might see the difficulty.

She chose not to. 'Lakshmi shall be our protector, Captain Hervey. We shall first make an offering at the temple.'

He had but a moment to decide.

It took an hour to reach the little village on the forest edge where the sampera, the snake-catcher, lived. Hervey was not especially afraid of the hamadryad, for he supposed they would view it from a safe distance. Rather was he chary of any return to the tumult of senses of the day before. Evil thoughts came as a temptation: he could not be condemned for the thoughts themselves. But if he indulged them – dwelt on them, took pleasure in them, or, worst of all, opened himself to them – then he stood condemned. Avoidance, he had learned, was always more effectual than resistance.

The village was a more than usually mean settlement. What passed for the main street also served as an open drain, in which lay repellently the domestic ordure of the ryots – a sad, tired-looking people squatting on their heels by fires of cow dung. Even the children were subdued – boys all, for infanticide was still a practice of the poorest. They were only three – the raj kumari, Hervey and the raj kumari's syce. Despite the obvious status of the party, however, the ryots made no show of deference or even greeting. It was more than the repose of the afternoon, for it was far from hot, even by his own reckoning. He judged the torpor spiritual.

She wore the Rajasthani breeches again, and with the sweat of her pony's flanks having its way, she was once more an image of allure as powerful as any of the temple carvings he had lately stared at in disbelief. But Hervey was now master of himself – of that he was certain.

An older man stepped from one of the earthen huts and made namaste, greeting her in what Hervey supposed was some dialect. He could get no sense of what then passed between them, but the raj kumari's familiarity with the place and the man was apparent. At length she turned to him and explained. 'The sampera says there is a hamadryad in the forest nearby and she is seeking a mate. He saw her this morning.'

'How does he know the snake is the female?'

'He *knows*,' she replied, with sufficient inflexion to suggest that there was some mystic power in his knowing. She told the syce to take the horses and beckoned Hervey to come with her across the open ground between the village and the forest edge, to the diminutive temple of the village's protecting deities. Here she placed three silver rupees in a bowl at the foot of an image of Lakshmi and motioned Hervey to do likewise. Then the sampera, singing a dreary, repetitive mantra the while, led them into the darkness of the thick-canopied jungle.

Hervey's encounter with the forest of his worst imaginings was come at last. He walked gingerly, stooping slightly, in the manner of one expecting to be assailed at any second. He searched the ground each time – albeit momentarily – before placing his foot down. He glanced about unceasingly, as a tiny bird at water. He searched with his eyes and his ears – and he saw nothing but green, and heard nothing but the faint rustle of his own steps. In front of him the raj kumari trod softly but without the same hesitation, and ahead of them the sampera moved as silently as if his feet did not touch the ground. They walked for a quarter of an hour along an old gaur track, the going easy, the track wide and clear of the bines which so easily arrested progress elsewhere. Here and there they had to crouch a little to pass below the branch of a tree that had fallen or bowed under its own weight, but there was little undergrowth even off the track, for the light barely filtered through the canopy of teak, tamarind and sal trees, and few seedlings were able to flourish in the gloom. Elsewhere in Chintal, where teak and sandalwood had been cut, allowing the sun to penetrate in great shafts to the forest floor, the undergrowth was profuse and their pace would have been that of the snail. But here was primal forest, virginal jungle. And it was, at this hour, silent – no birds singing, no monkeys gibbering or calling, no cicadas trilling. Silent, as it must have been at the Creation.

'"And here were forests ancient as the hills, enfolding sunny spots of greenery."' Hervey was slowly regaining self-possession.

'What is that?' said the raj kumari.

He thought he had breathed it to himself. 'Oh . . . a poet.'

'Which poet?' she demanded.

'Coleridge,' he whispered.

'Coleridge is mad, is he not?' she asked, scowling.

He cursed himself. Her father's knowing had been one thing, but how in heaven's name did *she* know of Coleridge? There were deeps not even Selden had perceived. 'Mad? Well, I, that is—'

The sampera made a hissing sound to silence them both. She turned back and frowned – a sort of half-smile, though its effect with Hervey was as potent as the fuller ones had been in the palace gardens. They walked in silence for another quarter of an hour, the conspiratorial closeness adding to the potency, for the raj kumari was stepping with growing care, glancing to right and left from time to time. Out of the sun it was cooler, but still warm, and the air, so laden with moisture that it was as some luxuriant shroud about them, seemed to be drawing Hervey by degrees into one with the spirit of the forest. The raj kumari had taken his hand when the sampera hissed, squeezing it in a gesture of reassurance, and he had not loosed it, so that now, moving a little ahead, she was leading rather than walking with him. Whether knowing or not, with every step he was further from the civilization that was his very being – and closer to a place of only primal forces.

In a while the sampera slowed, and soon he was stopped altogether, peering about him intently. And then with exhilaration, plain even in his whisper, he pointed ahead and to the right. *'Dekh, dekh, samne!'*

She pulled Hervey close, gripping his hand even more firmly. He could feel her pulse, faster and faster – so near must be the deadly spirit of the forest. They searched hard, as the snake-catcher told them. There was so much green on the forest floor . . .

And then both saw her. Even though she was partially coiled, Hervey knew at once she was a serpent of altogether greater proportions than the palace charmer's. She lay quite still, oblivious or not to their presence only a dozen yards away. He reached slowly, instinctively, for his sword – though he was not wearing it. The snake-catcher began to sway from side to side, humming to himself. The raj kumari began swaying, too; less extravagantly, but swaying nonetheless. The snake-catcher raised his hand carefully and began moving it, palm outward, across his face, eyes half-closed – slowly, gently, this way and then that, several minutes passing in a profound silence, nor with any motion on the forest floor, only the swaying of the sampera and the raj kumari.

The silence ended with the faintest sound, the merest rustle, difficult to identify and impossible to locate: a sound perceptible only to those whose senses were heightened, who were alert as if their very lives were threatened . . . The sampera froze, and then slowly lowered his hand. Hervey felt the tingling in his neck and down his spine, as intense as anything he had known. He put a hand slowly to the raj kumari's shoulder and held her, as still as if they had been the very trees of the forest, the danger as great as any he had faced – wholly defenceless. The hamadryad rose up. She stood two-thirds his height, as tall as the sampera himself. She looked at them, moving hardly at all, her great hood spread, exposing the creamy bands, her eyes cold, mesmerizing – as if she knew the evil she could deal them in a second. Hervey knew, too: she would be able to strike all of them before any might run clear. She turned slowly to one side, to the cause of her rousing: another hamadryad, a male, edging towards her, slowly, cautiously.

For what seemed an age he inched closer to her. She stayed upright, hood spread, ready to strike him in an instant. He crawled in a careful circle about her, and then, even more cautiously, crept the length of her body, to where it rose from the ground, never himself rising above an inch. He began to stroke her flank with his head – slowly, ever so gently at first, for any misjudgement would bring her needle fangs to his neck. As slowly, she lowered herself, and his stroking became more insistent. Gently but purposefully he began to coil about her – still slowly, *very slowly*. She coiled likewise – slowly, *very slowly*, watching him constantly, so that in a while it was not possible to tell which coil was which.

Hervey did not see the sampera slip away, spellbound as he was by the serpents' slow, deliberate writhing. The cold tingling had turned to heat: a curious, inflaming heat. The raj kumari, her leg pressing against his, was swaying once more, moving against him, as the male hamadryad had done with the female. The heat grew as she seemed to coil around him, aroused by the potency of what was happening only yards away. An age seemed to pass as the serpents coiled and moved against each other . . . And then the raj kumari was pulling him towards her, and he could hear nothing for the confusion inside, and he could

CHAPTER TWELVE

RACE TO THE SWIFT

The rajah's apartments, that evening

As Hervey entered, his host held out his hand. They were to dine alone, and all but the khansamah had been dismissed. 'Captain Hervey,' began the rajah, his face not as grave as in the morning, 'I have here a letter for you, just come – brought this day from the Collector of Guntoor by dak. And with uncommon velocity, I might say.'

Hervey wondered on what matter the collector might write to him, and took the letter curiously. Then he saw the hand.

'It is not inclement news, I trust?' asked the rajah solicitously.

'I do not suppose it to be, Your Highness. It is a letter from the lady I am to marry. I . . . I am astonished that it should find me here!'

'Do not be, Captain Hervey: we are hardly a primitive tribe of Africa here in Chintal.'

Hervey was discomfited by the rebuke. 'Sir, I did not mean . . . it is just that she had every reason to suppose me in Calcutta or even Haidarabad.'

'And how was the letter addressed?' he asked, still kindly.

Hervey glanced at it again. 'Captain M. P. Hervey, Aide-de-Camp to the Duke of Wellington, India.'

'In which case there can be no surprise, for such a letter, were it to be misdirected or delayed, would bring severe opprobrium on the official concerned. This is India, Captain Hervey: the duke's name still inspires a respect verging on reverence.'

Hervey nodded, gladly acknowledging his error.

'And now you would wish to read it in some privacy, of course. I shall retire for one half-hour and then, if it is agreeable to you, we shall resume our intercourse.'

When the rajah was gone, Hervey opened the letter. But he did so hesitantly, taking care to preserve as much of Henrietta's seal as he could. He unfolded the single sheet; only the one – not a propitious sign. He began to read, with every shade of feeling from trepidation to joy – and guilt, for the forest was all about him in one sense still. It was addressed from Paris not five days after his leaving.

> *My dearest Matthew* (a good beginning – as affectionate as ever he had seen),
> *Your letter from Paris was given to me upon arrival at Calais by the admirable Corporal Collins who was at once all solicitude, explaining that he had waited there for three days in vain, and feared that you would by then have sailed for the Indies. We set out at once, however, for Le Havre – a pleasant town where I learn that your name is now well known to the authorities for so fearlessly opposing the enemies of the King. Alas, I also learn that your ship has sailed two days before, and I am unable to find any which admits to the possibility of overtaking a frigate of the Royal Navy, and, in any case, Corporal Collins is insistent that your express wishes are that I should remain in France or England until such time as it is expedient for you to return or for me to follow you. And now I am in Paris at the house of Lady George, whose husband shows me every kindness and understanding – as, I may say, does your Serjeant Armstrong in equal measure. Tomorrow I shall call on the duke and make all our arrangements known – if, that is, he be in any doubt of them at this time – and thereafter shall return to Longleat with a heavy heart, though not so heavy as upon first hearing of your mission.*
> *Be assured, dearest Matthew, that I understand perfectly the duty to which you have submitted. I beg you do not have any*

concern that might stand in the way of affairs in India. I pray only that, in the fullness of God's time, we may be restored to one another and that thereafter there should be no unwonted putting asunder.

Your affectionate – nay, adoring – Henrietta.

He was at once overcome by two wholly different responses. First, great relief at learning of Henrietta's constancy. Second, shame at how close he had come in the forest to losing any honourable claim to it. He resolved in that instant to be done with intrigue in Chintal – for it had been that, he imagined, which had predisposed him to such conduct – and to press Selden for a speedy resolution of the matter of the jagirs. Then he might proceed with the business of Haidarabad. And when this was done he might return to Horningsham, or have Henrietta join him in Calcutta when the duke came there. By the time the rajah returned, he had steeled himself to his new course; gathering up the reins, so to speak, with a view to driving forward at last with some impulsion.

His face must have reflected this change, for the rajah felt obliged to remark on it. 'Is everything well, Captain Hervey? You look a little agitated.'

'Thank you, Your Highness; everything is well. There is not the slightest cause for concern.'

'I am very glad to hear it,' said the rajah somewhat heavily, 'for I wish to speak with you of certain matters, and it would not do for you to be distracted. I believe I may confide in you things that I scarcely dare think to myself, for to place trust in anyone in these lands is almost always folly.' There was sadness in his voice, but a note of optimism, too: 'You are an honourable man. That, or I am no judge of men at all.'

If the hamadryads had not so savagely ended their own coupling, might he still have been worthy of that esteem? What might have been standing now between him and Henrietta, between him and God – and between him and the rajah? He could not blame any great primeval power, as the raj kumari might, or Selden even. If there was nothing, in one sense, beyond a fervid embrace, there was much else in his heart that called for the most abject contrition. 'India will sweat the false civilization out of you,' Selden had told him. And he had not believed it for one instant. To his sins, therefore, he must also add pride. 'Sir,' he began hesitantly, 'I fear that I, as most men, have feet of clay.'

183

The rajah frowned. 'Englishmen are inordinately fond of their Bible.'

Hervey looked surprised.

'You think that I should not be acquainted with your good book? I have read the Bible many times from beginning to end. I read it every day. I would speak with you of it at some time. But I confess I do not remember with any precision whence come these feet of clay.'

'The Book of Daniel,' sighed Hervey. The knife – for such was the rajah's undeserved admiration – was going deep.

'Ah, yes – Daniel. Remind me of Daniel, if you please.'

Though bemused by the rajah's diversion, Hervey needed little time for recollection, for it was one of the regular stories of his boyhood. 'Daniel, you will recall, sir, was a Hebrew slave in Babylon, but he had become something of a favourite of King Nebuchadnezzar.'

'I trust you see no more than a superficial correspondence with your own situation here in Chintal, Captain Hervey?' smiled the rajah.

Hervey smiled too. 'No, indeed not, sir.'

The rajah rose from his cushion to take a book from a recess in the marbled wall. 'Here,' he said, holding out the black leather volume, 'here is your Bible. Read to me where is this allusion to feet of clay. I am much intrigued by Nebuchadnezzar and his slave.'

Hervey could not sense whether there was any design in the rajah's meanderings, but he opened the bible a little after the middle and turned the pages until he found the Book of Daniel. 'I think it must be in chapter two, or possibly three,' he said, searching. 'Yes, I have it – chapter two. The king has a dream, sir, a dream in which there is a graven image. I will read from verse thirty-two: "This image's head was of fine gold, his breast and his arms of silver, his belly and his thighs of brass, his legs of iron, his feet part of iron and part of clay."'

'Read on, if you please, Captain Hervey,' said the rajah, sitting down by a window and gazing out into his gardens.

'"Thou sawest till that a stone was cut out without hands, which smote the image upon his feet that were of iron and clay, and brake them to pieces. Then was the iron, the clay, the brass, the silver, and the gold, broken to pieces together, and became like the chaff of the summer threshing floors; and the wind carried them away, that no place was found for them: and the stone that smote the image became a great mountain, and filled the whole earth."'

The rajah remained silent for a moment. 'And what is its meaning?'

Hervey paused a moment too. 'Nebuchadnezzar was a great king. *He* is the head of gold, but the kingdoms that follow his shall be in turn weaker, until at last one – represented by the feet of clay – shall be shattered, and a greater one – ordained by God – shall take its place. It is a prophecy of the coming of the Hebrew state, sir.'

'And what said the king to this?' asked the rajah intently.

'He revered Daniel thereafter, sir.'

'Read it to me please, Captain Hervey. I wish to know exactly what is written.'

Hervey was growing uneasy, sensing now some purpose in the rajah which might run counter to his resolve over the jagirs. '"Then the king made Daniel a great man, and gave him many great gifts, and made him ruler over the whole province of Babylon, and chief of the governors over all the wise men of Babylon."'

There was a long silence. At length the rajah sighed. 'Captain Hervey, your father is a priest.'

Hervey confirmed, again, that it was so.

'And it is evident that you have much learning in these matters, too.'

'Sir, I cannot call it learning, only long exposure to scripture.'

The rajah nodded. 'I wanted first to speak with you of the nizam, for his coming to Chintal is exercising me greatly. But now I am minded to ask you more of scripture. Captain Hervey, I tell you things that I scarce dare think. Our sacred faith is become mere superstition here in Chintal, a constant endeavour to propitiate so many gods that may do us mischief. And some gods do each other mischief so that we do not know, in appeasing one, whether we anger another.'

'The Bible, sir, is not without its contradictions too.' He felt reasonably sure this did not go beyond the bounds of orthodoxy.

'Which is more than the nizam's religion would admit to,' said the rajah ruefully.

'And yet he is tolerant of faiths other than his own, is he not?' There were no rumours of conversions by the sword.

'Who knows what is the nizam's mind?' sighed the rajah. 'The best that may be said is that he despises tolerantly. Though he would not do even thus were there a Christian realm on his borders.'

'That is hardly likely, sir, from all I have heard. The missioners make few converts, even where they are active.'

The rajah frowned. 'Captain Hervey, the missioners would need to make only one convert in a Hindoo dominion.'

185

Hervey was incredulous. 'You mean, sir, that all a prince's subjects would be baptized with him?'

The rajah nodded. 'Indeed, yes – all save his Mussulmen, no doubt. So you see, Captain Hervey, it would take a ruler as great as the Emperor Constantine to adopt that alien faith.' And he smiled benevolently.

Hervey smiled too, for he knew well enough that Constantine's conversion had as much to do with the promise of victory as anything else.

As indeed did the rajah. 'His triumph over his fellow Caesar brought the Christians freedom to worship – yes. But I do believe his own conversion, a little later, was rather more profound.'

'On this, who could argue?' replied Hervey, 'for a man's heart – as the nizam's bears witness – is in the end impossible to know.'

The rajah was much intrigued. 'Mr Selden will never talk of that faith. He refers me only to the creeds. What is your opinion in this?'

Rarely did Hervey feel less adequate for a task. 'Mr Selden,' he began, confident that here at least he was on ground of which he could be moderately certain, 'does not believe. That is to say, he does not believe *yet*. For the rest, I fear that I could give you but an unsatisfactory answer. The Nicene creed is – by my understanding – a sufficient account.'

'You could not account more sufficiently for your own faith, Captain Hervey? I would be astonished if this were so.'

The challenge was as fair as it was difficult, he conceded.

'Perhaps, therefore, you may ponder on it until this time tomorrow, and then we may resume. I do so feel the want of scholarship here in Chintalpore in these times.'

Hervey agreed readily enough, pleased the rajah did not press him now. To what purpose this exchange was directed, he had not the slightest idea; nor why, indeed, the rajah should at this moment feel so driven to introduce it when so much else demanded his attention. How he wished himself free of intrigue. It was uncommonly difficult to share a man's table while at the same time being a deceiver.

Such escape was a vain hope, though. There was no dismissal in the rajah's invitation to ponder on the creed. Instead, his aspect became grave once more as he took the bible from Hervey and placed it back in the recess. 'Now I wish to consider with you the great danger that Chintal finds herself in,' he said, walking to the window and glancing with more than a suggestion of anxiety towards the city. 'I have today received intelligence that the nizam's artillery is being assembled close to our border.'

Hervey could scarce believe it. Only a moment before, the rajah was speaking of receiving the nizam here in Chintalpore.

'The nizam has very great artillery, Captain Hervey: he has pieces so big that the walls of any fortress would be quickly reduced.'

The exact import of the rajah's intelligence was beyond Hervey at that moment, but the movement of artillery was a usual presage of hostilities. 'I have heard of the formidable power of these batteries, of course, Your Highness – the nizam's beautiful daughters?'

'Just so – the nizam's daughters. The daughters of Eve no less, for such power tempts a man to more than might be his due. The nizam has three sons, also – the basest of men. They have often boasted what they would do with these guns. The nizam himself at one time I called a friend, but he is become enfeebled. His sons will not be satisfied until they have disseised me of Chintal. I know they have exacted plunder from the Pindarees, and encouraged them – and aided them – in ravaging us, but the gold which my Gond subjects extract from the rivers and hills, with all the skill of their ancestors, is what their minds are set on. Captain Hervey, would you consider it possible to fight the nizam when we have but a half-dozen light pieces?'

The prospect was absurd. Had not Bonaparte himself said that it was with artillery that war was made? 'Your Highness, I hardly know the particulars . . . And you have Colonel Cadorna to give you this advice, a man of greater experience than me.'

'But he is not with me at this moment, Captain Hervey – and you are one of the Duke of Wellington's own officers.'

It seemed pointless confessing his own narrow regimental seasoning. He wondered if the rajah somehow hinted obliquely at the obligation of the jagirs, as explained by Selden. Was this why the rajah had mentioned the duke's name? 'Your Highness, I am a mere staff captain. You ask me things which are of sovereign importance to Chintal—'

'I do, Captain Hervey,' said the rajah, softly but resolutely.

Hervey had now to think, as it were, on two tracks – as a horse responding to contrary aids. The rajah wished for his strategical opinion: that itself required the very greatest address. But he also had to consider what effect his opinion might have on the outcome of his mission, for whatever the true importance of the jagirs, his mission as stated demanded an estimate of Haidarabad's fighting capacity. And implicit in their speaking now was Hervey's acceptance of the nizam as the enemy – the nizam, 'our faithful ally' as Colonel Grant had called him. How he wished he had gone to Calcutta in the first instance. Yet how might the duke's greater purpose be served if a man as good as the rajah were crushed? Nor was it merely a question of the worthiness of men: the independence of Chintal – the collector had made it clear – was a pressing matter to the Company. And was it not the nizam's sons who were the enemy rather than the nizam himself? In any event, the rajah expected an answer. 'Your Highness, if the precepts on which war is made are universal, then I fear that I have no counsel but to seek terms. But something Mr Selden has said to me may indicate that in India it may not be quite so: bullocks, money and faithful spies are the sinews of war here.'

The rajah looked encouraged.

Indeed, Selden's words seemed to gain in substance even as Hervey spoke them. Peto's treatise on the art of manoeuvring, which had been his constant companion these past weeks, was coming alive at last as he began to imagine the rudiments of a strategy – a strategy, indeed, not without precedent. 'Sir,' he resumed, and rather more resolutely, 'the Duke of Marlborough, who mastered the French a century ago, used to say that no war can be conducted without good and early intelligence. I believe, therefore, that it is of the first importance that you should know everything there is to be known of the nizam's intentions, and in the case of your own intentions you must dissemble to the utmost.' He took another breath, half-surprised by his own authority. 'You have two able rissalahs of cavalry. They should be your eyes and ears on the borders with Haidarabad; they should deceive his spies as to your strength and intentions; and, perhaps above all, they should attack at once wherever it appears the nizam's forces are assembling, for though their material success might be limited, the moral effect would be incalculable.'

It was a faint hope, a very faint hope; scarcely grand strategy. But Hervey said it with enough resolve for the rajah to be encouraged. 'I am indeed fortunate to have two matchless rissalahs,' he agreed. 'But now, Captain Hervey, let us eat – and perhaps you might begin to elaborate on your plan.'

The sudden commotion outside made the rajah start. Hervey sprang up as, seconds later, the doors flew open and in stumbled a sepoy officer smeared in blood glistening still in its freshness. Hervey lunged towards him but saw at once he could be no threat to the rajah's safety.

The rajah's look of anguish turned to utter dismay. 'Subedar sahib, what has happened?'

Subedar Mhisailkar, a thickset Maratha officer who had served the rajah for thirty years, was crying like a child. 'Sahib, sahib,' he wailed, 'the sepoys are killing their officers!'

His Urdu was garbled but plain enough. The rajah was unable to speak. 'Call the jemadar,' Hervey shouted to a bearer ' – and Locke-sahib and Selden-sahib!'

The rajah, recovering somewhat, sent for his physician and sat the old soldier down on cushions, bringing him lime-water and dabbing at the blood about his eyes with a silk square. 'My old friend,' he cried, 'how could my sepoys do this to you, of all people?'

Hervey's admiration was now as great as his pity, for here was no native despot of popular imagination, no brutal prince who would bait tigers with village boys. Whatever had brought the sepoys at Jhansikote to this, it could not have been the rajah's tyranny.

The jemadar of the guard came running. He looked frightened. And then Selden, and Henry Locke.

'Remember what they say,' warned Locke; 'the first news of battle is brought by him that runs away the soonest.'

Hervey nodded. 'Yet I'm not inclined to believe it so in this case.'

Little by little, with many questions and diversions into Marathi, they were able to gain a picture of what had passed at the cantonments. Soon after dark, it seemed, the sepoys, led by some of their native officers, had broken into the armoury and the quarters of Colonel Cadorna and the battalion commanders, who, with their families, were the only white faces in the absence of the cavalry. All were now dead, said the subedar: wives, children, servants – everyone.

'They waited for the rissalahs to leave,' said the rajah, shaking his head.

'How long will it take for them to return?' asked Hervey.

The rajah smiled ironically. 'They are beyond the Godavari. It would take two days to get them back this side. These sepoy leaders have been clever. I see the hand of the nizam in this – or of his sons.'

One of the rajah's physicians had begun to examine the subedar's wounds, and the rajah himself made to assist despite the entreaties from both.

Selden took Hervey to one side. 'You must leave here at once.'

Hervey was taken aback by his insistence. 'Don't talk so: how can I walk away at this moment? In any case, you're assuming the worst.'

'There's nothing else to assume!'

'And you would leave, too?'

'Hervey, I have never had what would pass in the Sixth for courage; but there comes a time—'

'And this same time is the time for me to walk Spanish?'

'Matthew Hervey, you have duties elsewhere but to the rajah.'

He thought for a moment – not long. A look came to his eyes which Selden had not seen before: a cold, mercenary look, a grim smile almost. 'I shall stay. The rajah has no one else—'

'That's all very noble but—'

'Not noble,' said Hervey, his brow furrowing, 'not at all noble.'

'What do you mean?'

'The price is those jagirs.'

'For heaven's sake, man! You would throw your own life away to pull the duke's fat out of the fire?'

Hervey frowned again. 'I don't have any option. I've hazarded my mission by going against orders.'

Selden simply stared at him.

'There's only one means of redemption in the military,' he smiled ruefully. 'I want that page from the land registry.'

The raj kumari came, her face as angry as the jemadar's had been afraid. 'Father, have the rissalahs been summoned?'

They had not. The rajah looked at Hervey.

He ignored the question. 'What do you believe the sepoys will do now, Subedar sahib?' he asked instead, and then repeated himself as best he could in Urdu.

The subedar said they would wait for first light and then march on Chintalpore.

'And they would be here within three hours,' said Selden.

Locke was silent; so were the raj kumari and the jemadar.

Hervey looked back at Selden, whose nod sealed the bargain. 'Then we have until dawn,' he said gravely.

'No,' said Selden, 'until three hours after dawn – eight o'clock.'

Hervey shook his head emphatically. '*No*: we have only until dawn. If upwards of two thousand sepoys fall upon the palace it will be but a matter of time before it is taken – less time than there is for the rissalahs to return. We have to stop them leaving their cantonments.'

The rajah looked as astonished as Selden. '*How?*' they asked.

'I don't know,' he replied calmly. 'I cannot know until I get there. How many sowars do you have, Jemadar sahib?'

The jemadar looked even more worried: 'Only twenty, sahib!'

Hervey fixed him with a look he hoped would pass for steel. 'Do not say *only* twenty: say *twenty*!'

'Yes, sahib – *twenty*, sahib!'

'And galloper guns?'

'Yes, sahib – one, sahib!' The resolution, insane though first it seemed, was growing.

'Locke – lieutenant of Marines – you are with me?' said Hervey, turning square to him.

'Hervey, I shan't shrink from a fight, but is this one we are meant to be about?'

Locke's prudence did him credit, Hervey knew full well. If they were elsewhere now but in Chintalpore there would be no question . . . 'I could not in honour stand aside. I can say no more.'

A grim smile came over Locke's face, for it did not augur well for the return of Locke-hall to its rightful owner. But fighting was what he did best above all things. 'I say "Ay, ay", then!'

'Selden – will you stay to guard the rajah with your syces?'

'What choice do I have, Matthew Hervey?' The suspicion of a smile crossed his lips too.

'Sir,' said Hervey then, turning to the rajah, 'is there any safer place for you or the raj kumari than here? The forest perhaps?'

The raj kumari answered in his place, a note of defiance in her voice – resentment, even. 'We shall remain here, Captain 'Ervey. Shiva shall be our guard!'

There was a knock at the open door, an incongruous sound in the turmoil. 'Captain 'Ervey, sir, is everything all right?'

Now at last Hervey could permit himself a true smile, for Johnson's blitheness, his imperviousness to all beyond what intruded on the next minute, allowed nothing other.

When all but he and Selden had left the chamber, the rajah asked if what Hervey proposed had the slightest chance of success. Whether, indeed, it made the least amount of sense.

'The answer to both, sir,' sighed Selden, 'in terms that would be understood by me, or most men for that matter, is *no*. But, as says the Bible, the battle is not always to the strong. Matthew Hervey is a brave man, believe me.'

The rajah looked thoughtful. 'Where *exactly* in the Bible does it say that the battle is not to the strong?'

Selden was abashed. 'I am very much afraid, sir, that I do not have the slightest idea.'

There was, thankfully, a moon; enough to permit Hervey's little force to leave Chintalpore along the road to Jhansikote at a brisk trot. Four kos – nearly ten miles: they could be there by midnight. And then what? Three hours or so to think of something.

At the front of the column rode Hervey and Locke, the jemadar and two sowars riding point half a furlong ahead. Behind Hervey were six paired ranks of lancers, then the galloper gun, and then four more pairs. And at the rear was Johnson, his carbine primed and ready to fire at the slightest sign of riot (Selden had said that the sowars could be trusted, but Johnson was there to reinforce that trust). Hervey was content he could at least rely on his mount, for Jessye had more spring in her trot than he had felt in many weeks. How quickly she had regained her strength – faithful, honest mare! And he had his rifled carbine, the percussion-lock which had saved his life at Waterloo – probably the only one at the battle, and the only one in India, for sure.

They hardly spoke, for Locke had no idea how they might subdue Jhansikote's sepoys, and Hervey was absorbed in that very question. He could find no practical help in what he had said earlier to the rajah, that nothing could be done without good and early intelligence, and that it was with artillery that war was made. All he had by way of intelligence was that there were two thousand armed, mutinous sepoys readying to march at dawn. As for artillery, his amounted to one galloper gun that could throw a four-pound shot perhaps a thousand yards. Bold action in all circumstances, demanded Peto's thesis – the moral effect of surprise. Surprise, indeed, was the only thing they might have in this affair.

They made good progress to begin with, but the jemadar warned them that a mile or so before Jhansikote the road narrowed and passed through thick jungle. Here would be a picket, for certain. But the picket evidently was expecting no trouble since a fire gave away both its presence and disposition – fortified as it was by a tree felled across the road. Hervey's troop stopped well short. Hervey himself dismounted and advanced cautiously until he could hear the fire crackling, peering through the darkness with his telescope – as much an aid at night to seeing near to as it was to seeing distantly by day. He could detect no one his side of the tree. It was impossible to know how many were on the other, but he didn't imagine there would be many, since all they would be expected to do was raise the alarm rather than fight any lengthy action. However, they were less than a mile from Jhansikote, and shots would carry that far, even muffled by the forest. He could not risk an assault head-on. Back he stalked to the troop to tell Locke and the jemadar that they would have to approach through the forest and take the picket from a flank with the sword.

The jemadar looked alarmed. 'Sowars not like go in forest, sahib,' he stammered.

He knew some English: that much would be useful. Hervey might have owned to a dislike for the forest too, but instead he spoke briskly in Urdu.

'Sahib!' snapped the jemadar when he was done, saluting and turning back to look for his dafadar.

'What did you say to him?' asked Locke.

'I told him they would have more to fear from me than the jungle.'

Locke sighed. 'They're more likely to die with *you*, that's for sure! Shall we go left or right?'

'It seems the same to me. Shall we toss a rupee for it?' he replied lightly.

'For heaven's sake, man!'

'Very well. Which side is the moon?'

Locke glanced skywards. 'The left.'

'In that case we attack from the right,' said Hervey.

Locke said nothing for a moment, and then he could conceal his puzzlement no longer. 'Why then from the right?'

'Because as Hindoos they will sleep facing the moon, and we shall therefore have the advantage of them.'

Locke could not but admire Hervey's acquisition of such apt knowledge in the short time they had been in the country. 'Very well, then,' he whispered, 'right it is!'

The jemadar returned with his sowars, leaving but five as horse-holders. The dafadar looked a good man, a Rajpoot thought Hervey –

the high cheekbones and supreme confidence. Private Johnson came up, but Hervey said he was to stay to keep an eye on the horse-holders. Johnson took Jessye from him and started for the rear, for once without protest, though the muttering beneath his breath was all that Hervey needed to be reassured that his groom had not lost any of his former spirit. The remainder drew their sabres silently, and then, in single file, they slipped into the forest.

The moon was still good to them. They were able to see the road – now little more than a track – and keep parallel with it as they edged cautiously through the unearthly darkness, Hervey leading. There was more undergrowth than where he had spent the earlier part of the day, for the road allowed in light, and with that came growth on the forest floor. It was not enough to slow their progress, however. Anxiety to keep silence was what checked them. That and the dread of what lurked in the blackness. He shivered at the thought of the hamadryads.

It took more than a half-hour to cover the three hundred yards to where the tree lay across the road. They had slowed to the snail's pace as they neared it, for although the fire was an excellent beacon, and they were able to align themselves well, the undergrowth, the dead leaves on the forest floor especially, made for noise. Hervey stopped as he came level with the picket, only twenty yards into the jungle, and motioned half a dozen of the sowars to pass him so that he would be in the centre of the line as they broke from the forest edge. Five more minutes and they were ready. Something rustled on the ground not a yard in front. He froze, expecting any second to feel the creature's strike, or to hear a sowar shriek – or the picket to sound alarm. But there was nothing. Only the heavy silence of the jungle. He waited a full five minutes more and then motioned the line to advance. His heart pounded so hard he swore he could hear it.

The sepoy sentry at the tree, seeing them rush in, had only a second's horror before the dafadar's tulwar cut his head clean from his shoulders. After that it was easy. Simply a business of despatching the remainder in their sleep – eleven in all. Not one let out so much as a cry. It was a brisk, bloody business, over in less than a minute.

As they searched the dead, Hervey looked into the faces of the men who had just slaughtered their fellows. Whatever he saw he could not fathom, but one thing at least – they were more determined faces than before. Even the jemadar looked more resolute. 'Good work!' said Hervey. 'Well done, Jemadar sahib; well done!'

The jemadar's self-esteem grew visibly. It *was* good work: swift death to the enemy and no blood of their own shed.

'More men are flattered into courage than are bullied out of cowardice,' said Hervey to Locke as they sheathed their swords.

Locke seemed pensive. 'Hervey, you said they would be sleeping with their faces to the moon. They were sleeping the other way.'

Hervey smiled. 'I don't play brag, my dear Locke; perhaps I should! How in heaven's name was I to know which way they would be sleeping?' He turned to the jemadar: 'And now we must get that gun over this tree, Jemadar sahib!'

Locke was still shaking his head even as Hervey gave the orders for the gun-dafadar.

The jemadar assembled his NCOs, and there were words, increasingly heated, none of which Hervey could understand. In their haste to be away, the dafadar had not brought the tools to disassemble the piece and lift it – barrel, trail and wheels.

'Jesus, nothing's easy!' swore Locke. 'We could build a ramp and then haul it over, I suppose.'

'It would take too long,' said Hervey. 'Jemadar sahib, the dafadar will have to jump with the gun.'

The jemadar relayed the instruction but the dafadar replied with much shaking of the head. 'He says the horse does not jump, sahib.'

'Nonsense!' said Hervey. '*All* horses jump – perfectly naturally!'

'I do not think the dafadar will be able to do so, sahib,' he replied sceptically.

Hervey sighed. 'Very well, let *me* try.'

Locke voiced his disquiet too, but what was the alternative, said Hervey. 'We can't take all night building a ramp. The worst that can happen is that we'll end up with the horse and gun straddling the tree, and then we shall just have to cut it from between the shafts.' He chose not to speak of the ruinous crash they might have at any point of the leap. 'There is at least plenty of moon!'

He walked up to the gun-horse defiantly. 'He pulls to the left always, sahib,' said the dafadar, helping Hervey to shorten the stirrup leathers when he had mounted.

That was more the pity, thought Hervey, for he would need his right arm to drive the horse at the tree with the flat of his sword. All he could do was put him at his fence with so much speed that he would have no time to think about running out. The animal was a big country-bred;

Hervey thought it strange the dafadar had never jumped him. Was it *really* possible that he could not jump?

'Does tha want me to give thee a lead, sir?' chirped Johnson out of the gloom.

That was exactly what Hervey was about to ask the jemadar to do. But Johnson he could wholly rely on. And Jessye – the 'covert-hack' so much derided by his fellow officers when he had first joined the Sixth. 'Take her, then,' he said. 'Keep me close up behind, but we've got to hit the tree at a pace!'

A minute or so later they were ready, and he signalled the off. Johnson put Jessye into a canter in a few strides and Hervey was surprised by how the gun-horse was able to match her. He didn't need his sword until they were a dozen strides from the tree, and even then it looked unnecessary, for the gelding was chasing Jessye strongly. The teak barrier was plain to see in the moonlight – that much was a mercy – and Jessye cleared it easily. Hervey gave the gun-horse its head and slapped its quarters with the flat of his sword for all he was worth, feeling the beginning of a pull to the left.

He jumped. He jumped big! Hervey felt the gun lift behind him, praying that the shafts wouldn't break with the strain. The gun-horse landed square but on its off-fore, throwing Hervey's balance and almost tipping him out of the saddle. But he recovered just quickly enough to get both legs firm on as the gun bounced hard on the ground, the horse stumbling perilously for several strides, needing every bit of Hervey's leg to pick him up. It was a full fifty yards before he was able to bring him to the halt.

The acclamation that followed was too loud for his liking, but Hervey was pleased enough with his success to let it pass. The dafadar proffered his embarrassed apologies but Hervey made light of it. 'Only serve your gun bravely when the time comes,' he replied – and the NCO returned a look that assured him that on that, at least, he could count.

The remainder now led their horses into the forest, round the tree, and remounted the other side. Hervey decided they must now walk rather than trot, for he could not risk the noise as they neared the objective. Nevertheless, it was not many minutes before they were at the forest edge a quarter of a mile from the walls of Jhansikote. They dismounted once more, and Hervey, Locke and the jemadar went forward. The moon seemed even stronger now, but there was conceal-ment enough in the shadow-pools at the foot of the trees, and Hervey could soon see the white walls of the cantonment with perfect clarity through his telescope. They brought to mind the chalk cliffs that had welcomed him home, and the Sixth, two years before – and looked every bit as daunting to scale. Between the forest edge and the walls there was nothing: no scrub for cover, no nullah along which they might crawl. And this nothing was bathed in moonlight so bright that even a crouching figure would throw a shadow for any sharp-eyed sentry to see. Hervey was growing more dismayed, for the moon was still high and could not possibly set before dawn. 'How might a frigate take on a first-rate? For that's how it seems to me!' he whispered to Locke.

Locke grimaced: it was unthinkable. 'She would have to lay along-side her before the big ship's guns were run out, that's for sure. And I dare say she would have to board her before she could beat to quarters. But what ship-of-the-line would allow any other to do that? We need a ruse de guerre!'

'Just so,' sighed Hervey, trying hard, but in vain, to think by what subterfuge they could cross the ground unseen, let alone gain the walls. He peered through his telescope for some clue.

A minute or more later and he saw what first he had failed to. The merest glow, from a sentry's fire at the foot of the walls, revealed it. He had located the great gates easily enough in his first sweep of the field glass – immense teak barricades solid enough to withstand a whole battery of galloper guns. They stood out in the solid whiteness of the walls – Nelson-style – like the gunports of a man-of-war. And he had supposed them closed. Why, indeed, would they not be? Yet, why *should* they be? After all, the mutineers had a picket out, and the only troops loyal to the rajah were days away across the Godavari. He cursed himself for not seeing before. As he peered ever more intently through his telescope his heart began to race, for as his eyes became accustomed to the pools of darkness, and he gained a more accurate sense of perspective, he saw that the sentry's fire was *inside* the gates! He snapped his 'scope closed excitedly.

'What is it?' said Locke.

'The gates are *open*: they are *wide* open!' he replied, smiling broadly.

Locke was not immediately reassured that they were delivered of their difficulty. 'And your plan, therefore?'

'To attack – *at once*!'

'You mean . . . to ride straight at the gates?'

'Just so! *Through* the gates!' said Hervey without hesitating.

'Ride straight into the cantonment?'

'Yes.'

Locke paused a moment, in case he had missed some obvious key to victory. 'And when we are inside – what then?'

'We fight.'

Locke made himself pause again, certain that some vital element had escaped his understanding. Soon he realized it had not. 'Hervey, that's beyond a forlorn hope. It's suicide!'

Hervey smiled again. '*Racker! Wollt du ewig leben?*'

Locke began to laugh, and had to cover his mouth lest the noise carry. 'Matthew Hervey, it is *you* who is the rascal! Frederick the Great indeed! He was cursing a whole regiment of guards – as well you know! You mean us to gallop into their lines and just fight?'

'That's what a boarding party would do, is it not? It would clamber aboard and *fight*. It wouldn't have a plan!'

Henry Locke had to agree it was so.

'Well then, I wish you to take charge of the gun. I'll have the jemadar with me; he is not the stoutest of hearts but I believe he would wish to be one, and that in my experience is often good enough. The dafadar's a good man, and there is Johnson.'

'What have we to fear then?' replied Locke, clapping Hervey on the shoulder.

'*And* we shall have surprise,' he added with uncommon assurance.

It did not take long for the jemadar to relay the orders, for there were few to relay. They consisted, in essence, of galloping straight for the gates (the risk that they might be swung shut at their approach meant speed took precedence over stealth). Then they would bring the gun into action against the armoury and magazine, and fire the barrack-houses. 'We shall have to fight for our lives, Jemadar sahib,' Hervey had warned, and the jemadar's face had been filled with dread. Yet he spoke firmly to his men, referring several times to Hervey as 'son of Wellesley-sahib', and that they were about to relive the great deeds of Assaye. At the close of the peroration the dafadar raised a clenched fist and swore a chilling oath (there was no mistaking the meaning), and the sowars likewise.

Locke reported the gun primed, with a wad to keep the charge in place as they galloped; it would take but seconds to load the bagged grape, he said, adhering strictly to the naval term. 'I'll take at least a dozen of the murderous heathens with that first round – and we have nineteen more, and ten roundshot!'

Hervey, himself buoyed by the audacity, drew his sabre. He had already loaded both carbine and pistol, but it was with steel he expected they would first come to close quarters with the mutineers. When he had sheathed that same sword after Waterloo, he had somehow imagined that he might never again draw it on the battlefield – and, for sure, never in so distant a place. It had accounted for many men, had never let him down; Sheffield steel and always kept sharp. Before Waterloo they had all sharpened both edges, fearing that the cuirasses of the French heavies could only be run through with the point. He hadn't liked it since it spoiled the sabre's balance, and more than one trooper cut his horse's ears, or even his own arm, recovering it from a slice. He had let the concave edge of his blunt as soon as he could; he had no doubts he could run his point through any mutineer this morning. In any case, pointing was what a lancer did. A light dragoon fought with cut and slice. He smiled to himself: his first time in action with the lance on his side. But he didn't care to calculate the odds on being able to give an account of it later.

Johnson brought Jessye up. Hervey rubbed the little mare's muzzle with the palm of his hand, blew into her nose – as he had done every time before mounting since he had first backed her a dozen or so years before – then sprang into the saddle with sword still in hand. The troop formed in column of twos, the galloper gun in the middle, and the jemadar, with his trumpeter, took post just to Hervey's rear. Johnson closed to his side on his Arab (still napping as much as on the approach march), and for once Hervey did not order him to the rear, for he knew he would protest loudly – and ultimately disobey. He looked over his shoulder one more time, and then waved his sword aloft: 'Charge!' he shouted.

And the lieutenant of Marines said quietly, 'Here goes the last of the Lockes of Locke-hall.'

They burst from the forest edge like jack snipe. Jessye was at full stretch within a dozen yards. The noise, as hooves and the gun wheels pounded across the hard-baked ground, seemed that of a whole squadron. Hervey fixed his eyes on the gates, expecting any moment to see them

199

swung closed, and urged his little command forward with every word of Urdu he could recall. Still there was no sign of alarm at the walls. He glanced back: the jemadar was but five lengths behind, with the rest of the column close on his heels. Johnson was wrestling with the Arab mare intent on carting him off to a flank. At two hundred yards they could see clearly through the gates, but pounding hooves meant they could not hear the shouting. At a hundred they saw the picket running to the opening – then flashes, ragged shots. Seconds later Jessye flew through the gate arch, Hervey stretching low along her neck as the picket parted before him. Johnson and the jemadar raced likewise between the still-open gates, pushing the two wings of the picket closer to the walls. But the sowars behind had lowered their lances and took the sepoys effortlessly by the point as they galloped through. Those behind found quarry too, and tossed them here and there like bags of flour, fearful screams echoing in the gate arch and the inner walls. Hervey could see others on the walls, running – but away from the gates, not towards. Locke dashed through with the galloper gun, springing from the saddle to help the dafadar and his loader bring it into action. In less than half a minute he had the grape loaded and tamped, but to his dismay there was no rush of mutineers against which to discharge it. 'Come on,' he shouted to the NCO, 'wheel it over there!' pointing to the nearest barrack-house, a long, low wooden structure with a thatch roof. They strained every muscle to pull it the thirty yards to the corner of the building, swinging the trail round to aim obliquely along its front, point-blank. Locke seized the portfire from a sowar and put it to the touch-hole. The gun went off with a terrific roar, made all the greater by echoing from the walls. The devastation astonished them: the whole of the front – doors, slatted windows, joists, everything – was stove in, and bits of burning wadding set light to the thatch. Sepoys began tumbling out, yelling, screaming, to be caught in another enfilade by Locke's gun, reloaded with impressive address. Sowars cantered about the maidan, taking sepoy after hapless sepoy on the point of the lance. Scarcely a shot was fired in return, and none with any aim or success. But Hervey knew well enough this was but the crust with which they were engaged: there were hundreds – perhaps twenty hundred – mutineers in the lines beyond, and these must soon rally. He ran across to Locke. 'There's the armoury and the magazine,' he shouted, pointing to where the jemadar had told him.

They were more solid affairs than the barrack-blocks, brick-built, with tiled roofs. Nevertheless, the galloper gun's roundshot managed to dislodge many of the tiles, though it could make no impression on the doors. 'Jemadar sahib,' called Hervey, 'we must get through the roof.'

The notion of climbing to the roof now seemed no more impetuous to the jemadar than anything else he had found the courage to do that night, and he answered Hervey's imperative with equal eagerness.

The troop dafadar had rallied the rest of the sowars by the gun, keeping half mounted and half ready with their carbines. Hervey thought it unwise yet to take the assault deeper into the cantonment, for he could have little control once they were in more confined quarters. In any event, burning thatch had blown aloft from the barrack-house and set other roofs alight. He was well satisfied with the confusion as he and the jemadar now climbed through the smashed tiling into the eaves of the armoury. Private Johnson had detached himself from the fray, as so often in the past. His speciality was progging – with nothing express in mind, but with the happy knack of recognizing the potential in any removable device, solid or liquid. A building near the magazine, equally strongly built, looked promising. It had double doors, like a barn. Indeed, it looked as if it were just that. The doors were secured only by a padlock, and padlocks had never proved more than a fleeting hindrance to his work. A hoof-pick became a lock-pick, and in no time the doors were swinging open to reveal the spoils.

The stench sent him reeling, and before he was recovered a press of sepoys loomed. He drew his sabre – a magnificent gesture of defiance in the face of scores of mutineers. But it checked their egress none-theless, and for what seemed an age Johnson stood with his sword arm extended, holding at bay what he now supposed to be a whole company. At length, one of them stepped forward and bowed, making namaste. Johnson sensed a trick. Then another did the same, and another, and then more shuffled out, all silently making namaste. Private Johnson saw he had a company of sepoys his prisoner, but what he might do with them was not so obvious. Would they return to their quarters with as much docility as they had emerged? He took a step forward and gestured with his sabre for them to go back inside, but the leader bowed once more, held out his hands and spoke with sufficient entreaty in his voice for Johnson to know that something was not as he supposed. Why, after all, had there been a padlock on the outside?

201

Was this the guardhouse? Were they defaulters? Surely not so many? He cursed them roundly for having no English.

The same instinct for the potential in any booty now told him that these sepoys might be of use to his officer, for they appeared to have no weapons and seemed willing to obey his gestured commands – except, that is, to return to their stinking confines. 'Coom on, then,' he bellowed in his most stentorian Sheffield. They did. They formed fours and marched in step behind him out onto the maidan and towards where Locke and the gun stood steady as a Waterloo square. 'Mr Locke, sir, I think these men want to be us friends,' he called.

The dafadar shot to attention and brought his tulwar to the carry. 'Subedar sahib!' he snapped.

The sepoy who had been first to make namaste returned the salute with his hand. He said something unintelligible to either Locke or Johnson, but the dafadar relaxed and sloped his sword.

Locke was quick enough to surmise these were no ordinary mutineers, but he swung the gun round at them nevertheless. The column gasped, and the sepoys began to waver, but their leader calmly made namaste again. 'We are your prisoners, sahib; we are innocent of any offence,' he protested in Urdu.

'Go and get Captain Hervey from that building yonder,' said Locke, indicating the roofless armoury.

Johnson doubled across the maidan just as the armoury doors flew open to reveal Hervey and the jemadar about to torch a mound of kindling. 'Sir,' he shouted, quick to the mark, 'there's some 'Indoos as can use them muskets on our side!' pointing out the piled arms.

Hervey looked unconvinced, or at least puzzled.

'Sir,' insisted Johnson, ''ave found some prisoners! I don't know what they're saying but they seems to want to fight for us.'

The jemadar pushed past him, looked towards the gun and began nodding his head vigorously. It was so, he assured him. 'They are Rajpoots, sahib! The rajah has one company from Mewar. Rajpoots would not have mutinied like the others!'

There was no time for Hervey to make sense of this difference of loyalties, only to exploit it. Neither was there time for any lengthy interrogation: he must either trust and arm them or fire the armoury at once – and, in any case, he could have no exact idea how many weapons were already in the hands of the mutineers. 'Very well, Jemadar sahib, call them; let's arm them and stand our ground in the maidan!' He spoke, without thinking, in English, but the jemadar knew his thoughts by now, confident at last they could prevail.

The Rajpoots numbered a little short of sixty. At first they had looked a rabble, easily held at bay by Johnson's sabre. But as soon as they had muskets in their hands they were transformed. They were tall, proud sepoys again, even without uniform (for none was clothed above the waist). Their subedar barked a series of commands, and from this un-promising mass of half-bare disorder three ranks of soldierly-looking musketeers formed before Hervey's eyes. A company of Jessope's own Coldstreamers could hardly have had a profounder effect at that moment. He nodded approvingly to the subedar and indicated the direction from which at any minute he expected the mutineers to come like a great wave. The subedar barked more orders – *Left-form at the halt!* The three ranks pivoted half-left with speed and precision, and now Hervey too believed that winning was no longer dependent on an act of God. Locke took the gun off to a flank, supported by half a dozen sowars, to be able to sweep the maidan with enfilading fire. The armoury blazed, though they had been unable to make any im-pression on the magazine. But for the time being they commanded its approaches.

Hervey himself stood, dismounted, with carbine and sabre, at last with a moment to contemplate their position. He soon wished he had not, for the odds against them were, perhaps, a little short of thirty to one.

They did not have long to wait. They heard the wave before they saw it: howling, shrieking, wailing – chilling the blood quicker than the drumfire at Waterloo. And when the wave came, it was more fearsome than anything he had seen. Hundreds upon hundreds of sepoys, like the wildest beasts of the jungle. Not in any order, like a regular wave, but as a great foaming breaker about to pound upon a beach. The old feeling clasped at his vitals – the mix of paralysing fear and energizing thrill that came when life or reputation faced extinction. He had never faced an assault dismounted before, never had to wait at the halt rather than drive forward to meet it. His throat dried like parchment, and he swallowed rapidly to slake it sufficiently to give the order. Locke discharged the galloper gun as the wave rolled over the maidan. He had double-shotted it, and the two four-pound iron balls scythed through the mass of sepoys with brutal destruction. The great human wave had no knowledge of the gun, though. They heard its report, even in their lust to be about the little force by the gates, and they could hear the screaming and see the limbless and disembowelled. But none seemed to see the cause. Was it a part of their madness? Did any in that primitive swarm have any consciousness? The flames from the buildings dazzled them rather than lit their way, yet they slowed not a bit. Then came a flash like lightning in the face of the wave, and another loud report which for the moment overcame the animal clamour. And more men were writhing in agony. Then the same again as the Rajpoots' middle rank discharged its volley, and then the same once more from the rear rank. There were dead and dying mutineers where, only seconds before, their leaders would have promised them the blood of the intruders. Locke's gun thundered again and yet more roundshot felled lines of men in ghastly disorder. Then came the bugle, and the jemadar charged with his dozen lancers into the dazed mass, for whom now there was no hope of resistance, only flight or death.

For many it was both. No matter which way they ran – forward, left or right – they were met with fire or the lance. Or, for those who tried to clamber back over the bodies of their fellows, strewn across the maidan like pebbles thrown about the sand, there were the multiple bags of grape which Locke was now firing with double charges that sent the gun jumping ten feet in its recoil. Those sepoys who, in this economical yet lethal crossfire, were able to recover their individual senses began to prostrate themselves in abject surrender. One way or another, in a few more minutes there was no one left standing in the maidan.

Hervey knew what would happen next if he did not take action at once. The exhilaration – the *relief* – of being alive and in command of the battlefield would turn to a dangerous torpor. If he let go now he might never be able to rouse his eighty stout hearts again. They must not wait for the sun to rise, when those mutineers not prostrate before them would see just how few they were. He set about quartering and combing the maidan with the Rajpoots and corralling the surrendered in his new allies' former prison, using the lancers as drovers – all the while covering the entrance with the galloper gun, though it had little ammunition left. As day broke – rapidly, as always – they had cleared the maidan of the living and half-dead, leaving the lifeless – already the object of swarms of ants and flies – to impede the next wave, and were braced for another attack. Of the infantry at Jhansikote, sixty stood with Hervey, three hundred were secured in the granary, and as many were lying in the maidan. There might be a thousand yet to account for. He knew he could not suppose his position as strong as before: the Rajpoots had plenty of ball cartridge, it was true, but the gun had next to nothing and they no longer had the advantage of night. Spirits were high, though: they had not lost a man. The mutineers had scarce fired a shot.

Only now did it occur to him: *why* had they not fired? Why, indeed, were there no skirmishers harrying them from the walls? He ran forward, cursing, to examine a musket lying on the ground. It wasn't loaded, or even primed. He picked up another – the same. And another, and another – all without charge or ball! So their leaders were going to issue powder and shot only as they marched, said Hervey aloud; or perhaps only when they reached Chintalpore. Such was the insurance that perfidy required! 'The race *is* to the swift,' said Hervey aloud.

Johnson furrowed his brow. 'Tha's not quoting scripture again, sir?'

'I am,' replied Hervey. 'Indeed I am *challenging* it – Ecclesiastes no less!'

His groom looked bemused.

'Ecclesiastes – Solomon's great work on the vanity of man: "I returned, and saw under the sun, that the race is not to the swift, nor the battle to the strong . . . but time and chance happeneth to them all." Time and chance happeneth to all, Johnson!'

'Very pretty, Captain 'Ervey, but where does it get us next?'

'It takes us into the cantonment. It takes us right into their lines. And we shall not fire another round! Fetch Jessye and ask the jemadar and his troopers to assemble!'

CHAPTER THIRTEEN
LOST SOULS

Chintalpore, that evening

With an escort of two sowars and Private Johnson, Locke rode hard for the palace, through the heat of the afternoon, and arrived as the sun was beginning its descent beyond the hills west of Chintalpore. He had ridden through the city, and it was not its customary bustle. The nervousness among merchants and beggars alike was everywhere evident, for fifteen hundred mutineers descending on them was not a fair prospect. The palace was even more nervous. The water level in the lake that now served as a moat around three sides was higher than when they had left – testimony to Selden's address in attending to the defences – and the droog had piles of teak logs at intervals along its slope, secured by ropes which would be cut in the face of the advancing sepoys. A steady procession of elephants was still bringing logs as Locke and Johnson slowed their mounts to a trot for the climb to the palace gates. Once inside they found the rajah in his menagerie, alone, seemingly reconciled to the cataclysm about to befall his house. When he saw them it was with heightened despair, for their bloodstained clothes and grimy faces spoke of defeat. But they did not look like men who had fled slaughter, the enemy pressing hard on their heels. 'Mr Locke,' exclaimed the rajah, shaking his head in confusion, 'I had imagined—'

The raj kumari appeared, as close to running as a princess might. Locke saw little point in waiting on ceremony. 'Your Highness, the mutiny is put down. The ringleaders are restrained, and the rest have been disarmed and are confined to the cantonment. A company of Rajpoots remained loyal. Their help was capital: without it all might have been lost. Captain Hervey remains with them. Are your cavalry returning, sir?'

The rajah was speechless. His disbelief showed clearly as he turned to Selden, also come running, red-faced and sweating. 'Do we yet know if they return, Mr Selden?'

'We do, Your Highness,' he replied, gasping for breath. 'They will be here by dawn tomorrow.' And then he turned anxiously to Locke: 'Hervey – is he unhurt then?'

'Yes, we suffered little but a scratch – the entire force.'

The rajah looked even more incredulous (and Selden scarcely less so). 'Please tell us of it, Mr Locke,' he said, motioning him to a bower-seat close by and beckoning his khansamah to bring refreshment.

Locke recounted the story with such vivid grasp of detail that neither Selden, the raj kumari nor the rajah made a sound during its telling. He spoke of himself only when it was necessary for narrative completeness, he praised the jemadar and the dafadar, and many sowars by name, gave honour to the Rajpoots, especially their subedar, and even included Private Johnson in the paean. But throughout his account shone Hervey's resolution, his resourcefulness and courage. 'When dawn came,' he continued, scarcely able to believe it himself, 'Captain Hervey rode with a dozen sowars deep into the mutineers' lines and demanded they surrender and throw themselves on Your Highness's mercy. He had concluded they had muskets but no ammunition – but, even so, they had bayonets enough to make pincushions of us all. He told them that discipline was the soul of an army and that they had lost their souls when they had set themselves against Your Highness's authority. He told them they could never hope for paradise if they didn't redeem themselves now as soldiers.'

'And they took him at his word?' asked Selden doubtfully.

'He also said that if they did not surrender at once he would kill every one of them.'

'A skilful reinforcement of his appeal to their nobility,' smiled the veterinarian.

'Yes: he led them onto the maidan in formed companies and made them pile arms before attending their wounded and building pyres for the dead. They even gave up their leaders and those who had killed the European officers.'

The rajah expressed himself humbled by this account of the bravery of his loyal sowars and Rajpoots – and, even more, of those who were not his subjects but his guests. He turned to the raj kumari. 'What say you of this, my daughter?' he asked softly.

'I say that we are ever in the debt of Captain Hervey,' she replied, though without enthusiasm. Indeed, almost with a hint of discouragement.

The rajah turned to Locke again. 'And was there any indication of the cause that made my sipahis rise against my officers?'

'There was, sir,' replied Locke firmly.

The rajah waited silently for enlightenment.

Locke looked about to see exactly who his audience now comprised.

'Come, Mr Locke,' urged the rajah, 'you may speak as you find. All here are my loyal servants.'

Locke was uncertain on that point. Nevertheless he would conclude his report. 'It appears that the sepoys' *batta* has been withheld these past twelve months.'

The rajah looked puzzled.

Selden was yet more sceptical. 'But batta is an allowance, paid only when a sepoy must fend for himself – when there are no quarters or rations. And even then the money is held by the havildar-majors, who pay the merchants direct. The sepoy scarcely ever sees it.'

The rajah protested that the cantonments at Jhansikote were newly built, and that his sepoys should not have wanted for food or shelter.

'Just so, sir,' agreed Selden.

'But it appears, as well,' continued Locke (he had not thought any practice so elaborate could exist outside his own service), 'that the sepoys have been placed under stoppages for quartering and rations. This they would not have objected to had they been paid batta.'

The rajah looked more sad than angry. 'How might my own soldiers believe I would ill-serve them in this way? Who is responsible for this, Mr Selden?'

'I could not immediately conclude, Your Highness,' replied Selden, appearing still to be astonished by the revelation. 'There might be several, but it is probable that all are now dead. I shall begin at once – with your leave – to investigate the matter.'

The rajah said he would be obliged. 'Is there anything more, Mr Locke? I am eager to know what we may do to restore the peace that we hitherto enjoyed.'

'Sir, Captain Hervey pledged that every sepoy would receive a pardon if he had committed no direct violence against an officer. He has told them they must swear to serve for one year without pay in order to regain their honour. And all, indeed, were swearing thus before the sadhu as I left. But he believes that if you were to go there in person and release them from that part of their oath binding them to serve without pay then they would be doubly beholden to you.'

The rajah had no inclination to dispute Hervey's command of the circumstances. Indeed, he was impressed by his contriving this magnanimity. Yet he had his doubts. 'Why did the Rajpoots not mutiny likewise? Were they not deprived of their batta too?'

'I do not wholly understand this, Your Highness,' began Locke hesitantly, 'but the Rajpoots seem to believe they are in the service of the Maharana of Mewar, albeit seconded to yourself.'

The rajah sighed and raised his eyebrows sadly. 'My brother-in-law. Yes, one company of Rajpoots comprised part of the dowry of my late and most honoured wife. It seems that, even in death, she has been my deliverance.'

'I am perplexed, however,' said Selden, 'that the rissalahs seem to have been insusceptible to the cause of the mutiny.'

'It would appear, Your Highness,' replied Locke, 'that in their case no quartering or other charges were ever levied.'

'And what might therefore be the feeling of my sowars – and Rajpoots – when I tell the sepoys at Jhansikote that I will take them back into service? Might they not be resentful that they serve loyally on no better terms than those who have broken their trust?'

'Captain Hervey supposed that you would ask that question, sir,' replied Locke, unbuttoning a pocket.

'And what was his answer?' asked the rajah.

He reached inside the pocket and pulled out a folded note. 'He refers you to this, sir.'

The rajah took the paper and read.

Sir,

*St Matthew's Gospel, Chapter 20 – the labourers in the vine-
yard. And increase of pay for lancers and Rajpoots.*
                                    M.H.
                                    Capt.

The merest suggestion of a smile came to his lips. 'What an eminently
practical faith has Captain Hervey. Excuse me, gentlemen, if you will;
I have things on which to reflect. Mr Locke, I cannot begin to express
my gratitude. Mr Selden, would you please make whatever arrangements are necessary.'

Hervey returned to Chintalpore late next day. The rissalahs had
arrived that morning and he had been pleased – and confident – to
leave command of Jhansikote, and more especially its prisoners, in the
hands of Captain Steuben; and, too, of Subedar Mhisailkar, who had
ridden hard (as perhaps only a Maratha could) to join them as soon as
the native doctors had been able to staunch the wounds about his
head and body. Hervey did not doubt that the ringleaders would, and
should, face execution, but he had insisted that it should not be carried
out summarily – contrary to Locke's urging of robust naval discipline.
Instead he wished for trial by some duly appointed tribunal. He knew
not by what articles and regulations these men served, but he supposed
there must be some procedure akin to the court martial even in Chintal.
Locke had argued that there was but one decision to be made – the
firing squad or the hangman's rope. And Hervey had not been without
sympathy for that sentiment, especially after seeing how the European
officers and their families had been butchered. But he sensed that a
display of ceremony, of gravity, in the exercising of military discipline
would have a greater, more enduring, effect than would the mere
exercise of superior force. The latter might easily be countered by
greater force at some time in the future, whereas the former might
speak to something deeper in the sepoys' character.
    The rajah, not unnaturally, wished that Hervey be at once fêted, but
seeing his pulled-down condition allowed him instead to retire to his
apartments. There he bathed and lay a long time thinking of what he
must severally write in the letters now long overdue. It had been two
days only since the affair with the raj kumari in the forest, but it
seemed an age. He must write to Henrietta to lay before her his absolute

devotion. Until this were done his heart was still unfaithful. But first it was his duty to make a further report to the Duke of Wellington, for now the situation was materially changed. The rajah had seen the nizam's hand at Jhansikote, and the pretext of the batta did nothing now, in Hervey's view, to hide it. He knew sufficient of the state of affairs in Haidarabad, albeit entirely from third parties, to warn the duke that his expectation of a cooperating alliance might not be as favourable as he had hoped.

He had also to write to Fort George to reacquaint them with the parlous condition of the rajah's domain. Its contiguity with both the nizam's and the Company's must render Chintal of especial significance – as, indeed, the collector had indicated. He would now urge Philip Lucie to suggest to the Madras council that sympathetic overtures be made to the rajah, to offer him the Company's protection. And then he might with honour quit Chintal and continue on the duke's mission. Concerning the jagirs, he expected Selden to act without further delay.

But the letter to Henrietta – how should *that* be? What weight ought he to place on what passed in the forest? Was its remembrance to him grievous, its burden intolerable? Was his guilt encompassed sufficiently by those words from the General Confession? Or might he have to seek specific absolution, as his Prayer Book required? In truth, it was almost as nothing now. The sudden return to the simple essentials of his profession – the sabre in the hand – somehow ordered things clearly and set them into proper perspective. For the past six months and more he had scarcely been a soldier. He had skulked in the shadows, as it were, jeopardizing his soldier's honour. And honour was not divisible: a lady might not *partially* lose her honour, nor a soldier likewise. If he lived in the shadows then he would do things which did not bear light shining on them.

There was a knock at the door and, before he could answer, the raj kumari entered. He sprang to his feet and expressed himself certain that it was not proper she should be there.

'Captain Hervey, do you have so little regard for me – or yourself – that you would send me away without hearing what I came to say?'

'Forgive me, madam; I merely thought it best that . . .' His voice trailed off, allowing her to take the initiative once more.

'Captain Hervey, in India there are many demons which do battle with Shiva. They take possession of the mind and the body. Do not suppose that in the forest you or I were master or mistress of ourselves. We had intruded on the hamadryads, observed their most secret rituals of courtship, and in doing so had become possessed by their spirits.'

Here indeed was a convenient religion – one that might account no one responsible for his actions. Hervey was unsure of his response. Besides, the notion that it had not been the raj kumari who had writhed beside him in the forest, but instead a spirit of that forest, was hardly flattering to his manhood. He saw Henrietta in that dark beauty – strangely and unaccountably, for the raj kumari's looks were not in any detail those of his distant love. Rather was it, perhaps, the way she held her head, lowered and to one side, so that her eyes had to lift slightly to meet his: Henrietta's way when she teased, and tempted, him most – that challenge in her look and voice which made him weigh every word before he dare speak it, for she would give no quarter. Might he, therefore, take some comfort in the raj kumari's philosophy – that it was *Henrietta* to whom he had been drawn, and by whom he had been so fired?

Such an explanation could hardly serve. He bade her – cautiously – to take a seat.

'Captain Hervey, we are all in your debt,' she began, adjusting the throw of her saree as she sat. 'My father will express it better than I am able, but I wished also to thank you.'

He bowed self-consciously.

'But I confess that I am bewildered by your action. You are not bound by anything – least of all my father's hospitality – that should make you hazard your life in such a way. Why – and so far from your own people – might you do this? Is it that you love battle so much? That you glory in its dangers?'

'Not the latter, madam, I assure you. I have never, I believe, shirked battle, but I have never taken pleasure in it. Satisfaction, but never pleasure.'

'Then what has driven you to do these things here?'

Her suspicion was as artfully concealed as she was able.

How might he begin to explain his actions, with so great a gulf as their sex and their faith between them? 'Madam, there is nothing more repellent to a soldier than that others who share his calling turn their arms against those who have hitherto trusted them. There is never any justification for mutiny. Discipline is the soul of an army, and when it is gone there *is* no army – only a brute mob. No soldier can then keep his honour who merely stands by.'

She paused before pressing him to own to a further interest, though he did not guess that she supposed him to be working to some scheme. 'Captain Hervey, you will now entreat my father to accept the protection of the British, will you not?'

Her percipience did her great credit, and Hervey's admiration was the more. There was no question but that he must answer rightly. 'I shall. I would consider it more than prudent in any circumstances, but since the nizam's intentions are at best uncertain, and likewise the army's loyalty, I believe it to be the only possible course.'

The raj kumari looked closely at him, narrowing her eyes in a manner that conjured a startling menace. 'And do you suppose that Chintal would ever then be free of interference by the British?'

With what passion did she serve her father's interests! In that instant, Hervey was disavowed of any notion but that the raj kumari was quite unlike any woman he had known.

The rajah's utter dejection seemed, at one moment the following day, as if it might wholly pull him down. Selden was even fearful of some derangement, and all its unthinkable consequences. But the rajah would see no physician, native or otherwise. And then, towards the evening, he had seemed to emerge from his despondency, ordering that the state processional, held four times each year, and which occasion the following day no official of the court had dared to enquire of, should continue. He told Selden it would be a sign to his subjects that they might have confidence in the permanence of Chintal, and of the rajah himself. He would process with all his elephants, as was the custom, to the great oxbow of the Godavari, where the ashes of the dead had been ceremonially scattered for generations, and there he would have his sepoys drawn up. He would remind them of their destiny and then absolve them from the penalty which Hervey had imposed. Throughout evening and most of the night, therefore, the palace was all activity, with constant curses and laments: *Aré bap-ré, bap-ré!*

As Hervey walked towards the menagerie in the cool of the late evening, old Seejavi's mahout greeted him solemnly in his fractured Urdu, and Hervey returned his salutations with a smile. 'How go things in the *hathi-khana?*' he asked, knowing full well the mahout would be

213

flattered that Wellesley-sahib's captain wished to hear of things in the elephant stables.

'By the favour of the Presence, all is well. Tonight is old Seejavi's festival, and tomorrow he will go with the rajah to the river, if he wills – but with no man on his back.'

'And is he *very* old, mahout sahib?'

The wizened little man swelled with pride at both the thought of Seejavi's age and the captain's honouring him so. 'He is the oldest elephant in all of India – compeller of worlds, mover of mountains. He has been with the rajah since the Great Fear. Men say he carried Cornwallis-sahib. Gopi Nath has just repainted his head, and three *chirags* burn on his skull-top; will not the Presence come and see him?'

Of course he would come. And soon they were in the hathi-khana, the most peaceful quarters of the palace that night – although else-where, a dozen mahouts and many more gholams sweated to prepare the howdahs and trappings for the morning.

'See his tusks, mounted with gold: the rajah had that done when Seejavi charged through the Maratha hordes at the time of the Fear and enabled him to escape to the British. It was twenty years ago today, and the rajah always gives silver to the hathi-khana and decor-ates Seejavi, the *amir-i-filan* – the prince of elephants – lest he turn on us and kill his mahout. Seven mahouts he has killed in my memory, sahib. See the garland of roses the rajah sent him this morning: he will only wear them if his temper is good.'

Hervey contemplated Seejavi for many minutes. The old elephant stood swaying from side to side as if cogitating some equal mystery, the oil lamps atop his head flickering and dancing with frosty blue flames.

'Seejavi will soon begin to speak, sahib.'

'What?'

'Yes, sahib. We never know what he will say, but he tells of battles and sieges, of suttees and sacrifices, and of men he has killed.'

'Mahout sahib—'

'Prince-born, it is true, I tell you. He will speak to Shisha Nag, his favourite he-elephant. He will tell him secrets – how he threw the vile Sindhia's spy from his back and trampled him. And how, when he served the peshwa awhile, and they fought the nizam's army, they captured the guns worked by some French. And how they made prize of the French camp, among them a French woman whom the rao claimed as his share. He carried her off in a howdah on Seejavi's back that night, though she wept bitterly. The rao put his arm around her and she bit him till he bled, so that he swore again, but vowed she was a fit wife for a reiving Maratha. Seejavi took them across the Nerbudda, in full spate from the mango showers. And two sons she bore the rao! And Shisha Nag will listen respectfully – enviously, for the rajah does not use his elephants for war any longer.'

Shisha Nag stood a few paces behind Seejavi, swaying to and fro also, as if waiting for them to leave so that he might hear the amir-i-filan's stories. Hervey smiled to himself: why should such a beast as this, old and wise, *not* be able to speak of these things?

'Yes, Prince-born,' sighed the mahout, 'Shisha Nag has much to learn from him. And tomorrow Seejavi shall have nine full-size cakes for hazree, spread with best molasses. Tomorrow will be a grand tamasha – the very finest of parties, sahib.'

At eight next morning, the rajah emerged from his quarters into the great courtyard. There, in sunlight so bright that even the gold thread in his purple kurta glinted, he mounted a white Turkoman and, at the head of the palace troop, began the descent of the droog to where the procession had assembled on the maidan – a procession which, if lacking some of the order and symmetry of a parade on the Horse Guards, in its sheer colour and vitality surpassed anything Hervey had seen, or could ever have imagined.

He watched from the walls of the palace. The rajah had said nothing to him since the heartfelt greeting on his return from Jhansikote, nor had he sent any word, and although this might have occasioned some injury, Hervey confided that it was but a most conscious effort at self-reliance on the rajah's part. Again, he found himself filled with admiration for the rajah's attachment to duty, difficult for him – painful, even – though he knew it must be.

The palace troop – the lancers of the guard – wore purple also, thirty proud sowars on bays whose coats shone with the effort of many hours' brushing. Two half-rissalahs – four hundred lancers in all – were drawn up as advance and rear detachments, and six huge war-elephants, their tusks capped by gold sheaths, richly caparisoned in silk shabraques – purple for the rajah's, red for the others – stood with infinite patience. Ornate mounting steps awaited the dignitaries who would travel in the cupolaed howdahs. Awnings, extending like those which shaded the bazaar merchants as they sat in front of their shops, gave just sufficient relief from the sun's coming strength to the bare-legged mahouts. All the officials of the court were gathered in their most extravagant finery, and all made namaste as the rajah appeared. A fanfare of huge trumpets echoed the occasion beyond the palace walls, and the elephants, though their fighting days were long past, raised their trunks in salute. Out of a palanquin draped in silks and studded with semi-precious stones stepped the raj kumari. Hervey's telescope moved at once to her, for her purple saree set off everything about her which might make a man admire a woman. She bowed to her father, took his hand as he led her to the mounting steps, and most gracefully did they both ascend to the howdah. The rajah stood acknowledging the acclamation of the courtyard, and then signalled to Captain Steuben atop the magnificently accoutred Shisha Nag for the assemblage to move off (Steuben was the only European whom Hervey could see in the procession, for not even Selden was there). He watched them leave the maidan and went then to the stables, for although he had business enough to occupy him with a pen all day, the urge to follow the procession was too great. He wanted to see this singular cavalcade at its fullest extent, and the Godavari durbar where its design would be fulfilled.

Johnson, in the way that only he seemed able, had anticipated him, and Jessye and one of the rajah's country-breds stood saddled in their stalls. In five more minutes they were leaving the palace by a side gate, and heading for the low-lying hills which overlooked the river and the road to the oxbow, so that they might observe discreetly, respectfully.

The great basin of the upper Godavari was nothing like as green as at other times, except the forested slopes of the northern side, an abutment of the Eastern Ghats, whose dark canopy extended as far as the eye could see. On the flood plain itself there were comparatively few trees, and at this time of year the black cotton soil and rocky outcrops were bare of signs of cultivation. During the rains the tableland would become grass country once more, a vast grazing ground and fodder store for the thousands of placid beasts which served the people of Chintalpore. Between the city and the oxbow the river was a wide, sedate stream – as it was, indeed, for much of its length. The only obstruction between here and the sea 150 miles to the east was caused by shallowing across two or three sections of rocky bed where the river traversed the strike of the adjoining hills, barring the way to navigation when the water was low. On the eastern borders of Chintal, where the domains of the nizam, the Company and the Rajah of Nagpore successively adjoined those of Chintal, there were points of great beauty. Here the Godavari became enclosed between the Bison range (so called because of occasional visits by that stocky game) and the hills of Rumpa. The steeply shelving cliffs and crowded forests of bamboo, teak, tamarind and fig might have been those that overlooked the Lorelei, except that no castle or other work of human hand was to be seen.

In an hour or so they were nearing the oxbow, almost a full mile behind the cavalcade, on the higher ground to the south. But such was the brightness of the sun, and the clearness of the air, that the procession could easily be observed in all its detail without even a telescope. The saffron lance pennants first drew the eye to the escort, whose sowars still sat tall in the saddle. Then to the bullock carts and the camels which carried the means for the rajah's feast, and then to the gaggle of ryots who followed, as always, hopeful of some benediction of the rajah, or better still some material benevolence – and some blessing by Shiva or Kali or the spirits of the Godavari. In truth, they came because they had always come, for if they did not, then perhaps there might be no monsoon, no harvest. Such was the way with Hindoo gods.

But it was the state elephants that truly commanded Hervey's attention. At this distance their massiveness, their substance, their belittling of every living thing, was at its plainest. The howdahs added half their height again, and their golds, silvers, crimsons and vermilions stood in sharpest contrast with the baked colours of the land. No greater distinction between the highest prince and the meanest *hind* could there be than before him now, the rajah elevated beyond all reach in his jewelled and canopied throne, and the ryot behind, covered in the dust of his lord's retinue, legs bowed, back bent – closer to the earth than to the belly of the noble creature which carried his rajah and gave a face to God. At that moment Hervey knew in his vitals the eternal draw of this land.

Carefully he worked himself nearer to the oxbow, not wanting to be seen, for it seemed (for all its panoply) so private an occasion. He might have got closer still, but at a furlong from the rear of the great press of ryots, behind the ranks of sepoys, he halted shoulders-down in a nullah and took out his telescope.

217

'What d'ye see, Captain 'Ervey sir?'

He swept left to right along the whole line of the durbar – perhaps a quarter of a mile of tight-pressed souls, all silent. 'There's a sadhu haranguing them. I can't hear what he says but I think they're swearing the oath.' He allowed himself a faint smile of satisfaction: Locke's way had so nearly prevailed. He had come close to accepting Locke's counsel indeed, for the instant that muskets, powder and ball were placed in the hands of the sepoys they would be given the means of insurrection they had formerly lacked. But Chintal, of all places, could not be held subservient by mere force of arms. There must be a voluntary compliance in its subjects, both civil and military. The rajah knew it too. And that was why the rajah now had to meet the test four-square, knowing that if Hervey and he had judged things wrong his sowars might save his person, and that of the raj kumari, but his dominion would be lost.

Rousing cheers broke from the ranks of the resworn sepoys. The rajah descended from his state elephant, mounted the white Turkoman and rode along their front rank acknowledging the loyal greetings – testing their fidelity, even – by his very closeness. He rode back to the centre of the line, stood high in the stirrups and made his little speech of obligation and satisfaction. When he absolved them of the year's service without pay there was another full-throated roar of devotion, and he walked his charger directly towards them, the ranks opening to let him pass, the sepoys making low namaste. And as the great tamasha began – with its spit-roasts and rice, its breads and its spices – the rajah rode from the parade with a stature that even Hervey, through his telescope, could see was enhanced. An escort of but a half-dozen lancers rode with him, south and east towards the low-lying hills where earlier Hervey and Johnson had taken their ease as the durbar assembled.

He lowered the telescope . . . and then raised it quickly again. It was the sudden surge near the state elephants. Like the wind across a field of corn. Shisha Nag was it not? Throwing up his head, lashing with his trunk, raising a great dust. Hervey could not make out what disturbed him. All he could see was Seejavi standing close by, swaying gently, this way and then that. He rubbed his eye clear of moisture and put the telescope to it again. And he saw the body of a man being carried, as if it were a half-filled palliasse, from where Shisha Nag had raised such a dust. He wondered which unfortunate mahout or sepoy had fallen victim to the young male's bile – or even to old Seejavi's wiles.

A little trail of dust marked the rajah's progress. Hervey did not even have to broach the crest of the obliging nullah to keep station with him. Where the ground first began to rise, a mile or so from the oxbow, the dust settled and he edged a little up the nullah's banks to see where the rajah and his escort were halted. He could see them quite clearly, almost two full furlongs away, by an ancient pagoda in a secluded mango grove. The rajah waited as the lancers beat about the ground (for leopard were not unknown in these parts) and then, as his escort retired to the other side of the little hill which hid the pagoda from sight of the river, he dismounted and entered the sacred building. Hervey could see it all quite clearly from his hollow in the ground. He was about to lower his telescope, for he had no wish to spy on the rajah during his devotions, when he noticed, a hundred yards beyond the grove, under a banyan tree, a bullock cart. And then, after a short while, the rajah emerging from the pagoda and walking towards it. A figure emerged from the shade of the tree and made namaste – a shrivelled little man in a sunhat. Hervey turned his telescope back to the cart: two of the thinnest-looking oxen, cream-coloured, yoked side by side, stood patiently. How many oxen, carts and shrivelled little men there were in all of India he could not begin to imagine, but he knew he had seen these ones before.

That afternoon

Three pariah kites glided high above the palace with not a beat of any wing in the five minutes Hervey observed their ascent. They described a lazy but precise circle over the royal gardens, as if disdaining the city beyond, and without any apparent interest in prey on the ground. Perhaps the birds knew that now, in the heat of the day, though still no greater in this month than that of an English summer, few warm-blooded creatures left the shade. At length he walked to the stables, hoping to find Selden there.

'Hervey, come and take a look at this mare. Have you seen a foaling before?'

'Not since Jessye herself,' he replied.

'Well, you might this evening. She's waxed up, but she's not sweating yet, so she'll drop it after dark is my bet, as most do.'

The mare, a light-chestnut Arab, was standing calmly on a deep bed of straw, her syce keeping watch anxiously inside the foaling box. 'Very well then, Bittu,' said Selden to him in his native Telugu as he left. 'Send for me at once when her breathing becomes laboured.' And then, turning to Hervey: 'Come – tea and words, I think.'

Hervey agreed.

In the cool seclusion of Selden's apartments Hervey spoke his thoughts freely. He must leave Chintal as soon as possible – within the week, he hoped. The Jhansikote business was something he ought not by rights to have intervened in. 'Have you yet located the papers for the jagirs?'

Selden frowned. 'Hervey, it is a trickier business than you suppose. I don't have right of access to such documents. I must choose my time.'

Every day he remained here, Hervey protested, he prejudiced his chances of being received by the nizam – which was the duke's foremost commission.

'Yes, I understand full well,' sighed Selden; 'and I am conscious – acutely conscious – of your having gone to Jhansikote on my promise.'

Hervey would have said some words of mitigation (for he suspected he could never have stood aside, having accepted the rajah's hospitality), except that to do so might have lessened Selden's resolve to find the documents. 'Then you will try to bring matters to a conclusion before the end of the week?'

Selden nodded.

Hervey poured himself some tea and sat by the window.

'By the by,' said Selden, sitting in a chair draped with a tigerskin, 'you have heard of the elephant going must at the durbar this morning.'

Hervey, gazing out intently at the pariah kites still circling, could truthfully say he had not, for he had seen it at a distance, and no one had spoken of it since his return.

'Extraordinary business: it tore a man from its howdah. The fellow's back would have broken as it hit the ground, but the great beast trampled him for good measure. He was brought here post-haste in a doolie – dead as mutton.'

'Was it anyone of note?' asked Hervey, though not, in truth, greatly exercised, for he was becoming accustomed to death in India.

Selden raised an eyebrow and lowered his voice. 'Captain Steuben.'

'Good heavens!' gasped Hervey, turning back towards the salutri.

'Good heavens! The poor fellow. How perfectly dreadful . . . what ill fortune—'

'But not, I'm sure, *accidental* ill fortune.' It was now Selden's turn to look away, leaving Hervey to ponder the suggestion.

'Why do you say . . . on what evidence do you believe . . .'

Selden turned back to him, but he merely raised both eyebrows.

'Come, man: you must have *some* evidence!'

'I cannot suppose anyone to be innocent of the affair of the batta who had the opportunity to be otherwise.'

Hervey poured himself more of the cinnamon tea. He could not, he said, gainsay Selden's logic. 'And yet I cannot somehow believe—'

A sudden commotion below the window halted his speculation. They leaned out, to see several dozen of the palace staff babbling excitedly and calling on the salutri. 'Come,' said Selden, making for the door. 'Something's amiss.'

They followed the little crowd to the other side of the gardens, to one of the summer wells. Another babble; this time of outdoor servants as they pulled out the body of a man, gagged, and bound with ropes. They parted to let the salutri through. He needed only a glimpse of the smooth cheeks, the long straight hair and the doll-like upturned nose to recognize him. 'Kunal Verma,' he sighed, shaking his head.

'Who?' said Hervey.

'Kunal Verma – the rajah's dewan, keeper of his treasury. And of land deeds.'

CHAPTER FOURTEEN

THE SUBSIDIARY ALLIANCE

A week later

Chintalpore was becoming hot and the air heavy. The south-west monsoon, the yearly salvation of the tens of thousands of ryots who dwelled so close to the soil as to be almost indistinguishable from it, was a full three months away. Throughout the winter months, the sun being low, the surface of the earth in Hindoostan had been steadily cooling until now its temperature was lower than the seas adjoining it. By some as yet unfathomed effect no moisture-bearing clouds could be induced to leave the ocean and water the land. But from March onwards, with the sun higher, and its strength bearing directly on the land for longer, the surface of the earth would speedily become hotter than the ocean. And when this inversion came about, by some equally unfathomed effect, moisture-laden clouds from the south-west would march steadily landwards until, by about the end of May, they would be watering the Malabar littoral prodigiously, and as far north even as Bombay. By the middle of June, if the gods had granted a favourable monsoon, Chintal's fearsome heat and enervating humidity would be relieved by the daily downpours. Thereafter, there would be a bountiful harvest and plenty in the land. But if the gods were not propitiated and did not grant a good monsoon, then there would be misery, starvation, death. Which of these there was to be would increasingly occupy the prayers of the Rajah of Chintal's subjects in this onset of the hot season. But as for the rajah himself, what most occupied his mind, and filled his prayers, was the nizam.

Hervey had sent letters to Guntoor for Madras and Paris, together with a note for the collector advising him of his intention to leave for Haidarabad at the end of the (yet another) week. Having become more circumspect since Jhansikote, and now with the complications in respect of the jagirs since the death of Kunal Verma, he intended to proceed with more formality. However, Selden had been unable to transact the business with the land registry. It was not a propitious time, the salutri explained, for the rajah's ministries were in confusion. Another ten days or so, he believed, would see things better placed.

The letter to Colonel Grant had exercised Hervey a great deal. His immediate disposition had been to write a complete account of all that had passed, yet in successive drafts he had been unable to render any account that did not convey an inauspicious picture of his mission. This he partially ascribed to the difficulty of portraying the peculiar circumstances of Chintal, but mostly he knew it to be the result of his own misjudgements to date. And so he had in the end written a somewhat bland narrative, referring to one or two setbacks, but confident of ultimate success on all counts.

This and the letter to Madras urging the Company to come to the rajah's aid with an offer of subsidiary alliance had occupied the whole of one evening and most of its night, and so when the hircarrah left for Guntoor next morning it was without any letter to Horningsham. This had not done much for Hervey's spirits, and he had therefore thrown himself into lance drill with the rissalahs. It perfectly occupied his mind – though the price was heavy, with more than one crashing fall from misjudging the angle of strike on a tent peg. But neither did he think it time wasted in the wider scheme of things, for although the lance was merely his ostensible reason for being in India, the Chintal rissalahs were proficient with the weapon – skilled, even – and his findings would surely find a place at the Horse Guards as they considered at this very moment what should be the future of the lance in the British cavalry.

The Chintal sowars carried lances made of bamboo, ten and a half feet long, with a bayonet-shaped steel head. 'I dare not recall how close I came to feeling the lance's point at Waterloo,' said Hervey to Captain

Bauer one morning as they watched another round of tent-pegging, shaking his head at the thought.

'I am surprised you do not have lancers, after so many years' seeing their effect,' replied Bauer, his German heavy.

'Oh, do not mistake me, sir, for I myself am as yet unconvinced. The lance, for all its fearsomeness, has limited utility compared with the sabre.'

'Ach, Hervey – but its *moral* effect!'

True, he conceded, its moral effect alone could be overwhelming, even before the weapon was brought to bear. 'But in a mêlée, if only one can get in close, the lance is useless against the sabre. The lancer can scarcely parry, or wheel and thrust half so well as a sabreur – or even a resolute infantryman with his bayonet.'

'Ja, perhaps so – then he throws his lance down and draws his sword. But *first*, Hervey, how do you get to close quarters with a squadron of lancers?!'

'That, indeed, is the material point,' replied Hervey smiling.

Bauer joined in his enjoyment of the pun.

Hervey was still intent on serious study, however. 'What has determined its length? In England there is a regiment of light dragoons presently engaged with a lance some sixteen feet – longer even than a medieval knight's.'

'Ten feet, or thereabouts, is a good compromise,' said Bauer, nodding. 'It allows the sowar to pick off a crouching man and follow through cleanly, without surrendering any great advantage of reach. If he wants more reach then he must lean from the saddle!'

Hervey saw as much, as lancers galloped this way and that in front of him, effortlessly taking tent pegs further from their line each time.

'Of one thing I am sure, Captain Bauer: carrying a lance is a most effective aid. At the trot and canter it makes the man greatly more active, obliging him to ride his horse forward into the rein, and promoting a more independent seat. When it is in my power to do so I shall have my own troopers carry a lance at riding school.'

Bauer was delighted: exactly his sentiments when riding master many years before. 'Hervey, you would make a good German!' he beamed.

They did not speak for several more minutes, except to remark on one sowar's skill or another, but then Hervey's thoughts returned to the question of moral effect. The rajah's sowars could wield the lance with impressive skill; he fancied there was no sight more able to strike fear into an adversary than a line of their steel points lowered and approaching at a gallop – perhaps the only chance cavalry had of breaking an infantry square without support of artillery. And it was artillery the rajah was in want of. Yet even now as he watched the drill he could not but imagine that, if the infantry maintained their close order in the face of the moral effect, lancers would make no more *material* impression than would dragoons. The matter turned – as did every battle in the last instance – on how well-drilled was the infantry. 'Captain Bauer,' he said in a measuring way, 'do you not think a front rank of lances, backed by a second of sabres, and perhaps even the third, might have the same moral effect and yet have greater handiness?'

Alter Fritz did not hesitate. 'Hervey, I give you my opinion, but I am an old quartermaster only. You should have made these enquiries of Captain Steuben. He commanded a squadron against the French, you know.'

They had not spoken of Steuben since the accident. On the subject of cold steel, that German had been as passionate as at other times he had been distant. But now he lay in the palace's great marble crypt with the other honoured servants of Chintal. 'It was a swift death, says everyone, for he must have broken his neck at once.'

'Ja, a howdah is a fair height to fall from.'

'Captain Bauer, do you know . . . did anyone *see* what happened at this time?'

Alter Fritz shook his head. 'I heard tell only the mahout and two attendants.'

As drill ended, Private Johnson appeared. He had the sort of smile which Hervey knew portended awkward news. 'That Miss Lucie is 'ere, Captain 'Ervey, sir,' he announced.

And before Hervey could begin anything by reply, Emma Lucie, beneath a straw hat of huge diameter, came striding towards the edge of the maidan. 'Good morning, Captain Hervey,' she said in a matter-of-fact way.

Hervey and Bauer dismounted, the German's heels clicking together in the prescribed manner, while Hervey took off his shako.

'I heard that you were . . . how shall one say? – in trouble?' she smiled.

Hervey sighed. 'News travels quickly along the Godavari, it seems, madam.'

225

Emma Lucie sighed too. 'News, perhaps, but alas, not the budgerow: progress upstream is very slow.'

Hervey stood before her almost lost for further words. 'Madam, I am not sure to what news exactly you refer, but I am dismayed to think that any cause of mine should be occasion for your discomfort.'

Bauer gave a discreet cough.

'Oh, forgive me, sir,' said Hervey. 'Miss Lucie, may I present Captain Bauer, quartermaster and acting commanding officer of the Rajah of Chintal's lancers?'

'*Il me donne du grand plaisir de vous rencontrer, madame,*' replied Bauer, his accent clipped.

'Captain Bauer: Miss Lucie,' continued Hervey, in French. 'Miss Lucie's brother is in the Company's service at Madras.'

Emma Lucie made more of a bow than a curtsy. '*Von welchen Staat des Deutschen Bund kommen Sie, Herr Rittmeister?*'

'*Von Württemberg, gnädiges Fräulein.*'

But, happy though Bauer evidently was with the company of a lady who spoke his language, he had pressing duties to be about, and after a few pleasant exchanges he made his apologies and took his leave.

Hervey handed his reins to Johnson and invited Emma Lucie to walk back with him to the palace.

'Well,' she began breezily; 'it appears the reports of your perilous situation were but exaggeration!'

Hervey smiled. 'We have had our difficulties, Miss Lucie, but I believe them to be past.'

'Captain Hervey,' she smiled, 'in my experience of this country, as one misfortune abates another follows quickly on its heels.'

'A most depressing observation, madam.'

She chose not to respond directly. 'I was in Rajahmundry when I heard, and I thought what Henrietta would do in the circumstances. I had not seen Chintal – the river is very beautiful I heard tell – and had never met the rajah. Mr Somervile always speaks so well of him. And my brother would not too, I think, wish to hear of your lying untended in Chintalpore. So thus I am come.'

Hervey admired her spirit if not her judgement. 'I hazard a guess, madam, your brother will be greatly more alarmed at learning of your being here!'

'He will be greatly cheered when he learns of your dash at the mutineers. You recaptured the cantonments single-handed, I learn!'

'Hardly that, madam!' he laughed: 'that is far in excess of the truth. But may I enquire how you have learned of it?'

'From the rajah – to whom, of course, I first presented myself on arriving here. He is most happy to receive visitors from Madras.'

'Oh . . .' he groaned.

'Why do you make that noise?' she asked.

'Because the rajah's daughter, the raj kumari, is suspicious that I intend bringing Chintal under the Company's domination.'

'And what can I be to such a scheme,' she smiled, 'a mere woman?'

'The raj kumari is a "mere woman", madam, and I do not underestimate her power and influence!'

'But it cannot be supposed that I – travelling by budgerow up the Godavari with two servants – am in some way party to intrigue?'

'Miss Lucie,' said Hervey resolutely, 'I warrant there is more intrigue here than in Rome. There isn't a khitmagar who is not party to it. The sister of an official of the Honourable Company must be immediately suspect.'

'Ah,' she replied simply, though without concern.

'Do not trouble yourself, madam,' he laughed. 'I do not believe it will amount to much. I must tell you, however, that I shall in all probability be leaving Chintalpore within the week, and I would advise that you be escorted to Guntoor at that time, if not before.'

In the shade of the palace's great walls they were now walking more briskly, and as they passed through the gates a thought seemed to occur to her. 'You have, I suppose, heard of the latest depredations by the Pindarees?'

'The latest, as I understand, Miss Lucie, are those of which I had intimate acquaintance with Mr Somervile. I believe we were within half a day's ride of them as they fled into Nagpore.'

Emma Lucie seemed surprised. 'Why no, Captain Hervey: there have been more incursions into the Circars since then. There was terrible murder and rapine. They came within the civil station at Guntoor, even, and almost as far as Rajahmundry. There was great alarm.'

'*Post hoc ergo propter hoc?*'

'In what connection?'

'Earlier you said something about one misfortune following another. I have been at pains to understand events here. I was wondering if there might be some connection between what happened at Jhansikote and the Pindaree depredations.'

227

Emma Lucie nodded. 'Another thing I have observed in this country,' she said, lowering her voice, 'is that everything is perceived to be a consequence of human intrigue or the malevolence of the gods, no matter how apparent to us might its accidental nature be. If there is no connection between the events to which you refer, there will indeed be a connection in the minds of those who contemplate them, and there will therefore, in time, become a real connection in practice.'

'In that case, Miss Lucie,' said Hervey, with some foreboding, 'the situation here may be graver than I feared. But that cannot be a concern of mine – or, I venture, yours.'

'And there is not a frigate of the Royal Navy at hand,' she replied opaquely.

He did not catch her meaning. 'Madam?'

'Captain Peto and the *Nisus* are at present stationed at the mouth of the Godavari.'

'Then I am pleased for Mr Somervile. I trust that Captain Peto has been able to effect all the repairs he wished for?'

'I know not,' she replied, shaking her head. '*Nisus* was just come one morning – in some show of force, I believe. She was a most welcome sight.'

'A fathom of water,' smiled Hervey.

'I do not understand you, sir.'

'Something Bonaparte once lamented: wherever you find a fathom of water, there you will find the Royal Navy.'

'For *heaven's* sake, Johnson, can't you stop that horse from doing that?'

'No, it's 'ad ginger up its arse since I first took it out!'

'I *had* hoped for an easy ride this afternoon, and Jessye's in a muck sweat already.'

'D'ye remember that big geldin' that Captain Jessope 'ad afore Waterloo? I reckon that 'ad been figged right 'n proper when 'e bought it!'

'Enough about figging, Johnson. If *you* kept your backside a little stiller you might have more success.'

'Does tha want to change 'orses, sir?'

Hervey laughed. 'No!'

'Then we'll 'ave to make t'best of it. Like life.'

This was one of the rare deeper revelations of Johnson's philosophy, a unique distillation of barrack-room wisdom and the residual scripture of his poorhouse upbringing. Johnson saw little point in contemplation. Once, in Spain at the height of the campaign, he had modified the chaplain's rendering of the Gospel, and 'sufficient unto the parade is the evil thereof' had become for a time the axiom of the grooms. Johnson saw no difference in a parade in peace or in war, for each required strenuous preparation, each required him to follow precisely the commands given by word of mouth or the trumpet, and each ended when an officer decided that it should. The interim – whether bloody or not – scarcely mattered. Indeed, Johnson believed that he was alive *because* there was war, not in spite of it: it would otherwise have been the pit or the foundry for him had not the recruiting party happened his way ten years before (few orphans who found their way into those nether worlds saw more than a quarter of what scripture promised was their span of life).

'Johnson, are you content here?' asked Hervey, trying once more to urge Jessye onto the bit to stop the jog-trotting to which she had recently become inclined.

Private Johnson, whose Arab mare had done nothing but jog-trot since they had left the stables a half-hour before, was taken aback by the solicitude. 'Me? Ay, I'm content enough.'

Hervey knew this to be an expression of considerable satisfaction. 'You are not overly vexed that we might have been killed at Jhansikote?' he smiled.

'If it's all right by thee . . .' was all that came by reply.

'Johnson, do you ever think that it might be more prudent to follow some other line, perhaps a—'

'No.'

'So you are not ill-disposed to the country?' he pressed.

Johnson would have sighed had even he not thought it disrespectful. 'Captain 'Ervey, sir, I've 'ad more square meals 'ere than I can remember, and they cost next to nowt. Why is tha concerned abaht me all of a sudden?'

Now it was Hervey's turn to feel offended. 'I have never knowingly been *un*concerned! It's just that you're far from home, and there's no knowing when you'll see it again.'

'Captain 'Ervey, 'ow many times 'ave I told thee I don't 'ave a 'ome as I calls one!'

'No, forgive me. Perhaps what I meant is being among your own people – being with the regiment, even.'

'Ah well, that's another matter, but there's nowt I can do about it so . . . an' I tell thee, I've never eaten as well as 'ere.'

Hervey smiled again. For an enlisted man food was usually the criterion. 'And I have observed that you are popular with the rajah's establishment.'

'If tha means that lass whose father's one of t'rajah's fart-catchers – ay.'

Hervey was now smiling broadly.

'They must 'ave seen Englishmen afore, since they know a few words. But I can't make 'em understand much.'

Hervey shook his head, still smiling. 'Private Johnson, I am of the opinion that you lay on your diabolical Yorkshire speech deliberately to confuse!'

'It doesn't take much to confuse some officers!'

Hervey laughed outright. 'And how much of this lady do you see?'

'Tha means 'ow often?' he replied, with a wry smile.

'Johnson!'

'I eat with 'em most nights.'

'And native fare is to your liking?'

'I 'ad the shits all last week, but it weren't so bad.'

'There's good food enough,' Hervey conceded, 'though I confess to a pining for beef!'

'An' the women is friendly. Even Mr Locke seems to 'ave 'is feet under t'table with one of them naught girls.'

'*Nautch* girls, Johnson, *nautch*: there is nothing naught about them. They're respectable dancers. Their dance is a very ancient one.'

'Oh ay, sir?'

'*Yes.*'

'I bet Miss Lindsay wouldn't approve.'

Hervey felt chastened, even though he did not fancy it true.

'I reckon one of them girls would do Mr Selden a power of good, though,' he added mischievously.

'Now that's enough! There's to be no talk of those matters concerning Mr Selden – anywhere.'

'Well, my lass's family seem to know about it.'

'I thought you said they couldn't understand English?'

'We get along with signs and things,' said Johnson, matter-of-fact.

Hervey was at once diverted by the picture of their signing Selden's predilections. 'What Mr Selden needs more than anything is a good physician. The fever has laid him low again; he could barely raise his head this morning.'

'Well, there's a lot of talk about 'im 'n them eunuchs. My lass's folk reckon there's somethin gooin' on – fiddles 'n the like.'

Having become tired with the struggle to keep in a walk, Hervey decided they should trot slowly, even though both mares were in a lather. After a minute or so they were settled to a good rhythm, and Johnson felt ready to resume their conversation. ''As anybody found out yet about that 'Indoo as was fished out of t'water?'

'No, not a thing,' replied Hervey. 'He was the rajah's dewan, one of his ministers, that's all I know.'

'My lass's folk say that 'e must 'ave been on the take with them that was fleecing t'sepoys.'

'Yes, I had heard something of that too. But it's all speculation. The rajah is loath to speak of it.'

'What about Mr Selden: doesn't 'e know owt? Isn't 'e supposed to know everything that's gooin' on?'

'I've not had much opportunity to speak with him on the matter. It's not our concern, in any case. I want to move on to Haidarabad as soon as we can. There's a lot about this place that I wouldn't wish to know.'

''As tha got them papers yet for t'duke, sir?'

'No, not yet. I had hoped by the end of the week, but since Mr Selden is bedded down I fear it will be longer. And those papers, frankly, are part of what I mean by not wanting to know certain things.'

Johnson said nothing, leaving Hervey to his thoughts. Not wanting to know was perhaps the best policy – for both of them. Little was as it appeared. The tryst at the pagoda, for instance: what did that portend? And *did* Selden know everything? Was it likely that he did, a horse surgeon periodically racked by fever? Selden himself protested he did not, but . . .

They rode up to a bluff overlooking the approaches to the palace. Hervey liked to dismount here to take in the view. The horses were glad of the rest, too, picking at the dhak for a stem or two that was worth the effort of pulling, while their riders sat on the ground holding the reins – not, however, before Johnson had thrashed about the ground with his whip, as if he were flaying corn.

231

'Johnson, I don't think it's absolutely necessary to pound with quite so much vigour. The thud of the hooves will have been enough to drive anything away.'

'Tha mustn't 'ave been close to a snake 'ere yet then. I don't want one within a 'undred yards of me!'

Hervey blanched at the recollection of the hamadryads. 'Let us not talk about snakes.'

'They give me the cold creeps just thinking about 'em.'

'Enough!'

They sat a full quarter of an hour without a word, taking in the distant views, the horses as content. At length Johnson voiced his thoughts. 'Can we talk about what we're gooin' to do next, sir? It's not for me to say owt, but . . .'

Hervey sighed. 'I'm glad you do say something. I'm glad to have someone who I might speak freely to, for I can't with any other.'

'Not with Mr Locke?'

'Oh, indeed: I should be very happy to share everything with Mr Locke, but I am bound to secrecy in this matter, and I have already had to tell you and the frigate's captain.'

'But you could trust Mr Locke. You saw how he fought at them barracks!'

Hervey agreed that there was no one better to have in a fight: 'But he drinks so much at times – I could not wholly trust his discretion.'

'*You* might booze it, too, if you 'ad 'is looks.'

'I'm not making any judgement, Johnson; I am merely observing on his reliability.'

'*Jesus Christ!*' shouted his groom suddenly, springing to his feet and drawing his sabre. He sliced powerfully in one motion straight from the draw to the ground a few yards ahead.

Hervey was up a fraction of a second behind him, catching the Arab's loose reins. 'What the devil—'

'Bastard snake! Bastard, bastard cobra creeping up on us! It could've 'ad us both!'

The headless reptile writhed in the short scrub. Johnson sliced it into a further three parts for good measure. 'They can grow new 'eads, tha knows! Bastard cobras!'

Hervey was not inclined to question him on the regenerative properties of Indian snakes, but he looked as close as he dared – which was not very – before coming to the conclusion that they had been in no real danger. 'Not a cobra but a rat snake.'

'Is tha sure?'

'Moderately. Mr Somervile told me of the difference.'

'It sounds just as evil as a cobra. Why's it called a rat snake?'

'Because they eat rats?'

'Is tha tellin' me them's not poisonous?'

'That is what I understand; but believe me, Johnson, I would have done the same – only I fancy I would not have been so quick!'

The bluff had lost something of its charm to them, so they gathered up the reins. But as they turned for home Hervey's eye was caught by activity below, on the approaches to the palace.

'Looks like somebody important,' suggested Johnson.

Hervey got into the saddle and took out his telescope: 'Twenty, I can see. Half a dozen civilians with white faces. And the uniforms behind look the same as those Madras troopers we were with in Guntoor. Now what do you suppose *this* is about?'

That evening

Hervey rode back at no great pace and took his time bedding Jessye down. He saw no necessity to hurry, for he knew his letter could not yet have reached Madras, let alone elicited a response in the form of a visitation, and so he supposed that here was some initiative by the Company or even by the rajah himself. In either case he wished to be at arm's length from the proceedings. But how fortunate, he reflected, that he was able to address such a missive to someone with whom there was mutual confidence. Indeed, he owed much, did he not, to that felicitous meeting with Philip Lucie on the Madras foreshore, for, fever apart, he was close to securing the registry documents and he would soon begin making his journey west to see the nizam's forces. And it was perhaps as well that the nizam had cancelled his visit to Chintal, since he would now be able to observe him first on his own ground – perhaps a fairer gauge.

He went to his apartments, bathed and made ready for dinner with the rajah, to which he and Emma Lucie were invited alone. The rajah had of late become absorbed in a study of the Pentateuch, and Emma Lucie, he supposed, would be well versed in those books. Since the tryst at the pagoda Hervey had observed the rajah's manner become strange. Indeed, it seemed singularly ill-matched to the hour. Before, he had spoken frequently of the nizam's daughters; now they appeared to occupy him not in the least. Hervey wondered if money had changed hands at the pagoda, whether the shrivelled figure were an agent of the nizam's, or a spy of the rajah's.

Before the appointed time for dinner, however, he was summoned to the rajah's apartments, where he found the principal members of the party observed from the bluff – the Collector of Guntoor and Cornet Templer. 'You are acquainted with one another, I understand,' said the rajah.

All made bows and the usual gestures of greeting. The collector looked pulled-down by the journey, his thinning hair glistening with little beads of perspiration. Cornet Templer, on the contrary, looked enlivened by it, his eager features incapable of concealing his delight at being there.

The rajah resumed. 'Well, Captain Hervey, it very much seems that we are in peril both where the sun rises and where it sets. The nizam, I learn, is intent on striking in the west, and – from the intelligence which these envoys of the Honourable Company bring – the Pindarees are set to ravage the east of Chintal.'

But the collector looked puzzled by this appreciation. 'Your Highness, I brought intelligence of the Pindarees on the lower Godavari: why do you say the nizam is intent on striking Chintal? Are you not aware of the Pindaree depredations in his own domain?'

The rajah was not. The rajah knew only of the guns, about which, he revealed, he received daily reports, telling of their seemingly aimless movement about his border with Haidarabad.

The collector said he must explain the situation with the Pindarees at some length, and the rajah bade all sit, ordering his khitmagars to bring refreshment.

'Your Highness,' began Somervile, measuring his words carefully so that none of their import might be lost. 'Last October a body of – by some estimates – ten thousand Pindarees crossed the Nerbudda and swept through the nizam's provinces as far as the Kistna.'

'That I knew. And not even the Company's subsidiary force in Haidarabad could do anything to prevent this,' said the rajah accusingly.

'I regret not, sir.' Somervile cleared his throat and moved quickly on. 'The Pindarees then returned to their stronghold in the wilderness between the Nerbudda and the Vinhya Hills with so much plunder that merchants came from far and wide to purchase it. And, with such demonstrable success, they were able to attract even greater numbers to their ranks. In February, therefore, a force three times as big as that which had ravaged Haidarabad crossed the Nerbudda again, but this time their object was the Company's domain – the Northern Circars. They marched through Nagpore without, it seems, the rajah of that state raising a single musket to oppose them, poured into the Circars and sacked the civil station at Guntoor – not many days after you had left, Captain Hervey.'

'I have only recently heard of it, Your Highness,' said Hervey, turning to the rajah. 'The destruction of life and property was very great, I understand.'

The collector confirmed it. 'Over three hundred villages were plundered, many torched and razed to the ground. Two hundred persons put to death and three times as many grievously wounded. Thousands more – men and women – subjected to the vilest torture and defilement. Twenty-five lakhs of rupees – more than £300,000 – is my estimate of the loss of property alone.'

The rajah sighed wearily. 'I am troubled to learn that my fellow prince Raghujee Bhonsla should have connived at such outrages by letting through these marauders without hindrance.'

'It is now of no moment, Your Highness,' said the collector, 'for the Rajah of Nagpore died one week ago.'

The rajah looked alarmed: 'Raghujee Bhonsla is dead? I am very sad for it, but I am even more fearful, for Persajee – his son – is blind, palsied. He must not be rajah of so powerful a state as Nagpore!'

The collector remained wholly composed. 'You need have no worry on that account, Your Highness. The rajah's nephew Modajee – Appa Sahib – is, with the help of the Company, to be acknowledged as regent. We expect to conclude a treaty of alliance soon.'

'Consider, father: a subsidiary force and a resident in Nagpore!' said the raj kumari in a tone of disapproval.

Hervey had not noticed her beside the window, behind him.

The collector sought to reassure her. 'Your Highness,' he tried, 'surely it would be best to have a reliable neighbour, as would be guaranteed by the Company? The Rajah of Nagpore will be forbidden to make any alliances except with the approval of the Governor-General and his council, and it is an express condition of the treaty that Nagpore should never initiate hostilities against allies of the British. He could therefore be of no threat to Chintal.'

'But there is just such a treaty with the nizam,' she countered. 'There has been a British resident in Haidarabad these many years, and it has not made our position more assured.'

The collector was now seeing where the chief obstacle to his embassy lay. 'You are right, madam, to say that Haidarabad has not been without tumult. But there has been no eruption of warfare outside that kingdom's borders.'

'That is as maybe,' sneered the raj kumari, 'but Haidarabad has used every subterfuge to gain an equal result. The nizam's sons now throw the court into confusion while the resident is bribed into inaction!'

The collector bridled inwardly at the slur (though he would have admitted, privately, that there was truth in it), but forbore to show offence. Instead he tried to deflect the guilt. 'Madam, I own that the Governor-General would at present share your poor opinion of Moneer-ool-moolk, but—'

She would hear none of it, however. 'Sir, do you suppose we have no knowledge of affairs in Haidarabad? I speak not of the nizam himself, but of his vizier Chundoo Lall. *He* is the scourge of the nizam's kingdom. *He*, a fellow Hindoo, imposes his *dastak* on Chintal by threatening us with the very forces the resident has been so pre-occupied in bringing to such efficiency. And all in exchange for Chundoo Lall's gaudy bribes – a marble palace and gilded furniture from London, it is said!'

The collector knew he would have to trim. 'Madam, I assure you that I am not insensitive to the concerns of Chintal. That, indeed, is why I am come. With the greatest of respect, the danger to Chintal lies first in the Pindarees. The Governor-General – and take note that it is Calcutta now which acts, not merely Madras – the Governor-General hopes very much that the Nagpore subsidiary force which will be embodied once the treaty is signed will be of sufficient strength to deter them. Six, or perhaps seven, thousand will be the number. Colonel Leach, a Company officer of considerable distinction, will be placed in command. Yet more is needed if these brutes are to be prevented from finding booty *here*.'

The raj kumari was convinced this was but an incomplete explanation of their mission. 'And what is your design for us, therefore?'

'Your Highness, Lord Moira would welcome the assignment of the forces of Chintal to these efforts to keep the Pindarees north of the Nerbudda, or better still, to extirpate the menace once and for all.'

The rajah bade his daughter keep silent, and conceded there were fewer causes worthy of greater effort than the extirpation of the Pindarees. He thought for a while in silence, and then asked that the collector withdraw so that he might consider it more fully – which the agent of the Company did with all proper ceremony and deference. When he was gone, the rajah turned to Hervey and asked his opinion.

Hervey agreed wholeheartedly with the Company's proposal. Indeed, it was the very thing his letter, now en route to Madras, urged. He might wish these overtures had begun in a manner less pressing, for the implication of concerted action from Fort William – from the very place, indeed, where he expected the Duke of Wellington to be installed in but a few months – made him acutely conscious of another factor. He was obliged to consider what might be the duke's own wishes in the matter, for any alliances would constrain a new governor-general as surely as if they had been concluded by him in person. This much seemed easy, however, for a vigorous policy likely to promote greater peace would be entirely within the duke's notion of stewardship. But Lord Moira's intention to take vigorous action was so much at odds with what he had been told in Paris – that it was Moira's very passivity which was most likely to lead to the duke's being appointed in his place. 'Sir,' he began resolutely, but perplexed, 'I believe you may be confident of my respect for you and of my affection for Chintal: I would do nothing that would imply otherwise.'

The rajah bowed.

'I am strongly of the opinion that you should make an alliance with the Honourable Company – and with all haste. At least, that is, one limited in time or purpose, for a treaty is the greatest guarantee of your sovereignty in these difficult circumstances.'

The raj kumari turned on her heel and strode to the window, hissing. She would not engage in debate over the sovereignty of Chintal.

The rajah looked at her wearily, and then at Hervey. 'Do you suppose they would send an officer in command of this subsidiary force who was sensible of my condition, Captain Hervey?'

'It could only be to mutual benefit,' he replied.

237

The rajah looked at his daughter again, and then bade him leave them.

For the first time, Hervey was conscious that no matter where he went in the palace, or its gardens, he was observed – or, at least, might be observed. And overheard, too, should he speak in more than a whisper. He would have liked to meet with the collector and Cornet Templer, but to do so could only arouse suspicion that he was in collusion with the Company. He therefore avoided their quarters and went instead to look for Emma Lucie. He found her beside one of the fountains in the water garden, reading – as if there were not a care in the whole of the palace. 'Do I disturb you, madam?' he enquired.

'You do not disturb me, Captain Hervey,' she said with a smile, closing her volume of the natural history of Madras. 'But something disturbs you, evidently.'

Hervey sighed. 'For all its perils, the battlefield is at least a place of simple certainties.'

She looked at him quizzically.

'Events here have taken another turn.'

'Why should you, above other men, be privileged to a life without confusions, Captain Hervey?' she smiled. 'What are these events?'

The reproach in her voice was not excessive, but enough nonetheless to check him. 'You are right, madam. I accept the rank and position readily enough.'

'Well, let us not dwell too deeply on such matters. What exactly troubles you?'

'You are aware, I must suppose, that Mr Somervile is come?'

'Mr Somervile, *here*?'

Clearly she was not. 'Why yes, Miss Lucie: he is come with an offer of alliance with Chintal, this very afternoon.'

Emma Lucie rose as if to leave, and then sat down again. 'I had not thought that—'

'Forgive me, madam,' Hervey interrupted, 'but he comes with intelligence that there are to be further Pindaree forays, and next it is expected they will ravage Chintal.'

She seemed less agitated. 'I see. And this is what distresses you?'

'Indirectly, madam. I have been in India these past three months and I am become embroiled with a very minor potentate – albeit most engaging – whose interests are threatened by a man whose assistance I was intent on seeking.'

'Assistance, Captain Hervey?'

She had seized on it quickly. Had the hesitation in his voice betrayed him? 'Yes: you will recall that I am to visit his lancers.'

'Oh,' she replied, sounding not entirely convinced.

He judged it better to remain silent.

And she said nothing at first. But then she smiled – laughed almost. 'Captain Hervey, your friend Mr Selden – a most *intriguing* gentleman – has much entertained me this afternoon with stories which likened your time here to the trials of Hercules.'

Hervey frowned. 'Mr Selden is sick with a fever, madam. I had not thought him capable of receiving anyone.'

'Indeed – he is not at all well. But he had insisted on being brought to the rajah's stables, it seems, to examine a new foal. Such a pretty little thing. Yes, he was quite full of classical allusions to your time here.'

He did not see how it could be so.

'Oh, do not be modest, Captain Hervey: I have heard of your Herculean efforts to divert rivers, to capture boars, and even to confront the Hydra!'

He smiled at the rivers and the boars, but reference to the Hydra escaped him. 'You confuse me, I believe, madam.'

She frowned. 'Indeed? I had heard you saved the princess from a most fearsome two-headed serpent deep in the jungle.'

Hervey blushed a deep crimson. How could Selden have known of the encounter? 'I . . . that is,' he stammered; 'I confess that I ran from it.'

'*You*, Captain Hervey? *You* ran from it?'

'Well, Miss Lucie, in truth it was not one snake but two. They were entwined: perhaps that gave the impression of two heads.'

'Why were they entwined, Captain Hervey?' she asked, with all apparent innocence.

He blushed deeply again. 'It was part of their courtship, I understand.'

'And does such entwining always signal an inclination to mate?'

He felt almost as close to danger as he had been in the forest. What did Selden know, and how? 'I am not privy to the habits of the hamadryad, madam,' he replied, with as much an air of unconcern as he could manage.

But she was not inclined to let it pass. 'Do you know if the hamadryad mates for life?'

'Miss Lucie, as I said, I know little of the habits of this or, for that matter, any snake.'

She frowned once more. 'They are not so common in Madras, but I read in my natural history that the female will allow the male to make advances – even to mate with her – and will then kill him with a single bite. Do you know what is the habitual diet of the hamadryad, Captain Hervey?'

He shook his head as she leafed through her book to find the page.

'There,' she said, showing him the place. 'Its scientific name . . . see?'

'Oh,' said Hervey, tumbling to her meaning, 'Ophiophagus hannah.'

'Yes, Captain Hervey: Ophiophagus hannah – it eats only other snakes. Indeed, the female will even kill and eat a male with which she has just mated.'

Hervey shivered involuntarily, now convinced her purpose was more allegory than natural history. 'Perhaps we might change the subject, madam; I cannot even recall how it came about.'

'I spoke of the labours of Hercules,' she smiled.

He was partially relieved.

'It is as well, anyway, that we close that allegory, sir, for Hercules' eleventh labour would be most perilous.' She inclined an eyebrow.

Hervey saw it at once. 'Taking the world on his shoulders, do you mean, madam?'

'Just so. The rajah seems especially keen that you shoulder his burden, does he not?' She raised both her eyebrows, and smiled.

Hervey looked at her intently. 'You do not suggest that the rajah seeks to confine me in some way?'

She raised her eyebrows again, and tilted her head. 'I have been in India many years—'

'No!' he protested. 'If I am any judge of men at all, the rajah is incapable of such a thing!'

'I do not know the rajah,' she replied softly, 'but I believe any prince in his position would often as not be an unwitting deceiver. He may not have the cares of the world on his shoulders, but those of Chintal are quite enough of a burden for one man, by all accounts.'

*   *   *

240

Next morning, following a feast and entertainment as impressive for their improvisation as for their sumptuousness (which was nevertheless great), the rajah summoned Hervey once more to his apartments. He was quite alone, although the screens in his chamber might have concealed an entire council of ministers – a possibility Hervey would scarcely have imagined had it not been for Emma Lucie's caution.

'Captain Hervey, I have considered most carefully the position. Indeed, so long did I turn these things over in my mind that I saw the day break over Chintalpore. I have resolved to conclude a treaty with the Honourable Company.'

Hervey smiled and nodded appreciatively.

'I am glad you approve, for I make but one condition.'

Hervey nodded again.

'It is that you shall command the subsidiary force.'

Hervey's eyes were wide with disbelief. 'Sir, that is not possible, I—'

'Those shall be my terms.'

'Sir, allow me to explain. I am an officer of the Duke of Wellington's staff, albeit a junior one. But I have been given quite specific duties here, duties I could not discharge were I to command such a force. The second objection is that I am a King's officer, not a Company officer. I am not in the least certain that such a command would be lawful.'

'There is not a third, perhaps greater objection?' asked the rajah.

Hervey's brow furrowed. 'I, I do not think so, sir.'

'Then you do not feel yourself incapable of such a command? Insufficient for the responsibility of such a force?'

'Sir, I—'

But the rajah would not let him finish. 'No, of course you do not think yourself incapable. Captain Hervey, I should think there are few men more capable of exercising command than you.'

He blushed. 'I am flattered, sir – greatly honoured – but it does not diminish the primary objection.'

'Then,' said the rajah, sighing, 'we shall see what the agent of the Company has to say of the matter.' And with that he called for hazree. 'Take breakfast with me first, Captain Hervey.'

Instead, however, Hervey begged leave to speak with the collector at once.

*　　*　　*

He found him at breakfast in his quarters. It was the first opportunity he had had to speak with him alone, though even here he could not be certain that their conversation would remain private. There was little he could do about that, however, and, in any case, he proposed to say nothing – nor even did he think anything – that might not be laid before the rajah without embarrassment. That some of the rajah's establishment were in the nizam's pay left him no alternative, indeed.

Somervile seemed pleased, but not surprised, to see him, and beckoned his khitmagar to bring him coffee. 'These are momentous times, are they not, Captain Hervey?' he asked, smiling.

'I am beginning to think that I might not see otherwise in my lifetime,' replied Hervey, sighing.

'I learn that the Duke of Wellington is having a little difficulty in Paris, too.'

'Oh?' said Hervey. 'How so?'

'He has been assailed in the street. It seems that there is some resentment that he commands an army of occupation. The royalists feel that now the usurper Bonaparte is gone France should be returned to the French. And, I hear tell, there is trouble with one or two husbands . . .'

'I am sure that the duke is able to bear these things with fortitude,' smiled Hervey. 'How are things with Lord Moira?' he ventured.

The collector looked baffled by the enquiry. Hervey wished he had not made the connection so directly, for Somervile was quite astute enough to draw the inference.

'Lord Moira is, it seems, in the very best of sorts. He is quite determined on vigorous action in order to have peace from these Pindarees, and I understand that he now has the support of Leadenhall Street and the government. Or at least, there is quiescence in those quarters. I have it on the best authority, even, that he is soon to be ennobled with a marquessate.'

Hervey sensed that his next words were crucial to preserving his cover, but before he could speak the collector demonstrated the perceptivity of which Lucie had made so much.

'Captain Hervey, did you suppose that the Duke of Wellington were somehow to be translated here at the expense of Lord Moira? Are you in some manner his *scout*?'

Hervey was aghast.

The collector laughed. 'My dear sir, I have known as much since first we met! You forget that it is my business to be in the minds of men.

You suppose that what in London is plausible will be equally so in the Indies. Well, I may tell you that it is not. You may, so to speak, have a parade of Grenadiers pass muster on the Horse Guards, but in India the sun is so bright that the merest speck on a tunic will stand out like an ink-blot on parchment!' He laughed again, calling to his khitmagar in confident Telugu for more coffee – and then to leave them alone. 'Captain Hervey, you would be an adornment in Calcutta – for sure – but more importantly, you would come to see India as I do. And, since the wretched affair of Warren Hastings, there are fewer men each year who are prepared to see India as it *is*, rather than as it might be were only its rulers Englishmen.'

Hervey was not immediately convinced. 'Do you not confuse our purpose in the East, sir?' he asked boldly.

'"Let not England forget her precedence of teaching nations how to live"?'

Hervey all but scratched his head. 'That is familiar, but—'

'Milton,' he replied.

'Oh, Milton. My major was wont to quote Milton, but he had a decidedly melancholic turn. It does seem apt, though.' Then he had second thoughts. 'But have we not fought Bonaparte these past twenty years on that very precept?'

The collector frowned. 'Would that you knew your Milton better, for it is less contrived at polity than with private morals!'

'I think it dubious to suppose there is a distinction . . .'

'Oh, Captain Hervey!' groaned the collector, and then declaimed as if on the boards: '"I cannot praise a fugitive and cloistered virtue, un-exercised and unbreathed, that never sallies out and sees her adversary, but slinks out of the race, where that immortal garland is to be run for, not without dust and heat."'

'Milton again, sir? And what is *your* meaning by that?'

'*Dust and heat* – the essence of India!' said the collector, surprised.

Hervey looked blank.

'Captain Hervey, I shall speak plain: if you are the man I believe you to be, you will ever think meanly of yourself if you refuse the rajah's request.'

'Forgive me, sir, but I think you must perceive my difficulty at least. Such a course would be to stray a very great deal from that which I was meant to follow. I took a gamble in coming to Chintalpore because I believed it would be most expeditious to my mission. I must have the greatest care not to compound an error. And in any case, how do you know of the rajah's request?' he added, indignantly.

Somervile chose to ignore the question. 'Captain Hervey, officers are appointed to the staff of great men to exercise their judgement, being in the mind of their principal. There is nothing uncommon in your exercise of initiative in coming to Chintalpore. I dare say that you are in a better position today to instruct the duke in the actuality that is Haidarabad than if you had dutifully ploughed your way first up the Hooghly river!'

'Perhaps,' replied Hervey, mollified slightly; 'but how did you know of the rajah's request?'

'It is of no matter,' replied the collector dismissively.

'I consider that it *is*, sir!' insisted Hervey; 'I wish to know what collusion there has been in this concern!'

The collector smiled. 'Captain Hervey, you must not suppose there are spies everywhere. I said before that it was my business to know what is in men's minds. I knew perfectly well that that would be the rajah's stipulation.'

Hervey sighed again. 'See here, Mr Somervile, I make no admission by this, but the duties given to me by the Duke of Wellington do not permit of it. Nor, I believe, may a King's officer be so employed on Company business without express authority.'

The collector sighed too, and more wearily. 'The latter is but the refuge of the legalist. The former – well, I do not suppose that the duke is entirely ill-disposed towards initiative.'

'There is a perfectly able King's officer here in Chintalpore who could exercise command with equal address as I.'

'Who?' enquired the collector, incredulously.

'Mr Locke.'

'Locke? That potulent officer of Marines? From what I hear you would have the greatest difficulty hauling him off his little nautch girl!'

Hervey frowned in dissent. 'That is unfair. He fought like a lion at Jhansikote.'

'Hervey,' said the collector, his voice lowered in conspiracy, 'there will be no shortage of lions. What the rajah needs is a lion with the acuity of a mongoose!'

CHAPTER FIFTEEN

FEVER

_____

The following day

Hervey walked with Emma Lucie in the water gardens before the heat of the day drove all but the unfortunate to seek the shade. Despite the collector's best efforts she had insisted on staying in Chintal for a further week, for it was the first time she had seen a princely state (Mysore she dismissed as merely an outpost of Madras). Hervey was glad she had stayed. He was, perhaps for the first time, feeling acutely the want of support that was the community of the Sixth. Private Johnson was a greater strength than ever he could have imagined, but he could hardly share his doubts with a man whose life rested so completely in his hands. There was Locke. But somehow Hervey was unable to confide. There ought to have been Selden, but Selden protested that he supposed him more capable than he was. 'In the end I am a horse-doctor, that is all,' he had lamented. And Selden was abed with fever too – no doubt induced by the late confusions, but in periodic deliriums nevertheless.

Hervey had on his straw hat, but though it kept off the sun its leather brow-band made his forehead permanently moist. He took it off and wiped his brow with his sleeve for a third time. Emma Lucie, in a white cotton frock and a broad straw hat with a trailing silk band, looked for all the world as if she might have been in his father's garden at Horningsham. Years of acquaintance with the climate had conditioned her very comfortably to this spring season. As they reached the most active of the fountains Hervey stopped and bade her sit on its wall, for here he could be sure that no one might overhear them against the sound of falling water.

'The rajah has asked me to take command of the Company's subsidiary force when the treaty is signed.' His tone was less than resolute.

'You seem uncertain, Captain Hervey. I should have thought it a splendid thing for an officer.'

'I am anxious that it intrudes on the purpose for which I was sent to India.'

'To study the lance? Surely this would be a most opportune commission?' she replied, puzzled.

'Yes,' he nodded, not wishing to pursue it, for she was acute enough to conclude there was more to it than a bamboo pole. 'Quite so. The command is in any case to be a limited commission – until such time that the rajah gains more confidence in the Company.'

'And a good command, I imagine – rather bigger than has been yours hitherto?'

He smiled. 'I had the regiment for a day or so after Waterloo, but this would be the best part of a brigade – a thousand infantry, three hundred cavalry and a field battery. Yes, an exceptional command for a half-colonel, let alone a captain.'

'Let us call it a handsome command, then!'

'Not enough cavalry, though,' he mused aloud, as if he had already accepted the commission. 'Only rapid manoeuvre could make up for numbers if it comes to a fight. We should need to bustle troops from one end of Chintal to the other.'

'Then it seems doubly suited to a young head.'

'Positions can come early in India, Mr Selden always said – in the military as well as the civil. Your own brother has great responsibility, and the collector.'

'Positions come early, often as not,' she smiled, 'because men die younger or take their fortunes early and go to Cheltenham!'

Hervey made a sort of resigned shrug, and smiled too. Emma Lucie was no mere Madras hostess.

246

'So shall you accept the offer? Mr Somervile told me the rajah would not conclude a treaty unless you were to have the command.'

Hervey took off his hat and wiped his forehead again. 'As I was saying, Miss Lucie, my first duty is to the Duke of Wellington.'

She tilted her head.

No – it would not do. He had better place his trust entirely in his own judgement or else speak now to this woman who had, it seemed, wits, an understanding of the country *and* discretion. 'Miss Lucie, I must speak straight with you—'

'Speak that or not at all!'

'Yes, I am sorry. In truth, my mission here is more to do with the nizam than the lance.'

She drew back, as if suspecting some treachery.

'No, don't misunderstand me, madam,' he assured her hastily. 'The duke has need of knowing – and I beg you do not ask me why – how faithful and effective an ally the nizam might be in any future scheme of the Company's. You will see, therefore, that if I take this command – albeit for a short time until the rajah's confidence is won by the Company's nomination, a Colonel Forster – I may find myself set against the very man I am meant to be treating with.'

She thought awhile before replying. 'I see your dilemma,' she conceded. 'But why are you here in Chintal? Is it merely to reacquaint yourself with Mr Selden?'

'I beg you do not press me for an answer there either. I may assure you there is nothing dishonourable in it.'

'Oh, Captain Hervey! I did not suppose you capable of a dishonourable thing if your life depended on it!'

'I'm obliged, madam. And the more so for your hearing me now.'

'I do know a little about Company affairs,' she began tentatively. 'One is not always obliged to leave the table as the more interesting talk of an evening begins. You spoke of things coming to a fight, needing more horse than you have. But I thought the very presence of a subsidiary force would be enough to deter the nizam from any adventure. For those are the conditions under which his own treaty of alliance is concluded, surely?'

She was right. She knew exactly how the subsidiary alliance system worked. 'I am certain the nizam would be deterred – yes. But not the Pindarees, and it seems there may be some surrogation on the part of Haidarabad.'

She appeared to be contemplating the distinction. 'And what place do the rajah's soldiers have in your command?'

That, he was not sure. He knew it was the rajah's wish that he should also take command of his regiments, for since the mutiny there was little confidence in their loyalty, except the sowars and Rajpoots. But he was less inclined to take it. 'Its troubles are best dealt with from within.'

'*Is* there any danger from within?'

He was unsure of her meaning.

'Do you not think that until the cause of the mutiny is established—'

'Oh, but it *has* been established,' he replied confidently. 'The rajah explained last night – the withholding of batta, the sepoys' allowances?'

'Yes, yes, that much I am aware of, Captain Hervey, but to what purpose was the money misappropriated – and by whom?'

He had never been inclined to underestimate Emma Lucie, but he was surprised nevertheless by her inclination to question. 'I think it widely known that an official called Kunal Verma, the dewan, appropriated the money. Mr Selden, at least, is satisfied of his guilt.'

'His *sole* guilt?'

He made no reply.

'You had not considered the possibility that Mr Selden himself might somehow be implicated?' she said, her eyebrows arching.

'In no manner, madam!' The suggestion was outrageous.

'Captain Hervey, I have been in Chintal but a short time, and yet I have heard whispers—'

'You may always hear whispers. I have shared too many billets in Spain with Selden to believe him capable of anything so base!'

Emma Lucie arched her eyebrows again and waved away a persistent hornet. 'And the raj kumari?'

He was just as astounded. 'Why should the raj kumari rob her father's own sepoys?'

'Ah,' she replied, smiling. 'Now at least you are considering motives. Why, indeed, should she do so? But the material point is that *someone* must have been in league with Kunal Verma – or else his death was a most curious concurrence.'

Hervey had to concede her point. 'Miss Lucie, you have been here scarcely one whole day. The suggestion that the raj kumari—'

'I have not met the lady,' she agreed, 'and my knowledge of affairs is, I admit, principally that of the rajah's table last night, but I hear such whispers against her – beginning even on the Godavari. More, certainly, than against Mr Selden.'

'And of whom else have you heard accusations?' he asked, after a moment's contemplation.

'No one,' she replied. 'Is that not, perhaps, indicative?'

He confided that he had earlier suspected the white officers – perhaps even the Germans, for they had escaped the mutiny. And, indeed, Captain Steuben's death had been without adequate witnesses.

She took off her hat and fanned herself for a few moments. 'Strangely enough, Captain Hervey, you are the first *King's* officer I have known. I have met one or two, yes, but I don't believe I have ever spoken more than formalities. I will not say that Company officers are without loyalty, for they are fiercely loyal to their sepoys often enough.' She spoke with apparent authority. 'But in the end they serve a commercial enterprise, and they see most things in terms of the dividends which accrue to them. Were you a Company officer your decision would be a simple case of bookkeeping.'

He smiled. 'Well, I am gratified you see the irreconcilability of it.'

'Irreconcilable?' She was surprised. 'Not at all. If you accept the position under the *Company's* auspices, you and the nizam share an interest – you as a servant, he as a declared ally. There can be no subsequent difficulty there. If you were to take command of the rajah's forces too, then that would be a different matter – do you not see?'

It seemed so simple. He wondered if Philip Lucie's advancement in the Madras council was entirely on his own merits: his sister must have been of singular influence. But he was becoming restless with the heat, as well the debate. He stood up, saying he had troubled her long enough. 'Shall we walk to the stables and see the Arab foal? It's as white as snow – if you remember what that is.'

'Oh, I remember it, Captain Hervey,' she laughed. 'Only when I forget it shall I feel inclined to return to England!'

There was a great commotion in the stables as they arrived. Every horse's ear was pricked, there was whinnying in every quarter and the punkahs had stopped – the servers crowding the end doors to hear the news. A galloper from Jhansikote, a young jemadar, dust-covered, was demanding to know where the salutri was. The babble of syces, bhistis, grass-cutters and sweepers made as little sense to him as to Hervey. 'Where is the salutri!' he tried for the fourth time.

Hervey pushed his way though the crowd, the jemadar snapping to attention as he saw him. 'Very well, Jemadar sahib,' he replied, touching his forehead to acknowledge, 'what is the matter?'

The jemadar had a little English and some Urdu, and so Hervey was not long in discovering the cause. There was horse plague at Jhansikote. A dozen had already succumbed to choking, and many more were showing the same symptoms. Captain Bauer believed there would not be a horse left standing by the end of the month at this rate of contagion.

'What is the cause of the sickness?' asked Hervey, having managed to silence the babble.

The jemadar said they did not know. There had been no new horse arrive that might have been infected, nor had there been any change in feeding. The sickness was a mystery.

'And Mr Selden laid low with fever, too,' said Emma Lucie, her own Urdu quite good enough for the exchange.

Hervey nodded ruefully.

'But we are sure he is still indisposed?' she asked.

The ambiguity was not without its effect. 'I had better go and find him,' he sighed. 'I have not seen him in two days.' But he was already steeling himself to another ride to Jhansikote, for he could hardly expect Selden to be in hale condition, no matter how remitted was his fever.

'What do you suppose the horse sickness might be?' asked Emma Lucie once the jemadar had left. 'Do you suspect an evil hand?'

'I've never heard of one with such reach – that's for sure,' he said, shaking his head. 'But in India . . . as you keep saying. If the symptoms are as the jemadar describes, though, I should say glanders, or strangles perhaps – farcy, even. But who knows what fevers there are in this country? The heat alone must account for many.'

'Glanders, strangles?' she frowned. 'Have you met with these before?'

'No, I've never seen a case.'

'Oh,' she said simply.

'Just so, Miss Lucie. Let us pray that Mr Selden is in a sufficient state of consciousness to give me some direction – for I see no other course but to go myself. I can hardly stand by here, even if I *am* to leave at the end of the week.'

*   *   *

But Selden was not in a sufficient state. He was in a delirium once more, the punkah-wallah working hard to keep the stale air in his chamber moving, and his ringleted Bengali bearer sponging his forehead devotedly. Hervey sat in the chamber for some time, hopeful of even the briefest period of consciousness in which Selden might give his opinion. What a broken reed was the salutri, he lamented. Emma Lucie's allegations pressed themselves on him, and he found himself wondering what manner of vices and intrigues Selden had allowed himself to be drawn into. When he left him, after a full half-hour in which he had neither stirred nor made the slightest sound, his heart was heavy with the thought that even if he were to see him again, alive, it might indeed be under indictment for the sepoys' batta. He could not by any means bring himself to contemplate the connection with the murder of Kunal Verma, but the suggestion he could not escape. He needed to find Henry Locke.

Locke was not, as the collector had sneered, in the embraces of his nautch girl, but engaged in vigorous bayonet exercises with the sepoys of the palace guard. His powerful shoulders were unmatched by any in that mock combat, and he gave fearful impulsion to the two feet of steel at the end of his musket. The entire company was assembled in a half-covered court that served as an exercise yard to see Locke the gymnasiarch, and nautch girls watched coyly from a balcony. Even in the shade the heat was oppressive, and he was in a lather as great as a pony in a gallop, his cheesecloth shirt clinging to his chest as a second skin. He was smiling, nevertheless, enjoying the exhilaration of the combat and the adulation of the sepoys. 'So you are to be brigadier, or thereabouts,' he said with a broad grin as Hervey came up.

'You have heard, too? There's nothing, it seems, that waits to be passed in the usual way.' He handed Locke a towel. 'I've not yet said "yes" though. There's much to think about. You're not offended, I hope, by the manner of hearing?'

Locke smiled. 'Hervey, it was whispered in my ear by the most perfect lips I have ever tasted.'

Now Hervey smiled. At least there was one man in this princely state who took his pleasures as they came – and could face death with equal readiness. He was glad Locke had found a little happiness; no one deserved it more.

'So what vexes you now?'

Hervey explained the calamity that had befallen the rissalahs. 'I intend going there at once, for Selden's in no condition to. If they lose horses at the rate the jemadar reports then Chintal will be to all intents defenceless. The sepoys, we know, are less than wholly reliable. The Rajpoots are true, but they can't be in two places at once.'

Locke nodded his understanding.

'Would you take charge here?' said Hervey, a little unsure.

He smiled. 'If such a notion is conceivable, for it implies there's already some order! You know, Hervey, I think these sepoys are so much wind and piss. Any boarding party from a first-rate could take this place from the lot of 'em.'

'Yes,' sighed Hervey, 'perhaps so. Thank heavens the rajah has his sowars.'

Locke nodded, but the inclination of an eyebrow suggested something was amiss. 'Are you sure about the rissalahs? Why was Steuben killed? You don't believe it was an accident?'

'Oh,' said Hervey, as if the accusation touched him personally, 'I hardly think that—'

Locke smiled wryly. 'You mean it is inconceivable that a cavalry officer could do something so base? "*Un chevalier sans peur et sans reproche?*" Humbug!'

Hervey looked embarrassed, and struggled to find the right words.

'Forget it, man!' said Locke, clapping him on the shoulder. 'There's only one left anyway, isn't there?'

'Alter Fritz?' exclaimed Hervey. 'He is no more capable of anything so base than—'

'Than anyone else who's been deprived of Christian company for a dozen years!'

Hervey frowned. The trouble was – he knew full well – that Locke was the more prudent in this. 'By the way,' he whispered as he handed him another towel, 'I'm *not* going to take the command.'

'What? But I thought—'

'I had it all out last night at great length with the collector. I've said nothing yet to the rajah, but there's an officer coming here from Madras, and the collector's sure that once the rajah meets him he'll have every confidence. I'll then go to Haidarabad.'

Locke seemed to disapprove. 'And in the meantime, the rajah continues to think you will take the command?'

'I'm not happy with that. Heaven *knows* I'm not happy with it. But it's about the best I can manage in order to do justice to—'

Locke slapped him on the shoulder again. 'I'm sure you'll do the right thing. You're a King's officer after all: you can't just go fortune-hunting.'

'And shall you remain here for the rest of your furlough?' tried Hervey, not wanting any more discussion of where duty lay.

Locke glanced around him, and up to where the nautch girls stood, and simply smiled.

'Yes,' smiled Hervey by return. 'Why indeed should you not?'

Alter Fritz looked worried. 'Never have I seen so many horses with fever. Yesterday we had to burn seven more.' His German had the sound of one whose everyday tongue was no longer his own, its cadences distinctly native.

The first thing that puzzled Hervey was why no attempt had been made to isolate those with symptoms of the sickness. Although the stables were airier than many he had known – made more so by the enormous punkahs which swung night and day – there was still a vapour which assaulted the nose and eyes on entering, and on which he supposed the contagion was borne. Alter Fritz explained that, by the time the fever had taken hold, there was nothing they could do to reorder the lines, save making space in one building for the worst cases. And besides, he feared the contagion had now taken hold in the bedding and fabric of the stables. He had considered turning all the horses loose, but he had no means of corralling.

'You had better show me the worst cases, then,' said Hervey.

Alter Fritz took him to where two dozen mares and geldings stood motionless in their stalls, heads held unusually still, and silent but for an occasional muted cough. Hervey looked carefully at each of them. All were sweating, and there was discharge from the nose (in some cases as thick as syrup). There were fearful abscesses of the glands beneath and behind the lower jaw, too. Some had erupted, and a thick, creamy pus oozed from them. Alter Fritz said that those horses which had discharged in this way had not then died, but he did not know why some developed the abscesses and some did not. He had observed that if the contagion were retained in the body then the animal grew worse – certainly, the fever continued – whereas it seemed to remit if the abscesses came to a head.

'Have you lanced any of them?' asked Hervey.

They had not, replied Alter Fritz, but they had bled every horse.

Hervey had never liked the notion of bleeding; not since, as a boy, he saw a young horse sever an artery, and watched helplessly as blood poured from it, the colt becoming too weak to stand in but a minute. He could never comprehend, therefore, the principle by which the bleeding of an already enfeebled animal should restore its health.

Alter Fritz agreed they did not bleed as a rule. 'But when all else seems of no avail . . .' he shrugged.

'Very well,' said Hervey, 'but let us take the knife to these abscesses instead, since it's they which appear to be the point of contagion. Those that have died – what was the *manner* of their dying?'

Alter Fritz said their breathing became laboured, that they no longer had the strength to draw in breath.

'When did the last one succumb?'

'A little before you arrived – a mare.'

They went to find her. She was not yet consigned to the pyre since Alter Fritz expected there would be two more by the end of the day. She lay covered in marigolds (the sowars' customary mark of respect), and by a mound of brushwood that would later be torched. Hervey could not help but think it curious that, in a land where life seemed to be held so cheap, one troop-horse should be accorded such honour. In England it would be the limepit – or hound trenchers – and no ceremony.

The angle of the mare's jaw was sorely swollen but rigor mortis had not yet set in. He asked for a knife, and one of the farriers gave him his razor.

'What will you do?' asked Alter Fritz.

'I want to see if the abscesses have taken hold within,' he replied. But first he asked that the horse's mouth be opened as far as possible so that he could probe inside. Sowars crowded round to help or watch. He slipped his hand into her mouth, probing with a finger. 'The soft palate's compressed; she simply couldn't breathe.'

'Why is it swollen, think you, Hervey?' asked Alter Fritz, holding a handkerchief to his nose.

'Not swollen, *compressed*. I'm pretty sure it's the abscesses about the jaw and neck which cause the compression.' He pointed to the swellings, none of which showed signs of having discharged. And then, with the razor, he incised two of them and squeezed until pus spurted.

'*Ach, das ist schlimm!*' spat Alter Fritz.

'Yes,' agreed Hervey, his German unconsciously assuming the emphatic inflections of Alter Fritz's, 'very nasty indeed. I think it's a case of – I don't know how you say it in German – *strangles*.'

Alter Fritz looked puzzled.

Hervey put his hands to his neck: 'Strangle – *erdrosseln*?'

He understood. But he had not seen a case either, nor did he know anything about it.

'If it *is* strangles,' continued Hervey, shaking his head, 'we must try to bring the abscesses to a head and then lance them to take the pressure off the pharynx. Never have I seen sores so big. Everything in this country seems to grow to twice the size of what it would be in England.' He wiped his hands on some cotton waste and stepped back from the carcass. 'Tell your sowars to make poultices for their horses, and to keep cleaning the nostrils. Make up soft feeds which can be swallowed easily. Add syrup to make it appealing. And everything which comes into contact with any discharge must be burned, and the sowars must wash their hands before they attend to any horse that doesn't already show the symptoms. I'm sure the contagion is in the body fluids.'

Alter Fritz acknowledged the instructions. 'And you believe, Hervey, that we might save a few?'

'I see no reason why we should not. Except that – as I understand it – there's a complication to the disease known as *bastard* strangles, where the abscesses spread to the thorax and abdomen – and when they burst there's such corruption that the horse dies no matter what is done. I was inclined to cut her open to search for such signs, but the pharynx is so compressed that there's little purpose.'

Alter Fritz had begun to look more confident, but he now lowered his voice and screwed up his face. 'Hervey, there's one horse in particular you should see.'

'How so?'

'The raj kumari's mare shows these symptoms too. It has been here with the rissalahs this month past.'

'Oh,' he groaned. Why were there always complications? 'I'd better take a look at her at once.'

The little flea-bitten grey stood downcast in her stall on the other side of the maidan, separate from the main lines. Her head stayed still as they came in, her flanks were wet and her breathing shallow.

'How long has she been this way?' asked Hervey.

'About a week.'

He felt about her lower jaw and neck. There were the tell-tale swellings. 'Inform her syce that he must poultice at least three times a day to draw the poison to the surface. There's little more we can do. She'll be at her worst in another three days or so.'

He stayed with her until he was satisfied the syce could do the job properly, and then spent the remainder of the afternoon supervising the others to see they kept the discipline of burning the used wadding. Alter Fritz asked if strangles could pass from horse to man, to which Hervey replied that he did not know, but that he supposed it less likely if the men did as he bid in respect of vigorous hand-washing. And so all afternoon Hervey and the old German worked side by side – encouraging, demonstrating, upbraiding, labouring, consoling. Then, as the sun was beginning its descent over the forest towards Chintalpore, they retired to the officers' quarters for restorative measures of whiskey and seltzer, and the prospect of a good supper. Bearers brought bowls of hot water, clean shirts and hose, fresh decanters and bottles. In a quarter of an hour they were sunk into deep leather chairs, exhausted but still hopeful. Alter Fritz closed his eyes briefly, allowing Hervey to search his face for what signs of perfidy might be etched in those sun-weathered features. He saw none. Indeed, he saw nothing but the bluff openness of an old quartermaster – wily, perhaps, but never a deceiver.

But then the prospect of their good supper was rudely dispelled by the arrival of the last person they would have wished to see in the circumstances. The raj kumari came in without ceremony, though, her anxiety quite evident. Hervey sat her down and called for the khitmagar. Dust fell from her shoulders still, and the same long breeches she had worn for the hunt clung to her with the sweat of the fleet young Arab she had galloped from Chintalpore. He offered her seltzer, which she accepted with the addition of the whiskey. She had come at once, she explained, for Gita was the issue of her own mother's mare. Hervey told her what he had found, and what they were doing. She seemed thankful, but asked if a sadhu had attended. When she learned not, she gave instructions for one to be brought without delay to say prayers and perform his rituals. A naik was despatched to the bazaar, and he returned within the hour.

The holy man was but skin and bone, and covered in white ash. His hair was thickly matted, he carried a begging bowl and flute, and he made repeated namaste to the raj kumari. They took him to her mare, and he stood contemplating in silence for several minutes. At length he breathed into her nostrils, sat down cross-legged in front of her and began a sing-song mantra, shaking violently all the while. Hervey watched from the corner of the stable, glad of the excuse for respite. The raj kumari stood close by, swaying to the sadhu's mantra as she had that day in the forest. After five minutes the holy man stopped abruptly, rose and bowed deeply to the little mare. Then he turned to the raj kumari and spoke to her in Telugu. He explained that the horse was very small and there was much poison in her. He might revive her for a short while, but he could not thwart the will of Shiva. He had done his best to draw out the malignant spirit of the poison, but . . .

With great composure, the raj kumari thanked him and placed a purse of silver in his begging bowl, asking him to visit each of the sick horses in turn. The sadhu returned her thanks, bowed low again, and shuffled off with the naik in the direction of the other lines. 'He does not expect her to live,' she said as he left. 'He says there is too much poison in her body – too much poison.'

Hervey measured his response carefully. There could not, to his mind, be the slightest possibility that the sadhu's ministrations could have any effect on the outcome of the sickness. He did not even know whether or not the raj kumari herself believed that they would. But evidently she believed that they might. He had a strong desire to dissuade her from her superstition, yet he had already known her antagonism, and he did not wish it greater now. 'Your Highness, do you wish me to continue with my treatment? I am merely trying to draw out the poison to which the sadhu refers.'

His sensibility did him credit. She smiled at him for the first time in many days and nodded her assent. There was moisture in her eyes, though she was trying hard to hide it.

For three days the raj kumari tended her little mare herself, allowing the syce only to clean the stable of the few droppings the horse managed. She used sponges to cool her, she wiped the discharge from her nostrils with cotton waste, she applied poultices to the swellings, she coaxed her to eat – handful by handful of bran and crushed barley, sweetened with syrup. And she slept for the most part in the stable, with her chowkidar as sentinel and only a zenana to attend her. When all was done each day, she would cross the maidan and tend the others. Half the horses were now showing symptoms of the plague, and since her arrival a dozen more had breathed their last. Hervey visited her mare as many as a dozen times each day, but the fever was not abating. Nor were the swellings coming to any head.

'It is as the sadhu said: the poison in her is too great,' said the raj kumari on the fourth morning.

Hervey had not supposed her capable of the devotion she had shown these past days. Even the sowars remarked on it: a princess who would do the work of a sweeper, who would sleep in a stable. More than once he had felt a powerful urge to encourage her by an embrace, but after the forest there could be no question of it. And as to any notion of her implication in the affair of the batta, he could no more contemplate it now than he could of Alter Fritz, for her honest affection for these men was plain to see.

But this morning it looked as if the sadhu's prophecy had been right, for as they stood trying to coax Gita to a barley sweet she suddenly fell to the ground, struggling violently to draw breath. The raj kumari began to sob quietly. Hervey was only grateful the mare's ordeal – and hers – was coming to an end. But there was one last effort, he knew. If, that is, the raj kumari could bear it. He had never before done it; nor even had he seen it done. Long ago, Daniel Coates had shown him the point at which he must make such an incision, and he had never forgotten – as he had never forgotten a single thing that Daniel Coates had told him, for such were that veteran's years of experience.

He took out the farrier's razor and began to feel along the mare's throat for the point to cut.

'What do you do?' exclaimed the raj kumari, seizing his hand. 'You would not slaughter her in the fashion of the nizam's people?

'I am going to open her windpipe,' he said, indicating its line, 'so that she can breathe in air from beyond the obstruction at the back of her mouth.' The raj kumari did not grasp the principle and seized his hand again, but Hervey persisted gently. 'The horse breathes *through* its mouth, not with it,' he explained. He pointed to the heave line: 'See, the muscles are trying to draw in air, but can't because of the obstruent in the mouth. If I make a hole in the windpipe, air can be drawn in directly. It will relieve her for the moment.'

'But she will bleed to death!' protested the raj kumari.

Hervey was only too aware she might be right. 'She need not,' was all he would allow himself.

'Make the hole then,' said the raj kumari resolutely.

He took a deep breath and tried to locate – to avoid – the jugular groove. At last he felt sufficiently confident, and in went the point of the razor about half an inch. There was no blood – a trickle only. That was encouraging, not to say a relief. He used the blade's edge to elongate the incision, and there was a loud sucking noise, at first alarming but then reassuring as he realized it was the sound of success – of air being drawn down towards the lungs. He held wide the hole with his fingers and told the orderly-dafadar to bring him some cartridges.

'How many, sahib?' he asked in Urdu.

'Just a handful.'

The dafadar looked puzzled, but he doubled away nevertheless, soon returning with a half-dozen carbine cartridges.

The raj kumari asked him what was their purpose, and Hervey explained that he needed something to keep the incision open, for Gita would have to breathe this way for several days. He told the dafadar to remove the bullet from the paper cartridge, and to shake out the powder and open the closed end. Then he pushed the makeshift breathing tube gently but firmly into the windpipe and turned to the raj kumari with a smile of satisfaction. 'It will do until I can find something more apt – a reed, or bamboo perhaps.'

She could say nothing, tears running freely.

Once the mare was comfortable he left the raj kumari with her and went to find Alter Fritz. The old German looked exhausted as he laboured with a dozen sowars to free a big gelding cast in its stall. 'Rittmeister Bauer,' said Hervey, with considerable resignation in his voice, 'I believe we are losing the battle. We have to take drastic measures. I want you to set up lines the other side of the river, the horses with at least ten lengths between them, and I want you to put a torch to these stables.'

Hervey expected him to protest, as would any quartermaster, but the old German simply looked at him and nodded.

It took all day to move camp. The sowars had the running-ropes up quickly on the other side of the river (they were, after all, well practised in bivouacking), but it took time to ferry the animals across. Three horses that could not rise were put down where they lay, and for a while Hervey thought they would have to do the same with Gita, but towards evening she was coaxed to her feet, and she even managed a small feed before being led, unsteadily, to the ferry. Once night was come, and the worst of the heat gone, so that the thatch on the rest of the cantonment buildings was not so tinder-like, Alter Fritz and the officers of the infantry posted a line of fire pickets, and the torch was put to the rissalah stables. By dawn, all that was left was blackened walls. Everywhere smoke drifted upwards.

Hervey was standing contemplating his destruction – the razing of some of the best stables he had ever seen – when a voice broke the silence. 'He maketh wars to cease in all the world: he breaketh the bow, and knappeth the spear in sunder, and burneth the chariots in the fire.'

He looked round. 'Selden! I am *very* glad indeed to see you!'

'I thought the burial service apt,' he smiled. 'It's the only scripture I've heard these past five years.'

Hervey had no wish to contemplate the Prayer Book at this moment. 'You are restored, then?'

'Ay: quinquina spooned to me by a faithful Bengali – which is more than I could have expected in England. Now, tell me: what exactly have you been doing – other than making work for Chintal's builders?'

Hervey recounted the tribulations of the past week, Selden nodding his approval at both diagnosis and treatment. And of the burning of the horse lines he seemed positively admiring. 'No doubt you superintended the conflagration like King Charles at the Great Fire – astride your charger?'

'The fire did burn out the plague from the City, as I recall,' replied Hervey in mitigation.

'Of course, of course!' said Selden, smiling even wider. 'A refiner's fire!'

He was able to laugh for the first time in days. He had had doubts about every action he had ordered. The only thing of which he was certain was the *need* to take action. Selden's presence was, indeed, a great comfort. As they walked about the new lines, the sowars greeted the salutri's arrival as a sign that their trial was at an end.

And so it proved. In the next twenty-four hours only six horses developed the strangles' symptoms, and on the fourth day there were no new cases at all. Gita's abscesses were lanced the day after she crossed the river, having come rapidly to a head with poulticing, and her breathing returned to normal soon afterwards, allowing Selden to remove the bamboo tube and sew up the incision. There was a great roast of pig to celebrate the passing of the contagion, the sowars dancing and carousing until dark, and the sadhu filling anew his bowl with silver. When Hervey retired that night, he felt more content than he had been in many months, for he had been – as it were – on campaign with his troopers, and they had triumphed. *This*, he knew, was his proper calling; not the affairs of the staff, with their errands, diplomacy and deception. He was sure he must return to it as soon as he decently might.

CHAPTER SIXTEEN
WEAKLY TO A WOMAN

Chintalpore, 3 April

Pleasure, though intense in India, seemed fated to be brief. Hervey was in his quarters with pen and paper once more, about to write to the collector to hasten both the subsidiary force and, in his view just as important, the officer who was to win the rajah's approval and thence take command. Since returning from Jhansikote three days ago, he had heard of so many causes for alarm that he was now certain that Chintal faced the most pressing danger. He had written on the first evening to Guntoor to urge the collector to send, in advance of the subsidiary force, any troops he could spare, for a mood of deep foreboding seemed to have settled on Chintalpore – on merchants, beggars and courtiers alike. Rumours abounded and there had been signs in the heavens. Shiva himself had been incarnated several times, had murdered good and bad alike and ravished many virgins. There was, as yet, no riot, no general hysteric passion, but Hervey did not imagine such seething would end in ought else. His chief alarm, however, lay in what was reported to him by Locke (who was increasingly privy to the gossip of the bazaars), that there was a widespread supposition that Chintal was soon to be attacked by a confederacy of Haidarabad and Calcutta, and that the European officers were the harbingers of this aggression. It troubled him principally because, until the Company officer arrived to take command, he considered himself obliged to the rajah; yet any order he gave would be questioned, especially if its purpose were equivocal – in which case attempts at deception would carry grave dangers.

It did not help that the demeanour of the rajah himself was daily more unfathomable. He neglected the usual formalities of the court, would receive no one without their absolute insistence, and remained for the most part in his quarters, forsaking his menagerie even. All this Hervey had laid before the collector in the first letter, and he repeated it now – together with further intelligence of the nizam's malevolent intent (so alarming, indeed, was the intelligence that on receiving it this very morning the rajah's first minister had fled the city). Officials in the west of Chintal had reported movement of Haidarabad's sepoys all along the border, and – worse – cannon. Even more alarming, and more perplexing, were similar reports from the other side of the country, where the nizam's territories reached over the Eastern Ghats and abutted Chintal on the plains of the lower Godavari. Hervey could divine no purpose in these movements, except the crudest attempts to overawe, and he asked for the collector's assessment. Next he gave his estimate of the fighting power of the rajah's army in the light of the recent depredations. It was not encouraging. At his instigation, since the mutiny, the rajah had removed those officers who he considered had shown insufficient discernment when trouble was fomenting, or who had shown particular vindictiveness when rebellion actually came. Locke had urged Hervey to dismiss all of them – indeed, to blow them from the mouths of the galloper guns in front of the rest. But Hervey had resisted: he could not, in one sweep, remove all the facility for order and fighting. Instead, he had urged the rajah to keep a core of the most junior officers (no one above the rank of jemadar, except the Rajpoot and Maratha subedars) and to make each of them swear, at the oxbow durbar, by all that was sacred to their faiths, their unquestioning loyalty to him personally. He had had the rajah promote several of the Rajpoots – paragons, he was now convinced, of the martial spirit. But in all, he wrote, the rajah could muster only one battalion of fewer than a thousand sepoys. The reduction of his cavalry was, however, Hervey's gravest concern. Alter Fritz could mount, serviceably, fewer than a hundred sowars, for the horses that had survived the strangles were in so poor a condition that it would be at least a month (perhaps more in this oppressive heat) before they were fit for service. He had sent to Nagpore for remounts, but anything that the collector could arrange, begged Hervey, would be of inestimable value, for there were no means to patrol the border with Haidarabad while at the same time keeping any sort of handy reserve in Chintalpore and Jhansikote for interior security. He implored the collector to send him a full troop of Madrasi cavalry at once.

All this he read over a second and then a third time before attaching his signature and seal, hoping he had managed to convey the necessity for prompt action, yet without its appearing too importunate a plea, as if he were anxious at any price to leave the city. Yet leave was all he wished, profoundly, to do. Every day he delayed – every *hour* – lessened his chances of being received by the nizam, and therefore the success of his mission. The first part of that mission – the jagir deeds – was in any case still unfulfilled, for Selden had found nothing but confusion in the chancery since the death of Kunal Verma. Hervey knew he stood in default of reporting to Colonel Grant, for it had been many weeks since he had sent any despatch to Paris. But so damning a testimony to his own shortcomings would such a despatch be that he had put down his pen, dry, on every occasion he had attempted the task. This letter for Guntoor, however, ought to bring him the means of at least presenting himself to the nizam, and therefore of having something of substance he might relate to Paris. He would thus entrust it to Cornet Templer, who had arrived only the day before to assist with arrangements for the subsidiary force. He could ill spare him, but who else might he send? Without Johnson, who would have done it admirably, he was at a loss over so many things, and Locke's standing with the sepoys might be invaluable: indeed, without him he was not sure they could be relied on.

Private Johnson was unconvinced by Hervey's eloquence when he heard the contents of the despatch. As they watched the farrier hammering in the last nail of a new set of shoes, Jessye standing as patiently as if they were at the forge in Horningsham, he gave his candid opinion. 'Tha's not said owt about them Pindarees, and no matter 'ow quickly them Company troops comes they won't 'ave big enough guns to take on them that you said t'nizam 'ad.'

Johnson's dalliance with a daughter of the palace these past weeks had done nothing for his elocution or refinement, thought Hervey, but, as so often, he had addressed the material issue. 'In truth,' he replied, frowning, 'I'd been calculating that the Pindarees would not trouble the rajah this year – not this side of the festival of Dasahara, at least. And I saw no reason for the nizam to bring his so-called daughters into the field. For since he knows that Chintal has no artillery he would manage perfectly well with smaller pieces – which we ought to be able to deal with by other means.'

Johnson snorted. 'Tha always used to say that 'ope wasn't a principle of war!'

And Hervey was inclined to concede the point, except that there was an entirely reasonable element of calculation: it was not strictly hopefulness that made him optimistic – if indeed that word could be used to describe his condition. Before he could get too far into a justification of his optimism, however, they were interrupted by a jemadar with an urgent summons to the rajah's quarters. 'What occasions this?' asked Hervey cautiously, knowing how reclusive the rajah had become in recent days.

'There has been fighting on the upper reaches of the Godavari, sahib,' replied the jemadar, measuring his Urdu so that Hervey was able to grasp it first time. 'And a sahib has been found murdered on the road outside Chintalpore.'

'A sahib? Which sahib? Who?' demanded Hervey anxiously, though hardly wishing to hear the name.

'His face is not known, Captain sahib.'

That much at least was a relief. 'I'll come at once. Has Locke-sahib been summoned also?'

The jemadar did not think so.

'Then please send for him too.'

Fighting proved perhaps too strong a word to describe the incident on the Godavari, and Hervey thought he might have misunderstood the Urdu. The rajah's dastak officials had been roughly handled by the nizam's men, and though that hardly bode well it did not constitute an attack. But the officials also reported seeing guns with uncommonly long barrels.

'Captain Hervey, an official of the Company was found dead this morning on the road from Guntoor.' The rajah seemed perfectly composed as he handed a letter to him, unlike several minor officials also gathered in the audience chamber. 'He seems to have been travelling alone, and set upon by thieves, for his pockets were empty and his horse gone. But sewn into the lining of his coat was this letter, addressed to you.'

The seal was unbroken. Hervey was astonished – and then thought meanly of himself for supposing it would be otherwise. He read the letter with mounting despair.

'Does it reveal who was this man, Captain Hervey?' said the rajah, still perfectly composed.

'It does, sir – though a man I never met. He was Colonel Forster, whom the Company – and, indeed, I myself – hoped would take command of the subsidiary force once he had gained your confidence.' As he spoke the words he could feel the fetters closing fast on him, and his stomach heaved at his abject failure to discharge the duke's mission. 'The letter also bears disturbing intelligence, sir,' he continued, his voice once or twice betraying his turmoil. 'Word has come from Nagpore that several thousand Pindarees have been swarming along the Nerbudda river, and that the Nagpore subsidiary force is not yet embodied – and that Appa Sahib, the regent, earnestly requests you to lend him all support at once.'

The rajah still seemed remarkably composed at the news. Yet, to Hervey, the situation could hardly have been graver – and he said so. Chintal faced threats on both flanks simultaneously, there was in-sufficient intelligence of what the nizam's forces were about, especially in the east, and in the west they appeared to be staring in the face of the most powerful guns in India.

The rajah was not convinced. 'Captain Hervey, for many years we have lived with the nizam's fearsome daughters. Like many women, they spit and they make a great deal of noise. But, truly, must they trouble us so?'

Hervey was as close to exasperation as he had been since leaving England. This was not *his* fight: he had never even formally accepted command of the subsidiary force. Truly the rajah was a *gentle* man, but . . . 'Sir,' he began emphatically, 'as I am given to understand, the nizam's daughters are French iron guns of the very largest nature. Their barrels are long – almost ten feet. They may throw a projectile with considerable accuracy, therefore. And they may do so at great range – a mile, easily. You may suppose how they will command the approaches to any fortified position.' He paused to allow the notion to sink in. 'The projectile itself weighs thirty-six pounds – three times greater than any which the subsidiary force now being assembled possesses!'

'War itself is an option of difficulties,' replied the rajah simply – complacently, even.

Hervey checked himself. 'You quote General Wolfe, sir, and that is most apt, for he was only able to take the heights at Quebec after stumbling on an unguarded path. It seems to me that we too must find one.'

'Captain Hervey,' smiled the rajah, 'you do not know how pleased I am to hear you say it is *we* who shall have to find that path. I had begun to suspect you would desert us!'

Hervey counted himself fortunate, always, that the griping in his vitals – the fear of death or dishonour in equal measure – had never rendered him incapable of thinking. Indeed, in some respects it stimulated it. In an instant he had chosen to say 'we', for although he knew his mission for the duke was all but rendered impossible now (and by his own making), he could at least redeem some tiny part of his reputation by facing up to things squarely in Chintal. 'I am at your service, sir,' he said resolutely.

'Do I therefore send my sepoys to Nagpore, Captain Hervey?'

'No sir,' he replied at once. 'That would be to leave Chintal a prey to Haidarabad – and there may already be Pindarees down the Godavari on Nagpore's borders.'

'But we do not know what the nizam is to do with these guns,' protested the rajah. 'If I am able to recall my history, Quebec was a fortress, its defences fixed. Perhaps that is the nizam's intent only – a fortress on his border?'

'Sir, why should the nizam build so strong a fortress when there is no threat whatever? No, the only purpose those guns serve is either to be brought to the palace here, probably on boats down the Godavari, to cannonade you into submission – or else they are a lure.'

The rajah had looked anxious at the suggestion that his palace might be thus despoiled, but positively intrigued at the notion of a lure. 'Please explain yourself more fully, Captain Hervey.'

At the rajah's bidding, the assembled company sat down, no longer having need of the map spread on the table. Selden, who had arrived after the conference began, but silent throughout (his influence much diminished by the most recent attack of malaria), started coughing violently. The rajah gave him iced water, which revived him as much by its expression of continuing regard as by any medicinal property. Once the coughing had ceased, and the rajah was again seated, Hervey took a deep breath and began his estimate – a calculation which, if wrong, might soon spell the end of the rajah's sovereignty over Chintal. 'The nizam will not invest Chintalpore,' he opened confidently. 'His treaty of alliance with the Company forbids any such aggression without the Company's compliance – and that, we know, is unthinkable.' The raj kumari cleared her throat. Hervey looked at her and saw the suggestion that he could not be so assured on this point. He decided to press on rather than be drawn into deliberation on the perfidy of the Company, however. 'Your Highness, as I was saying, it is wholly inconceivable that Haidarabad should undertake overtly offensive action against Chintal.'

'Unless, that is, those brutish sons of the nizam have a hand in matters,' responded the rajah. 'I have heard much of the enfeeblement of the nizam these past months. Nor would I place any faith in that badmash Chundoo Lall, his minister. Their long-held designs on Chintal – or, rather, the wealth of Chintal – are about to be thwarted by our alliance with the Company, about which they will have surely heard, since nothing remains secret in Chintalpore. Is this not now the only remaining opportunity they have to wrest that wealth from me?'

'I cannot gainsay that hypothesis, sir, but I cannot believe the resident in Haidarabad would not have knowledge of such an enterprise. And, that being so, the Company's agents would have been alerted, and in turn Chintalpore. We must discount it as the least likely eventuality.'

'And yet we hear,' said the rajah, with a hint of reproach, 'that the resident in Haidarabad is not all that he should be.'

A high official of the Honourable East India Company seduced from his duty by pecuniary advantage: it was a grave charge. Hervey scarcely considered an Englishman was free from the mark of original sin, but he was not inclined to see perfidy in that quarter – though Selden would, no doubt, remark that India sweated the false civilization out of the best of men. He knew he could have complete confidence in one official at least. 'Your Highness,' he replied, in careful, measured tones, 'we know, regrettably, that things in Haidarabad may not be as they should. But I have the utmost faith in the Collector of Guntoor. He would not dissemble.'

The rajah conceded. 'Then what is it that you suppose the nizam is about? What is this ruse you speak of?'

Hervey considered for a moment how best he might explain his thesis

– which was, in essence, simple, however ingenious. 'If Haidarabad may not attack Chintal, then Chintal must be induced to attack Haidarabad. If, as I suspect, the nizam is at this time building redoubts on Chintal soil – not very distantly across his border, so that he might say that its precise line was in some doubt – it is a gauntlet thrown down in challenge. If you do not take it up then there will be some further encroachment, but all the time falling short of anything to which Calcutta could have substantive objection.'

There followed a long silence during which the rajah appeared to be praying, and the raj kumari calculating. At length the rajah pronounced himself in agreement with the appreciation. 'But, Captain Hervey, we now come to the most painful part: what is to be done? Do I appeal to Calcutta? Do I journey to Haidarabad to ask for terms? I have read that a good tactician is he who knows what to do when something must be done; whereas strategy must from nothing derive what that something *is*. What *should* be our strategy?'

There was scarcely an eye but on the rajah as he spoke. Now there was not an eye that was elsewhere but on Hervey. He was all too aware of it, all too conscious of the expectations of him. He had nipped in the bud the mutiny at Jhansikote with little more than a whiff of grapeshot, just as resolutely as Bonaparte had defended the Convention. But did his art lie any more than in the skirmish? He had, in the rajah's conviction, made a thorough and accurate estimate of the situation that faced them. Yet it had been one thing to make an appreciation – that much could have been done, with varying degrees of percipience, by anyone in the chamber. It was quite another to determine a strategy. And he dared not betray any doubt, for to do so would challenge the resolve that each would need for his strategy to have the remotest chance of success.

He began resolutely. 'We know that we have not one-hundredth of the power needed to fight the nizam's army.' It was not an auspicious beginning. The rajah looked all but dismayed, which hastened Hervey to his purpose. 'We must therefore take care to fight only those of his forces that it is supremely necessary to fight. By the boldest action we must prevent the enemy from reaching the battlefield in the first instance. These great guns of his – the nizam's daughters as everyone seems wont to call them – are the cornerstone of his attempt to overawe us. If we are able somehow to neutralize that advantage then the nizam's own stratagem is thwarted. Then we may turn our backs on him, so to speak, and make ready to deal in turn with the Pindarees on the plain of the Godavari – for that, surely, is where they will erupt from Nagpore.'

The rajah looked disappointed. Was this a strategy of substance or of evasion? he asked himself. How, for instance, were the nizam's guns to be dealt with by so insufficient a force as Hervey had at his disposal? Had he placed too much faith, after all, in this captain of cavalry – *cornet* a little but a year ago? 'Captain Hervey, how, by all that is reasonable, do you suppose we may confront guns as powerful as these? Did not Napoleon himself say that it is with artillery that war is made?'

Hervey blanched at hearing the imperial name, for 'Bonaparte' was the best that any Englishman would allow. But it was no time for strict form, and he had to counter the rajah's proposition – difficult though that task was. He could think of only one response, turning on the rajah's own exposition of the strategic and the tactical. 'Your Highness,' he said, smiling confidently, 'you have had occasion already to place your faith in my tactics, and not without gratification. Treating with those guns is merely an affair of tactics.'

The rajah, even if he retained doubts, looked intensely relieved. He left for his temple prayers with something of a smile, too.

'I see you have reconciled where duty lies then, Captain Hervey,' whispered Emma Lucie with a wry sort of frown.

'Have I?' he sighed. 'I fear I have merely chosen the easier course.'

Later, in the seclusion of the palace gardens where they could not be overheard, Hervey spoke with Locke. Henry Locke, stout-hearted, in love with the most beguiling of the Maharashtri nautch girls because she looked him full in the face; though their positions of a decade before, when Hervey had stood in awe of him at Shrewsbury, were reversed, he bore no sign of disaffection. 'What do you wish me to do?'

'My dear friend,' sighed Hervey, 'this isn't your fight. It's not even my fight. I cannot tell you everything, but—'

'Matthew Hervey, don't try to send me away!' Locke protested

He smiled. What simple loyalties fighting men enjoyed! 'You don't understand. I'm doing this because I've left myself no other course – because I've made such a hopeless job of the thing I was sent here to do!'

'I could not care less. I have my reasons too. Just tell me what it is you would have of me!'

Hervey would lose no time with any expression of gratitude, for he knew he could not express it sufficiently with brevity. 'First, you could see that no harm comes to Emma Lucie. Get her out of Chintalpore – to Guntoor if you can.'

He nodded.

'And then I want you to go to Jhansikote and take charge there.'

Locke nodded again, and smiled broadly. 'I do have one question though. Would it not be better to see off the Pindarees first before turning to the nizam's redoubts? If, as you say, he will take no offensive action against Chintal, what's to be feared having him at our rear?'

He had a point, though not one that Hervey had overlooked. 'Do you recall what the Duke of Marlborough was said to have declared about campaigning – that no war could be fought without good and early intelligence?'

Locke nodded.

'Well, that's more the essence of our problem than those guns themselves. We are, so to speak, like a prizefighter who's blindfold. We surmise the purpose of the nizam's men on the lower plains is no more than to rattle our nerve, that they have no offensive intent.'

'Ay,' said Locke, furrowing his brow more, 'but you claimed – and convincingly – that the nizam could not risk taking such action. And for him to do so on the plains, which are so much closer to the Company's territories, makes no sense at all.'

Hervey nodded. 'Yes, but what if his troops gave battle not as soldiers of Haidarabad but as Pindarees? They would be able to throw the whole of lower Chintal into confusion, cause the rajah to flee and give the nizam pretext for marching in to restore order.'

Locke's mouth fell open. 'Hervey, that's fiendish. Why did you not say all this in the rajah's chamber?'

'For two reasons. First, I could not be sure who might hear – nor even could I be sure of the discretion, perhaps even the loyalty, of all that were in the chamber. And second – and I am most loath to say this, for I admire so much in the man – the rajah is not of the most resolute disposition, at least for the present. If he flees Chintalpore it will be the end.'

Locke blew out his breath in a gesture that acknowledged the true extent of the danger. 'And you still believe that disabling those guns is the key?'

'Yes,' said Hervey, and with some assurance. 'We may take our chances with the Pindarees, but if they were backed by those guns, I think it another matter.'

'You think the nizam could simply move those great things the other side of Chintal?'

'Let me put it to you thus, my dear fellow,' replied Hervey, smiling. 'From my reading of history, whenever a plan has depended upon the enemy's *not* being able to move guns into a certain position, it has been overthrown by the very fact of his doing so!'

'Yes, but *here*—'

'Even here – even with these forests and hills. What about the Godavari? Now that Haidarabad appears, in practice, to have immunity from dastak, who knows *what* is moved along the river? Don't lose heart, though. We shall be fighting the Pindarees with relief at hand – for I can't think it will be long before the Company is able to despatch the subsidiary force. In any case, I'll send urgent appeal to the collector this very day. What I want *you* to do, my dear Locke, is to drill the rajah's infantry as light companies, for we shall have to bustle them about as nobody's business. And have them ready, if you will, in three days' time to take to the field. Tonight I shall leave with half a troop and the galloper guns for the west – I would do so earlier if this heat were not so punishing. And first I shall have it spread abroad that *all* of the rajah's troops are to march on the nizam's redoubts – for having us so march is their purpose. There are agents aplenty in Chintalpore: the false news will not take long to reach the guns.'

Locke looked puzzled. 'Why do you want them to believe that all the rajah's men are marching west?'

'So that, my good friend, they are not tempted to move the guns. If they do, I cannot very well destroy them!'

Locke, knowing now the full risk of the enterprise, would hold Hervey in even higher regard than he had after the mutiny. He knew he could never match the acuity with which his erstwhile junior examined a problem. He could count himself just as brave in battle, but he knew that courage was more than that. It required nerve. That, indeed, was how Nelson and Hoste would have had it. And he did not, in his heart, trust he had nerve in the same measure.

All this he admitted freely to his nautch girl, the Maharashtrian beauty whom Hervey had first been suspicious of for her cloying attachment, but whom latterly he had come to believe was, in her affections, wholly genuine. She helped him make ready for his ride to Jhansikote, bringing him ripe figs from the palace gardens for the journey. And as he set out, when the full heat of the day was beginning to abate, there were large tears in her eyes, and entreaties that he would return to her unharmed. Had Locke given it but a second's thought he would have known it an unlikely possibility – about as great as leading a boarding party against a deck swept by carronades. But his relish for the fight was growing by the hour, and after Jhansikote nothing seemed impossible. He kissed each eye gently – and then her lips with all the passion that was welling for the battle to come. 'I shall be back,' he said defiantly; 'and then you shall come with me to England!'

Half an hour before dawn, Hervey stepped down from the saddle in a nullah close to the nizam's redoubts. He had ridden hard all night. There had been – just as on the ride to Jhansikote on the night of the mutiny – an obliging moon, and there had been stretches of the road on which he could put Jessye into a hand-gallop. For the rest of the time they had trotted hard, except when she was in need of respite or where they came upon a hackery travelling by night to escape, as they, the heat of the day. Those travellers who were on foot – and there were many – simply stood aside as they heard the pounding hooves. Hervey, Johnson and the Maratha subedar had made the forty miles between Chintalpore and here in six hours, and their horses had yet something in reserve.

Behind them, hurrying at best speed, was a half-troop of the rajah's cavalry (Hervey had specified not fewer than thirty sowars) and two galloper guns. But since these were coming from Jhansikote they would be four hours behind at least. He wanted all the time he could to think of some way to overcome the guns, however, and he knew, from long experience in the Peninsula, that if he could observe the routine of a defended position at first light it would reveal the best means of proceeding against it. He loosened Jessye's girth and unfastened the noseband on her bridle so that she could pull at the couch grass: he would give her some of the oats he carried later. As he stood rubbing her ears, wondering what he might see when the sun revealed the redoubts to his telescope, Johnson handed him a tin cup. 'Tea, sir,' he said simply.

'Tea?' said Hervey incredulously. They had only just arrived, yet the cup was hot to the touch. Not even Johnson could have brewed tea in the saddle!

'Ay, tea.'

'Well tell me, man: how in heaven's name have you hot tea so quickly?'

'I'll show you,' and he went to retrieve the tea's conveyance. 'Here, can you make it out?' – it was very dark now that the moon had set – 'It's a stone bottle which keeps 'ot with this charcoal 'ere in a cooker underneath. And it all fits together in a tin 'arness. I bought it in t'bazaar.'

Dark as it was, Hervey grasped the principle and wondered why he had not seen the same on campaign. Perhaps, however, in the everyday of the Indian bazaar or the London emporium, such a thing seemed over-contrived for its simple product. Yet no one who had been on campaign would ever undervalue hot tea before stand-to on a day when battle was expected. 'Johnson,' he said simply, with a note of disbelieving admiration, 'I do not know how I should fare without you!'

They ate some chapattis and gave the horses a little corn, and soon the first shafts of daylight were piercing the darkness behind them. He told Johnson to take the three horses a little way back along the nullah, and then he and the subedar ascended its sides, and a hillock no wider than a dewpond, so that they might spy out the strength of the nizam's lure. He was confident they would be able to do so undetected: the subedar knew the ground well from many a patrol, and the dastak official whom they had sought out at the village a mile or so back had confirmed that here exactly was where they would see the redoubts. He would have wished the sun were not rising behind them, for it risked their exposure in silhouette to an observer still concealed by the darkness. But then, had the positions been reversed, he would not have been able to use his telescope for fear of the sun's reflection on its lens. In any case, avoiding a silhouette was but part of the scouting cavalryman's art: he must find some background cover – a bush, or suchlike.

They found a handy euphorbia and crawled under its protecting greenery. Hervey took out his telescope and searched in the direction the official had indicated. He had first been surprised there were no campfires, and now, with the glass to his eye, he could find no flame, no movement – no activity whatever. And there was not a sound, either. These, truly, were soldiers of high discipline, he muttered to the subedar.

274

As the light grew, almost with each tick of Hervey's full hunter, he was able at last to make out one of the redoubts. 'The guns must be run in: I can see nothing of them,' he whispered, rubbing the condensation from the eyepiece before taking a further look. It was the same with the second redoubt: the embrasure could be made out clear enough, but again the gun appeared to be run in. He found the third: it was the same. Surely the guns would be run out for the dawn stand-to? Yet each of the eight redoubts looked, in the half-light, asleep, inattentive – not even the sign of a sentry. If only he now had the half-troop and the galloper guns: he wagered he could storm each in turn and take them at the point of the sword. Scarcely would the enemy have time to rouse! He even thought of rushing the nearest redoubt himself and, with the subedar, turning the gun on the other seven. But he knew well enough that, so alerted, they would overpower him first. No, he would have to wait another night and take each by stealth. But then he had spread word that the rajah's troops were advancing: they would be waiting tomorrow, alert – surely?

The sun was now glinting over the hills to the east, the light growing ever stronger. After five more minutes, still peering through his telescope, Hervey started suddenly: 'Great heavens! There's no one there – no one at all!'

The subedar looked at him in astonishment. 'Why would they build redoubts like that and then abandon them as quickly, sahib?'

'I don't know, Subedar sahib; I simply don't know.'

He called for the horses, but as he did so there was a fearful squeal from one of them, and then squeals from all three. 'What in God's name is Johnson doing?' he rasped as they scrambled down the hillock and into the nullah. The squealing continued as they ran to where Johnson was struggling to keep hold of the reins of the three terrified animals – rearing, jumping and kicking in a manner he had rarely seen. 'What is it Johnson? What's got into them?'

'I don't know, sir; they was all just 'aving a bit of this couch grass and suddenly they all goes barmy!'

'Snake, sahib! They are panicking because of snake!'

There was no sign of a snake, however.

'They know when there is snake, sahib; it is most likely gone by now, though.'

The horses were, indeed, settling. Hervey took Jessye's reins and brought his hand up to her muzzle to reassure her. 'Oh God,' he said suddenly. 'Subedar sahib, come look here: there's blood on her nose!'

The subedar took one look and sucked in air between his teeth. 'It is snakebite, sahib – no mistake.'

Hervey looked closer and saw the tell-tale pinpricks from which the blood oozed. He went cold with dread: he had heard of horses dying within minutes of a snakebite. Jessye was now standing stock-still, her legs spread as if to keep herself braced. She began to pant. Only a month before Waterloo he had read of a condition described as 'shock', explaining why he had seen horses most cruelly mutilated on the battle-field which had not succumbed, and yet others with little apparent injury failing to recover. The paper suggested it was a collapse of the respiratory system – and Jessye's quickened breathing, and now her sweating flanks, pointed to just this. He called for a knife, but then decided against making free with it across the bite since the poison would already be deep. He took off the saddle and bridle as she began to shake.

In a while her forelegs began to buckle and she almost fell to the ground, just managing instead to drop unsteadily to her knees and then to roll onto her side. She lay sweating prodigiously, her breathing now growing shallow. 'Sahib, send to the village for sadhu,' pleaded the subedar.

Hervey had to check himself: the subedar's plea was well meant, but he wanted no fakir dancing about his mare. He knew in his heart that nothing could be done for her, nothing that could arrest the poison's evil, now deep in her vitals. Would Selden have bled her? The poison was in her blood, and bleeding would remove some of it, would it not? But Selden had always been so sceptical of bleeding. He would surely urge that not one drop of blood was better placed than in a vein. Jessye had survived so much – three years of the Peninsula, and then Waterloo. To succumb now to something that slithered in the couch grass was ignoble, the basest of ends – like Edmonds's death to the first volley in that battle. He pulled his pistol from the saddle and began to prime it. He would not let her end come from a serpent: better that she die at the hand of a friend. He lifted her head, and she grunted. He pulled her ears, blew in her nostrils, wiped the blood from her muzzle, keeping the pistol out of sight as tears streamed down his cheeks. 'Is she in pain, Subedar sahib?'

'No sahib, she not in pain. Snake's poison in horse only make it sleep in peace. Let me fetch sadhu, sahib. He know many mantras to draw out poison.'

'Thank you, Subedar sahib, but no. I can feel her slipping away even as we speak.' He brought the pistol to her head, gently but firmly putting the barrel to the fossa over her left eye so that the ball would not strike bone. He pulled the hammer back carefully to full cock, the 'click' as it engaged in the notch of the trigger arm seeming louder than he had ever heard. He prayed it would take just the one round . . . and then he drew the pistol away. 'If she is in no pain, let her lie in the sun at rest, Subedar sahib. Let her remaining time be peaceful. I don't want her to hear another shot: she's heard too many.'

'Yes, sahib; let her pass in peace with the sun on her.'

It had been no more than five minutes since he heard the commotion, but he knew he should now be about the business of the guns. Every instinct, every precept he had been taught and every lesson from life told him so, for in war, time was the only commodity which, once lost, could not be regained. 'Johnson, stay with her until . . .' He found himself choking on the words. 'And then have her buried – I don't want her on a pyre.'

'Ay sir,' replied Johnson quietly, just as moved at her plight, for he had been with Hervey, and therefore Jessye, for more than three years.

He cradled her head to his chest and whispered a farewell in her ear, tears now running freely. He gave Johnson a handful of silver to see to her burial. 'There will be men in the village who will dig. Find whatever horse you can to get back to Chintalpore.'

Then he sprang up with all the resolve he could muster and leapt into the saddle of Johnson's mount. 'Come, Subedar sahib,' he called briskly, his face streaked where the tears had washed the caked dust. He dug his spurs into the little Arab, and did not look back.

The redoubts were as empty as if they had never been occupied. Except that there was the unmistakable spoor of heavy guns – and easy to follow, for their wheel-ruts were as deep again as those of the wagons that had accompanied them. Hervey soon found the tracks of eight pieces converging beside the Godavari. This could not be a fording place, surely? There was no exit that he could see on the far bank. Had the nizam withdrawn his guns, therefore? Surely not on hearing that the rajah's troops were marching west. There must therefore have been some interior cause for withdrawal, but it seemed unusually coincident. Which left only the possibility that the guns were taken *down*stream. To Chintalpore? Or to the Pindarees? If Haidarabad had known that the rajah's forces were not moving west after all – that they were not, indeed, to be drawn by this lure – then the nizam's men would have removed the guns at once. But how might Haidarabad have learned of this? Hervey had, after all, told only one man. Surely he and Locke had not been overheard? Surely Locke had not . . . ? And then came the awful realization: the Maharashtri girl. Like the wretched Samson at Gaza, groaned Hervey, who 'weakly to a woman revealed it'. He groaned again: Locke – brave, true, foolish. 'O impotence of mind, in body strong!'

But what was the purpose now of railing? Indeed, the guns, if they were on the river, were powerless. With the lightest galloper gun he could force them to surrender, or even send them to the bottom! He looked again at the river, to the middle where the stream seemed fastest. A tree trunk bobbed obligingly by, giving him the chance to assess the speed. It seemed little more than marching pace, and since there was no breeze he estimated that barges carrying the guns could not exceed a horse's jogtrot. They had had, perhaps, six hours' start at most. They might be, say, forty miles downstream – at Chintalpore. His heart sank. But his duty was clear either way: if the guns were making for Chintalpore, his place was back at the rajah's palace. And if they had *not* been able to make such speed . . .

He swung the mare round. 'Subedar sahib,' he shouted, 'the guns are on the river between us and Chintalpore. We are going to destroy them!'

He had two options. To pace his mare so that, if the half-troop and the galloper guns had made slow progress (perhaps not yet even arrived at Chintalpore), they did at least reach them; or else he could make all speed at once in the hope of meeting the troop in time either to inter-cept – or at least catch up – the boats. Hope was not a principle of war, he reminded himself, yet surely the second option was the only one?

Now he would do something he had never done before. He would push his horse until it fell of exhaustion. Had he contemplated the act coolly and at length, he might have balked at it. Yet now, scenting the distant possibility of a kill, he felt nothing. He unfastened the holsters from the saddle and flung them and their pistols into the river. He unbuckled his sabre – a fine tulwar from the rajah's armoury – and hurled that into the river too. And when the time came – when he needed just another mile from his mare – he would throw off shako and tunic, and discard the saddle to ride, as Xenophon prescribed, bareback. The subedar followed his example: everything – his own sacred tulwar included – he cast like Hervey into the waters of the Godavari.

After two hours at a truly prodigious pace, their horses tiring desperately with every stride, Hervey was suddenly inspirited by the distant appearance of the lancer troop. He pushed his little mare back into a gallop to close the remaining quarter of a mile, and kicked up so much dust that the troop was taking guard as he hallooed them. 'Have you seen any boats on the river?' he shouted.

The rissaldar looked confused. Hervey tried again, this time in Urdu. Still there was no reply. He cursed and looked at the subedar. 'In heaven's name ask him if he's seen boats on the river – a dozen, maybe more; big boats, big enough to carry the nizam's guns!'

With a concoction of English, Urdu and Telugu he eventually established that a small flotilla that might answer thus – certainly unusual in appearance, with several craft roped together, and having an uncommonly large number of people aboard – had passed them by almost an hour ago. Hervey's face lit up at the news. He explained what he wanted and soon the rissaldar's face was lit up too. The troop's officer trotted back down the column to relay the intention, and the sowars' faces took on the same aspect. Hervey wanted one more thing, however: paper and pencil. The rissaldar obliged, handing him his sabretache, and in less than a minute he had scribbled his message for Locke. It read simply, 'Nizam's daughters on river. Shall intercept. Make speed to Chintalpore in case elude me. There is spy in palace who knows our last conversation. Hervey.' He gave it to a dafadar with instructions to ride for Jhansikote at all speed.

Changing horses to a big country-bred which tried to bite his arm as he mounted, Hervey hastened to the head of the column. 'Very well then, Rissaldar sahib, let's be about it!'

Though the rissaldar knew not the precise meaning of Hervey's Urdu, the sense was clear enough, and, with an appeal to Shiva, he put his thirty men and the guns straight into a gallop.

Sooner than Hervey expected, they caught up with the flotilla of shallow-draught vessels taking the most powerful guns in southern India deep into the territory of the rajah. The sight filled him with a powerful sense of violation, and a glimpse into the eyes of the sowars behind him would have revealed the same. They had not hated these men from Haidarabad before. Though most of the nizam's soldiers were Mussulmans they were brothers nonetheless. Perhaps it was the outrage of sibling betrayal which now fired these Hindoos of Chintalpore, for when they saw the boats they quickened the pace without orders. Soon they were in a flat gallop, the guns bouncing behind the bigger country-bred geldings. As they drew parallel and then overtook the boats which, here on the curve of the river, were much closer to the sowars' bank, the nizam's gunners realized what was to come, and there was at once commotion where before there had been only torpor. The guns themselves were covered by canvases – not that they could have been fired from such flimsy craft even had they been ready – and some of the gunners sought the meagre protection of concealment beneath them.

The sowars unhitched the galloper guns before the wheels had even stopped turning, swinging them at the boats with frenzied heaving. They opened fire so quickly that Hervey thought they must have been loaded ready. He urged them on with the most sanguinary imprecations. He wanted no measured action, only the most ferocious assault: what might these sepoys of the nizam be capable of if they were not subdued rapidly and with the greatest violence? The rissaldar, suffused with that same resolve, and without waiting for orders, spread his men along the bank to deal with those who were, willingly or otherwise, about to enter the water. The galloper guns found their mark easily. Although the Godavari, even before the monsoon, was wide at this point (perhaps as much as two hundred yards), it was a placid – even a sluggish – stream, and the guns needed no elevation. Against river barges a single four-pound shot did the most fearful destruction (they were just beyond the range of canister), and with targets that stood practically still, the business of re-laying was nothing. The first to strike home carried away the head of one of the sepoys, leaving his body standing for several seconds before it toppled forward and over the side. Blood spattered about the others and sent them into a frenzy. An officer tried to rally them to some resistance, but he fell to a carbine ball, coolly discharged from the saddle by a diminutive Tamil who was not prepared to wait for the sabre. The others were soon loading theirs, but next the second galloper gun fired a corrected shot, low, which smashed through the gunwale and sent a torrent of splinters as lethal as grape across the deck of the third barge, leaving not a man standing for'ard. Sepoys on the fourth barge began a brisk return of fire, but to little effect, and Hervey ordered the jemadar to have the sowars direct their carbine fire at this and the following barges, which were much closer to the bank, to suppress the resistance until the galloper guns could play on them in turn.

The lead barge was now ablaze, the first gun having fired one of its precious fused shells into the shrouded cargo, and sepoys were soon jumping from the sides. Some could not swim: they thrashed wildly, calling upon Allah until the Godavari claimed them. Some struck for the distant bank, but a dozen sowars put their horses into the river after them. There could be no doubting who would win the race. Others, accepting their fate or hopeful of mercy, made for the nearer side. Sowars waded in to meet them, slinging lances over the shoulder to draw sabres instead, and the shallows soon ran red – brackish though the river was. Some of them, impatient of waiting for the remaining fugitives to leave the barge, swam their horses towards the craft to assail the would-be survivors with the steel point of the ten feet of bamboo. The second barge was now sinking, its gunwales below water, its sepoys, seeing the slaughter of the first, unable to commit themselves to the fate attending whichever course they chose. Those on the third made no attempt at resistance, climbing instead into the water on the cover-side, holding on desperately, doubtless hoping that the barge would somehow drift out of reach of the guns. But it edged instead into the second, which was wallowing midstream. Both guns now turned on it. The first round struck just below the waterline, and the barge's fate was sealed, if slowly. But the other gun still had one fused shell, and it took only seconds to have the vessel ablaze, forcing the sepoys finally to choose their fate. However, none were to feel the sabre or the lance's point, for before the most resolute had made a dozen strokes the barge blew up, sending a fountain of matchwood higher than the tallest mathi trees on either bank. On seeing this the sepoys on the fourth barge began throwing down their muskets and jumping into the water. Hervey guessed that the powder was carried on just two barges, this and the third, and he shouted for the galloper guns to play now on the last two, whose sepoys were returning fire briskly but with almost no effect from behind the cover of the gunwales.

The guns were now fiercely hot, despite vigorous sponging, yet still their sowars showed no fear in serving them. Indeed, the jemadar ordered double charges and canister, believing he could just reach the nearer barge. Two discharges put an end to the volleying from behind the gunwales, allowing the sowars to fire with more measure at the hull. The third shot, perhaps finding some weakened part of the clinker-built side, stove in a dozen feet of timber just on the waterline. The barge began to list at once. Those sepoys who had not been hit by canister sprang up in dismay from behind the gunwales, only to begin falling again to the sowars' carbines. And then the barge, under the weight of the two giant cannon – now exposed as the canvas covers fell away – turned on its side like some great beast of the river, the cannon plunging free of their lashings into the Godavari, and then rolled over completely before disappearing. All attention now turned to the last barge, but Hervey wished to make it a prize: the nizam's guns would be of incalculable value in the rajah's service, and the sepoys would surely have intelligence of the nizam's intentions. But before he could make his orders clear to the jemadar, the sepoys began trying to stave in the timbers, their officers having at least determined that the cannon should be denied to Chintal. Hervey ordered the galloper guns to reopen fire at once with canister, and the sowars with their carbines, to try to prevent the destruction. Guns and carbines worked terrible havoc – men fell almost continuously for a full five minutes – but still the sepoys hacked away with whatever they could find. In another five they were dead or dying to a man, sixty or more of them. But they had done their work, and the barge began to settle in the water. In five minutes it would be gone. Silence now returned to the Godavari. Hervey looked slowly from right to left, up and down the river, along its banks and its shallows. He had seen butchery of this kind before – but never so fervently and efficiently done.

CHAPTER SEVENTEEN

GOOD AND EARLY INTELLIGENCE

Later that morning

Hervey threw up violently. The slaughter at the river had been no greater than at Waterloo or any number of affairs in the Peninsula, but he had never seen men so drunk on blood. When the sowars had killed every last one of the nizam's gunners they had turned in their frenzy on those they had killed first, until there was scarcely a body that had not had a limb sliced away or been several times impaled. He had tried to stop it, but it was futile. Had he not, in truth, encouraged it? He had shouted 'no quarter' when they came on them, for he could spare no quarter until the last barge was destroyed. None of the nizam's men had held up their hands – except to Allah – and none had called for mercy. War was fury, not sport – victory the only consideration, was it not?

He now sat under a tree scribbling a second note for Henry Locke, out of sight of the river carnage. The rissaldar marched up as if on parade. 'Sahib! We have counted all bodies,' he announced. 'More than two hundred, sahib!'

Two hundred: what did it matter? It wasn't as if they were British, or even French. Just a lot of heathen natives. He would have slaughtered a hundred more to bring Jessye back. How the soul grew cold, he mused, even in so hot a place as Chintal.

'What is it, sahib? Is sahib unwell?' The rissaldar bent to take his shoulder.

This was absurd. He couldn't see the bodies now. Throwing up because he felt nothing? 'No, Rissaldar sahib – I am just a little winded still from the ride.'

'Brandy, sahib?'

'Yes, brandy would do very well, Rissaldar sahib.'

He took the canteen – water and brandy mixed, as reviving as it was slaking.

'Take it all, sahib – there is plenty more.'

He took it all. Then he threw up a second time.

The rajah, like the King of Spain in his chapel when the Armada sailed, would do nothing but pray. To the exasperation of those courtiers who had not fled or given way to a debilitating panic, he remained inaccessible, ministered to solely by a sadhu. Hervey, sick with killing, full of brandy but unquestionably triumphant, stormed into his apartments in fiery resolve.

The rajah stared at him, eyes fearful.

'Your Highness, the guns are now at the bottom of the Godavari. I shall ride tonight for Jhansikote and I urge you to follow as soon as you're able. Your sepoys must see you. We do not yet have complete victory.'

The rajah expressed every degree of relief, gratitude – obligation, even. But he was reluctant to leave his capital. Not for fear of the enemy on the plains but for fear of what might be done in Chintalpore were he now to quit it. 'I am convinced of the need for me to remain, Captain Hervey. And of my prayers in this place.'

Hervey sighed. How he wished for less of the pious inactivity of the Spanish king, and more the spirit of the English queen rallying her sailors. But no amount of reasoning could change the rajah's mind. 'With your leave, then, sir,' he said at length before retiring.

He left the rajah's apartments unsteadily, taking deep breaths to force out the brandy's ill effects. But the air was heavy and gave him no relief. More than once he turned the wrong way in the labyrinth of marble. Where in heaven's name were Selden's quarters? Instead he found a door opening into the courtyard, the sun strong in his eyes, an overpowering smell of horses, donkeys, mules, bullocks, elephants, sweating bearers – almost making him throw up again. And there was the raj kumari, and all about her treasures being loaded into hackeries and yakhdans.

She showed no surprise at seeing him. She already knew of the affair at the river. As soon as firing began she had galloped one of her Kehilans straight to the sound of the guns. He seized her roughly by the arm. 'What—'

'My father sends me away; that is all you need know.' She struggled free.

'The danger to the palace is gone, but beyond the walls—'

'I have no care. I take what is mine and leave.'

'For where?'

'You need not know!'

He seized her arm again, then the other, pulling her round to face him. The jasmine scent of loose hair drew him closer. He searched the sullen eyes for their secrets, but they yielded none. They never had. The same mastering urge as at the slaughter swelled again, a lust he would later revile just as much. He let go, turned about and walked away without looking back. Had he done so he would have seen her look of defiance turn to one of despair.

He saw the squatting shape as he turned the corner to his quarters. It was too early for a chowkidar to have taken post, and his senses returned with the recognition of danger. The figure rose in one easy movement and made namaste. The long black hair, falling loosely about the shoulders, the gaudy saree, the earrings, the bangles, the fat necklace hiding the Adam's apple – the creature's profession was unmistakable.

The hijda looked him up and down insolently. Hervey was close to scourging him. 'May I speak with you, Captain Hervey?' The English was heavily accented but confident, the voice that of neither a woman nor a man – and without the deferential 'sahib'.

'Of course you may speak,' replied Hervey warily; 'about what?'

The hijda looked at him as if to say he would not tell while they stood outside.

'Come, man!' snapped Hervey, only then realizing the incongruity of calling him thus.

'Mr Selden,' replied the hijda.

Instinct made him look about, but there was no one to overhear. 'Come,' he said, opening the big teak doors.

Inside, the hijda glanced here and there in a sort of sneering approval, before pouting in the way the troupe had done that first night at the rajah's banquet.

'Well, come to it!' demanded Hervey testily.

'Mr Selden is most sick of the fever which comes and then goes again.' The English was delivered in a modulating half-strangled alto.

'Where is he?'

'At our hijron. He is better cared for there than he would be here,' he sang defiantly.

'Why do you come here then?'

'Because Selden-sahib wants very much to speak with you. He is too ill to come himself. I will take you to him.'

'Very well – but not now. Be at the palace gates at three,' he snapped, intending to keep him at a full arm's length.

The hijda made namaste as if playing to a fuller stage, took a peach from a bowl and bit into it suggestively. Hervey cursed him roundly, making him cackle like a bazaar harlot as he fled the room.

When the hijda was gone, Hervey lay with his arms outstretched on the great bed. A pair of collared doves outside his window were enjoying a vocal courtship. Before the female had finished answering the male, he was asleep.

He was awakened soon after midday by a bearer who shook him with all the resolve he would a sleeping leopard. 'What in heaven's name—' He felt blindly for the sword that was not there.

The bearer was saying something but the Telugu made no sense.

'He says that I would have words with you, Captain Hervey,' came a voice from near the door.

Hervey got to his feet, as full awake now as he had been before he closed his eyes. 'Miss Lucie!' he exclaimed, blinking. 'I had thought you were gone to Guntoor.'

'No, indeed: it seemed to me the very best time to be in Chintalpore!'

Outside, the usual silence of the afternoon was broken only by a peacock calling from the menagerie, for all the world as if Chintal was a place of profound peace.

'How may I help, madam?' he tried.

Emma Lucie came to the middle of the room as the bearer left. 'Soon after you were gone last night a hircarrah arrived from Calcutta with this letter.' She held out a wax-paper package. 'His orders were that he should deliver it only into English hands.'

'And yours were the only ones to be found?' asked Hervey, taking it.

'As you see,' she smiled.

'You will excuse me?' He broke the seal and took out the letter.

She showed no inclination to leave. He read the copperplate with dismay, until his anxiety became evident to her.

'It is ill news, I take it?'

He nodded. 'It is very *late* news, madam. A letter from the agent of the Company – my facilitation – who died before I was able to meet with him.'

She smiled. It was the sort of knowing smile that only increased his discomfort. 'And it reminds you of the need to do things which are quite contrary to those you do now?'

'Just so, madam.'

She smiled again. 'I can scarcely give an indifferent opinion since my own brother's view I would know perfectly well. The treaty between the Company and the rajah is of the first importance. But you may know something that they do not, and if your Duke of Wellington troubled to send you here it must be with good reason.'

He could not but concede both points. And he would have wished to share more with her, but that would have been indulgent. 'What shall you do now?' he essayed airily. 'I myself have an assignation with Mr Selden somewhere in the city. It seems he has something of moment he must tell me.'

'And I fancy that, in general terms, I may know of what he will speak,' she replied, and none too cheerily.

'Oh?' he said. Was there no end to her discernment?

'Mr Selden asked me to assist him in examining what pass for the accounts in the rajah's treasury. They are ill-kept but conceal nothing – now that they are at hand, for certain of them came to light only when the babus fled three days ago.'

Hervey made as if to speak, but she held up a hand.

'Two and a half lakhs, approximating to the batta which had not been paid to the sepoys, was sequestered. It is evident that Kunal Verma did this, but other entries referred – I'm very much afraid – to payments to the "gora log". There are no white people in Chintal other than the European officers, are there?'

Hervey could scarce make himself believe it.

'You had better believe it, I think, Captain Hervey, for *there* is the very canker which has need of a knife!'

He knew it well enough, but it was for the rajah to dispose of the corruption, he said. 'And he is as like to go into a faint as soon as he hears of it!'

'Then perhaps you might leave that to me?' she said resolutely. 'Yours, I think, is a more pressing duty down the Godavari.'

That much he was more than happy to leave to her. How favoured he felt himself, for he doubted that wiser or more resolute counsel would have come from her own brother, or even the collector. 'Is there any other account on which Selden must see me? Does he have more *especial* intelligence?'

'I don't know, but I should be surprised if he did not, for I believe the company he keeps is – how shall we say? – *fertile.*'

Hervey looked astonished. How had she learned so much?

'Merely by observation. And, I might add, an ear for the native languages – which all who wish to make their fortune here would do well to acquire. But one thing I must tell you, Captain Hervey, for earlier I sowed seeds of doubt in your mind about Mr Selden – so that even now you may think him not without a hand in this. To me, however, it is quite inconceivable that Mr Selden had any part in the business, or even that he knew of its occurrence.'

He was more glad to hear this than anything: 'I had begun to doubt whether *anyone* might be trusted in this country.'

The hijron lay in one of the quieter parts of Chintalpore. Hervey had expected – inasmuch as he had given it any thought – quite the opposite, that the hijron would be in a place of some bustle and squalor. But instead it was a pleasant-looking haveli, a sizeable single-storey building with well-pointed brickwork, a good tiled roof, a courtyard swept clean and full of sweet-scented mimosa in pots, and an air of calm not unlike that he had known in some of the religious houses of Spain. His hijda guide beckoned him inside one of the open, slatted double doors, where the scent of mimosa turned to one of incense. He was conscious of other figures scuttling away, like mice. It should have set him on his guard, but here, unaccountably, he felt no fear of ambush. The hijda led him along a dark passageway, to an inner room where light streamed through tall windows at which muslin curtains hung perfectly still in the sticky, airless heat of the afternoon. There, in a large bed, its sheets perfectly white, lay Selden, his face as ochreous as that day in Toulouse when it looked as though the fever would finally carry him off. He was, however, without the delirium into which the fever periodically cast him, and he greeted Hervey with an attempt to raise himself on an arm. It ended, nevertheless, in a bout of coughing that was only relieved by lime-water and the hijda's gentle ministrations.

Hervey sat on the edge of the bed. 'Selden, this is a wretched business. Is there a physician who treats you?'

He coughed again. 'No, and there is no need, for there is nothing to be done but to sweat out these attacks. It will pass: I *feel* it.'

But Hervey could at least alleviate his discomfort now by telling him that the nizam's guns were no more a threat.

Selden, though he had heard the nizam's forces had received a check, was so amazed that he began another bout of frenzied coughing, which only brandy from Hervey's pocket flask was able to put a stop to. 'I should never have thought it possible, Matthew Hervey – not even with your address. In truth I feared I should never again see you alive!'

Hervey smiled. 'There is still business to attend to *down* the Godavari!'

'Just so, Hervey, just so. And there's more danger there than you might suppose. Three lakhs and more have been drawn off from the pay that was due to the rajah's sepoys, and it seems that some may have gone to the pockets of his white officers. And one of them remains – the German.' He began coughing so violently that Hervey thought he would expire, but more brandy eventually stayed the paroxysm. 'But it is worse. The nizam learned of this through one of his spies – Kunal Verma no less, the same that was found in the well. And, so my own spies inform me, he will use it to coerce that officer into taking absence of leave while the Pindarees are active – or even to throw in with them in the field.'

Hervey was more sickened by this news than before. That an officer should steal from his men was beyond his comprehension, but that he should then abandon them, and the rajah, to whom he must have taken some sort of oath, beggared belief. A more ignoble deed he had not heard of in all his time in the Duke of Wellington's army – an army which had had more than its share of rogues and felons.

'Don't be fooled, Hervey: jewels here – and there are many – will buy most men in the end.'

A month ago, perhaps two, Hervey would have railed against the betrayal, cursed the dissipation. But instead, wearied with both the heat and the intrigues of the past fortnight, he simply sighed. Yet, perhaps strangely, his resolve was not diminished. Rather was it strengthened – as had been the resolve of many at Waterloo when they saw others break and quit the field. 'Well, so be it!' he pronounced. 'We shall see how the rissalahs fare under their *native* officers!'

'I'm afraid there is more – worse, indeed,' said Selden, shaking his head.

Hervey could not have imagined it.

'The nizam now has guns on the lower Godavari.'

Hervey did not know what to address first – this new intelligence or Selden's knowing it. In the end he was pragmatic. 'But how did they get there?' he demanded. 'Not a single one escaped our ambuscade.'

'It seems they have been taking guns downriver – disassembled – these past several months. The rajah's concession to dastak enables any Haidarabad vessel to navigate the river unmolested.'

'And how have you learned of all this – and *now*, at this time?'

'My dear Hervey, I remember once your quoting to me what the Duke of Marlborough was wont to say – that no war is won without good and early intelligence. And I have told you that in India war is made with spies and bullock carts. The people who nurse me now, the hijdas as we know them, have been my trusty spies these last dozen months. And an exceptional source of intelligence are they.'

Hervey sat silent, his admiration increasing with every word Selden spoke.

'There is a hijda brotherhood which transcends other allegiances, and there are many hijdas in Haidarabad – perhaps more than anywhere in India. They have of late fallen prey to the nizam's sons, whose greed has exacted too high a tax on their possessions. They have a means of communicating that would stand tolerable comparison with the Admiralty's signal chain – though how it works I don't know. Nor need I. Well, suffice it to say that the hijdas of Haidarabad have communicated with those of Chintalpore.'

'And is there any *more* intelligence?' asked Hervey, now so thoroughly bemused that nothing, it seemed, could come as a surprise. 'Some plan of action to spike the nizam's guns, perhaps? Some subterfuge or stratagem?'

Selden raised his eyebrows and furrowed his brow. 'I am but a horse-doctor with a few friends who are – shall we say – *demi-rep*?'

Hervey had feared as much. Perhaps it was as well that the rajah was occupied with his prayers, for without any plan he might become wholly cast down. 'Do we even know who it was that murdered Kunal Verma?'

'And *Steuben* also.'

'Steuben! He was murdered? I thought his death an accident.'

'I don't know for sure. There were no witnesses.'

'Then do you know who murdered Kunal Verma?'

Selden thought for a while. 'No.'

Hervey sighed.

'What shall you do, now?' asked Selden after a suitable pause.

'What options do I have?' smiled Hervey.

'You ask a fevered horse-doctor for a military appreciation?' said Selden, at last managing a smile himself.

'Then I shall ask myself what the duke would do were he here!'

'Hah!' said Selden, managing another smile. 'Is that entirely wise? I hazard a guess what the duke would do, for we had three years and more of it in the Peninsula!'

Hervey returned the smile faintly, expecting the worst.

'He would find some bit of ground with a few bumps and hollows – would he not? – and then wait for the enemy to give battle. Scarcely an option in this case: the Pindarees would never be so obliging.'

Hervey frowned. 'You forget the battle of Assaye,' he countered. 'The duke still thinks of it as the best fighting he has ever done.'

'I do forget it. I never, indeed, knew much of it.'

He gave a little shrug. 'Sindhia outnumbered him by so many – horse, foot *and* cannon – he appeared to have no option either.'

'And?' said Selden, still not conceding.

'*L'audace!* He attacked. He simply attacked!'

CHAPTER EIGHTEEN

IN THE CANNON'S MOUTH

The plains of the lower Godavari, four days later

The rajah's modest force at Jhansikote was better found than Hervey expected. It cheered him greatly, for though he had left Chintalpore with his head full of heroic thoughts of Assaye, he had almost become resigned to a hopeless outcome. Defeat for the rajah, confusion for the Company, was what any reasonable appreciation would suggest. And for himself . . . oblivion, at best. What a loathsome month it had been – a month like no other he had seen: not before Corunna, neither after Toulouse, nor even before or after Waterloo. *Then* there had been a discernible strand of purpose – some clarity, even – in their endeavours. However, the rajah's two rissalahs of cavalry, albeit with remounts in want of schooling, and the three battalions of infantry had the stamp of a brigade drilled with purpose and infused with confidence. That much was obvious at once, testimony to Henry Locke's aptitude and determination. How the marine had managed it Hervey could not imagine, for the sepoys spoke in so many different tongues and Locke had no Telugu or Urdu, nor even any German, and no others had any English beyond the here and now. It was all the greater surprise, therefore, when Hervey learned that the force was now under the command not of Locke, but of Alter Fritz.

Alter Fritz could not explain why Locke had taken leave of his command. The old Württemberger had even less English than the native officers, and Locke had not been able to convey his thoughts well, it seemed. He had therefore given the Rittmeister a letter for Hervey, but in a comedy of errors it had been rendered unreadable when the German's sabretache had proved not to be waterproof. All that Hervey could now glean was that Locke had become cast down on receiving his note, learning that the nizam's guns had slipped from their grasp at the border, and that he had left some hours before the news of the destruction on the river reached Jhansikote.

Hervey was now plunged into deep gloom. If he had ever truly thought there to be a chance of overcoming the Pindarees it was only with the resolute help of Henry Locke. What had made him discouraged – Locke, the staunchest of men, the doughtiest of fighters? It was inconceivable that he should take counsel of even his most deadly fears. And yet he was not at his post. Could the sodden letter have contained any explanation that might remove from Hervey's reluctant thoughts the word 'desertion'? Surely it must.

But what, now, was he to make of Selden's fear that Alter Fritz might be implicated in the business of the batta? The officer's very presence signalled the improbability of guilt – unless he were scheming to deliver the rajah's lancers into the nizam's hands. Hervey knew he must trust to his judgement in this. He had not in the beginning always judged men right, but years with the duke's army had taught him well enough. Taking Alter Fritz to one side as they watched a procession of grass-cutters bearing their loads to the stables, he chose to confront him more or less directly, and in his own tongue. 'Rittmeister Bauer, could the sepoys have been placed under stoppages without knowledge of their officers?'

Alter Fritz seemed surprised by the question – a not unreasonable reaction, thought Hervey, given their circumstances. 'Not without the quartermaster knowing,' he replied unflinchingly.

So plain an answer augured well. 'And therefore the sepoys were cheated by a European officer?'

'Yes, and he is dead, I am pleased to say.'

Hervey thought it base to continue in this way: he would speak openly. 'Certain papers have been found in Chintalpore which suggest that more than one officer may have been guilty.'

'They are all dead but me, and so you wish to know—'

Hervey, deeply embarrassed, made to stay his words.

'No, Hervey. It is right that you should consider it – your duty as a soldier.'

Hervey's look indicated his gratitude.

'But there is nothing I can say. No papers will show any guilt of mine, yet I can do nothing to prove that I am without it.'

'You are here: that is enough, perhaps?'

'*Ja*, Hervey – I am here.'

Rani knew why Locke had been downcast. Rani, the hijda whom Hervey had asked to accompany him, knew everything about the gora log. Yes, Rani knew the reason Locke had gone, and now he spoke. There was only one person who knew in advance of Hervey's intentions, he said in his squeaking Urdu. It was Locke. And Locke had told the nautch girl with whom he shared his bed. Pillow talk had given away the secret, said the hijda, running his tongue between his lips. And now Locke-sahib could not face the shame.

Hervey felt the shame strongly enough just hearing him speak of it.

But Rani knew not quite so much of the gora log as he supposed. An hour later, just as the little force was about to leave Jhansikote for the lower plains, Cornet Templer returned from his galloper duties and was able to disavow all thoughts of Locke's perfidy – if not of his want of judgement. The dust of the cornet's hard ride, turning his uniform to the colour of the earth, and caked hard to his hands and face by sweat and the baking heat, neither obscured his fine features nor shrouded his golden hair. Rani's excitement was all too apparent, but Templer merely smiled where Hervey recoiled, for he had been in Hindoostan long enough.

'Well, then, man!' demanded Hervey, his frustration with everything and everybody getting the better of him. 'What is it that Mr Locke thinks he is about?'

Templer smiled winningly. 'I saw him on the road to Guntoor – or, rather, to Rajahmundry: the two are as one for much of the way—'

'Yes, yes, Templer: let us have it directly!'

'Well, he would not tell me what he was about, only that he would deal with the nizam's guns in his own way. He said that he had written a full account for you, and had given it to Captain Bauer.'

Hervey could only raise his eyebrows. 'The Godavari has claimed the account as well as the nizam's daughters – some of them, at least.'

'Sir?'

'It is no matter – not at this time. Continue, if you please.'

'That is it, sir. Except that Mr Locke said that he was having to work on the presumption that you might be dead!'

'I could have no quarrel with the logic of that, be assured of it!' laughed Hervey, pleased at least that Locke's steadfastness could no longer be doubted. 'And now, is the collector able to render us any assistance?'

'Yes indeed, sir!' beamed Templer. 'Two rissalahs of Colonel Skinner's irregulars!'

'No artillery?'

'Artillery? Yes, sir: a troop of the Gun Lascar Corps from Madras.'

Hervey looked at him despairingly. 'Mr Templer, it is artillery which we have greatest need of; you might have told me of them first!'

Templer was unabashed. 'You have not seen Colonel Skinner's Horse, sir!' he grinned.

Irrepressibility was not to be undervalued, Hervey told himself, however trying it might be. 'Well done, sir!' he acknowledged. 'And when might we expect them?'

'Gallopers were sent to Rajahmundry, where Colonel Skinner's regiment have come from Calcutta. And the Gun Lascars have already set out from Guntoor. Their progress will not be rapid, for the artillery is hauled by bullocks. Two days, perhaps three?'

'Oh,' said Hervey; 'not as felicitous as I was beginning to imagine.' And then, as if he remembered an obligation to be at all times optimistic, he added: 'But a great deal better than nothing.'

All that was a day and a half behind them. As, too, were sixty weary miles of marching, part by day and part by night, until they were come from Jhansikote to the plains of the lower Godavari, the plains where Hervey had first become acquainted with Chintal through the distress of the rajah's favourite hunting elephant. Now it was so much hotter than then, and more parched, for the monsoon was a month at least in the coming – if, indeed, it came at all. Green was no longer a colour of any prominence on the plains, except in the jungle itself. It was but an hour after sunrise, and already the heat was distorting any image beyond a few hundred yards.

The rajah's men were breaking camp after hazree – eggs, ghi, pulses, dakshini rice, dried fish, mutton, poori. It was a breakfast, said Alter Fritz – a quartermaster of very singular ability – that would send them into battle with not a doubt as to the rajah's generosity (and, therefore, their loyalty). Mention of the rajah set Hervey brooding once more: if only he had insisted on his coming here, for sepoys and sowars alike would need more than a good meal to inspire them for what was to come. But they had at least slept well. He had estimated that the enemy would not risk an attack during the night. Why, indeed, should they? Their greatest strength (and, certainly, their superiority) lay in the guns which stood immobile in the redoubts half a league across the kadir. There was little point in attacking at night when that advantage would be at nought. Selden had said they would not attack at all. Pindarees never attacked: they *awaited* attack and, if it looked to be over-whelming, they simply fled. So Hervey had stood down all but a company of sepoys, and these in turn had been able to pass a restful night in surveillance of the approaches to the camp abetted by the fullest of moons.

But not all of the rajah's men had passed the silent hours in sleep or on watch. Hervey himself had spent the early part of the night writing letters. He was not without hope for the outcome. Assaye had, after all, been a battle which by rights should not have gone to the duke. But he had much to explain – to Paris (he scarcely dare think of the duke as he wrote), to his family, and to Henrietta. Sleep, he knew, would not in any case come easily. And then when the moon rose, at a quarter to midnight, he had accompanied a little party of sepoy officers and NCOs to dig and set fougasses with the dafadars in charge of the galloper guns. There had been no shortage of powder in Jhansikote, but after the affair with the nizam's guns at the river there was now an abundance, for several barrels had floated to the bank, their contents as dry as dust with the tar sealing, and one of the two powder barges had fallen into their hands intact. When first he had explained his intention the dafadars seemed incredulous. Indeed, Hervey himself had never actually seen a fougasse, nor even heard of its making – except that years before he had read some dusty tome in the library at Longleat about the ancient fougasse chambers along the Maltese coast. How strange, he thought as they dug, that a childhood foray among the marquess's bookshelves should come to such a fruition. Templer had asked him why he made this effort, to which he had replied that since he could not increase his cannonading, explosive pits packed with stones and musket balls must suffice – 'poor man's artillery' he said they were called. And, he declared, their value might be even greater than cannon in the complete surprise of the sudden eruptions.

The work took until after two, and by then a portion of the kadir forward of their right flank, which Hervey already intended to picket, and extending to two furlongs, was peppered with his medieval devices. He had resolved not to make his final appreciation, however, until first light. Then the kadir would be revealed by the sun's searching power, rather than by the moon's deceptive glow. And, perhaps even more important, he would have the results of the night's reconnaissance, for since shortly after dusk his spies had moved freely about the Pindarees' camp, and even among the nizam's gunners in their bivouacs beside the cannon. Never could he recall hearing of so free a play of spies. But then the hijdas were no ordinary agents. Before they had left Jhansikote Rani had been joined by a half-dozen others from the Chintalpore hijron, and several more later from that at Polarvaram, and all night they had capered and debauched their way among the enemy's camp-fires until the cockerel booty had warned them to leave. An hour before dawn they had slipped back into Hervey's lines, waking a good number of sepoys by their squeals and laughter, and assembled outside his tent. Torches cast an unflattering light on their gaudy sarees, but, all revulsion at their ambiguity overcome (holding them in some affection, even), he had listened carefully to what they had discovered, only occasionally finding his Urdu insufficient. But their night's work, though valiant, yielded nothing that provided the key to unlocking the great task before him. True, they had been able to confirm that there were eight guns, whose barrel length was that of the tallest of the hijdas (Hervey had tried not to squirm as that individual related in lewd detail how he had come to be able to judge the length so exactly), also that there were many horses, tethered properly, and arms piled in soldierly fashion in parts of the camp. Behind these disciplined lines, however, lay a host of camp followers, whose fires stretched so far that it was impossible to estimate their number or extent. The only opportunity which the hijdas' intelligence brought was in this mass of camp followers – no doubt laden with the spoils of their past weeks' depredations, as tight-packed and immobile as their reputation for intoxicated indolence promised. They might well impede the retreat of the fighting men, for there was the river on one side, and the forest on the other.

297

But how was Hervey to compel any retreat? The kadir between his lines and the Pindarees' would be swept by the fire of those eight guns (by the hijdas' description, the fearsome thirty-six-pounders, with a range of one mile). Equally, the forest and the river limited his chance of manoeuvre. Late in the afternoon of the day before, as they were about to set up camp, he had contemplated doing what he had done the night they had galloped to Jhansikote and found the tree and the picket barring their way on the forest track. But that night they had traversed – what? – half a furlong of jungle? Not more than one and a half, certainly. And their progress had been slow, tiring and unsure. Here, at night, they would have to steal into the forest half a mile at least from the Pindaree lines. They could not reach the lines before dawn, and once the sun was up they would surely be detected if the enemy had taken the slightest precaution of posting sentinels. By day they would have to cover three times that distance, for there was no closer concealed entry to the jungle. They could, perhaps, make the best part of the distance before dark, leaving the last furlong or so to the night, but it would still be risky, and they would lose a whole day in which the Pindarees might even go onto the offensive. It was a doubtful option.

And so, with the sun's growing heat threatening the most uncomfortable of fighting – but also beginning to put life back into the weariest of the sepoys – and with the cooking fires and spices already sweetening the habitually fetid air of a military camp, Hervey surveyed the kadir through his telescope. He made one resolution at least. He would not make the mistake of fighting when or whom there was no need. The guns were his objective: counter those and the day would be his. But although this helped concentrate his attention on that to which he must direct the principal effort of his force, it did not provide him with an answer to how he might achieve his object. How *might* he subdue the guns? How might he even reach them without challenging – head-on – the Pindaree cavalry? They greatly outnumbered his and would not be inclined to run, as usually they were expected to, while the guns covered them. What was his little force capable of? He could not consider what the promised augmentation from Guntoor might allow, for there was no knowing when they might arrive. He could dispose six companies of infantry which had been trained, during the past few days, to work as light troops capable of skirmishing and responding to the bugle rather than to fight as dense-packed bearers of volleyed musketry. Without the nizam's guns to play upon them he was sure they could reach the Pindaree lines. If only there were not the guns! Every time it returned to that question. But just as bewilderment was turning to desperation a thought occurred to him. He reined about and trotted back towards his tent, jumping from the raj kumari's handy second Kehilan – which she had insisted he take when finally they had parted at the palace – and shaking the sleeping hijda on the ground outside.

'Yes, Captain sahib?' he said, blinking.

Hervey did not even have to think of the Urdu. It came at once. 'Rani, did you visit *each* of the guns last night?'

'Yes, sahib, all of them.'

'How strongly built were the redoubts – the little forts that the guns were in?'

'Very strong, sahib.'

'Not easily knocked away?'

'No, sahib.'

To the hijda's puzzlement, Hervey looked pleased. 'And how narrow were the embrasures – the spaces through which the guns fired?'

'Not more than a woman with voluptuous hips could pass, sahib,' replied Rani, pouting and describing the shape with his hands.

The Urdu escaped him, but the hijda's hands said enough. He smiled to himself. Could it be that the nizam's men had made the mistake of doing what many an embattled gunner had done before, and sacrificed traversing for protection? *Yes*: this was their Achilles' heel! This was where he would direct his lance!

He was already back in the saddle when he heard it. First a murmuring, then a buzzing, and then – if not cheering – sounds of distinct approbation. He turned to seek its cause, and there was a sight as glittering as that before Waterloo, when the Duke of Wellington and his staff had made their progress through the ranks. But, he smiled, what a contrast with the duke's sombre, civilian attire that day was the court dress of the Rajah of Chintalpore!

'Good morning, Your Highness,' said Hervey, saluting. He could scarce believe the felicity of the timing. Five minutes before and the rajah would have found him with no plan, and each would have fuelled the other's despair. Now, though, the rajah was inspired by Hervey's sanguine air, and he likewise by the rajah's substance and dignity.

'Captain Hervey,' he replied with a smile, 'you see before you a very indifferent soldier but, I hope, one that may have some utility.'

'Sir, your coming here now is most welcome to me, and I have no doubt it is everything to your sepoys,' he replied, bowing.

'Is there time for you to explain to me what is your design for battle?'

Hervey returned his smile willingly. 'Indeed there is, sir. It is, in any case, a simple plan. First let me point out to you the ground – the sun is not too bright for you to make out the Pindaree lines in the distance?'

The rajah shaded his eyes and peered across the kadir. 'Oh yes, Captain Hervey, I see them very well. And the guns like the walls of Jericho. How shall you tumble them?'

Hervey smiled again. 'If I may first explain the ground, sir. See how on our right the Godavari constrains our manoeuvre – and that of the Pindarees too. It is too deep to cross in force: it cannot therefore be the means of outflanking the line of the guns.'

The rajah nodded in agreement.

'On the left is the jungle. It constrains our manoeuvre as surely as the river, except that, for a short distance at least, it might afford cover. But progress on foot would be too slow, and with horses impossible.'

The rajah nodded again.

'The distance to the guns is about one half-league, and the distance from the forest to the river, at its widest part, the same, though it narrows to no more than a mile where the guns are – as you may see.'

The rajah saw it all with perfect clarity.

'There are eight guns, sir, and they command the approaches across both the kadir and the river—'

'But how can we possibly advance in the face of such a cannonade?' said the rajah, unable to contain himself.

Hervey nodded respectfully. 'Ordinarily, Your Highness, we could not. But the embrasures in each redoubt are extremely narrow, which means that the guns are not able to traverse to their extreme left or right. Neither will they be able to depress far enough to sweep the final approaches. They are also strongly built—'

'Then that is more ill news, is it not, Captain Hervey?' the rajah protested.

'Not really, sir. If they are strongly built then the gunners will not be able to break them down quickly when they discover their mistake. If we could capture just *one* of the redoubts and use powder to blow up a wall, we could enfilade each of the others, reducing them one by one.'

The rajah looked at him in dismay. 'That is not possible, surely?'

'It is an option of difficulties, certainly, sir – but what other do we have? Awaiting the collector's reinforcements risks being overwhelmed in an attack once the Pindarees discover our strength – or rather the want of it.'

'I see your reasoning well enough, Captain Hervey, but how do you intend capturing a redoubt?'

'Quite simply, sir, I intend getting sepoys along the cover of the forest edge to a point where they may enfilade the Pindarees – and perhaps even the redoubt nearest the forest, for the flanks are not wholly walled.'

The rajah pondered the notion before nodding his head slowly. 'But one more question, Captain Hervey: how have you discovered this critical information about the guns? Your telescope alone would not reveal it.'

'No, indeed, sir. I sent spies into the Pindaree lines last night.'

The rajah eyed him sternly before nodding again, but this time with a smile. 'As did Joshua?'

'As did Joshua, Your Highness,' said Hervey, smiling.

'And is there a Rahab in the Pindaree lines?'

'No, sir; merely some brave hijdas, now returned.'

'Hijdas. Always hijdas,' he tutted. 'But now you have to be about your business?'

'Yes, sir. I have my orders to give.'

His officers assembled in the lone shade of a flame tree in full bloom. Locke's absence he now felt all the more as he looked into the faces of those on whom his plan depended. Templer, for all his youthful enthusiasm, was no substitute, and Alter Fritz was . . . old. The faces of the native officers revealed a mixture of eagerness and apprehension. Hervey explained his design to tolerable effect in a mixture of Urdu and German (which Alter Fritz then rendered in Telugu – and not once was the rajah's facility called on). The sepoy officers, hearing the plan, now looked keen. The rissalah officers looked disappointed, however.

'You want us only to make a demonstration, sahib?' they said disconsolately.

'Yes, to begin with. We must tempt their attention away from the companies as they advance along the forest edge on our left flank. We must therefore convince them that we intend moving along the river's edge in strength. We might tempt their cavalry to a charge and lead them onto the fougasses.'

The cavalrymen looked a little happier.

Hervey turned back to the infantry. 'When you sepoys reach your enfilade position I shall gallop our guns to join you, and bring them to bear at close range on the embrasures, or even on the flanks of the redoubts if we have got far enough round.' He now turned to Alter Fritz: 'Have you the taste for the sabre still, Captain Bauer? Shall you take command of the cavalry?'

Alter Fritz's face lit up. 'Hervey, with sword in hand I die here!'

Hervey smiled and clapped the old Württemberger on the shoulder. 'Then let us begin, before the sun makes our work even hotter than will the nizam's daughters! But first,' he said, turning to the rajah, 'Your Highness, do you wish to say anything?'

The rajah looked around benignly at the dozen or so officers crouching in the flame tree's welcome shade. 'Only this,' he began in Telegu: 'today I believe is a day when honour shall return to us all in full measure. May your god be with you.'

All stood. Alter Fritz saluted, his face still aglow, and the rajah walked with his officers towards where their bearers waited.

Turning to Templer, Hervey said simply, 'Now you know what is my design. If I should fall then it is you who shall have to see it through. I want you to leave your horse and go with the sepoy companies.'

'But—'

'There can be no "but". Alter Fritz is well able to see to the demonstration. The point of decision will be with the sepoys on the left. That is where I shall be as soon as the Pindaree cavalry is drawn across to the right and you have reached a position of enfilade on the left.'

And then they shook hands.

The sepoys' blue coats stood a better chance of going unnoticed than the scarlet of the British infantry would have, but a diversion nevertheless seemed prudent. Hervey therefore ordered one rissalah to advance along the river bank with the galloper guns to draw fire – which he was confident would be opened prematurely by the nizam's gunners in their eagerness to begin work. 'Double your charges,' he told the gunner jemadar. 'Do not concern yourself with any effect but that on the enemy's attention.'

Though he knew where he *wanted* to be, Hervey knew where necessity demanded he should be, and he now took post in the centre of his depleted brigade, drawn up with four companies in line and a half-rissalah on either flank. From here he would watch his design for battle unfold, and judge the moment when and how to make the dash to join the sepoys' enfilade. And as he sat, keenly observing the flattest, emptiest arena on which he had ever faced battle, his thoughts turned not to home, as they had done before Waterloo, but to that very battle, with its many, many times greater numbers – horses, guns and men. Yet though the numbers were vastly greater at Waterloo, he fancied his situation now not entirely unlike the duke's that day: at least, in the closing stages of the battle. He sat astride a horse not much bigger than a pony, in front of a body of men who, though stout-hearted enough, faced what must be overwhelming odds.

And yet there was one test they would not face – the test that had been Major Edmonds's and then Captain Lankester's as they had had to judge the effect of the enemy's cannonading on their line. For this morning Hervey's brigade was outside the guns' range, and he intended that it remain so. Nevertheless, he knew that the smallest misjudgement would see them all perish.

Alter Fritz and his rissalah advanced in two ranks at the trot. The lance pennants, though there was no breeze, fluttered with the forward movement – a pretty sight, thought Hervey, and unusual for its not *facing* him. He watched through his telescope as they proceeded with admirable steadiness towards the Pindaree lines, Alter Fritz sitting erect in the saddle, as proud, no doubt, as when he had first been a trooper on parade for Duke Charles Eugene. When the rissalah was half-way to the lines, there was a long, rolling eruption of flame, smoke and then noise from the nizam's guns. The range was extreme, yet Hervey held his breath as the rounds arched lazily towards the lancers in a graceful parabola: he could see each one of them quite clearly. All fell short of the rissalah by a furlong at least, one ball bouncing into the river, sending up a fountain of water and steam, followed by another and then another. Two balls bounced straight at the lancers, but with each bounce their velocity was diminished, and the ranks opened to allow them to pass through harmlessly. The three remaining shot were what interested Hervey most, for they were so wide of their mark (fired, he supposed, by the guns on the Pindarees' left) that he knew their traverse must indeed be severely limited, with only the narrowest of arcs. Though the battery was able to sweep the whole of the kadir, and very effectively out to a quarter of a league, they were not able, it seemed, to concentrate on one target. It was exactly as he hoped. And then, a minute later, Alter Fritz having most daringly advanced a further hundred yards, the second salvo was fired (equally without damage) and Hervey realized the full import of the limited traverses: at half the distance between the cannons' first graze and the muzzles themselves there would be a significant extent of frontage which the guns could not cover at all. He had never been especially good at geometry – and he would have wished now for paper and protractor – but, by his rapid calculation, at that distance *half*, indeed, of the front would be uncovered.

Now here was an opening. Between salvoes he could take the whole of the cavalry in a gallop from as close as where Alter Fritz and his rissalah stood presently in safety, and in the time before the gunners could fire another round they could be through the belt entirely swept by fire (he supposed the enemy must have explosive shells as well as roundshot) and into that where the arcs could not interlock. From then on the odds would change in their favour until, in the final furlong or so, the guns would scarcely be able to bear on more than a fraction of his front.

A frontal assault on any guns was, however, a calculated gamble, for there were bound to be casualties, especially close in when they began firing canister. It was, therefore, merely attrition – and a cynical attrition at that. Any cavalryman felt a deep repugnance towards confronting guns with nothing but the breasts of horses and brave men. And Hervey not least: he could not throw away the lives of any of his command in so premeditated a fashion. But the effort in this appreciation might not be wasted yet, for he saw clearly now that to disrupt the fire of the two guns on the Pindarees' right was to open up an approach by which he could, perhaps, turn their flank.

Alter Fritz and his rissalah were doing sterling work drawing the guns' fire – and, thereby, the Pindarees' attention – to the right flank. The old quartermaster judged it prudent to advance no further except to send forward an open line of mounted skirmishers to try to draw the fire of the Pindaree cavalry mustered in a dense mass before the guns – by Hervey's estimation, perhaps a thousand or more. And his stratagem was working, for all attention seemed fixed on the river flank. A calm settled once more on the kadir, as the gunners perceived their powder to be wasted at that extreme range, and all of Hervey's force stood motionless in place. All, that is, but the two companies making their way on the left – still undetected – along the forest's edge, and the mounted skirmishers advancing with deliberate slowness on the right.

It was now becoming uncomfortably hot: not yet the heat that seized the whole of the body in a vice, but fierce nevertheless, and salty beads of sweat were making their way down the back of Hervey's neck. He took off his shako and wiped his forehead with his sleeve, and rubbed dry the leather cap-band. He envied the sepoys at the forest edge who, though their brisk step would not have been without effort, at least had some shade. He replaced his shako, adjusted the neck-flap, though the sun would not bear directly on it for several hours yet, and took a long drink from his water bottle. He had been worried about water. He had been worried that the Pindarees might have poisoned the wells near where they supposed he would make camp. He had been relieved, therefore, to see villagers using them as they approached, and Alter Fritz, whose proud boast was never to have had a moment's gripe since coming to Chintalpore, had pronounced the water sweet. But how he wished for Private Johnson's chirrupy humour at this moment – that and the brew of tea he would have had at daybreak, and no doubt another canteen for him now. In Johnson's mind a brew of tea was a kind of military elixir during whose making and drinking all priorities were resolved and all possibilities became apparent.

But with thoughts of Johnson came thoughts of Jessye, and a moisture about the eyes that was not the fault of the heat. He had always known that Jessye must one day succumb to . . . any number of things. Such was their precarious profession. But he had always promised her that the final blow would, if need be, come from him, and that she should pass peacefully with him by her side. And this promise he had not kept. Had he truly believed him when the subedar said she felt no pain lying there full of the snake's poison? That letting her slip away with the sun on her back, rather than with the crack of a pistol in her ear, was a truer kindness? Or had he simply not the courage to see the oldest friend he had in the service lifeless at his feet? It was a cruel and ignoble end for her, and he had not been there at the final moment. Yes, Johnson had been with her, the man who loved her almost as much as he did. But Johnson had not seen her slip wondrously in that soapy membrane from between the haunches of her dam ten years or so before, nor watched her instinctive struggling for her mother's milk only minutes later, nor her clambering to her feet and her first, tentative steps not long afterwards. These were what bound a man more closely to his horse than anything might – even if the man might find admitting it beyond him.

For the first time since coming to India he felt alone, though the rajah was close beside him. Every time he had awaited battle he had been surrounded by faces he knew and voices he recognized, and they had talked incessantly. There was *always* something to talk about: if it was not the battle to come it was the battle that had been. And then there was the encouragement of juniors by seniors, and the reassurance by return. But he did not know these native officers, and the impassivity of the sepoys and sowars unnerved him somewhat. He thought of riding up and down the ranks to hail them with an appropriate word, but his grasp of Urdu was still precarious, and he had none of Telugu, so the enterprise might be worse than unproductive.

Suddenly they were all attention to the right flank, where Alter Fritz's skirmishers had opened a brisk, if scarcely effective, fire on the Pindaree cavalry.

'What do they do there?' asked the rajah, a little shakily.

Hervey reassured him. But contrary to everything he had expected – or, indeed, could have hoped – half the Pindaree host now surged forward in a trot towards the skirmishers.

The rajah became anxious. 'They come upon us!' he called.

'No, sir, I believe they mean only to overawe the rissalah. Your cavalry' (he was most particular in his choice of adjective) 'do great service there, drawing the enemy's attention. See over on the left how your sepoys make progress towards the guns unnoticed.'

The rajah was further reassured.

But Hervey was surprised when he saw that the sowar-skirmishers did not turn about to rejoin the rissalah, but stood their ground and fired further volleys at close range – this time with lethal effect. It was, he told the rajah, as steady a conduct by cavalry as he had seen. And then, when another few seconds' delay would have seen them overrun, they turned for safety and galloped back to where Alter Fritz and the rest of his men stood.

Again, he expected that the Pindarees would not press their advance – certainly not beyond supporting range of the guns. But they did – perhaps five hundred of them. What, indeed, could they fear? Alter

Fritz's one hundred could not withstand them, for sure. Would he charge them, as was the practice? The seconds passed, the rajah growing more anxious with each (and, indeed, Hervey too – though not as conspicuously). Another ten might spell disaster. Then Alter Fritz's front rank fired their carbines, turned about and retired at a steady trot, leaving the second rank to send their volley into the mass of horsemen. The effect was not, perhaps, as devastating as the smoke and noise portended, but a good many men and horses were tumbled nevertheless.

Still the Pindarees did not check. If anything they increased their pace. The rissalah was now in a gallop – and in the highly irregular order of two columns. Hervey was full of admiration for their drill, if perplexed by the formation. Until, that is, he saw that the columns were making for the two clear paths through the fougasses. 'Great heavens!' he exclaimed, alarming the rajah even more.

'What is it, Captain Hervey?'

'Your Highness, you will see in a short while. I believe that the Pindarees are about to receive a very great shock. They are about to have a taste of what is sometimes known as – if you will excuse my saying so – "poor man's artillery"!'

The rissalah columns wheeled left and right into line, fronting fifty yards to the rear of the fougasses, the galloper guns unhitching and making ready before even the last of the lancers had taken post. Alter Fritz galloped along the line shouting orders to the NCOs who had been lying concealed with their slow matches at the end of each powder trail. Before he reached the flank they fired the first of the fougasses, followed immediately by another, and then more. The ground heaved, great fountains of earth spouted high, and those rocks which had not been projected forward rained down on the Pindaree rear ranks. Horses and men tumbled in their dozens as shot, nails and pebbles swept like a scythe into the packed lines. Hervey counted fourteen or fifteen explosions. No more than five or six must have misfired – not a bad rate of success.

The rajah was at first speechless. And then overjoyed. And then sickened.

But Hervey scarcely heard him, intent as he was on observing what the Pindarees would do next, for they still had more horsemen than stood with Alter Fritz. However, the old Württemberger was even wilier then he had supposed. The Pindaree host had been checked: it stood motionless in a sort of collective contemplation. All it would take was resolute action by their commander to renew the attack, but doubt was evidently creeping into their minds. This was the time that Alter Fritz chose to make up their minds for them. He fired two more of the fougasses, and then another two, and then the galloper guns opened up with explosive shell. His trumpeter sounded the advance, and the rissalah lowered its line of lances and began to march forward.

It was enough. The front ranks of the Pindarees turned. But their way back was blocked by the rear ranks, who were thrown into confusion by the retrograde movement. There was panic, suddenly, and many of the horsemen turned to the river for escape, followed by many more in the rear who must instinctively have believed that water rather than their own lines would be their salvation. Alter Fritz put his left wing into a canter to envelop their right. When they saw what was to come, all order among the Pindarees disintegrated and there was a headlong dash for the river.

The rajah, roused from his sombre thoughts, grabbed Hervey by the arm. 'Why do you not send the rest of my lancers to assist their comrades? We can surely finish those devils in the river?'

Nothing would have given Hervey greater pleasure – or, at least, satisfaction. It was just what a cavalryman should do, for this was the moment when, if he threw in even half his remaining rissalah, the Pindarees who had advanced would be destroyed to a man. 'Your Highness, my object must remain the guns: it is not necessary that we finish those at the river. And there is, I must point out, at least their number again still at the redoubts. If they were to attack then we should be deuced hard-pressed to withstand them.'

The rajah sighed. 'Captain Hervey, forgive me for seeming to doubt you. What now is your intention?'

Hervey took in the whole of the kadir at a glance. It was not difficult to do so, for the attention of the enemy seemed entirely focused on the slaughter at the river, the nizam's guns keeping up a furious but ineffective fire, shot falling wide or well short of the press of horsemen. The rajah's sowars had slung their lances to set about the fleeing Pindarees with their tulwars, and still those Pindarees by the guns made no move to their comrades' relief. Perhaps they were wise not to do so, thought Hervey, as those at Waterloo who had gone to the aid of the Heavies – himself included – might have been wiser to stand their ground. But it was alien to every instinct of a soldier to stand by while a comrade was in trouble. If only the sepoys on the left were closer to the Pindaree lines: now would be the perfect opportunity to take the remaining rissalah to the enfilade. 'Your Highness, I had wished that we might tempt the rest of the Pindaree cavalry to advance, to tie them to a fight on our right so that – as I earlier explained – we might then advance to the guns on the other flank. But they will not be tempted. Though I hope that is more by lack of courage than judgement.'

'And so, Captain Hervey?'

'And so, sir, I must chance to gallop for the flank and hope that your sepoys are able to come to our relief before too long!'

The rajah looked alarmed.

'Do not concern yourself, sir. I cannot suppose that the enemy has much appetite left after seeing what has just befallen those at the river. And they are not to know that we have expended all our fougasses. Nor, I suspect, do they truly know what they are.'

But Hervey had judged it wrong. He galloped the half-rissalah and his two guns (he would have taken the other half had he not needed to leave it as the rajah's lifeguard) along the edge of the jungle without hindrance from either cannon or horsemen, and they were even able to dismount and take cover just inside the forest not fifty yards from the nearest redoubt. But two things stood against him then. First, the side of the redoubt *was* protected, contrary to what the hijdas believed (though he could see now that the sides of the others were not). They would not be able to enfilade it to any effect, for his galloper guns would make little impression on the revetted walls. Second, and more pressing, the Pindarees made immediately to counter-attack. This move was halted by brisk flanking fire from the sepoy companies who had begun doubling forward as soon as Hervey had overtaken them – but not before Cornet Templer had been hit twice in the legs by musketry. He made not a sound as he fell, and would have lain there as if in cover had not one of the sowars seen him hit. Hervey crawled back to him and managed, with the sowar's help, to staunch the bleeding. But the cornet was no longer for the fight – despite his pleading to be left to work his carbine – and Hervey called to two others to drag him back into the shade of the forest.

There was now, therefore, impasse – a bristling triangle, no side of which could move without drawing withering fire from another. Hervey knew that the initiative was not his, however, for the Pindarees

309

could – if they were both resolute *and* skilful – outflank his two sides of the triangle, though he was not strong enough to do so with theirs. Now, perhaps, was his aptness for command to be most truly tested. He had already first unnerved and then impressed the rajah by his bold insistence on not throwing all his men into the fight against the Pindarees at the river. Now he would retain the same single-mindedness in pursuing his objective. He would *not* try to fight the Pindarees pressing upon him: he would strike at the guns.

It was as well that he did not attempt to explain his plan, for it was essentially inexplicable. He threw off his shako, threw down his pistols, gave his carbine and cartridges to the sowar who stood temporarily in Johnson's place, and ran forward with no encumbrance but his sabre in one hand and a length of tethering rope in the other. A furious musketry opened again from the Pindarees, but, being aimed shots, they were all wide of their fast-sprinting mark – and indeed of the sowar who, without bidding, ran at his side. They threw themselves to the ground at the foot of the redoubt. It was so much bigger now they were close – half the size of a windmill, and much the same shape. Hervey expected at any minute that fire would come at them from above. But they were unseen by the gunners. The cannon overhead – a good ten feet above where he crouched – was silent, though run out and there-fore, he supposed, shotted. The instant it fired, the recoil would take it back inside the embrasure, and he thus risked all even if he were able to do what was in his mind. But had he any option now?

The gun projected as proudly as if it had been one of *Nisus*'s main battery. Hervey made a running loop of the rope and stood to cast it over the barrel. His first attempt failed, and he froze for several seconds, expecting it to have been seen. He cast again. This time the rope looped the muzzle and he pulled the end tight closed. He waited a few seconds – again, no one had seen – then began to pull himself up, his feet scrambling for footholds on the rough face of the revetments. How many gunners did he expect to find inside? Better not to think. Even his rifled carbine would have been too slow. The sabre hanging from his wrist by its sling was his only chance. He swung his leg over the barrel and pulled himself upright, straining every muscle to do so, expecting the gun to explode at any moment or a pistol or musket to fire point-blank. And then he was through the embrasure and in among the gunners like a terrier among rats – except that these rats did not fight.

They squealed, though. Squealed and squealed and squealed as the sabre slashed and cut and thrust – without anything stronger than a raised arm to parry it. Two gunners escaped its work by diving head-long from the redoubt, but five more soon lay still or dying at Hervey's feet. He rushed to the embrasure to call for support, and at that instant a huge roundshot crashed into the redoubt furthest from him. He saw it strike – carrying away the earthwork and dismounting the gun. He saw a second, ploughing into the debris wrought by the first, sending earth and brickwork skywards. He was dumbstruck. What? Where? How? He peered out further, towards the Godavari whence only the fire could have come . . . and there were the ensigns, unmistakable! And then another 'broadside' of such regularity that before it could strike, the nizam's gunners were pouring from the redoubts like rats fleeing before a flood. 'Great God!' he gasped. 'A fathom of water! A fathom of water and there'll you'll find them!'

But the Pindaree horsemen stood firm. Hervey saw with alarm that all they needed to do was assail the half-dozen budgerows on the river, from which the *Nisus*'s quarterdeck twelve-pounders enfiladed them, and with a modicum of resolution they might yet carry the day: the Godavari was shallow enough at the edge, and not all would have fallen to grape as they charged. Alter Fritz was engaged with the remnants of those that had earlier attacked him, and evidently did not see the danger, and all Hervey's half-rissalah were dismounted and their horses with holders inside the forest. He looked back towards his night camp and the lancers with the rajah – and to his great relief saw them advancing at a canter.

But the Royal Navy was not yet done with its fighting. A thin line of red was also advancing, muskets at the high port, as steady as if on parade at Portsmouth. And there, in front, was Henry Locke, sword held high. The Pindarees seemed rooted to the spot, incapable even of dealing with two dozen marines. Never had Hervey seen cavalry so supine – as feeble as Sackville at Minden. And then, at fifty yards, Locke lowered his sword to the engage, the marines put their bayonets to 'On guard', and they began to double. At thirty Hervey distinctly heard him shout '*Charge!*' and the Pindarees – hundreds upon hundreds – turned and broke. But a handful first discharged their firearms – perhaps more for safety as they retired – and a ball struck Locke in the throat.

Hervey rushed to where he fell, through ranks of horsemen who wanted nothing but to be away. Locke's serjeant was already trying to staunch the bleeding as he reached him, but so much blood was there that the end could not have been in doubt. His eyes were open and something of a smile came to them as he saw Hervey. He gripped the soldier's wrist, squeezing with that strength which Hervey had so admired, trying thereby to tell him something.

Hervey smiled back. 'Thank you, my dear, dear friend. Without you it could not have been done!'

Locke's eyes smiled even stronger, his breathing like the raj kumari's mare when the incision was made. His other hand reached for his gorget and pulled it from his neck, snapping the chain. He held it out to Hervey, his eyes somehow managing to tell him why.

'For your . . .' he cursed himself that he did not know her name.

Locke nodded his head.

'I will see she is well provided for,' he said, tears now running down both cheeks.

And then Locke's eyes closed, and his head rolled gently to one side in his serjeant's arms.

Hervey swallowed very hard. 'Samson hath quit himself like Samson,' he stammered.

CHAPTER NINETEEN

RECALL

Chintalpore, two weeks later

Jessye nuzzled him, searching his pockets for some favour. Hervey put his nose to hers so that their breathing spoke secretly for them, as it always had. He rubbed her muzzle with his palm. The pinpricks, through which the krait's venom had spurted to mix with her blood and scheme its way to her vitals, were now healed, her body purged of all poison. He found her a piece of candied fruit and she took it gently from his hand, not greedily as would the Kehilans in the stalls either side of her. Tomorrow he might take her out – an easy ride, a walk only – in the cool of the morning, to coax her back to the hale condition in which she had been before the snake's assault.

'Mr Somervile is greatly interested in village medicine,' said Emma Lucie, watching from a discreet few paces.

Hervey nodded. 'Would that I had had greater faith, too. The subedar begged me to let him go to find a sadhu, but I couldn't bear to have a stranger dancing round her, throwing ash about and blowing on a pipe.'

'And it was a Brahman who came, you say?'

'So Johnson says. He gave her a potion, though I can't imagine how

313

she could have been induced to take anything, prostrate and her heart failing. It was mungo root, apparently a native cure for snakebite.'

'Ah yes, indeed: Ophiorrhiza mungos is its botanical name. I was reading of it in my natural history only yesterday.'

'Oh – so it *is* more than village magic?'

'I believe so. It is a well-known antidote with grass-cutters, but I have never heard of its use with equines.'

'You are very ingenious, Miss Lucie. You have extensive learning, and are yet open to all you see in this country.'

'It might very well be fatal not to be,' she said, smiling.

'In its most literal sense, too,' he conceded. 'For the snakebite I should, myself, have trusted to potash, but that would have been of little account had it not been used at once. And I had none.'

Hervey pulled Jessye's ears again, and gave her another piece of candied fruit. 'I've sent Johnson with a purse of silver. I should have liked to go myself but time is pressing.'

'How long do you have remaining?'

'I can't delay beyond tomorrow.'

'Philip will be sorry he shan't see you before you go.'

'And I him. Not least to be able to tell him in person all you have done.'

'Not *all*, I should suggest!'

He looked away sheepishly. 'I cannot thank you enough. When did you make the discovery?'

'Soon after the rajah had set off to join you. It was the only ledger I had not looked at.'

'And you read through every page?'

'That was my intention, but it was there on the third – very plain.'

'Even so, its significance might not have—'

'Captain Hervey!' she scolded. 'I cannot think that anyone would *not* connect the Duke of Wellington's name in a land register and the presence of one of his ADCs! I wonder, though, that you did not give me any more direct indication of your mission.'

He glanced around awkwardly, but there was no one else about. 'Perhaps so, madam. I'm obliged none the less. And the evidence?'

'The ledgers are wholly beyond redemption: they were sodden by the time they were recovered from the well. It has saved you and me a difficult choice.'

'I have thought a great deal about that, I may say, Miss Lucie.'

She simply smiled and shook her head.

'And still there is no idea who might be the culprit?' he asked, leaving the trickier matter.

'It would seem not. All the ledgers and documents were taken from my room while I was with the rajah and thrown down the same well in which Kunal Verma perished. But the rajah is sure that his spies will soon begin to speak now that his position is more secure.'

'As you say, their taking removed a fearful temptation. And so now the disposal of the jagirs is a simple matter for the duke's new agent in Calcutta. How very fortunate things have turned out, when only days ago all seemed lost.'

She did not reply, merely raising an eyebrow instead.

Jessye was contentedly chewing the best hay that could be had in Chintalpore – though that was no better than Daniel Coates would feed his sheep in winter. He patted her neck. 'I wish Selden could have seen her recovered,' he sighed. 'His was a tortured life, I think. I pray his soul finds more rest.'

Emma Lucie said not a word.

'I am sure that nothing will ever be found to implicate him in the batta fraud.'

'Let us hope not,' she replied.

Silence descended on the stables once more, broken only by the slow grinding of hay. Hervey seemed perfectly content to watch his mare restored to her proper appetite, content with no more thoughts, let alone words, of the perfidy that had sapped Chintal in the late months.

It was Emma Lucie who chose to speak first. 'I have been reading some of the most sublime verse from the rajah's shelves.'

'Indeed?' said Hervey, imagining it – without very great enthusiasm – to be some profound native poetry.

'You have read Herbert?'

She surprised him. Herbert on the rajah's shelves? '*George* Herbert – yes. I have more often sung it, though.'

'And I,' she smiled. 'It makes fine hymnody.'

'I believe I can say that my father has never coveted anything so much as Herbert's former living. His parish lay a little further down the valley. I was thinking about those parts as you came into the stable. You must visit with my family in England, Miss Lucie. I think that Henrietta would very much like to see you again too.'

'Yes, I should like that; but you distract me,' she chided, smiling.

'I found a poem which seemed most apt for you and Captain Peto.'

'Oh?'

'Yes,' she continued, smiling more, 'called simply "Discipline".'

'I do not know it,' he replied, shaking his head.

'"Love is swift of foot; Love's a man of war, And can shoot, And can hit from afar." *There*, Captain Hervey: do you not think that apt?'

He smiled ruefully. 'I think Captain Peto would heartily approve. All his philosophy seems but one vast naval allegory!'

'Just so,' she nodded. 'And in speaking of shooting from afar, would you tell me what really happened in your battle?'

'Well, madam,' he began, thoughtfully, 'we are obliged as always to the Royal Navy. It seems that Bonaparte once lamented that wherever there was a fathom of water, there you would find the British. When Mr Locke heard that the guns were gone from the border with Haidarabad he assumed at once that it was he who had betrayed our stratagem through careless talk with his . . . ahm—'

'Paramour?'

'Er, just so. Well, it seems that he thought the only recourse was to enlist the firepower of the *Nisus* standing off Guntoor. Perhaps there is not a single frigate captain in the Royal Navy who could then have resisted the challenge, but Peto of all men would have been determined to demonstrate the truth of Bonaparte's lament. He took *Nisus* up the Godavari as far as he could, and when he could go no further he had six cannon dismounted and transferred to budgerows, and these he was able to bring into very timely action.'

'But it was not Mr Locke's fault that the stratagem was out?'

'No, his . . . the *native lady* had said not a word, for she was given so big a draught of laudanum when he left that she lay insensate for two days. No, it seems that as soon as the nizam's men heard that all the rajah's forces were marching upon the border – as we had intended they should hear – they put their guns on the river. We do not know why – yet. Indeed, it may never be known. Everything in India seems unfathomable!'

'Unfathomable? Perhaps. And how did Mr Locke die?'

Hervey fell silent. At length he sighed and raised his eyebrows slowly. 'Bravely – though that hardly needs saying. He advanced with twenty marines, in their scarlet, against hundreds of the enemy, as steady as if on parade. A ball struck him in the throat, and he died almost at once. I cannot say more.'

Emma Lucie saw the moisture in his eye and turned towards Jessye, giving her another of the favours she had brought. A pair of hoopoes in the eves was all there was to be heard: '*Poo, poo, poo*,' called the male, his crest lowered. His mate answered – '*Scharr*.' Hervey looked up; for an instant he was a boy in Horningsham again, stalking the jays in the churchyard.

The silence stretched a full five minutes. 'There was much to admire in Mr Locke,' said Emma Lucie softly. 'His fortitude, his . . . *simplesse*.'

'Indeed,' coughed Hervey, wiping an eye.

She let him be for a while again. 'But we may thank God that Cornet Templer is set fair for a full recovery.'

'Yes . . . yes indeed,' said Hervey, now recovering himself too. 'He is the very best of fellows. And he loves India.'

After a few minutes more she asked what were his thoughts on being recalled.

He answered readily. 'I must confess that, anxious though I am to return to England, I am myself more than a little intrigued by these lands.'

'You are relieved, nevertheless, by your letter of recall? It does – does it not – permit a reunion with all whom you love?'

There could be no other conclusion, he replied, knowing he would have six full months to contemplate it. 'We shall say farewell tomorrow, Miss Lucie. But let me say again how greatly in your debt I am. You have been kind beyond words.'

'Let us just say that my brother – and Henrietta – would have had it no other way.'

'So, Captain Hervey, you are to leave us – never, I suppose, to return to Chintal, or even to India, again?' The rajah was disappointed but philosophical.

'Your Highness will understand where my duty lies.'

'And your heart.'

'I am engaged to be married, sir, yes.'

'We in India never see a British grey hair!'

Hervey smiled. 'Oh, I think that Mr Somervile's head will become white in these climes, sir. His will be a lengthy residency, I feel sure.'

'I trust so, very much. And, I had hoped, Mr Locke's too. The grant of jagirs on the plains would, I think, have been eminently to his liking. They shall, at least, provide some comfort for the Maharashtri dancer.'

'I was not aware that you knew of the liaison, sir,' replied Hervey with some embarrassment.

The rajah smiled. 'Captain Hervey, this is my dominion.'

'Yes, sir,' he nodded sheepishly. 'The Fates dealt ill with Mr Locke, Your Highness. I pray that they are not cruel to his memory now.'

'Most delicately put, Captain Hervey. But the *Fates*?' he smiled. 'And you a Christian officer of most exemplary practice!'

Hervey smiled again. 'I believe you know that I was speaking figuratively, sir.'

'Just so, just so. And your own jagirs: you are content for them to rest in Mr Somervile's stewardship?'

'I am, sir. You have been more generous than could be imagined. There was no need, as I have already said: I could have done no other but what I did.'

'And now you will return to your Duke of Wellington and continue upon advancement to high rank.'

'That is every soldier's intent, sir; though not all are permitted to achieve it.'

'Just so, just so. And I have been unable to persuade you to remain in Chintal for a colonelcy and command of all my sepoys and sowars.'

'I am a *King's* officer, Your Highness. And your princely state is now secured by the subsidiary force – and an admirable officer in Colonel Bell.'

'Perhaps, perhaps,' smiled the rajah, 'though I can understand but little of what he says. He speaks very ill – Scotch, you say?'

'Your Highness, I happen to know that his Urdu is faultless!'

'Urdu? Yes, though I had rather wished we might discourse in English – read poetry, scripture and the like – as you and I have, Captain Hervey.'

The Englishman bowed, acknowledging the compliment.

'Well, I take my leave of you for the time being,' said the rajah. 'Do you have further business today, or may we have the pleasure of your company once more this evening?'

'I shall do my utmost to be there, Your Highness, but first I must seek Captain Peto. He, too, has letters of recall, but he cannot wait and we must make our arrangements directly.'

The rajah nodded; he understood. '"And the gilded car of day, His glowing axle doth allay, In the steep Atlantic stream."'

'You quote one of my favourite works, sir.'

318

'Yes, I know it – the masque at Ludlow Castle. Near Shrewsbury, is it not?'

Hervey smiled even wider: truly this rajah was a man of uncommon learning and sensibility. 'I hope, one day, you will visit England, sir. It cannot compare with Italy in the magnificence of its past beauty, but I believe you would be excessively diverted.'

'Thank you, Captain Hervey. Let us pray that it may come about. Now to one last matter – the raj kumari. It is, perhaps, not possible for you to judge anything but the gravest ill of her. What she did, however, was for no baser reason than out of love for me and for Chintal. In time she will return to the palace, but not yet, not yet.'

Hervey shifted awkwardly. There was immense sadness in the rajah's voice.

'You know all, I suppose?'

'I cannot tell, sir,' he replied, for how much there was in this most convoluted of stories he could not hazard.

'This land is made of spies, Captain Hervey. It was perhaps destined that one day the secret I have borne for many years – my Christian baptism in the place that St Peter himself was most cruelly put to death – should be discovered, and traded for the highest price. Kunal Verma learned of it, skulking in shadows, and, like Judas, traded his secret for silver – two and more lakhs of it. The raj kumari and some loyal but misguided courtiers connived at his extortion – the batta fraud – but when silver was no longer to be had, and he threatened to travel to Haidarabad, my daughter ordered him killed.'

'And Captain Steuben, sir?

'An entirely innocent victim, I fear.'

Hervey sighed. One day he might reconcile the raj kumari's actions with the necessities of war, but for now that prospect looked distant. 'Must you still hold your secret, Your Highness?' he asked, his voice hushed.

'For the moment,' replied the rajah. 'Perhaps for ever. There is room within the Hindoo religion. You cannot understand, for I believe truly that it must come with birth alone.'

'I hope you *will* visit with us in England, sir,' said Hervey once more.

The rajah smiled again.

Hervey hoped fervently that the raj kumari might somehow appear, her exile more figurative than real. Too much had passed between them for there to be no leave-taking, for their association to be just fractured

319

in this way. But she did not come. Deep in the forest of the Gonds, with but a few attendants, she listened all day to the sadhu and served out her penance. The rajah did not know whether he himself would ever see her again, for her restoration was given entirely into the hands of the holy men.

Captain Laughton Peto was pacing the terrace of the water garden as he would his own quarterdeck. Hervey almost saluted as he came up the steps.

'Well, sir,' he huffed, 'I hear those despatches included your letter of recall.'

'Yes, the duke is not after all to come to India. He's to be appointed to the cabinet.'

'Deuced lucky for you in the circumstances, I should say – eh, Hervey?'

'Yes, I should say it was.' He tried to keep his reply free of the relief he had felt on first receiving the order.

'Am I to suppose, therefore, that you now seek passage to England?'

'If that is in order, sir,' replied Hervey, maintaining all due ceremony.

'And, of course, for your groom?'

'I would be obliged.'

There followed a purposeful silence, but Hervey saw no obligation to hasten its end.

Peto could no longer contain himself. 'And I suppose you wish a berth for your horse!'

'I am *ever* in your debt, sir.'

'Great heavens, Captain Hervey, my ship is become nothing more than a packet! But I suppose I should count myself lucky the rajah has not presented you with a deuced elephant!'

Hervey smiled sheepishly.

'*What!*' exploded Peto.

'Not an elephant but a Kehilan. Let me explain . . .'

HISTORICAL AFTERNOTE

The following year, 1817, the armies of the three presidencies, together with those of several Indian states, undertook a coordinated campaign to extirpate the Pindaree menace – what is sometimes known as the third Maratha war. The Rajah of Nagpore was treacherous; consequently, most of his state was occupied by the Company and a new ruler placed on the throne. But the nizam remained loyal, as did successive rulers of Hyderabad (its later spelling) up to the very end of British rule. In the north, the Rajput states concluded subsidiary alliances with the Company, so that by 1820 the British were the strongest power in India. This Pax Britannica was the first peace which many a poor ryot had ever known. Only in the north-west, in the Punjab, did the Company have a serious rival left: the Sikh kingdom of Ranjit Singh. About which, perhaps, more anon.